Hold ON TO Hope

A.L. Jackson

NEW YORK TIMES BESTSELLING AUTHOR

A.L. Jackson
www.aljacksonauthor.com
Cover Design by LJ Designs
Editing by Susan Staudinger
Formatting by Mesquite Business Services

Print ISBN: 978-1-946420-39-8
eBook ISBN: 978-1-946420-38-1

Hold ON TO Hope

More from A.L. Jackson

Hollywood Chronicles, a collaboration with USA Today Bestselling Author, Rebecca Shea
One Wild Night
One Wild Ride

Disclaimer

Hold on to Hope utilizes American Sign Language within its pages. In order to give better ease of reading, they are not written in true ASL format.

prologue

Moonlight poured in through the window where I leaned over the desk, soul twisted in two as I struggled with the decision that had to be made.

Memories spun through my mind in the most violent storm.

Battering and bruising.

I felt chained by them. Forever tied to the past where I'd been condemned.

I'd tried to change it. Tried to fix it. But I'd already caused more pain than one person should have to bear.

The only thing I could do now was sever the ties.

End this before it was too late.

Loving her had been the easiest thing in the world.

Letting her go the most brutal.

Every cell in my body wept with the sorrow of it as I leaned over the piece of paper.

The words flowed over the page.

Bitterness and regret and the little bit of hope she'd left me with.

Before I could do something selfish like change my mind, I

stood, grabbed my bag from the floor, and tossed it over my shoulder.

Then I walked out the door and I didn't look back.

Because I knew there was no atonement for this sin.

No amends that could rewrite what had been written in stone.

Nothing that could change who I was . . .

one

Frankie Leigh

"*O*h, God, why is that so good?" I moaned as I swirled my tongue around the finger in my mouth.

You know, all kinds of ladylike.

But hell, when it came to food, manners could jump themselves right out a skyscraper window.

A giggle rippled from my closest friend, Carly. "Um . . . I'm pretty sure the answer to that is sugar. All the sugar."

Right.

Which was probably why the entire world was staging a war against it, considering it made everything so damned delicious and it was hard to stop once you started.

And here at A Drop of Hope, we were in the business of delicious.

And this frosting was out of this world.

Score.

"God, get this away from me before I eat the entire thing," I said, shoving the bowl away but not so far that I couldn't dip my finger in for another taste.

Aunt Hope grinned like she'd won a prize where she worked on whipping up a second batch of lemon drop cupcakes.

"Good?" she asked, teeth raking at her bottom lip as she focused on getting the new recipe right.

"Describing that as good is nothing but a disservice. That is orgasmic," I said through another mouthful I'd scooped onto my finger.

Sue me.

And besides . . . this was a tester batch. It wasn't like I was defiling a single health department code. At least, I didn't think so.

Soft laughter rippled from Aunt Hope where she stood opposite Carly and me at the big work station in the industrial kitchen at the coffee shop and bakery she owned with her best friend, Jenna.

Carly and I had basically been working there for all of forever, ever since we'd begged her to let us have summer jobs way back in high school.

"That good, huh?" Aunt Hope asked.

"Oh yeah. I think this might be my new favorite."

Carly shook her head with a short chuckle. "You realize you say that about every single recipe Hope creates, don't you?"

"All except for the bacon cupcakes," I corrected with an exaggerated gag. "Bacon is for breakfast, or if you want to really get crazy, maybe add a slice or two to your burger. Puttin' it on dessert is nothing short of blasphemy."

Aunt Hope laughed. "Always so dramatic, Frankie Leigh. Only you would rank cupcakes up there with heaven and sex. I bet Jack appreciates that." She said it with a wink, like we were nothing but girlfriends who got to shoot the shit.

I tamped down the roil of heartbreak that surged. A flashflood of it that nearly knocked me off my feet.

She didn't have a clue of what she was saying or implying. Where my thoughts would actually go when heaven and sex were mentioned together because there was only one place in this world where those two things went hand in hand.

I wondered what she would think of me if she actually knew the truth.

I tacked on the biggest grin.

You know, nothin' like living your fakest life.

"Hey, our job here is serious business," I told her around the shot of unease. "Don't go knocking the importance of sweets. We make a whole ton of customers very happy every single day."

I let the suggestion ride into the words.

She giggled and blushed.

Okay, Aunt Hope wasn't really my aunt. She was married to my godfather, Kale Bryant.

Growing up, Kale was best friends with my daddy and their other friend, Oliver Preston. The three of them had been inseparable. Closer than mere friends. Tied in a way that bound their lives together permanently.

Now, all of our families were intertwined so tightly that's exactly what we'd become.

Family.

Blood didn't matter. Love and connections were about devotion and loyalty. The fact you'd do absolutely anything to support someone you cared about, and that same care was returned to you.

That was family.

So there was something else you should probably know about Aunt Hope—about why my spirit shivered every time I was in her space.

She was also Evan's mama.

Pain staked through me at the thought of his name. It was an effect that happened damned near a thousand times a day.

Evan had been my best friend.

The boy who'd been at my side since I was five years old.

Through those years, he'd become the biggest part of my life.

The brightest part of my soul.

He'd left me three years ago, and still, I could feel him everywhere.

Echoing from the walls.

Taunting my spirit and teasing my mind.

He'd abandoned me when I'd needed him most.

Packed his things and left nothing but a note.

It'd nearly killed me.

But somehow, someway, I'd clawed my way out of the darkness.

Oh, but that sure didn't mean it didn't still hurt.

Refusing to spiral, I focused on the task at hand.

Creating something spectacular, a new recipe that kept our customers flooding through the door.

Aunt Hope smiled one of her soft smiles. "Yes, we sure do keep our customers satisfied. And I have to say how thankful I am that both of you are here to help me and Jenna do it."

When I'd first started working here in high school, I'd thought the title of barista sounded way cooler than working at my mama's diner a few streets over.

Maybe it was a teenager thing.

Needing to spread my wings to experience something outside the watchful eye of my mama.

Somehow, through college, I'd just . . . stayed.

Thing was, every time I walked into this kitchen, I had a sense of belonging so intense that I didn't know how to up and leave.

Now that I had my marketing degree, I couldn't help but imagine all the places we might be able to take it.

"You know that, don't you? We couldn't do this without you," Aunt Hope prodded. A flash of the sadness she'd worn for the last three years made its way into her expression.

It gutted me.

Seeing her worry.

Her confusion over what Evan had done.

Her first son had caused her so much joy and grief.

The boy special in so many ways.

Extraordinary.

Unforgettable.

I gazed over at her, wishing I could take it away. Tell her it would all be fine.

I just didn't think I could tell a lie that big.

Her red hair danced around her shoulders, the smattering of freckles on her face glinting like specks of red glitter under the glaring kitchen lights.

I swore, looking at her was like looking directly at the sun.

A ray of sunshine that'd made itself home right in Gingham Lakes.

Hardest part was it felt so much like looking at *him*.

"I'm just glad we get to do this with you, Auntie. That you put up with us." I gave her a little tease, hiding the quivering in my voice.

She huffed at me. "Put up with you? If you tried to leave me, I would hunt you down and drag you back. Place hasn't been so profitable in years, all thanks to you."

She set her sparkling green eyes on me. Eyes the same color as the ones that had watched me for years with an affection so intense I'd felt like I was the center of a great big, magnificent world.

The center of Evan's world.

Maybe that's why I'd felt so off-kilter, so lost, when he'd gone away.

No longer sure of my direction when my life had always been intertwined with his.

"Hey, way to make a girl feel like a third wheel over here." Carly was all feigned tsks and anger.

I laughed. "I'm sorry, but your literature degree does nothing for us."

"Um, hello, have you read the store's bio on the website? That shit is amazing. Customers come running, mesmerized by the words. And that coupon I put up yesterday? Sheer brilliance."

"You just keep tellin' yourself that," I told her, tossing her a grin as the timer dinged on the oven behind me. I slipped mitts onto my hands and pulled out the tray of triple berry scones.

Hit with the scent, I leaned over them and inhaled deeply.

God, they really did smell like heaven.

"Don't even think about it," Aunt Hope warned when she saw my taste buds getting the best of me.

I laughed. "Just one?"

"I'm about to start docking your pay."

"I'm okay with that," I told her, setting the tray on the cooling rack.

Aunt Hope picked up the batch of key lime cupcakes she'd already frosted. The cupcakes were massive, the frosting a light green and decked with the cutest slices of lime candy and a sugared key.

She knocked her hip into mine. "Just keep doing what you're doing, and we're even."

I fought for a grin. She had no idea how much I adored her. How much I wished that I could erase the pain she kept hidden in the warmth of her caring eyes.

Sometimes I wondered if it was my fault.

If maybe I'd pushed him too far and too fast or maybe if I'd loved him too fiercely.

If he would have stayed if it hadn't have been for me.

"Thank you, Auntie," I whispered low.

She smiled and started for the swinging door that led out to the main lobby. "I better get these restocked and check on Jenna. She's probably ready for a break by now. Can you grab some fruit tortes and vanilla crème cakes? Last time I was out there, we were running low."

"Sure thing," I told her, shaking off the mitts as I headed for one of the warming ovens at the back.

The sound of customers filtered in through the thin walls, and the aroma of freshly brewed coffee filled the space—vanilla and hazelnut and sweet cream—all mixed with the mouth-watering scent of the confections baking in the oven.

It was no wonder A Drop of Hope was just as popular on people's trips home at the end of the workday as it was to help them get their days started.

Aunt Hope disappeared through the swinging door, and I situated the things I needed before I started to head out behind her.

A satisfied smile was taking to my mouth as I listened to the bustle of activity right outside. Voices carrying, the bell on the door dinging every few seconds.

No doubt, the line would be building up.

Half the time, we had people winding all the way out the door.

We always went from dead to completely slammed in a second

flat.

It was go time.

I started to step out, then froze for a beat when I heard a sudden crash. Metal clanged as it slammed on the floor, and a gasp shocked the air.

It was followed by a sticky-sort of silence that bled through.

Climbing into the atmosphere.

Apprehension and distress.

My chest fisted tight, and a sense of dread came over me that made me feel like I was stuck in quickly drying cement.

My pulse hit a sluggish thud, thud, thud.

It took about all I had to push the rest of the way through the swinging door, my feet so heavy I might as well have been wading through a vat of liquid steel.

But my eyes? They raced. Quickened to take it all in.

The customers at the counter looked around in confusion, cupcakes rolling around at their feet, and Jenna's eyes had doubled in size where she stood stock still with a twenty clutched in her hand.

Aunt Hope was frozen right outside the door.

Her hands pressed to her mouth like she was trying not to weep.

It didn't matter how hard I tried to keep it locked in my throat.

A sob broke free.

Echoed through the room while my heart nearly failed where it thugged and hammered and clenched in my chest.

Three years. Three years. Three years.

That was the amount of time that had passed since Evan had gone away.

Three years since a part of my heart had stopped beating.

Three years since the last time I'd seen his gorgeous face.

And now, he was there, standing inside the entrance with a flood of sunlight pouring in through the bank of windows behind him.

Lit up like an apparition.

A ghost roused.

Before he'd left, he'd long since grown out of being a boy. But now? He was all man.

Changed in every way, and somehow exactly the same.

Lean but rippling with strength.

Tall but no longer gangly.

Healthy.

Beautiful.

But I was pretty sure the biggest change was the tiny child he had hooked on his right hip, this little thing with his fist clutched at the neck of Evan's shirt, the child clinging to him like a little froggy sticking to a tree.

Grief gusted and blew.

My hand darted out to the wall to keep myself standing beneath the weight of the green eyes that were so familiar. The baby's gaze overflowed with confusion.

I didn't know if it was horror or relief that hit me hardest.

The fact that Evan was standing there alive and breathing and whole, or if I was crumbling under the weight of witnessing what I would never have.

My attention was back on him. On Evan who was frozen like me.

Shocked.

The two of us stuck in that second as I was assaulted by the memories.

By the oaths and dreams we'd weaved.

The fact he'd promised me all of his days, and then he'd just walked away.

That break in my heart quivered. Threatened to crack wide open.

Suddenly, I couldn't breathe.

Air gone.

Knees weak.

I struggled around it, trying to get it together, to focus on the fact that he was there.

But I couldn't stop shaking.

Couldn't stop the crash of hurt that rolled underfoot.

Tears spilling free, I started to back away, unable to stand, unable to watch. I fumbled through the swinging door because

there was no chance I could remain standing there.
And I fled from the boy I'd always love most.

Evan

*H*ave you ever heard the sound of silence?

The echoing nothingness banging through the stillness?
I'd lived it my entire life.
Like moving through a stifled ocean of complete, utter quiet.
Deaf from day one.
But I didn't think I'd ever felt it more profoundly than when I stepped through the entrance of A Drop of Hope as my mother came through the kitchen door.
Like it was all playing in slow motion, a tray slipped from her hands, the metal hitting the ground, bouncing twice before it skidded.
The treats she'd made my entire life tumbled across the floor.
Every single person in the bakery froze as a shockwave of confusion blistered through the air. I felt it like a hushed anxiety clawing across my skin.
The stilled vibrations that shivered and shook.
They shouted louder than a voice ever could.
Had I expected a different reception?

A prodigal son coming home to a ring on his finger and a feast at the table?

My mom's hands flew to her mouth, holding back what I knew was a shout of pain. Her eyes were rounded, though they were pinched at the sides, bleary with an overwhelming shock of emotion that I was one-hundred-percent responsible for.

Disbelief and hurt oozed from her like a flood.

Only solace was that in it, there was the most stunning kind of relief.

Sometimes it only took one single moment to realize how badly you'd fucked up.

My moment was right then.

But there was nothing I could do but come here.

Desperate.

Hopeless.

Hell, I'd get on my hands and knees and grovel and beg if I had to.

I hiked Everett up a little higher against my side, and he dug his little fingers tighter into my shirt, tipping his trusting gaze toward me in question.

My throat tightened.

Fuck. Still didn't know how to deal with it. What to do with the crush of fear that pulsed through my veins like a flash of fire. A million different emotions I couldn't seem to process.

They all came at me in strobes.

Only thing I did know was I had to return. No matter the consequences.

"It's okay," I told him, sure my voice cracked with the tremor of dread.

I started to say something to my mom. To plead with her.

That was until my own shock was jutting from my lungs when my attention jumped to the door swinging open behind her.

Frankie Leigh stumbled out.

A kaleidoscope of that energy boomed through the air.

She was there.

Of course, she was there.

My tightened throat fully constricted, and my heart tried to climb out through the stricture, like it recognized its home and it couldn't wait to lay itself at her feet.

No regard to whether it was going to get all busted up on the way to get there.

It'd been broken since the day I was born, anyway.

Didn't think there was any hope for reconciliation now.

Might as well take a swim in the pain.

I stood there watching the horror etch across her face as she jerked to a stop.

Didn't matter if it made me a fool.

My eyes climbed to hers as if they were searching through the rubble, fingers bloody and knees scraped from the time it'd taken to claw my way back to her.

I felt her like a goddamn stake to the heart.

A scourge.

A balm.

Didn't fucking know.

Brown eyes with the cinnamon flecks I could never forget roamed over me, like she was trying to reach out and touch me through the distance.

To remember.

But then that gaze was twisting.

Morphing.

The disorder whipping into a frenzy when her attention landed on the child I was holding.

My son. My son. My son.

The words spun through my mind like a windstorm. A vortex that was going to suck me into oblivion.

Still unable to process it myself.

But Frankie Leigh?

Her head rocked back like she'd been punched in the face.

Blindsided.

I wanted to shout at her. Beg her to understand. To not look at me like I'd completely shattered her because it was the last fucking thing I'd wanted to do.

I knew immediately her face was wrought with the same expression I'd been too much of a coward to stand in front of three years ago when I'd left. Knew this was the kind of pain that would have been written on her when she found the note.

Crushed.

Absolutely demolished.

There wasn't one goddamn apology that was going to fix this. No explanation. No reason that would be deemed sufficient.

But I had to remember the mess I'd left between us wasn't the reason I was there.

I had a child to protect.

I swallowed, tried to shove the turmoil down, to ignore the fact that this girl's sweet body still made me ache with a need that had chased me through every night of the last three fucking years.

Ignore the force of her spirit that rippled and shook.

Ignore the connection that pulled and tugged and demanded to know how I could have betrayed her the way that I did.

Still, I felt like I was getting peeled apart when she started backing away.

Fleeing.

Desperate to find a safe place.

Those locks of wild brown curls all around her face.

Mouth parting in shock as she stared at Everett like she was trying to force it all to make sense.

Then her eyes snapped to mine in a blast of alarm before she turned and was gone.

I wanted to run after her.

Touch her.

But I had to focus on what I'd come back to Gingham Lakes for in the first place.

I forced my attention back on my mother—this woman who would have laid down her life for me—the one who'd protected me and sacrificed and instilled in me what a real man should be.

Failed that, too.

"Evan." Her mouth moved in a plea, no sound to touch my ears.

Didn't matter.

I *felt* her.

My focus locked onto the motion of her lips, carefully watching my mom deal with the idea that I was really there while I tried not to completely lose my shit. No doubt it was the fact I had a kid hooked to my hip that almost knocked her on her ass.

That made two of us.

"Mom." I forced it up my throat, knowing the word was probably distorted and garbled, though most people could understand me when I spoke aloud.

Everett scratched his fingers into my chin. Without a doubt, this little man felt my anxiety. I had to wonder if he'd been born with a sixth sense.

One that could tap into emotions in a way that wasn't natural.

Like he'd taken all my amplified senses and multiplied them as his own.

We'd connected in an instant which scared the shit out of me, too. Didn't have the first clue how to care for him. How to help him. And still, there was nothing I could do but cling to him, anyway.

I shifted him to bring us chest to chest, his little heart beating erratic. Or maybe it was just mine.

"Mom, I need your help."

That was all it took to send my mom flying across the bakery floor, confusion pouring from her as she ran toward us. Tears streaked down her cheeks, her eyes roving like she was taking in every inch.

She came to a grinding stop a foot away, hands lifted and trembling, like she wanted to wrap me up and didn't know where to touch.

Like she'd become an outsider.

I hated it.

Hated that I'd put so much distance between us that she no longer knew how to reach me.

Everett pressed one ear against my chest, his head way up high under my chin while he stared out at his grandmother. I splayed my hand over his back, giving him comfort, and I knew it was a sob that was busting from my mother.

Guttural.

Broken.

The way her entire chest swelled and shook, the roll of her throat, the twist of her jaw.

Pain lanced through my spirit.

Regret and remorse and every-fucking-thing I wished I could take back.

"Mom," I said again.

Frantically, she began to sign.

E-V-A-N. WHAT IS HAPPENING? WHAT IS GOING ON? I CAN'T BELIEVE YOU'RE HERE. YOU'RE HERE.

Her watery gaze turned to Everett, a trembling hand reaching out to trace his chubby cheek. Her mouth was quivering all over the place when she looked up and asked, "Oh God, Evan . . . is this your son?"

It wasn't much of a question considering he pretty much looked exactly the way I had in my baby pictures. But I knew exactly how she felt.

Shocked.

Hurt.

Dread taking hold at the truth of what that meant.

"Yes," I told her, admission cracking with a grief I wasn't expecting.

Everett gave one of his tiny-toothed grins when I said it, and fuck, that feeling I kept fighting was twisting around me again.

I wanted to tuck tail and run.

I wanted to stay.

Wanted to fight.

Protect.

Maybe curl up in a ball like I used to do when I was a kid and pray my mom could make it all okay.

But those days were long since gone and it was time I manned up.

"Oh God," Mom whimpered and she swayed, and suddenly Jenna was in action, rounding around the counter, rushing for us. Jenna wrapped an arm around Mom's waist when she looked like she might faint.

Jenna angled her head at me. Pissed. Dazed.

I couldn't blame her.

"Think it might be a good idea to take this homecoming party into the back, don't you?" She rushed through the statement so quickly, it was hard to read her lips, but I got the full gist.

I was about to get my ass handed to me.

I gave a tight nod.

Itching to reach out for my mom.

To hug her and do a little of that begging myself. To tell her I was so goddamn sorry. That I hadn't meant to hurt her. That I'd believed I was doing the right thing for everyone.

I'd been so sick of being a burden.

Of their lives revolving around mine.

Waiting for the day it would end.

Once I'd started the spiral of hopelessness, I didn't know how to get out of it.

Climbing out of it now was the only choice I had left.

I gave an apologetic glance to the customers who were standing there gaping, unwilling parties witnessing this shitshow going down.

Jenna led my mom to the back, and I followed, knocked in the guts again when I stepped into the kitchen and found Carly floundering in through the back door.

Flustered and rushing and attention darting all over the place.

If I had to put down money, she'd just chased Frankie out.

When she saw me, a tear burst from her eye, and she was shaking her head through the disturbance, looking between me and Everett like she didn't recognize me, either.

Apparently, we were making quite the entrance.

Welcome to the family, Everett.

But I knew them well enough to know they would welcome him. Do anything for him. Protect him and keep him, which was exactly why I was there.

As soon as we got into the kitchen, Mom whirled on me, her nails scratching at her chest. "You broke my heart, Evan."

Her words scraped my skin. Hit me like a blow. No, they made no impact on my ears, but fuck, I felt them all the way to my soul.

Shame slammed me. "I'm sorry. I'm so goddamn sorry. The last thing I ever wanted to do was hurt you."

I hugged Everett a little tighter because the last thing I wanted was for him to be in the line of fire.

None of this was his fault.

It was mine.

She blinked frantically. "You didn't want to hurt me? God, Evan . . . you destroyed me. I . . . I . . . I haven't slept a full night in three years. Three years, Evan. Because the only thing I've been able to do was worry about you. Wonder if you were safe or sick. Happy or alone. If you were *alive*."

She clutched her chest again on the last like the thought made her physically ill.

"And now you show up here with a child? A child who looks like he's at least a year and a half old? How could you do this to me? How?"

There's a thing about growing up the disabled kid.

People watched you like you were different.

Treated you like you were different.

With too much care or with outright disdain.

Fawned over you, made concessions, or treated you like you were dirt, unworthy to breathe the air.

I'd been called both *special* and a pussy a thousand times.

Thing was, the only times I'd ever cried in my entire life was over this woman.

When she was in pain. When she walked in fear.

When I'd been a little boy, and the only thing I'd wanted was to be able to protect her from my piece-of-shit biological father, but there'd been nothing I could do to stand up for her because I was just a weak little kid.

Now, standing there as a man? I wanted to fucking weep because it'd turned out that I was a pussy after all.

A coward.

One who'd run when everything had felt too dark and bleak.

Turning away for a beat, I gripped at my hair, hardly able to look back at her because Mom was sure as hell not making concessions right then.

Wasn't about to give me an easy out.

I didn't deserve one.

Could feel Jenna and Carly watching in their own horror, and everything trembled when I forced myself to speak. "And I've spent every day of the last three years hating what I did and feeling like it was the only decision I could make at the same time."

WHY? she begged.

I hesitated, warred, then finally said, "I just . . . needed to find myself. Away from all of this."

It was bullshit.

She knew it was, too.

Because grief was striking on her face and then she was throwing herself at me.

Wrapping her arms around both of us.

The same arms that had fought for me my entire life.

Through all my disabilities.

My genetic defects.

My deafness and this fucking transplanted heart that some days I wondered how it was still beating.

Because of her. That was why.

This woman who'd wrapped me in comfort and joy and steadfast belief.

Refusing to give up hope when she'd been told there was nothing left to be hoping for.

She hugged us tight, tears seeping into my shirt. Could feel her sobs. The tremble of her body. After a long time, she pried herself away, her face full of anguish, only to shift and pull Everett into her arms.

She was whimpering, hugging him and murmuring and kissing the side of his head.

And she didn't even know his name.

It was the reason I'd come.

The reason I'd known this was the only place I could go.

She looked over at me through the tears in her eyes.

Silent questions pouring free.

Is he healthy?

Does he carry your disease?

God, how could you let this happen?

I lifted my hands and gave her the only answer that I could.

HIS NAME IS EVERETT. EVERETT CHASE.

Everett Chase who I hadn't known existed until three nights ago.

Everett Chase who had been thrown into my arms in the middle of the night with a plea and a warning.

Everett Chase who I didn't know but was determined to protect.

Whatever it took.

It was surreal pulling into my parent's circular driveway. Massive trees stood like age-old sentries around the property, sheltering its borders, a vast canopy that stretched out to protect the big white house tucked at the back. Yard immaculate. As immaculate as the wrap-around porch that fronted the first level.

Nostalgia whipped through my entire being as I pulled to a stop. It was in the same neighborhood where Frankie Leigh had lived. Where her parents and brothers still lived two houses down and across the street.

After my mom and Kale had gotten married, they'd purchased this place. Frankie's father, Rex, and his company had come in and renovated it.

Made it better than brand-new.

Putting my car in park, I scrubbed my face with my palms, hoping it might break up the disorder.

Blowing out a strained breath, I cranked open the door and climbed out. I went straight for the back-passenger door, and I swung it open to Everett who was smiling so big at me it made everything hurt.

My heart and my spirit and my mind.

Guts twisted.

How the fuck did this happen?

The kid was sixteen-months-old. All emerald eyes and dimpled, chubby cheeks and trusting face.

"Hey, Chunky Monk." I rumbled the nickname I'd given him that first night when I'd held him for hours to try to calm him down because he freaked the fuck out every time I'd tried to set him down. As I'd comforted him and he'd clung to me and I'd paced for hours as I'd tried to figure out what to do.

Probably should have gone straight to the police, and somehow, I'd shown up here.

Everett made a bunch of sounds that I felt rather than heard.

His sweetness skating my skin. Fisting my heart in a tight clamp.

I undid the buckles of his car seat. "It's going to be okay, Everett. I promise I'm going to figure out what the hell is going on. Promise I won't let anything happen to you," I swore to him, not even sure if the words coming off my tongue were making any sense, while he babbled a bunch of indecipherable things that I wanted to read like brail.

To be able to get to know this kid—for him to know me—and wondering the whole fucking time if he was going to be ripped out of my life as quickly as he'd come into it.

A wall fought to go up around my heart every time I thought of it, a guard against the coming pain, and the kid knocked it down every time he looked at me with all that trust.

Awkwardly, I hauled his little body against mine and slammed the door shut just as I felt the energy erupt from the house, and I looked up to see the front door bang open.

Kale barreled out, his chest heaving and his demeanor wild, so different than my dad who'd always had it together.

He came to a rigid stop at the top of the five steps that led to the house, staring down at me in outright disbelief.

In grief and hope and confusion.

The man who'd become my father when I was eight years old.

The man who'd saved my life.

Literally.

It was one thing to be deaf.

It was another to know your days were numbered, your heart metered with a timestamp.

But Kale?

He'd given me more days than I'd been destined to live.

I clutched Everett to me.

Making some kind of statement.

Taking a stance.

I didn't know.

Only thing I knew was I wanted to wrap this kid up and protect him for all my days.

My throat bobbed heavily while Dad stood up there like he wasn't sure how to breach the space.

E-V-A-N.

He signed my name like a petition. Like desperation. Like terror.

Could feel all of them rushing down.

Slamming into my being.

A reminder of what I'd done.

Everett buried his face in my neck. No doubt, he'd felt the force of it, too.

I rubbed his back. "It's okay, sweet boy. It's okay. I've got you. It's all going to be okay." Just prayed it was the truth.

I edged for the wooden steps, meeting my dad's eye.

Dad's hand clamped down over his chest, like looking at me caused him physical pain. "Evan."

Emotion clogged my throat, and I blinked, trying to see through the years. "Dad," I forced out.

Shame written in the word.

A plea.

"God." His lips moved. Distraught. Overwhelmed.

And then he was stumbling down the steps, his eyes flickering frantically between me and my son.

Like he was readying himself. Prepping himself to have to step in the same way he'd had to do when I was a kid.

Like he was reliving it all over again. With a shaky hand, he reached out and ran his hand over the back of Everett's head.

Tenderly.

Like he was making his own statement.

A promise.

I felt it like an earthquake.

Then he shifted his gaze to me, hesitating, before he hauled me in for a hug that shouted so many things.

Distress and hope and gloom.

He seemed to have to pry himself away, his expression full of apprehension. "We should go inside."

"Yeah," I responded.

I followed him up the steps to the porch and into the house.

This house that was just as cozy as the one Mom and I had shared when she'd run with me.

When she'd saved my life, too, doing every single thing she had to do to keep me alive.

To keep me safe.

I finally understood it now.

A parent's willingness to give it all.

Sacrifice everything.

No matter the cost.

I noticed the whir of movement upstairs, and my attention snapped up to find my little sister blazing down the steps, her hair this unruly mix of red and blonde.

My heart clutched.

She'd grown at least five inches, no longer a child, now fourteen, so much that I had missed.

She didn't slow. She hit the bottom of the landing and dove right for me. Her arms around my waist and her cheek against Everett's back.

Pinning us all together.

With my free arm, I fumbled to return her embrace. "Charlotte." Was pretty sure it was some kind of whimper. It was taking my all not to lose my shit right there.

To drop to my knees with the crash of emotion.

I'd known coming back here was going to be hard, but I hadn't prepared myself for it to feel quite like this.

She squeezed tighter before she looked back at me, her face a blur of tears. "Evan. I was so worried about you. I can't believe you're here. And you have a baby. Oh my God. How did you get a baby?"

She was rushing. Rambling.

Good thing, too. There was no chance in hell I was answering that.

"I'm here, I'm here," I told her instead. "I'm not going anywhere."

The promise came out without thought. I cringed. Unsure if it was the truth or if I was just placating her.

At the same time, I was hit with the devastating realization that I hadn't felt *right* in three years. That I hadn't felt whole or real during all that time.

Lost.

Drifting.

As messed up as my current situation was, there was no question that this was where I belonged.

"I need to talk with Mom and Dad." I touched my sister's cheek, meeting her eye in a promise that we would talk later. No matter what. That I wouldn't disappear.

Her attention darted between Everett and me before she nodded frantically. "Okay," she said as she swiped at the tears beneath her eyes.

"I love you," she said.

"I love you, too," I mouthed back.

Angling around her, I took the short hall to the left. I passed by the formal dining room on the right and stepped through the arch at the end that led into the gourmet kitchen.

A custom nook was built at the far end under the windows that looked out over the yard and the forest beyond. The kitchen huge and brimming with warmth. It'd basically become our family's gathering spot.

My mother was already there, her eyes wild, her arms eager as she pulled Everett from my hold. Hugged him to her chest.

Ripples of angst undulated through the air.

Unease and questions and speculation.

I moved right for the refrigerator. This conversation was going to require alcohol.

I grabbed a beer.

Popping the cap, I chugged half of it before I let the refrigerator door shut, and I turned around to meet their faces.

Their judgment.

Their doubt.

I deserved it.

Still, I was heaving out an unsteady breath.

WHERE THE FUCK HAVE YOU BEEN, EVAN? Dad's anger bled free, the movement of his fingers and hands hard as he made the demand.

I swiped my free hand over my mouth and set the beer aside.

Wasn't sure if I was surprised that he was starting there or if I'd expected it.

If they'd be more upset that I'd disappeared for three years, or if they'd be more shocked by the fact I'd returned with a child.

Not that I was a kid. It was just the fact I was never supposed to have one of my own.

CALIFORNIA, I told him.

I KNOW WHAT STATE YOU WERE IN. WHAT I WANT TO KNOW IS WHY? WHY YOU FELT THE NEED TO CUT US OUT OF THE LAST THREE YEARS OF YOUR LIFE?

Sadness blew through the air. Their pain so stark I felt it like the stab of a knife.

I rubbed my palms together and exhaled a harsh breath.

"I needed to go," I finally forced out, tongue close to tied. "Needed to find out who I am outside all of this."

I gestured around the room like it could embody the pressure I'd felt on my shoulders. Too bad my hand was shaky as shit. Nothing but a tell.

Dad's face twisted, like it was hard for him to hear the sound of my voice. Maybe he'd thought he would never hear it again.

AWAY FROM US, EVAN? FROM THE PEOPLE WHO CARE AND WORRY AND LOVE YOU? FROM YOUR FAMILY? AFTER WHAT HAD HAPPENED?

Didn't he fucking get it? That was exactly it. I was so over being their albatross.

But looking at them now, through the dust and the ash and the debris? I knew what I'd become was an affliction.

IT WAS TIME YOU TWO COULD TAKE A BREATH WITHOUT HAVING TO BE WORRIED ABOUT ME. LIVE WITHOUT FEAR.

Could feel the weight of his incredulous laugh riding on the atmosphere. "Are you kidding me, Evan? You think that was easier? That you could walk and we'd forget about you? Your mom . . ."

He planted his hands on the island and dropped his head, like he couldn't bring himself to even say it. To even delve into what I'd put her through.

Grief and guilt constricted, and my attention flew to Mom who was still hugging and bouncing Everett and kissing his little knuckles like he could be her relief.

Both my hands went to the ache in my chest. "I'm sorry. I'm so damn sorry. But I had to go. You have to understand that."

Could they?

Could they get it?

That I had to go for them.

That I had to go for Frankie Leigh.

Didn't want to live my life an obstacle.

Still didn't.

But there I was.

Laying myself at their feet.

Asking them for mercy.

For forgiveness.

Something I had to do for my son.

Dad turned the weight of his gaze back on me. "Have you even seen your specialists? Continued on your medication? Jesus, Evan, if it weren't for the few letters you've sent, I would have thought you were dead."

His hurt cut through me like a dull, rusted blade.

Slow and excruciating.

I heaved a sigh. "I'm healthy."

REALLY HEALTHY, I signed in emphasis.

Was probably healthier than I'd ever been. Pushing myself to the limits. Over the last year, I'd been working out. Eating right. Doing everything my cardiac specialist had told me to do and doing it to the T. Finally crawling out of that hole I'd dug myself into.

Doing my best to discover myself.

That was until three days ago when my entire world had been

flipped upside down. Rug ripped free, leaving me face down and on my knees.

That seemed to give him some sense of relief, and then his attention was drifting to where Mom had Everett against her, my son with her necklace in his fist, babbling up at her like he wanted to tell her his life's story.

I wished to God I knew it.

Dad's eyes swung back to me, his worry fierce. "You have a child."

Second he did, I signed. *YES, AND I THINK WE'RE IN TROUBLE. DAD, I NEED YOUR HELP.*

Three

Frankie Leigh

I burst through the door of my parents' house. I was gasping for
the breath that I hadn't been able to find for the last thirty minutes,
trembling and nearly bent in two.

I'd come straight here.

Home had always been my first solution, but I wasn't sure that
was going to remain true today.

"Frankie? Is that you?" My mother's voice echoed across the
great room from the kitchen.

"Hey, Mama," I called from the doorway.

Her diner, Pepper's Pies, would already be closed up tight for
the night.

Of course, because she was Rynna, she would still be doing
what she loved to do most.

Cooking.

I followed her voice and the scent that wafted from the
kitchen, stumbling a bit on my wobbly legs as I angled around the
couch as I made my way over to the wide threshold that separated
the two rooms.

White pillars rose on both sides.

Both ornate and welcoming.

I peered through to see Mama had a big pot of stew on the stove. The aroma of it wrapped me in a blanket of comfort.

A shiver rolled my spine as I was struck with the enormity of it.

The safety and sanctuary of this place. I was staggered by the sudden urge to run to her and throw myself in her arms and beg her to chase away the demons the way she used to when I was little.

This was a woman who hadn't birthed me but had become my mother in every way. Stood by me. Never left me.

Had never deserted me.

Hurt crested in waves.

So maybe I had some abandonment issues.

Scars that had been written in the deepest, darkest recesses.

I guessed that's why my first thought had been to seek reprieve here.

Her goodness filled the space, her devotion so fierce I could feel it weaving through my spirit. "Frankie?" she asked with almost a laugh in her voice. "What are you doing, lurkin' back there?"

I sucked all the turmoil down and tried to come off as chipper as could be as I strode in. "Lurkin'? What are you talking about? I'm right here. Just came to see you. I got off work a little bit early today, and I thought I'd stop by and see what's goin' on. Goodness, that smells delicious. You really are a food genius. Remind me why I moved again. I mean, that's just downright crazy, right? Up and payin' rent when I could live here with you and eat all your food? What kind of psychopath am I?"

Okay, so maybe I was known to be a bit chatty.

But there was no missing the tremor that rolled out with the ramble as I moved for the refrigerator, opened the door, and stuck my head inside.

Cold air blasted out.

I wanted to climb all the way in.

Maybe it would cool the heat that was burning me up, flames that were going to leave me nothing but ash.

Mama knew it too.

Could sense her shifting, her awareness, her keen eye turned on me. "Sweet Pea . . . look at me."

Hesitating, I heaved out a breath before I forced myself to turn around and look at her. Guessed it was just then I felt the hot moisture covering my cheeks.

Great.

Now I was straight-up cryin'.

Mama reached out and gathered up a tear. "Oh, sweet girl, what's wrong? What happened?"

I chewed at my bottom lip so hard I was sure I was drawing blood, and I angled my attention to the side and mumbled the name. Maybe if I quieted it, saying it wouldn't hurt so bad.

"Evan."

Nope.

It slayed.

A sharp, searing pain that cut right through the middle of me.

Intensity and worry blustered through her expression, and she was searching mine for a sign.

Blinking through the bleariness, I forced myself to meet her worry. "He's here, Mama. He's here. He walked right into A Drop of Hope like he'd never left, all except for the fact that everything has changed. God, Mama, he has a baby. This little boy who's so adorable and sweet and looks just like him—"

And it's never hurt to look at someone so much.

I had to stop myself from actually saying the last part aloud.

Questions toiled and raged.

Had he found someone? Had he fallen in love? Oh God, was he married?

My weakened knees faltered, and the walls spun, and I was pretty sure I was two seconds from passing out right there on my mama's floor.

A hand was pressing to her mouth, her chocolate eyes that were just as warm and comfortin' as her food going wide with her outright concern. "Is he well?"

I didn't know if she was asking about Evan or the child, and I was blinking through the disorder, trying to make sense of what

A.L. Jackson

I'd seen. I swallowed around the grief lodged like a tumble of jagged rocks at the base of my throat. "I don't know, Mama. I don't know anything. I found him standing in the doorway and I just . . . hightailed it out of there. I couldn't stay."

"Oh, Frankie."

A flash of a second later I was in her arms, and she was hugging me hard, and I was releasing my pain and my rage and my sorrow.

All the hopes that boy had left shattered inside of me.

The dreams that were scattered.

I sank to the floor like maybe I could gather them up.

She came with me, pulled me onto her lap, and held me, rocked me the way she'd done when I was a child.

Sobs heaved, and she kept whispering at the top of my head, "It will be alright, Sweet Pea. It'll be alright. You'll see."

"How could it be?"

Tears kept streaming free, and I was clutching her like a lifeline, searching for air, for reason.

My lungs squeezed.

Painfully.

Agony stretching me thin.

Ripping me in two.

"How could it be?" I whimpered. "He left me, Mama. He left me." And just because he was there didn't change the fact that I could still feel that void echoing inside of me.

That little face pushed into my mind like a storm. Raging and rampant. Beautiful and terrifying. Old wounds rushed in with the darkened, churning clouds.

It doused my soul in anguish.

The deepest, ugliest kind of affliction.

I gasped and choked.

Mama brushed her fingers through my frizzy curls. "He might have walked away, but that boy left a huge piece of himself with you. He's etched himself in places that helped to mold and shape who you are. And I know you did the same to him."

She urged me up to sitting, forcing me to meet her eye, and she set her hand on my cheek. "You two were always something more, Frankie Leigh. Something so powerful that it scared me that you could share a connection that great so young. That's not just going to go away."

My eyes dropped closed, and I shook my head. "But what if I want it to? What if I want to erase all the pain and the scars and the hurt he left behind? Forget him?"

Her smile was sympathetic. "Love doesn't work like that, Frankie Leigh. We cut ourselves wide open when we love. Make ourselves vulnerable. Our hearts reliant on the other. I have to wonder if that connection wasn't so strong that Evan's heart didn't have the strength to bear it."

"But everything has changed."

Jack's face moved through my mind.

Guilt gripped me hard.

God, I shouldn't even be thinking any of these things. Having these feelings.

Her brow pinched as she studied me, her brown hair tied up in a messy but stylish twist. I swore my mama was the prettiest woman in the whole world. Meant for us in every way.

Our savior when me and my daddy had needed her most.

"I'm not sayin' everything hasn't changed, Frankie. I'm not saying that the two of you could ever get back to the way that you were, even if you wanted to. All I'm saying is you don't have to be ashamed of the way you feel. That it's okay to hurt because we can't hurt if we don't love. And a life without love is the most tragic thing."

I jolted in dismay when I heard the back door whipping open.

"Crap," I muttered, frantically trying to wipe the soaking mess from my face. "I don't want them to see me like this."

Mama pushed to standing and held out her hand. "Come here, Sweet Pea."

She rushed over to the sink and wet a cloth under it, wiped my eyes as we listened to the chaos of the guys spilling in through the backdoor, nothing but a ruckus of laughter and carrying voices.

My daddy and my two brothers. Daddy hadn't exactly approved of the relationship Evan and I had shared growing up. The way we were always sneaking off. Holding hands. Far too close for little kids.

He'd always been super protective of his little girl.

He sure hadn't liked it any better as we'd gotten older, either. Forbidding things that I had to believe now were just gonna happen, anyway.

Unstoppable.

I only wished I'd been strong enough to stop it myself. Before it'd been too late. Before I'd let it destroy everything.

"You okay?" she asked, dabbing under my eye.

No, I was absolutely not okay.

But I was gonna fake it for a minute.

With an erratic nod, I struggled to get myself together. To gather up the pieces littered all over the floor. No idea how I was going to recover from the aftermath.

Ryland and Preston clomped down the hall from the back, jostling and pushing each other the way they always did. I swore the two of them were louder than a stampede of bulls.

"Call was solid, man. You're just going to have to accept it." Ryland's deep voice echoed through the air. Ryland was five years younger than me, close to no longer being a child.

Sixteen and as burly as a beast. Hair and eyes super dark like Mama's.

Could hear Preston trying to be just as much a man. "Hell, no. That take down was all me. Ref was blind. Total bullshit."

"Hey, language." My daddy's voice reverberated the hall behind them, the sound of his work boots banging on the floor hitting me with a rush of perfect familiarity.

I had the urge to press my hands to my chest to hold the feeling in.

To remind myself of the relationships I had been given.

To be grateful.

Not to live my life in the grief of the one I wasn't strong enough to keep.

I pinned a smile to my face when my brothers rounded at the end of the hall.

"Yo, Frankie," Ryland called with one of his massive grins when he saw me. It was almost as massive as the guy. Ryland was all wide, hulking shoulders, and thick muscles. Sweat and grime covered every inch of his practice football uniform. "What are you doin' here? Didn't think we'd see you until this weekend."

Oh, you know, just having your everyday, run-of-the-mill meltdown.

"I just wanted to stop by to say hi." I actually managed to keep the warble out of my voice.

Mom pointed at him when he started to plop onto the couch. "Don't even think about it, buddy. Shower."

He laughed. "Ah, come on, Mom, can't handle a little man in the room?"

She arched a brow at him. "*Little* being the predominant word."

He chuckled low and swiped a hand through his drenched hair. "Wow, kick a guy in the nuts, why don't you?"

Preston raised his hand. "I'd be glad to do the honors."

I almost laughed.

God, I loved my family.

Loved them that way that Mama was talking about. Wholly. So big and powerful and fierce that I couldn't imagine what my life would possibly look like without them in it.

My brothers were so wild and crazy and fun.

Growing up, our home had been a constant madhouse, two of them in an unending battle to outdo the other.

Was pretty sure Ryland could take Preston flat out.

Preston was only two years younger than Ryland, but they were worlds apart in size. Preston was still this little stick figure with blond hair and thin arms and the most carefree smile you'd ever seen.

Was pretty sure he was getting ready to grow into his skin, though, even surer that he was going to look exactly like our daddy, tall and sinewy with lean, packed strength.

Speaking of Daddy, he trudged in, wearing one of his crooked, coy grins. He went right for Mama, kissed her firm on the mouth. "Hi, baby. How was your day?"

My insides clutched at the sweet, tender sight.

It was a rare, precious thing to find a love like that.

"Better now that you're home," she murmured up at him.

He swatted her on the butt.

"Ah, gross, you two. Get a room," Preston gruffed the tease over his shoulder, going for the refrigerator to grab a Gatorade.

"Plan to," Daddy baited right back.

Preston pretended to gag as he twisted the cap. "Why'd I even go there?"

"Because you're an idiot, that's why," Ryland tossed out, leaning a hip on the counter.

A frown took hold of Preston's face. "Way to be rude, man. You really do want me to junk punch you, don't you?"

Ryland gestured at himself. "Bring it and see what happens."

Preston gulped down his Gatorade, pointed a finger wrapped around the bottle at Ryland. "Don't worry, brother. Your boys are safe. At least for now. But watch yourself tomorrow. Or maybe in your sleep."

"You even look at me when I'm sleeping, and you die. Think I'll just take you out right now." He started for Preston, and Preston cracked up, jumping into action, sliding behind the round dining table situated in the nook and grabbing onto the back of a chair like he might have to use it to propel himself back over to the other side.

Ryland scrambled for him, a shimmy and fake lurch.

Preston squealed like a pig.

Affection floated, and a small giggle slipped free.

It was no wonder I came here.

The reminder that life went on. That there was joy all around me. Drawn to the chaos and the loyalty.

I just wished Evan would have felt some of it.

"Hey, hey. No roughhousing in the house." Mama shooed them both.

"That is the very definition of roughhousing, Mom. Can't do it outside." Preston tossed her the smart-mouthed tease while Ryland relented and started for the archway so he could go upstairs, canting me a smile when he paused. "You sticking around for dinner?"

I rubbed my sweaty palms up my arms. "I don't think so. I was just stopping by to say hi."

He frowned like I was crazy. "Have you smelled what Mom is

cooking?"

I smiled at him. "Yeah, but I'm pretty sure after you get to it, there won't be any left for me."

"True story," he said, sending me a wave as he headed for the stairs. "See you this weekend then."

Preston loped along behind him. "See ya, Frankie! Love you. Way more than Ryland does." He cracked up at that as he started up the stairway behind Ryland.

"You wish, asshole." Ryland pushed him back down a single step.

"Language," Daddy shouted again.

"Love you both," I hollered after them. I thought it was a small miracle that the words didn't crack.

That I didn't come loose again.

Crumble to the floor.

"Boys." Mama rolled her eyes with all her affection, though her worry was still blatant as she turned her gaze on me.

Soft and concerned and filled with her undying support.

Uncle Kale and Carly were the only ones who really knew.

But I thought Mama had some inclination. Mother's intuition that her little girl had been completely shredded in some way.

Decimated.

Utterly destroyed.

Daddy grinned like he hadn't picked up on the mood quite yet as he swung his attention to me, hitting me with the adoration that always glowed in his eyes.

He was pretty much the most awesome daddy around.

Except that made him about as intuitive as Mama.

His smile slipped.

"What's wrong, Sweet Pea?"

"Oh, absolutely nothin'." I pinned on a bright, fake smile.

Lies.

All lies.

Honestly, there was no reason to beat around the bush. No doubt, that news was going to spread like wildfire.

Hell, I had no idea how he didn't already know.

"Evan's back," Mama said where she was pulling off the lid to stir the bubbling stew, her voice deep with implication.

Daddy hissed, gripped a handful of hair in his own shock and dread. "What?"

Evan disappearing had done a number on all of us.

It was like Daddy's attention didn't know where to land, the weight of it whipping back and forth between Mama and me, demanding answers.

He loved Evan. Of course, he did. But all those fatherly instincts had always landed on the protective side of his little girl when it'd come to us.

But I knew how worried he'd been when Evan had left. Had heard him up pacing the floors while I'd lain in my room and cried.

None of us able to find sleep.

No one able to believe he would do something so horrible to Kale and Hope.

That he would leave that way.

Little did my daddy know that he had been devastating me in a way I would never recover from.

Nodding, I went for as casual as I could, talking around the torment crushing my windpipe. "Yeah, he took us all by surprise by just waltzing into A Drop of Hope late this afternoon."

"He good?" Real concern moved through Dad's expression. Seemed all of our thoughts immediately went that direction when it came to Evan.

Unable to stop it.

"He looked like he was, at least. Healthy." I realized I was hugging myself, tighter and tighter, the words coming thinner with each that I released until the breath was leaving me on a haggard rasp. "He's got a baby."

Daddy's eyes raked me like he was looking for the possibility that it was mine.

I wanted to weep.

"With who?"

I flinched. Hard. He might as well have driven an ice pick into my eye. "Who knows? I didn't get a chance to talk to him. You know, I figured he and Aunt Hope needed to talk first before I got in the way and started monopolizin' all his time the way I used to do." I tossed it out like it was no big deal, but my voice was shaking all over the place, and again, I was thinking I was goin' to get sick right there on the floor. "Well, I'd better go. It's getting late."

Mama frowned her worry from behind Daddy, hating that we couldn't talk freely, giving me a look that she was there for me, no matter what. "Are you sure you don't want to stay for dinner? I do have plenty."

"I think I need to go. Jack mentioned us grabbing dinner."

That sent nausea rebounding for a third round.

Just awesome.

Daddy glowered. Was pretty sure he didn't believe a word. He reached out and took me by the arm.

Softly.

In all his care.

"Frankie." His voice was hoarse, the man so gruff and raw and masculine that you wouldn't think he would have the capacity.

But underneath all that rugged exterior was the gentlest man.

My eyes squeezed shut. "Please, Daddy. I can't talk about this right now."

He hesitated, warring, before he gave a tight nod. "Okay. Just . . . know you can come to us with anything."

Sorrow pulled my lips into a twisted, vacant smile. "Thank you. I'll . . ." I started to back away. "I'll talk to you tomorrow."

Daddy used to call me his Sunshine. Same as Evan. I wondered if my daddy had recognized that it was three years ago that light had gone dim.

He huffed out a worried sigh. "Frankie."

"It's fine, Daddy. I'm fine."

More lies.

But sometimes telling yourself them was the only way to make it through the day.

I hiked up on my toes and pressed a kiss to his scruffy cheek, did the same to my mama, fighting tears as I turned around and beelined for the door, needing to get the heck out of there before I fell apart again.

Because I could feel it coming on.

The hopelessness.

The helplessness.

The loss that screamed and wailed.

Not that it was going to magically disappear when I got home. To the quiet and silence and the questions that I knew were going to consume me the second I was alone.

Topple me into a spiral I might not recover from.

But at least I could do it in private.

I turned the knob on the front door, and I stepped out onto the side deck and rushed down the steps, only to stumble to a stop when I hit the bottom.

Twilight danced through the tall, towering trees, and a wistful blue filled the sky that was just getting dotted with a few stars. The air dense with the scent of honeysuckle and humidity.

I felt stifled by it.

Stuck in it.

Maybe the whole reason I'd shown up here was because my spirit had called out that this was where he would be.

Drawn.

Compelled.

Just like my sight that was racing up the opposite side of the street toward Evan's childhood home.

The pull intense.

The power fierce.

Stunning and striking and unrelenting.

I tried to inhale against the clot in my throat.

To stand and not cower when it felt like the sky was toppling down and spilling to the Earth. Every star falling free. Crashing to the ground.

I tried to see through the turmoil. Through the tears blurring my eyes.

But the only thing I was seeing was Evan standing at the side of a car that I didn't recognize but I had to believe was his.

This beautiful, beautiful boy that my fingers itched to remember. That my spirit demanded to once again know.

Impossible.

No one had ever loved me the way Evan Bryant had.

And no one held the power to hurt me the way he could.

He'd left me when I'd needed him most.

Destroyed and decimated.

Still, I couldn't do anything but stand there and watch as he ducked into the backseat and pulled out what I was pretty sure was a diaper bag, and my heart was panging with horrible, horrible things.

Thoughts I couldn't entertain.

He turned around. Awareness jolted through his body, and immediately his gaze landed on me.

Our eyes got tangled.

Tangled like the tendrils of our spirits that were thrashing wild.

Reaching for the other.

Hurt and desperation and need.

The bag slipped from his hold, hitting the ground at his feet with a thud, and he stood there, fisting those big hands.

Hands I couldn't help but remember the way they'd felt against my skin.

There was nothing I could do but move.

Carried toward the desolation.

Just needing to feel him one more time.

To make sure he was whole and safe and real.

Feet numb below me, I fumbled over the loose gravel of my parents' drive, not pausing when I floundered across the street.

My gaze raced over him like he might disappear, sight filling full of his chiseled jaw and his full lips and the distinct angle of his nose.

And I remembered and I remembered and I remembered . . .

But I was noticing all the differences, too.

His brow darker.

Everything a little harder.

His demeanor strong and stony and rife with a plea.

To me, he'd always been the most beautiful boy. Now the man was making my body ache in the most painful of ways.

Acute.

Piercing.

His presence this violence that wracked my insides.

He worked that jaw, his thick throat bobbing heavily.

And suddenly, I was dropping everything.

My pride and my fear and the questions and hurt that spun their wrath in the space that separated us.

Howling and whipping and screaming.

I braved it.

The distance.

The pain.

Every obstacle that stood in our way.

I ran through it.

Heart first.

Until I was throwing myself at him, wrapping my arms around his warm, strong body.

The feel of him intoxicating.

Dizzying.

I pressed my ear to his chest. Against the bang, bang, bang that thundered at his ribs.

Life. Life. Life.

He hesitated, his hands glued to his sides.

Could almost feel the years rise between us like a barrier.

"Frankie." My name scraped from his throat. Raw and grating. It didn't matter how badly he'd hurt me. I was sure his voice was the best song that had ever been written. "Frankie. I'm sorry. I'm so fucking sorry."

I pulled back, my hands against his chest when I signed frantically, telling him the one truth that still remained.

YOU ARE MY FAVORITE.

He heaved out a breath with the impact of my statement.

Then I tore myself away, stumbling as I wept, unable to look back as I ran for my car.

Wishing that loving him didn't have to hurt so bad.

four

Frankie Leigh
Five Years Old

Frankie heard the voices getting louder out on the back patio. She

scrambled to her feet, dropping the unicorn toys she was playing with onto her bedroom floor.

"We gots ta go, Milo!" she shouted at her favorite, favorite puppy. Scrambling to his feet, he chased her right down the hall, nipping at her heels, barking his own excitement.

Frankie was grinning so big.

Today was a special day.

Such a good, good day and she couldn't wait.

Her mama had told her she was gonna get a new special friend and she felt so, so, so excited, and her belly was full of butterflies flappin' their wings all over the place.

At the end of the hall, she cut to the left, and she raced through the kitchen, rounding around to the back door.

She burst out of it and onto the porch, the screen door smacking behind her. Milo did a circle around her feet.

Her uncle Kale was standing at the top of the porch steps. Her heart nearly burst. She loved him all the way to the moon and all the way back times a million. Without slowing, she wound through the tables set up on the patio, her feet pounding on the wood. Excitement blazed through her whole body, and she threw her arms into the air, shouting, "Uncle Kale! Uncle Kale! You came to see me!"

Then she came to a skidding stop when she saw the boy who was holding her uncle's hand, his hair almost like the sun, red and orange and white, all mixed together, his eyes so big in his glasses.

Green like the trees.

"Is this mys new friend Evan?" she rushed to ask, looking up at her uncle.

Her new special friend who her Mama told her she had to play all, all day with because he was super, super special because he didn't have no hearing and he had a special heart that he got when he was just a baby.

Her mama even taught her how to talk to him a little tiny bit.

Her uncle knelt down. "Sure is, Sweet Pea. This is Evan, and he's really special to me, so I hope you spend the whole day playing with him because he doesn't know anyone else here."

Frankie made the sign she and her mama had practiced so much last night, her belly feeling a little worried because she wanted to do it just right. She lifted her hand and put it to the side of her forehead and pulled it away like a little wave.

HI.

And then the boy signed it back with a big grin that made Frankie grin even wider. Oh, she did like him, the way his eyes were big and funny and he kinda looked like a froggy.

And then he was moving his hands at his mommy.

His mama said, "Wonder Woman."

Frankie laughed out in glee. Wonder Woman was what her daddy called her and it was the best name in the whole world and made her feel special, too. She liked it that her new friend called her that.

Her uncle Kale looked at Evan. "Yeah, buddy. This is Wonder Woman."

Her uncle looked at her and swept his hand toward the boy. "And this is my little Hulk."

Giggles came floodin' out of her. "I likes the Hulk . . . but he's not as strong as my daddy and my uncles! Thor and Cap'in 'merica."

The boy didn't look a whole lot like the Hulk, she thought. He wasn't very strong. But that didn't matter none. She liked him, anyway.

"Wanna play? I gots my puppy and he's so fast and he likes to jump and lick and he's so funny!" she rambled, pushing the curls out of her face when the hot breeze came blowing through, and then she was rememberin' that her mama told her to talk slow because Evan had a special super power and it was that he could read lips!

And oh man, she thought that was so, so cool because she could barely even read a whole book that had ten pages.

Evan nodded fast, and he dropped her uncle Kale's hand and chased right after her.

He clamored down the steps, his feet pounding to keep up, and she rushed out onto the lawn. Her puppy raced between them, darting around their ankles, running out ahead and running right back.

She laughed.

Laughed and laughed.

She gave it all she had as she ran across the yard, and Evan chased her, a funny noise rushing up his throat.

It was rough and strange, but when she looked back, she saw that he was laughing, his head tipped toward the sky, those sounds scraping up his throat and riding on the breeze.

Frankie thought she liked that sound, too.

The little dots on his face glowed bright in the sun, and she wondered if she could count high enough that she could count them all.

He chased her and they zig-zagged and they hid and they played, and she was sure she'd never had so much fun.

Finally, she slumped down onto the lawn, all out of breath.

Evan's breath was super loud, too, huffing and puffing, and he fell down onto the ground beside her.

"You tired?" she asked where she was on her belly and looking over at him.

He nodded frantic. "Rest."

He made a word come out of his mouth and Frankie squealed. Nothing but delight.

"You can talks, too!?"

He held up two fingers, just a pinch.

"And you gots a new heart?" she asked, remembering her mama telling her he was even more super special because he got a new heart when he was a baby and she thought that was weird and scary but kinda cool.

And she thought her uncle had it all wrong.

He wasn't the Hulk. He was Iron Man.

Evan nodded again, let her put her hand on top of it, and she liked it even better when he put his hand over hers and pushed tight so she could feel it go boom, boom, boom.

He felt warm and safe, her eyes dropping closed as she felt the way his chest thrummed and beat.

Finally, she peeled open her eyes to see him staring at her really close.

"That's so, so good you gots a new a heart." Her voice came out a whisper. "You want to be my best friend?"

Because Frankie was sure Evan was her favorite, favorite.

He nodded again, so fast that it made her laugh.

She gave him a thumbs up.

He laughed that sound again and gave her one, too, his breaths loud and hard.

And she felt so happy and full, and she rolled onto her back. Milo curled up to her side, sniffing along the grass, digging his paws into the dirt until he got comfy.

She gazed up at the clouds that rolled slow across the sky, a gazillion different pictures written in puffs of white and blue, blue, blue.

And she wanted to tell her new best friend so many things.

That she liked spaghetti and unicorns and her favorite color was pink.

That she was afraid to be alone and fire was her most scariest thing.

Instead, she grabbed his hand and just stared at the sky.

He squeezed it back.

And she knew she'd never been any happier than that.

five

Frankie Leigh

My tires crunched on the gravel drive of the little duplex I shared with Carly and Josiah. The house attached to us was the exact replica, only mirrored.

Jack lived there.

My spirit gave a shudder at that, my movements stagnant and slowed as I eased to a stop in front of the house. Killing the engine, I sat there staring through the windshield as the shadows from the branches overhead lapped and played, the sun sinking behind the house and hitting the horizon in a blaze of blinding red and orange glory.

I gulped, trying to figure out how to just . . . move.

How to exist in the same town and world where Evan was and him not be a part of my life.

It felt so wrong.

Sacrilegious.

Filthy and obscene.

And at the same time, I felt completely terrified of being in his space. The wounds he'd left raw and throbbing, this pain I was experiencing so intense I wasn't sure how to stand.

But he couldn't come close to understanding the depth of the scars he'd left me with.

The front door cracked open, and Milo squeezed his way through, his tail waggin' like crazy.

Carly stepped out onto the small porch, watching me with apprehension and distress.

I forced myself to get out of my car.

Milo bounded down the two short steps, as fast as his old body could take him, my sweet boy's back bowed and the whiskers on his face grayed with his age. I knelt down in front of him, petting his neck and landing a kiss to his wet snout.

He wiggled all over the place, loving me the way only a dog could.

Unconditionally.

Absolutely.

I sniffled and somehow coerced myself into standin', meeting the worry and questions in Carly's eyes.

"Are you okay?" she asked. "I didn't know what to do when you took off."

My shoulders hiked to my ears, my arms crossed over my chest, hugging myself like that would be sufficient to hold the pieces together. I laughed out a weary sound and looked to the hedge that was blowing in the breeze. "I don't think I've ever really been okay . . ." I shifted my attention back to her. "Have I?"

Her lips pursed, and she edged forward, leaning her forearms on the railing. "I think you've done the best you can after that type of loss. Better than I expected, honestly."

I huffed out an ironic chuckle. "You mean you expected me to crumble into a big ol' ugly mess?"

Her laugh was a little freer, a tease winding through. "Well, you kinda did. You were lucky I was there to help pick up the pieces."

Even though I appreciated her trying to lighten the mood, my sigh was heavy, and she leaned forward a little farther. "Did you talk to anyone about him? Find anything out?"

"I went to my mama's. She hadn't heard anything about it, either. I don't really think anyone knows what's goin' on."

Sorrow shifted through her being. "I'm worried something is not good with that little boy. Evan seemed . . . distraught. He left with his mama right after you took off. He told her he needed help. Jenna and I closed up, and we didn't hear anything after that."

Unease crawled beneath my flesh. Hot and sticky. "Evan was at his parents' house when I left my family's."

"You saw him?"

My nod was jerky. "I saw him outside when I was leaving."

"Did you talk to him?"

My head shook, my teeth clamping down on my bottom lip to keep myself from crying again. At this rate, I was going to gnaw the entire thing off. "No. I . . . not really."

Her brow lifted in speculation. "Not really?"

God, part of me wanted to deny my weakness. The effect this boy still had over me. But this was Carly I was talking about. "Okay, fine. I ran over and hugged him hard and then got right the hell out of there before I went and said something that I couldn't take back. Are you happy?"

"Oh, Frankie. How could I be happy when you're not?"

The breeze whipped through, and I dragged my fingers through my frizzy curls, pushing them out of my face. "He's moved on, Carly. And so have I."

Only saying it hurt real, real bad.

All the way down deep like I was getting a stake jabbed right through the most tender spot in my soul.

"Bullshit," Carly spat. Somehow it still sounded like encouragement.

"Don't," I told her, rubbing at one of Milo's ears where he sat leaned against my leg, as close as he could get.

"Don't what? Point out the truth? Because I'm pretty sure enough lies have already been told."

Grief crested and crashed.

My stomach getting twisted up in a mess of knots that I didn't think could ever be undone.

I glanced over my shoulder at Jack's side of the duplex. His car was out front, parked crooked the way he always did. No doubt, he was inside, sitting in front of the television, unwinding after a day of manual labor since he was the foreman of one of my daddy's construction teams.

I looked back at her. "The only thing I want is for Evan to be happy." It came out a plea.

She leaned back against the wall. "Well, he sure didn't look all that happy to me. He looked . . . terrified. And every bit as broken as you."

Disquiet stirred, my thoughts getting whipped into a frenzy.

Carly was right.

There was just . . . somethin' off.

Way off.

Not that the situation could even be remotely normal, Evan showing up after being gone for three years.

What he'd done to all of us had been so damned wrong.

But it didn't matter.

Didn't matter how much time had passed. How much pain he'd meted. How much distance had separated us.

I knew Evan.

Knew him with a glance.

Something was definitely wrong.

Horribly wrong.

That little boy's face flashed.

The spark in his green eyes.

The way Evan had held him like he was petrified he might slip away.

My guts clenched.

Pain and shock.

I tried to block it out.

Maybe if I focused hard enough, I could will the love away.

Guessed I always had been accused of being a dreamer.

"You should come inside," Carly said. "Josiah's making dinner, and I just opened a bottle of wine. Thought you might need a glass or maybe six."

"You're my hero."

She arched a brow. "Ah, we know who your hero is. We're done with the lies, remember?"

I relented with a nod, knowing I wasn't going to be able to eat. But that wine? I was game.

Five minutes later, I was standing at the counter with a glass of red while Josiah worked his magic in the kitchen.

"You're almost as good as my mama," I told him with a smirk, fighting for normalcy.

"I wouldn't dare aspire to such great things," he teased, sending me a wink that was wound with worry and understanding.

Josiah was awesome.

The biggest nerd you'd ever met.

Spent his life in front of a computer screen playing video games.

He was also Evan's first friend, the two of them introduced by their pediatric cardiac doctor since they'd both had heart defects.

Josiah's had been much less significant, and he was considered completely cured.

Carly, Josiah, Evan, and I? We'd become as tight as could be, even in the days when I'd been running around in junior high and high school, thinking I was all kinds of awesome, wantin' to be a cheerleader. On the A Team. Varsity.

The center of attention.

A dancer and a star.

But a star didn't shine without the reflection of the sun.

"She's pretty amazing, that's for sure," I agreed, taking another good guzzle of the wine.

"Kind of like those recipes you and Carly have been whipping up at the bakery." He angled a shoulder toward her since his hands were busy dicing and chopping.

"Pssh." Carly waved him off. "I am there purely for supervision. Have to keep Hope and Frankie here from running wild with their crazy-ass concoctions."

"Hey, those concoctions are gonna make us famous."

Josiah let his attention move over me, searching. "Are you finally going to employ that marketing degree you worked so hard to earn? Apply it to the bakery?"

I bit down on my bottom lip. I'd graduated this last May. I think everyone was waiting around on what I was goin' to do. If

I'd find some small firm here in Gingham Lakes, or if I'd move away to a big city.

Maybe I'd contemplated it for a day or two.

Running away.

Getting free of the memories that bound and chained.

But I'd come to accept that idea was about as far-fetched as it came.

Because I knew leaving A Drop of Hope would be impossible.

Felt like I'd been etched into those walls.

As if the years had seeped into my bloodstream until it was written in me.

Carly hopped up onto the counter, swinging her legs as she sipped at her wine. She tipped her glass at Josiah, though her head was angling for me. "You know she wasn't about to leave A Drop of Hope. She's been waiting around there for the last three years for Evan to show back up."

Was she serious?

My mouth dropped open. "Carly. I have not. I can't believe you would even say that."

I was gonna throttle her.

"Lies, lies, lies." She singsonged it in the middle of taking a sip of her wine.

"You're just trying to stir up trouble," I warned. Did she really have to go and point out the obvious?

Last thing I needed was for her to rub it in.

"And you're just trying to live in the delusions you've been living in for your whole life. Sweet Pea Frankie Leigh and her fantasies. Only this one is straight-up ridiculous. You're really gonna stand there and deny it?"

Sadness billowed through my being, and I tried to swallow around the lump. "You're right. Maybe it is time I finally stopped living in a fantasy world. Maybe it's time I accepted that Evan is my best friend and that was all he was ever meant to be."

Maybe then we could figure out how to get back there. To the days when our trust was bigger than the worries of our world. When our friendship could conquer all.

Carly laughed.

Loud.

This cackling sound that rattled against the kitchen cabinets.

"Are you hearing this?" she asked Josiah in exaggerated disbelief.

"Loud and clear, Nutter Butter."

"You should have seen her face when Evan walked through that door." She hummed in some kind of morbid satisfaction because her mind going that way was nothing but sadistic.

Like she was taking some kind of joy in causing me more pain.

"This isn't funny, Carly," I told her, voice starting to tremble.

She frowned in true sympathy. "Nope. It's not. But you claiming that Evan isn't your soul mate is damned near hysterical."

My heart clutched all over the place, then it was tipping out onto the ground when I heard the knuckles rapping at the door.

Milo started barking like mad, scrambled to get on his feet, and trotted for the door.

"Damn it," I managed to mutter.

Carly smirked. Josiah laughed under his breath.

"That should tell you something right there." She pointed toward the door.

I scowled at her from over my shoulder.

She sure wasn't gonna make this any easier, was she?

I crossed the small living space to the door, and I worked through the lock, cracking it open and praying I could act like a normal person and not some crazy loon who was gettin' ready to lose her mind.

Heart had gone missin' a long time ago, so I guessed the ailment was fitting.

Jack was on the other side, like I'd known he would be, all dark brown hair and thick beard and tattooed sleeves.

"Hey," he said in his casual way.

"Hi," I mumbled. Even that one word felt like a lie.

Jack frowned. "Bad day?"

"You could say that."

"She's spun-up because her best friend, Evan, is back," Carly shouted from the kitchen.

I was going to throttle her.

Jack frowned. "Evan?"

I forced a bright smile. "Yep. Remember I told you about him?"

Only I'd barely mentioned him. Unable to speak his name, to confess what he'd meant to me.

"Guy you'd told me about who took off? The deaf one?" Jack's voice was edged with hardness.

I tried my best not to throw the defensiveness I felt right back, wishing that I'd never said a word at all. "That's him."

"What is he doing back?"

I shrugged like it didn't matter. "Who knows."

Could see he was getting ready to ask more questions, so I cut him off. "You'd better get in here. Dinner is almost finished. I bet you're starving."

six

Evan

Night clung to the walls of my old childhood bedroom.

A palpable quiet echoed through the space. Stagnant and constricting. Like maybe the air had gotten caught up in a bad dream.

Held in a single moment of the night that threatened to go on forever.

It only amplified the silence that screamed through my mind.

A flood of fear. A torrent of confusion.

All of it tumbled and mashed and taunted.

Made me feel like my flesh was suddenly two sizes too small, and I was getting ready to split apart.

I stared at the ceiling, roughing a hand over my face, wondering what the fuck I was going to do.

The darkened expanse was only illuminated by a thin stream of moonlight that streaked through the break in the curtains and landed on one side of the room.

A spotlight directed at the one thing that was important.

What had brought me back to Gingham Lakes, though I had

to wonder if I wasn't getting drawn back here all along.

The glow struck down on the spot where we'd placed Charlotte's old crib that Dad had brought up from where it'd been stored in the shed out back.

It was the spot where my son now slept.

Didn't matter the overwhelming distress and concern that had radiated from Dad.

Slowed his movements and sent his eyes constantly slanting toward me.

He'd stayed there. Helped me put it together the first day when I'd gotten back.

He'd always promised he would support me no matter the situation. Maybe that's why I'd had to go. Completely remove myself because they would never make that decision themselves.

Selfless.

Dread chugged through my veins when I thought about what I might have gotten them into this time, yet I knew I was willing to take the risk, anyway, because how could I not?

I knew, no matter what, they would stand for family.

Fear constricting my throat, I sat up and reached over to snag the crumpled letter I'd found in the front pocket of Everett's diaper bag tonight. I'd been getting him ready for bed after Mom and I had been out running around most of the day picking up things that he would need.

A letter I didn't think had been there before, though I wasn't sure.

Everything had been so chaotic that night when he'd come into my life, the quick decision I'd made to come here as the dawn had been breaking. I'd grabbed a few things before we were in the car and headed for Alabama.

I studied the words in the lapping shadows that clawed through the room.

A whisper. A will.
A lie. A debt.
You can run. It doesn't matter. I will collect.

A shudder rolled my spine.

I mean, what the fuck was this bullshit? A joke? Some kind of twisted threat? Some inconsequential thought she'd scribbled on a scrap of paper and then stuffed into the pocket and left it without realizing it was there?

Only thing I knew was I couldn't stop the flash of Ashley's face from blazing through my mind. The way she'd looked that night when I'd opened the door to find her frantic, trembling and shaking, this girl who I hadn't seen in over two years who was shoving this kid into my arms.

A kid I'd never seen.

A kid who looked exactly like me.

The sheer terror in her eyes, the way she'd met mine with a plea.

"I'm so sorry. I'm so sorry for everything. I swear I never meant for this to happen. I . . . I . . . Take care of him. Please." Her hand flew over her mouth and tears raced down her cheeks.

"Ashley," I'd shouted as she'd turned to flee, no clue how to even hold the child in my arms, the weight of him foreign.

She whipped around to look at us from over her shoulder. "I'm sorry."

Two seconds later, she was gone, and I was suddenly a dad.

We already had plans to contact an attorney tomorrow.

Dad suggested it was the best way. Track her down and figure out what her intentions were. Get the gist of what her frame of mind was when she left him.

Of course, that meant I had to decide on what my intentions were, too.

Where I stood.

Long term.

Forever.

That and we had to get him immediate testing.

Nausea coiled in my stomach, this sickness I would never outrun clawing and ripping, like I could feel the rise of the disease that lived inside.

My teeth gritted, and I scruffed a hand over my face to break up the disorder. So I could see through the turmoil to the one thing that mattered. I pushed to my feet and eased over to the crib, this crazy feeling running a circuit through my body.

A connection like I'd only ever experienced once before in my life.

Knew firsthand how dangerous it was.

How that feeling could destroy.

The destruction that came when the bond was severed.

Warily, I peered down into the crib.

Everett was face down, his knees tucked up under him, his butt in the air, his little hands fisted in the sheets. Mouth moving like he was sucking something.

Affection and fear pulsed.

I couldn't distinguish one from the other. Or maybe they were one in the same.

Intense.

Unrelenting.

Like a fist was driving itself right into the middle of my chest and tearing out my heart and giving it to this kid.

But that's what this was, wasn't it?

The sudden awareness that I'd give him my life.

Whatever bullshit his mother had gotten herself involved in? I was going to make sure it didn't affect him.

That he would be safe.

Guilt stalked through my insides like a monster preying on the innocent. The selfishness of those nights. The way I'd been overcome with the desperation to do anything to erase the loneliness that had howled and begged.

Like fucking some other girl was going to erase the pain.

Blot out the loss of Frankie Leigh.

Fill up the vacancy.

Because of it . . . I'd done this.

I stared down at this child. Heart seizing in my chest, I sent up a thousand prayers that I hadn't condemned him to the same life I'd endured.

That he would be spared.

That he hadn't inherited this curse.

Consumed by it, I reached into his crib and picked him up, needing to feel his weight. The little motion-activated light Dad had set up to draw me from sleep in case he woke up in the middle of the night flickered to life in a dull haze.

Only thing it did was light up his cherub face.

These fucking chubby cheeks and double chin that I had the overpowering urge to kiss.

He barely stirred, just snuggled deeper into my hold.

I carried him back to my bed.

Lay on my back with him nestled on my chest.

His little heart thrumming its life beat against me.

I wrapped my arms around him.

Held him tight.

And for the first time in days, I actually slept.

"Okay, big man, this is going to be a little cold." Dad pressed the stethoscope to Everett's bare chest, kid without a shirt with all his adorable jelly rolls pudging out over the top of his diaper.

I cringed the second the metal hit his breastbone. Struggled to breathe. To slow my pulse that was beating mad.

Was pretty sure I was two seconds from passing right the fuck out.

Dad glanced at me in worry. "It's okay, man. Just . . . take a seat. Relax."

Relax.

That was not going to happen.

"I'm good," I told him.

"Good, huh?"

YUP, I signed.

Dad studied me for a beat before he turned his full attention back to Everett and his eyes dropped closed.

Listening intently.

Everett was grinning, grabbing at the tubing, tugging hard and thinking it was some kind of fun game when he managed to yank out one of the earpieces from Dad's ear.

"You are a little stink bug, aren't you?" Dad teased, poking him in the belly.

Chubby legs kicked all over the place, his joy spilling out.

Dad reached over to grab a plastic toy from the desk that was some kind of bug that hung from a short string, its body made of rattles. He dangled the decoy in front of Everett's face.

"How about this instead? Look how awesome it is . . . a little grasshopper . . . just like you."

Those full lips of his puckered in a little 'O' and his eyes shined with glee.

Dad tapped it to his nose.

Everett threw his head back in a fit of laughter.

"Boink. Got you," Dad said.

Everett grabbed it from him and held it up like a prize in his little fist. "For Ehvie! Ehvie, please." Everett nodded this emphatic little nod that left me a puddle on the floor.

How the hell was the kid so damn cute?

"Yours? That's mine." Pure affection radiated from my father. His gentle care so clear as he distracted my son from the exam. Made him feel comfortable and safe.

Dad had practiced here at Gingham Lakes Children's Center since he'd come into mine and Mom's lives.

A room almost exactly like this one had brought us together.

Our paths crossing.

Colliding.

My dad was probably the best doctor in Gingham Lakes.

Caring.

Intuitive.

Didn't think there was anyone else in the world I would trust with Everett.

Still, I felt sick.

Legitimately sick.

I hated these fucking rooms.

Hated them with every fiber of my being.

Hated the needles and the fear I could feel creeping across my skin, the memories of the pain I'd suffered through.

Loved them the same.

Because if it weren't for exam rooms like this, I wouldn't be here today.

Could feel the squeals of laughter Everett was exuding, could feel the warmth in the murmur of words that Dad spoke to him.

Moments like these were when I really wished I could hear.

Wished that I could hear Dad tell me he was completely fine.

Tell me he didn't inherit the scourge from the family I didn't want to be a part of.

The illness that came from my biological father's side of the family.

My aunt had died from it.

Chances were that someday I would, too.

I almost scoffed at the memory of when the attorney had shown up at my apartment here in Gingham Lakes about a year before I'd left, the knock at the door that had let me know I'd inherited five million dollars.

My estranged grandfather had passed.

Wasn't like he wanted to take care of me after he was gone. Hell, his son, aka the piece-of-shit who had fathered me, had wanted me dead.

My congenital defects nothing but a blemish on their superior blood line.

What bullshit.

Only reason I was still breathing was because my mom and Kale had been willing to fight the fight. To war and contend.

Refusing to stop until they'd brought the corrupt into the light.

Once my father and grandfather had been exposed, the will had been rewritten.

I hadn't wanted anything from either of them, but there it was, my bank account now boasting so many zeros I doubted I could spend all of it in my entire life.

Had to admit right then, I was thankful I had that cash. Didn't matter where it'd come from.

Dad sat back, swiveling around in the low wheeled stool he sat on, his hand still on Everett to make sure he was safe.

"From where I'm sitting, his exam is completely normal."

Relief hit me hard.

YOU'RE SURE? Couldn't help but go back to my first language, signing like instinct.

Dad wrapped the stethoscope around his neck. "Going to talk to you man to man, Evan. As a doctor to a parent. All of this is preliminary. Basic. But right now? This second? The only thing I can see is that he is a healthy sixteen-month-old boy. Fiftieth percentile for height and ninetieth for weight. You might need to put him on a diet."

The last was a tease.

Felt like deliverance that sloshed through my bloodstream.

I sank down onto the chair.

"Thank God," fell from my tongue in a slur as the weight I'd been carrying since the second I'd had Everett in my arms lessened a fraction.

Dad touched my knee to get my attention. "Hey, Evan. Need you to hear this."

I held up a finger for him to give me a second, and I stood up and moved for Everett where he was swinging that toy all around.

What I needed right then was to wrap him up and hold him close.

I pressed my lips to the back of Everett's head where he sat facing out on my lap.

"He's beautiful, Evan." For a beat, the white coat was gone, my father in its place. His eyes warm and brimming with the faith he'd raised me with. "Beautiful. I can't believe I have a grandson."

Dad lifted his hands to sign, like he needed to be direct, ensure that I was understanding what he was saying. *IF HE CAME IN HERE WITHOUT YOUR FAMILY HISTORY?*

I nodded understanding, my heart going spastic at the reference.

The curse.

I WOULD HAVE NO CONCERNS. I'D BE CONFIDENT HE WAS ONE-HUNDRED PERCENT HEALTHY, he continued, hands moving distinctly, emotion packed in the emphasis. *I'D CLEAR HIM AND SEND HIM HOME AND SAY TO FOLLOW UP FOR HIS EIGHTEEN-MONTH WELL-CHECK.*

More relief.

Dad leaned forward a little more, the rhythm of his hands growing more forceful.

RIGHT NOW, I'M NINETY-NINE PERCENT SURE THAT IS THE CASE. BUT BEFORE WE CAN COME TO THAT CONCLUSION, HE HAS TO HAVE A COMPLETE GENETIC WORKUP. IT'S THE ONLY WAY WE CAN BE CERTAIN HE DOESN'T HAVE THE SAME DEFORMITIES THAT YOU WERE BORN WITH.

Dad's throat tremored, and I could see his own ghosts and demons simmering deep in the well of his eyes.

BECAUSE OF YOUR MEDICAL HISTORY, I'D ALSO LIKE HIM TO SEE THE PEDIATRIC CARDIOLOGIST.

It was instinct.

The way I hugged Everett fiercely.

Like if I held him close enough, I would never have to let him go.

Dad watched me with pure hesitancy. "Do you have any of his prior medical records?"

Regret shook my head. *NO. THE ONLY THING SHE LEFT ME WITH WAS A DIAPER BAG.*

That and a car seat she'd left sitting outside the door.

"All right . . . we'll just . . . go about this the best that we can. Hopefully the attorney can track her down quickly. Get the judge to order temporary custody so you can sign to obtain his records."

That was a worry, too.

If the state would come in and snatch him up and place him in foster care.

Deem the situation too chaotic.

My care unfit.

I'd already given a blood sample this morning so I could at least prove paternity before we got the law involved.

The attorney said that was the first step.

Then getting me on his birth certificate.

The rest of it would have to go from there.

"He needs us to do the best that we can for him, Evan."

"I'll do absolutely anything. I just . . ." Misery twisted my brow in a plea. "How am I supposed to be a father when I have no fucking idea if I'm gonna be around?"

Grief streaked through Dad's expression. "None of us gets the luxury of knowing that, Evan. Not one of us. And I know your situation is different, but being a father is giving your child every single one of your days. However many of them there are. That's what matters."

"I just . . . want to be enough."

And that was the problem.

Wasn't ever sure that I could be.

Emotion welled in his eyes. "You've always been, Evan . . . more than enough for all of us. I don't think you ever really realized what a blessing that you are. How you made us all better people for being you. How you changed our worlds and in a better way."

My gaze drifted to my son who'd slid off my lap and was standing between my knees.

"You want to tell me about his mother?" Dad hedged.

Last night we'd tiptoed.

Only the barest facts given.

Not that I had a whole lot of information to contribute, anyway.

HER NAME IS ASHLEY. Decided to sign it, not sure I could get it out if I attempted to say it aloud.

"And who is she?"

In discomfort, I roughed a hand through my hair. "Girl from my complex."

Speculation and confusion lifted his brow. "And . . . you were in a relationship with her?"

Didn't matter that I couldn't hear him. Could feel the degree of hesitation his questions were coming with.

Didn't know what it was that shook my head—shame or remorse or just plain surrender. "More like I was drunk and lonely."

Just trying to fill up that vacancy.

I touched Everett's hand, still unable to comprehend that something so magical could come from something that had been so superficial.

"We hooked up a couple times. She moved a few weeks later. We weren't even close enough that she felt the need to say goodbye. Hadn't seen her until she showed up at my door in the middle of the night a few days ago."

Dad's head shook, and he bounced his knee, like he was trying to come to grips with this. "I get it, Evan, trying to fill a void when you know something is missing. What I don't understand is if you were so lonely, why didn't you come home? Why did you think you needed to separate yourself from us? We love you. You really think we considered you a burden?"

I huffed out a sigh, hesitated, lifted my hands, dropped them before I was speaking aloud again, "I know that I was."

Everything quavered with the memory, and my tongue darted out to wet my dried lips. "You think I couldn't see it, Dad? See it in all of your eyes that day when you came rushing into the emergency room? The fear? The agony? I didn't want to be the person who brought that on anymore."

When I'd finally felt I'd reached a peak in my life, finally accepting what I'd always wanted, I'd collapsed. Heart function dropping and sending my blood pressure into the danger zone. They were able to adjust my meds.

But there had been something that had changed that night.

A realization that had come on when I'd seen their faces.

I'd known it immediately. It was what they had been waiting on all those years. For the day when they would get the news that I was gone.

I figured I was nothing but selfish if I stayed and continued to put them through that.

"Yeah, Evan? Well that agony only increased tenfold the day you took off. And it never went away. So maybe it's time you stopped fooling yourself into thinking you are less than you are."

He hesitated, warred, his attention flickering away before he was pinning me with the force of it. "Frankie."

He said her name like mourning.

My fucked-up heart shook. Shivered and fisted and pulsed.

He knew. I should have known that he would. I didn't think I could keep a truth that bright and beautiful concealed.

I met his eye. "She deserved to have a life that I couldn't offer her."

And I knew, if I was being honest, the root of the problem had been that I couldn't stick around to watch it happen.

Sorrow billowed through the air.

Dad's.

Mine.

The years of loss and the question of where the hell I was supposed to go from here because there wasn't a whole lot that had changed.

Nothing but this child who stood like a beacon in the middle of us.

He exhaled through the tension, fighting whatever war I could see going on in his mind. "She loved you."

He said it so simply.

With so much remorse and disappointment that I wasn't sure how to remain sitting in the regret of it.

His hands fisted on his thighs. Like he was having to hold himself back. "Leaving her like that? It was wrong, Evan. I would have supported any decision you had to make, except for that one."

My chest felt tight.

Achy.

Everett grabbed my index finger and shook it all around. Kid rooting me. Grounding me. Making me feel like there was a bigger purpose for my life than I'd ever imagined.

I lifted my attention to Dad. Could feel the confession coming raw, a jumble as I forced it off my tongue. "I never wanted to hurt her. I never wanted to hurt you or Mom. Ate at me every single day, and with each day that passed, I felt more out of reach. More distanced."

Lost.

My throat tremored. "Sometimes it hurts too damn bad to stay."

"Yet you came back?" he pressed in an encouraging challenge.

I gazed down at Everett.

Affection took me whole.

I looked back up and gave my dad the truth he had instilled in me, his promise forever etched on my spirit, one he'd issued when I was eight-years-old. "You find your purpose when your love for someone else becomes bigger than your fears."

After Everett's appointment, I pulled my car to the curb in front of A Drop of Hope. Maybe I should have kept right on driving. Gone back to my parents' place and spent the day with Everett getting to know the kid who I kept glancing at through the rear-view mirror.

Mom would be home in a couple hours, but stopping to see her was an easy excuse.

Hell. Almost a mandatory excuse. She'd barely been able to pry herself away when she'd left to open the café this morning.

But I knew better.

Knew why my heart felt like a fucking rock that might crumble where it sat so heavily in my chest.

Knew why my breaths felt short and my head felt light.

I thought I could feel her from a hundred miles away.

Sense her presence.

Feel her turmoil and questions.

Didn't have the right to stop, but I didn't think I could leave things how we'd left them yesterday, either.

Could barely stand under all the vulnerability she'd let spill out on the ground between us when she'd come running across the street. Like she was crossing a river of hurt and she was willing to feel it if it meant she could get to me. All the while my spirit had gone mad with the need to hold her. Body demanding the girl it'd been missing for the last three years.

Knew I didn't deserve her.

Fuck.

Probably even more so now.

But I couldn't help but put my car into park, kill the engine, and climb out. I went right for the back and pulled out my son.

He smiled one of his smiles and patted both my cheeks and for the flash of a second my entire world felt whole.

Purposed.

It should be enough.

Still I rounded the front of my car, hit the sidewalk, and headed for the entrance.

Wasn't really paying all the much attention until I was right there, when the super tall, lanky guy stretched his legs out in front of me from where he was sitting at one of the bistro tables in front of the café.

My attention darted that way.

His dark hair was unkempt, his jeans ratty.

"You got a few bucks to spare?" he asked.

I shook my head. "Sorry, man, don't carry cash on me."

"Bullshit."

My hand instantly went to Everett's ear, holding him tighter in a protective stance, because there was just something about this guy that was off.

"Don't owe you anything," I told him.

Not money or an explanation.

Not that I wouldn't have given him some change if I actually had any, but still, what the hell was this guy's problem?

"No?" It was purely a challenge, and my pulse started to pound harder. A warning blaring somewhere deep in my mind.

My eyes narrowed, and it was one of those times I really wished my voice was normal. That my words wouldn't be a tell that would give this prick the idea that I wouldn't gladly throw down if he even looked at my kid wrong. "You should probably move along."

He laughed, and I got the sense the sound coming from him was cynical.

Mocking.

There was something in his eyes that set me on edge.

That alarm screamed louder.

He pushed to standing, angled his head, got in close. "Whatever you say, freak."

The last he spat, his unwarranted grudge hitting my cheek, but it was my own venom that pooled on my tongue. I glared at him from over my shoulder, watching him as he swaggered off the sidewalk, not going to the crosswalk but instead loping across the street like the fucker thought he was invincible.

Apprehension seethed.

Another thing about being deaf?

I'd learned to read people really goddamn well. Sense their spirits. Read their movements. Listen to their intentions.

Didn't even have to look that hard to smell the vileness seeping from his flesh, and it didn't have a damn thing to do with the fact he looked homeless.

I watched him until he hopped onto the sidewalk on the other side of the street. Whole time, I held my son protectively, making another silent promise that I wouldn't allow anyone to touch him.

I pressed a kiss to his temple, breathing relief when the guy disappeared around the corner, realizing I was probably being overprotective.

Judgy.

But when it came to your kids?

There were some things you just didn't risk.

seven

Frankie Leigh

*H*ave you ever felt like you were hooked on a moment? Waiting

for a specific second to unfold, not sure which it would be, but one-hundred percent certain it would come?

You might not know exactly where you'd be standing.

Where the sun might sit in the sky or if the moon might be glowing from the heavens.

Oh, but did you ever know precisely how it would feel.

How it would rock you to the core and send the ground rumbling below you, your heart taking off at a sprint, bang, bang, banging against your ribs that suddenly felt too tight?

That precise second for me?

It was when the door to A Drop of Hope swung open during the typical time of our afternoon lull. When we were working to restock and clean up and regroup.

But I doubted there would be any recovering from this. No reprieve from the sight of him, so tall where he stood in the doorway, sun shining all around him.

A blaze of light lit him up, a beacon so powerful, it was enough to draw me home.

Same as he had yesterday.

Only today, my spirit had known he would come. I'd known with every fiber of my being that there wouldn't be a way to avoid the fact that Evan Bryant had returned.

I was just goin' to have to face it.

Accept it.

He stood there, holding his son.

His son.

His son.

His son.

I heard it like an echo shouting in my soul.

Reverberating. Rebounding. Slamming back into me with little pulses of pain with each pass.

The child clung to his side like a little froggy with sticky, clinging hands.

Just like his daddy.

Cute as a bug when he was so little like that. A smattering of freckles speckled beneath his eyes and running the bridge of his nose.

Full lips all twisted up in a shy-sort of glee.

Agony clutched me by the throat, and somehow, my shattered heart threatened to expand. I struggled to remain upright, to fight for the good in all this mess.

"Did you come to see Grammy?" Aunt Hope's expression lit up like a kid watching fireworks for the first time on the Fourth of July.

Wow.

Had she ever gone from horrified shock yesterday to sweet grammy mode in a quick shift of gears.

It wasn't like I would have expected anything less from her. Wasn't like her givin' nature wasn't going to come out on top.

Not that there was a soul in this whole wide world who would be able to resist that smile, anyway.

Not the child's and sure not Evan's.

Evan who sent his mama a wide though unsettled grin.

Like he didn't know how to stand on the ground that seemed

to be undulating, either.

Everything crooked and off-balance.

Carly sent me a look. There was hardly any sound coming from her mouth, her words secret and covert and packed with implication. "Oh girl, you are in so much trouble. Have you ever seen anything as sexy as that? I mean, Evan was always cute and all . . . but holy hot damn. He came back with his A-game."

Why did she feel the need to do this to me?

Like she was pointing out what was plain as day.

Besides, what Evan and I had shared had never been a game, even though he looked like he might as well suit up for a not-so-friendly match.

Evan rumbled something to his mama, and my stare got tangled in the action, in the way Aunt Hope was over there kissing on that tiny boy's cheek, the way Evan was staring down at the kid like the child was the one who'd personally placed the stars in the sky.

The one who'd given Evan a reason to stare at them all through the night.

Carly reached over and lifted my chin where my jaw had gotten away from me and was hanging down to the floor.

"Clean up on aisle 4. You're droolin'," she said.

I shot her a glare. "Stop it," I hissed.

"What?" She shrugged, all kinds of innocent.

"You know what."

Carly's brow lifted.

Clueless.

Except she was grinning.

I mean, seriously, did she think she was gonna play some kind of cupid? Because Cupid had struck me a long-damned time ago and I was still bearing the wounds of that arrow.

Bleeding out.

She started wiping down around the coffee urns, her back turned to the lobby, her voice for me. "You know he came here to see you."

"He did not. He came here to see his mama."

"Um . . . pretty sure he's stayin' with her. Not a whole lot of reason for him to stop by when she's gonna be getting off here in a bit."

I scowled at her. "You're just dreaming up more drama. Drop it. It's over, and I'm over it."

I tried to build up all the fortitude that I could find.

"You are literally the worst liar I have ever met."

My attention got snagged on the trio when the little boy's giggle filled the air. So light and sweet and carrying the promise of agony.

The child threw his head back, grabbing his daddy's strong jaw and cracking up laughing as Evan nuzzled his face into the little boy's neck.

The whole scene was so tender that the flood waters sloshed and dribbled over the side.

If I wasn't careful, I was gonna get drenched.

Carly angled behind me where I'd been leaning over to restock the Blueberry Button Bliss cupcakes. She knocked into my hip as she passed. "Liar, liar, pants on fire," she taunted beneath her breath.

Awesome.

We were back to bein' ten.

"I will stab you," I warned.

She chuckled. "I'm super terrified of you, Frankie Leigh. I might have pissed my pants. Oh wait, that was just because I was laughin' so hard."

I pinched her side.

Hard.

She yelped, then mouthed, "Vicious."

"I'll show you vicious."

And then my head was snapping forward, a slow-slide of chills rolling down my spine when I felt the shift in the air.

Aunt Hope was bouncing the child in her arms and murmuring sweet nothings that I knew really meant everything. She rounded to the back of the counter. "Did you eat, my chunky boy? Let's see what we can get for you. I bet Grammy has something special that you'll like. You are so sweet . . . yes you are, aren't you?"

But that wasn't what had me trembling.

Evan had set his sights on me.

Watching me with this confusing expression that I wanted to pretend I didn't recognize.

That I didn't know firsthand.

Need and want and this crazy passion that I remembered all too well.

God. He was not allowed to look at me like that.

I just might pass out.

This was too much.

But there I was, standing there with a big ol' grin plastered to my face.

Faked.

Feigned.

Forced.

Thing was, there was a tremor rolling underneath that was real. Joy and hope seeping into the vacant spaces, right to the parts of me that had only wanted Evan to be happy. All the nights I'd spent so lonely and still praying that he could find himself.

To my left, Aunt Hope was approaching, carrying that little boy, and my heart started to speed, jumpin' a beat, getting erratic and flustered and blundering out of control the closer they came.

Aunt Hope slowed when she was three feet away.

Was that sympathy on her face?

Empathy seeping free?

Could she possibly understand?

No, not even close.

But still, her smile was filling right up with all her warmth and affection, her eyes softer as she looked between the two of us. "Frankie Leigh. I figured you might want to meet Everett."

I got worried I'd swallowed a grapefruit because there was suddenly a lump so huge sittin' at the base of my throat that it was constricting airflow. Only these little wheezing, choking sounds were getting free.

He babbled some more, and my stupid heart that was running wild tried to leap right out of its hold, cracking my ribs wide open as it went.

Hand shaking like mad, I reached out and touched the back of the little boy's plump hand.

"Everett."

It felt like a whisper somewhere in my mind. A taunt. A plea.

"You are so precious, aren't you? I'm Frankie Leigh." Affection tugged at one corner of my mouth, sorrow and cheer.

And the little boy?

Everett.

He smiled a smile that could shatter the entire world. Rid it of hate.

It was enough to send a stake of misery to impale my spirit.

It was funny when you thought you'd gotten over things, healed of them, and you hadn't healed at all.

And it was all right there, suddenly almost too much to bear.

He pointed one of those chubby fingers at the display of treats, his lips pursing in a tiny 'o' and his green eyes going wide with excitement.

"Ball? Ball? Ehvie ball?"

My attention darted that way. He was pointing at the colorful cake pops in the display.

"You want one of those?" I asked.

"Ehvie, please?" He patted his chest, his mouth twisting into that same smile again.

Oh God.

This was too much.

Torture.

Still, I was looking over the top of the counter at Evan who had edged closer, his big hands shoved in his pockets and his own fear racing through his features.

Everything hurt.

Every cell in my body felt like it had gotten compressed. So tight it was going to explode.

Cracks getting busted up and vacancies getting filled.

"Can he have one?" I attempted to ask, the words getting locked around that grapefruit that had grown spikes where it was getting tossed like a bowling ball up and down my throat.

Those eyes flashed regret and something that looked way too close to desire.

Evan nodded tight, though a frown dented that strong brow.

He pulled his hands free to sign. *I THINK SO.*

He thought so? I was pretty sure it was issued as a question.

What the hell did that mean?

And suddenly I was wishing I would have pelted Aunt Hope with the million questions that had roiled in my brain all day. Problem was, I'd been too terrified to force a single one from my mouth.

To terrified to hear the truth.

Last thing I wanted to hear was that Evan had moved on and he'd left me behind and there was absolutely nothing that my broken heart could do.

We both looked to Aunt Hope. She smiled a wary, knowing smile, like she was wading through the unease lapping between Evan and me. "I think that should be fine, as long as he ate lunch?" she asked, looking at Evan.

"We ate with Dad at the cafeteria," Evan said with a tight nod.

Oh, was I ever a glutton for punishment because the masochistic side of me went on a hunt of his stupid ring finger, desperate to know what his situation was—if he was happy and in love and if he was there to show off his family, or if he was as lonely as he looked.

I did my best not to gag while I braved the inspection.

Bare.

I nearly buckled in two at the relief.

And that was just about the faultiest thinking I'd ever endeavored.

I jerked my attention away from his hand, only for it to go and do something even more foolish, like land on that gorgeous face.

Emerald eyes flashed, pinned on me, reading my intentions like they were projected on a lit-up marquee.

Shit.

Damn.

Hell.

This was gonna be the end of me.

"What color is your favorite, Everett?" Aunt Hope all but sang, leaning down so Everett could pick.

"Dis."

He basically pointed at the entire tray, that tiny finger jabbing at everything he could see.

A little laugh escaped the turmoil.

Aunt Hope giggled, too. "Only one, sweetheart. How about blue?" she asked, reaching in and grabbing one of the pops so she could hand it to him.

Everett squealed and kicked his feet.

"Can you say 'thank you'?" she asked in that encouraging way.

"Fank ooo," he cooed with his nose all scrunched up. His voice a balm and the steely blade of a knife. He shoved the cake pop into his mouth, his chubby cheeks instantly smeared with frosting.

Pure affection filled Aunt Hope's face. I didn't want to be jealous of it. I didn't. But God did it feel impossible to stand there and not get all busted up watching it.

She looked back over the counter at Evan who was standing there, invading my space. "How about you, Evan? It's been so long since you've had one of my treats. I have some of those strawberry cupcakes you always loved so much . . . even have a few A Lick of Hope lollipops. Of course, they're not the same now that you haven't been around to help me make them."

My attention went to the lollipops that were on one of the cute display tables set up at the front of the lobby where we featured A Drop of Hope merchandise—cups and T-shirts and aprons and trinkets.

But the lollipops? They were the focus of it all—one-hundred percent of the profits from each sale went to the nonprofit Hope had started up when Evan was just a little boy—A Lick of Hope.

Hope had poured her heart and soul into the organization that supported children with heart defects—Evan such a huge part of it that I was sure a piece of him had been ingrained in each one.

Let me tell you, every single time someone came up with one of those lollipops over the last three years, it'd been brutal. A constant reminder of what we'd lost.

Evan watched his mom and Everett and somehow simultaneously watched me.

As if he were wielding some more of his special super powers.

His hearing deficit only amplifying his awareness of everything happening around him.

Reading.

Calculating.

Then his attention dragged across the selection, to the lollipops and back across the glass display at the danishes and cookies and every kind of treat.

That gaze climbed to me when he said, "Actually, think I want one of those unicorns."

His voice was jagged and low, the way it always had been. Raspy. The syllables always a bit clipped or elongated.

Shivers raced.

The out-of-control connection we'd always shared fired and blistered and made it all sorts of crazy-hard to breathe.

Because I knew what he meant.

Knew exactly what he was referring to.

My hand instantly went up to fiddle with the necklace he'd given me, the words engraved that had meant so much and the unicorn that dangled from one end.

Unicorn Girl.

Why was he doin' this to me? How could he walk out of my life and then come ridin' back in and stand there and imply these things?

Like nothin' had changed?

Like he hadn't left me completely shattered and crushed and alone. Those wounds were barely scars. Just flimsy patches he was threatening to rip right off.

"You're sure that's what you want?" I asked, unable to keep the hurt out of my voice. The accusation.

"Yeah." His response was hard.

Huffing out a disbelieving breath because it was a whole lot easier to give into the anger that was threatening to rise than the sorrow that scraped below the surface, I quickly plated the stupid unicorn cupcake that was a rainbow of candy and sparkles and a cookie horn for the topper.

They were pretty much a boon for adorable little girls who came in with their parents and immediately gravitated toward them and were sold out half the time.

If I would only have been so lucky today.

I set the plate on top of the display, hand shaking like mad, getting jolted by a blast of that energy when he reached over and touched the tip of my finger when he took it.

Like I'd been burned, I stumbled back, but that didn't mean I could tear myself from the intensity of that gaze as he continued to stare at me from over the counter.

Pinning me to the spot.

Heart going frantic and wild and my skin feeling sticky.

God, I was gonna burn up right there.

I needed a good jump in the lake.

Maybe that would wash away all this insanity.

I forced out a smile and tried to smooth out my hair. "Well, since it looks like y'all have things under control, I think I'm gonna . . ."

Run, flee, get the hell out of Dodge.

I gestured awkwardly toward the back door. ". . . go."

You know, only three hours before I was supposed to get off, but desperate measures and all.

Because I couldn't stay there with Aunt Hope bouncing that baby and him making all these adorable noises as he got lost in the sugary bliss. Couldn't stay there with Evan watching me like he was a starved man when it was abundantly clear that he wasn't.

A bumbling smile curled my mouth, and I probably looked all kinds of nuts, but I'd take it as long as it got me out of this mess.

I started for the door.

Carly grabbed me by the wrist, her face angled so her words were only for me. "Hey. Are you okay? Let me drive you home. You don't look so good."

I didn't feel so good.

"I'm fine."

Her expression shifted. Silently shouting, 'liar'.

That little voice was going to town behind me, that tiny boy telling a story that only he knew, and my heart was going haywire. If it beat any faster, I was sure it was going to explode.

Before I completely lost myself, I burst through the swinging door, going for the bins where we kept our things, hands trembling so hard that I could barely dig out my keys from my bag.

Somehow, I managed to get them free, and I slung the strap of my bag over my shoulder and flew out the back door into the dirt lot that was basically an alley.

The Alabama summer smacked me in the face.

Hot, sticky humidity an oil slick on my flesh, or maybe it was just the heat I was trying to escape from inside.

I started to stride for my car I had parked next to Carly's, only to stop in my tracks when I felt the presence cover me from behind. The shift in the air and the punch to the atmosphere.

Shivers curled down my spine, spreading far and wide, and for a second, I froze.

Froze at the feeling of being in Evan's space again.

Froze beneath the memories.

Beneath the hope and the love and the outright grief that had chased me for years. The problem was I had never figured out how to breathe beneath the magnitude of them all. The pendulum shift that I could never stop.

Could feel the force of his breaths coming at me like shockwaves.

An earthquake that shook my world.

Finally, I convinced myself to turn around.

To face the boy.

The man.

His hands moved, Evan communicating in his first language. The only one I was sure my heart truly recognized.

DON'T LEAVE. I watched the tremor roll down his thick throat when he swallowed.

PLEASE.

Could feel the despondency, the fierceness as he pled with me to stay.

It sucked that he hadn't given me the chance to do the same. That he hadn't stuck around to see the wreckage he'd left behind, for him to feel the torment of what living without him might be like.

That he *chose* it.

Old wounds convulsed in the middle of us.

Energy alive and weeping.

Still drawing and begging.

That was the hardest part.

This connection that remained so real and intense that I could barely force myself to continue to stand in place without getting sucked right into the beauty of this boy. Into his beautiful heart and spirit and mind.

Oh, that body sure wasn't helping things, either.

I forced that wayward thought down.

Bad, Frankie.

There was no way I could allow my mind to start going there.

E-V-A-N.

I signed slow, every letter emphasized, my mouth moving with his name.

A whisper of regret.

A murmur of praise.

I blinked at him, my hands and fingers quickened in their plea. *I'M NOT SURE I KNOW HOW TO STAY. HOW TO STAND IN FRONT OF YOU AND HAVE TO WITNESS THIS.*

I gestured toward the café, heartbreak spilling out with the motion. My own selfishness and greed getting loose of its chains. Then my hands were clamping down on my chest, words tumbling out like a confession.

"You're a daddy. He's so incredibly beautiful. I'm so happy for you."

It was funny how both emotions could be completely true.

Evan watched me.

Knowing me the way he always had.

I wanted to cower behind a bush or maybe throw a towel over my head to hide what I was feeling. This boy reading me like I was a story that only he could tell.

"I never meant to hurt you, Frankie."

Tears broke free.

YOU DIDN'T MEAN TO HURT ME, EVAN? YOU NEARLY KILLED ME.

Evan

I stood out in the deserted parking lot, chest heaving with pants like I'd just run a goddamn marathon. On some account? It felt like that was exactly what I'd done.

Run all the way across the country only to end up right back here.

Standing ten feet away from her.

Begging.

For what? I wasn't sure.

I'd been convicted of my reasoning then, sure the path was right, and now I was standing there wondering if the only thing I'd been was a fool.

But how could I stand there in front of this girl and expect her to give her entire life to me when I might not have one to give her in return?

It seemed so fucking selfish.

So fucking wrong.

Yet there I was, wanting to walk up to her, drive my hands into her hair, and claim her.

Because I saw it.

She was mine.

Same way as she'd always been. Same way as I was always going to be hers.

Guilt blustered through the wind, and I tried to get it together. To say something that would mean something when the only thing I was saying again was, "I'm sorry. I'm so fucking sorry."

I could feel the way the laughter that tumbled from her was brittle. "You left me, Evan. You walked out of that hospital and out of my life without looking back. Only a note that explained absolutely nothing. You had told me you were gonna *marry me.*"

She was clutching her chest again, but her upper body was angling toward me, like she couldn't help herself. "And you're really goin' to stand there and tell me that you didn't want to hurt me? You chose to leave me, Evan. You picked the pain. You chose the hurt. And now all you can say is that you're sorry?"

Regret churned and coiled. Problem was it was getting all mixed up with the lust that curled my guts.

The only thing it took was the sight of Frankie Leigh to bring it surging back.

Fingers itchy.

Dick hard.

Had no right to it, but my eyes were drinking her in, mouth watering as I dragged my gaze over her.

Would never forget the way it felt to be lost in this girl. In her body and those hands and the caress of her fingers.

She stood there seething and soothing under a spray of the blazing sun.

The sight of her a balm.

A punch to my soul.

Tall.

Always a little bony and skinny.

All sharp angles and subtle curves.

She stood there wearing a pink frilly skirt that landed under her knees over a pair of black leggings.

Of course, she'd paired it with a pair of pink high-top Chucks.

Frizzy, brown curls blew all around her.

Wild child.

My unicorn girl.

"I would have died for you, Frankie, and that's what it felt like when I let you go."

Disbelief curled through her expression, and her head was shaking, those tears streaking down her cheeks and across her mouth, wetting her lips. She huffed out a sound that I knew was derision. Felt it like a lash on my heart. "You think you did me a favor? That you were actin' noble?"

My hands curled into fists.

She took a step toward me. "Is that what you think, Evan Bryant? You took the coward's way out, that's what you did. That wasn't noble. I needed you."

A sob followed the words out, and shit, there was nothing that I could do but erase the space, pull this girl into my arms and bury my face in her hair and listen to the thrum of her heart. It'd always felt like the beat of it had led mine.

Frankie lost it the second we touched. The girl weeping in my arms, her fingers clinging to me.

Shame spiraled.

But in the middle of it was something new. Something that should have been there all along.

Determination.

Because she was fucking right.

I'd been a coward. A goddamn coward. That ended now.

I pressed a kiss to her forehead, and fuck, the taste of her skin nearly sent me spiraling.

Wanted to sink into her.

Dig deeper.

Crawl inside.

"I am sorry, Frankie. I am. Need you to know I thought I was doing what was best. That in the long run you'd be better off."

She pulled back to look up at me. Couldn't do anything but set my hand on her precious cheek.

Tears kept streaming free. "You had no right to make that decision for me. None at all, Evan. Did you even consider the consequences of what you leaving would be?"

Dread tightened my chest.

Something about the way the words dropped from her lips felt final.

Like she was saying I was too damn late.

Frantically, she scraped the moisture from her face with the heel of her hand. Almost as frantic as I could sense the frenzy of the laughter that tumbled out of her.

Disturbed.

Disbelieving.

She twisted herself out of my hold and took a step back.

That tiny space screamed.

"You know the sad thing, Evan?" She seemed almost frustrated with herself. "All this time? All this time I've been worried about you? All the nights I laid awake terrified that you were alone or sick or maybe hurt? Or the nights I was sick thinkin' about you with someone else? The times I was angry with you or hurting for you and just all around praying to God that I could just forget about you? You want to know the most pathetic thing? Last night when I crossed the street, when I was in your arms for that fleeting second, it was the first time in all those years that I felt almost complete."

Those cinnamon eyes glistened and glimmered.

Grief and love.

Grief and love.

Warm honey sprinkled with the hottest flecks of red.

Mouth painted a dizzying, sparkling pink.

I needed to get my physical reaction to her under control.

But that was the thing about going without what you craved most for years.

It made you half mad, delirious with the need.

I swallowed hard, hands curling into fists to keep from driving greedy fingers into her hair. "That's because we belong together."

More of that laughter.

Barking and harsh.

Could feel the sharpness of it slice across my skin.

She dropped her gaze to the ground with a shake of her head before she looked up so I could read her lips. "You're right. We did. But it's too late for that now, isn't it?"

It wasn't a question.

But I was answering it like it was. "No. Fuck no, Frankie."

"It is."

I surged forward and gripped her by one hip, our bodies pressed together.

Her breaths turned shallow, the girl's chest heaving, her tongue darting out to swipe across the moisture still wetting her lips.

Wanted to trace it with mine.

Kiss this girl the way that I used to.

My hand burrowed deeper into her flesh. "You're wrong, Frankie Leigh. There is no amount of time that could ever erase who you are to me."

Frankie gulped, her delicate throat tremoring, and she lifted that fierce chin that she'd always worn.

"I have a boyfriend, Evan. I've moved on." She glanced over my shoulder before she returned her gaze to me. "And clearly, you have, too."

The words were frail.

Feeble in their defense.

Still, I felt the impact of them like a kick to the gut.

Giving Frankie the chance to move on, for her to find the kind of life she deserved, had been the whole goddamn point. So she could have a family. So she didn't have to wait around for the day that I died.

But facing the reality of it was like the blunt stab of a knife.

She took advantage of my shock and stumbled back, trying to pry herself away from the energy that rippled and shook and circled us like a black storm.

Terrifying and beautiful.

Our connection had always been that way.

Almost too much because living without each other was nothing but devastation.

Sniffling, she stepped back and dropped her attention to the ground, trying to gather herself before she turned her gaze back to me.

In the depths of it, I saw a thousand lies. A million truths.

I watched the mess of them move on her mouth. "I'm so glad you're back, Evan. And I truly, honestly hope you're happy. I hope that you've found love, and I hope even more that sweet boy has filled up the vacant places I know existed in your soul." She brushed her fingertips over my chest. "I don't know any of the details of your life, but I really hope someday we can remedy that and we can be friends again. But I hope you know, after everything, that's the only thing we can be."

Then Frankie turned and fumbled for her car like she couldn't stay standing there for a second longer without crumbling.

Her argument valid but completely false.

She struggled to open her car door, and I stood there watching her trying to get away.

Maybe that was the second I realized neither of us could ever get that far.

"Frankie," I called, knowing her name had to have cracked with the way it scraped my raw throat.

She froze, and I waited until she finally twisted around to look at me.

That gorgeous face staring back.

Fuck.

I had no idea what the hell I thought I was doing. But I couldn't stop the statement from bleeding free. My hands moving powerfully with the importance of what I had to say.

I KNOW I HURT YOU, FRANKIE. I KNOW IT. AND I KNOW I KEEP SAYING I'M SORRY, BUT THE TRUTH IS, I AM. I'VE BEEN SORRY EVERY SINGLE DAY.

My head angled in emphasis.

YOU REALLY THINK THERE'S A CHANCE THAT I'VE MOVED ON? YOU REALLY THINK THAT'S POSSIBLE? THERE HASN'T BEEN A SINGLE DAY SINCE THE DAY I MET YOU THAT I DIDN'T LOVE YOU, FRANKIE LEIGH.

I kept moving closer as I signed.

SO YOU CAN GET IN YOUR CAR AND DRIVE AWAY. YOU CAN GO BACK TO WHOEVER IT IS WHO IS WAITING FOR YOU. BUT AT THE END OF THE DAY?

HE'S NOT ME.

Frankie shivered from where she watched me at her car, standing in her open door. I swallowed down the pain. The regrets. Everything I'd done.

YOU BELONG WITH ME. JUST LIKE I BELONG WITH YOU.

An instant of the fear I'd been wearing for years attempted to rise to the surface with the confession.

I shoved it back down.

Because that cowardice no longer had a place.

It was no longer welcome.

Frankie stared back like she was terrified because she knew it was the truth. Without responding, she finally tore herself from the tether that tied and fumbled into the driver's seat of her car.

She started it and lurched out onto the road.

I looked back to the café where I knew my son was waiting with my mom as Frankie Leigh was accelerating down the street.

Everything crystallized in that moment.

My reason.

My purpose.

Everett and Frankie Leigh.

Everett and Frankie Leigh.

And I finally knew exactly what it was that I was supposed to be fighting for.

"You're going." Mom was all smiles as we finished off the desserts at one of the lobby tables. My pulse was still beating a little too hard from the interaction with Frankie Leigh fifteen minutes before.

Anxious and excited.

But for the first time in three years, it felt like it might be beating right.

"That's final." Mom grinned.

I shook my head, unable to believe I was actually considering this. "Uh, think we're going to have to sit this one out."

Pushing up to standing, she leaned over and set her hand on my cheek. "You sat out the last three years. There is no chance I'm letting you get away with that this year, too."

There might have been a hint of playfulness spinning through her eyes, but I also heard the relevance of it.

She needed us there.

To reestablish some of the traditions we'd lost.

The holidays and the celebrations and the family gatherings that I'd missed more than I'd wanted to admit.

My gaze moved to Everett who'd basically been painted blue—cheeks and lips and teeth and hands.

YOU THINK HE'LL BE OKAY?

Reassurance filled Mom's expression. So maybe it was readily clear that I had no idea what the hell I was doing. Best I could do was figure it out along the way.

YES. ABSOLUTELY.

Softness tugged at one side of her mouth. "Everyone has been bringing their babies out to the lake for years. The first time your sister went, she was four months old. He'll love it. I promise."

Everett banged at the table, babbling one of his songs that I felt vibrate to my bones.

I jerked when something nailed me on the shoulder, and I whipped around to watch as a wad of crumpled paper tumbled to the floor. My gaze traveled the rest of the way to the culprit.

Carly who was standing behind the counter.

Busted.

She didn't even care. She just grinned. "Frankie's going to be there."

I heaved out a sigh. I wondered if that was going to be half the problem. Not sure either of us were ready for that. Not sure how I was supposed to be in her space and act like it was chill and good and we were only friends when I was dying to get us right back to where we'd been before it'd fallen apart.

Old fears flickered. Feelings of selfishness and inadequacy.

I ignored them.

I wasn't going back there.

Not ever.

Mom's brow lifted in hope.

I blew out a heavy breath. *FINE. WE'LL GO.*

Mom clapped and jumped around like she was twelve, swooping in to dot a kiss to Everett's nose, kid laughing and laughing and laughing.

Joy bounding free.

And I knew this was right.

That he deserved to have this family. These amazing people surrounding him even when I still didn't know what direction this was going to go.

Maybe it was more unsettling now, knowing exactly where I wanted it to.

I pushed to standing and dipped behind the counter to grab a towel, dampened it under the faucet, Carly watching me with a grin and knowing eyes.

I rolled mine at her.

I watched her silent chuckle.

Forever the pot stirrer, and I couldn't help but love her for it.

I went back and cleaned off Everett's hands and face, kid leaning his head back to try to get away. "It's okay, buddy. We just need to clean you up. Then we're going to go home."

Home.

Emotion fisted and crashed.

That's what this place was. And I wasn't going to give up until he was a permanent part of it.

"We're out of here."

Mom popped up and kissed Everett on the cheek then squeezed my hand. "I'm so glad you're here."

I nodded. "Me, too, Mom. Truly."

Her smile was soft and a little sad, and I waved a hand over my head toward Carly who was helping a customer before I ducked out the door and headed to my car. I slowed when I saw the white paint on the side window.

FREAK.

Instantly, my attention whipped around, doing a complete three-sixty of our surroundings. Searching as my throat closed off. Rage and fear becoming one, a violence unlike anything I'd felt before jumping into my bloodstream as I looked for the asshole who'd stopped me outside the café.

People strolled the sidewalks, scrolled through their phones, came in and out of stores, headed toward their destinations without any care of mine.

Dude was gone.

Thin air.

Unsettled, I cast another look, finally giving up and buckling Everett into his seat. I set my hand on his chest like some kind of instinct, needing to hear it beat.

Maybe it was a little obsessive.

I didn't care.

I wasn't taking any chances.

I used my shirt to wipe off the paint before I climbed into the driver's seat and drove the ten minutes back to my parents' house.

By the time I was pulling into the drive, the fury had lessened by a degree.

That was until I saw some guy I'd never seen before sitting on the porch steps.

Dark styled hair and nice jeans and a printed t-shirt.

Didn't matter that he looked totally innocuous. Younger than me. Arms rested on his knees.

That ferocity still lingering from the asshole at the café instantly came galloping back.

Muscles flexing and bowing in a sharp swell of protectiveness.

I glanced at Everett in the rear-view mirror. He was jabbering incessantly, fisted hand bobbing in the air, completely oblivious that anything could be amiss.

On guard, I came to a stop, not sure if I should throw it in reverse and get the hell out of there or gun it and just do away with the possible threat.

I forced myself to cool it. To take a deep breath. Overreacting wasn't going to solve anything.

The guy on the porch steps slowly stood. He appeared uneasy, though nonaggressive. I turned off the car and stepped out, keeping my attention pinned on him the whole time.

The guy slanted his head. "Are you Evan?"

I gave a tight nod. "Yeah."

He exhaled a tense breath. "I'm Chris, Ashley's brother."

Didn't know if it was relief or apprehension that hit me hardest.

I studied him, realizing why something about him felt vaguely familiar. "Is she okay?"

"I was hoping you could answer that."

Warily, I edged back to the passenger door, unbuckled Everett, and picked him up.

When I shut the door, Chris's gaze moved over my son.

I held him a little tighter, fighting the urge to fucking run and hide him away, not having the first clue what this guy's intentions were.

Air huffed out of Chris's nose, and he minutely shook his head. "She left him with you?"

Part of me wanted to be pissed that he'd known about Everett before I had.

"Yeah," I found myself answering again.

"That's good."

I angled my head in question. "Why's that?"

He shrugged a little, roughed a hand through his hair as he stared out into the distance before he looked back at me. "She's got issues, man. She's a good girl, but she goes off the deep end every year or so. Severe depression. Was worried about her having a kid when she told me she got knocked up."

I flinched at the way he threw it out there.

Couldn't tell if this guy was just concerned for his sister or being a dick.

But there was also a huge part of me that was feeling relieved. Gaining some perspective. That also meant the other half of me was certain I wasn't going to like it when Ashley came out on the other side and wanted Everett back.

I glanced down at the child who grinned up at me.

My heart fisted.

There was no going back.

"She seemed . . . distraught. Like she was scared when she left him with me," I chanced, hoping he could give me some insight on where to go from there.

He shrugged again. "She does that. Gets paranoid." His eyes narrowed. "You're the deaf dude, right? Your voice is all screwed up."

Nice.

"Yup. That's me."

"She said you were cool."

I didn't want to tell him that she didn't even know me.

I hugged Everett closer. "How did you find me?"

He gave a small smile. "Last time I talked with her, she was talking about you, mentioned what town you're from. She'd said something about maybe trying to find you. I hadn't heard from her in a few weeks so I went to her place to check on her. When she wasn't there, thought I'd take a chance and see if she'd hooked back up with her baby daddy. I was worried about the kid, but it looks like he's fine."

Everett started fussing a bit, getting squirrelly in my hold. I shushed him, brought him to my chest, rubbed his back in attempt to calm him down. "And what about your sister?"

"She'll come around."

"And when she does?" Was sure it came out hard. Was sure he knew exactly what I was implying. What I was asking.

He pursed his lips and shoved his hands into his pockets. "You got the means to take care of him?"

Wasn't so hard to figure out what he was implying, either.

Money was the language of the corrupt.

My arms tightened around Everett who was starting to cry, his head rocking back in his unrest, mouth twisted in a wail that I felt impale my skin. Something frantic bottled in my chest. This feeling coming over me that felt like an omen. Like I could taste something wicked and wrong riding in on the air.

"Yeah."

"And you want him?"

I hugged Everett like his life depended on it. Had the horrible sense that maybe it did. "Yeah."

He smirked. "I'm sure my sister could be handled then."

Was he serious?

That's what this was about? What Ashley wanted? It just . . . didn't make sense. Not with the way she appeared that night.

He strode toward me, angling to the side as he passed, turning around and walking backward when I whirled around to watch him go. "I'll be around." He jutted his chin toward Everett. "Since he's here, I figure this is where she's gonna show."

Then he spun around and kept walking casually down the street.

While I stood there feeling like I'd just got shoved off a bridge.

No foundation underneath.

And I had no fucking idea where I was supposed to land.

nine

Frankie Leigh

"*J*ack will be here in fifteen minutes. You need to get your lazy butt out of bed."

Groaning, I barely cracked open an eye from where I had been hiding under my pillow for the last three days.

So yeah. I'd been calling in sick. It wasn't exactly a lie. It wasn't called heartbreak for nothin'.

Carly leaned against my doorframe, sporting all kinds of judgment in her expression.

"No, thanks." It was nothing but chipper sarcasm before I was rolling over and dragging the pillow over my head.

A disbelieving huff hit the room, her feet stomping on the floor as she stormed to the side of my bed.

"It wasn't a suggestion." She ripped the pillow out of my hold and tossed it to the end of the mattress.

"What the heck? That was so uncool. And here I thought you were supposed to be my best girlfriend. You are so fired," I whined, flopping over onto my back with a pout.

"Up."

"I already told you there is no chance in this whole wide world that I'm going. It's not gonna happen. Forget it."

Carly crossed her arms over her chest. "Oh, it's gonna happen if I have to drag you there myself."

On a moan, I flung my forearm over my eyes. "Remind me to kick you out."

"Please do. Turns out my roommate is prone to sudden bouts of self-pity and moping. It's kind of gross. Almost as gross as her stinky ass that hasn't seen a shower in three days. Seriously, Frankie, you're gettin' ripe. Josiah's worried we're goin' to have to fumigate."

My lips pursed. "You two are so mean."

"And you're pathetic. Now get up, Pig Pen, before I haul you out back and douse you with a hose."

"Fine." I tossed off the covers and sat up on the edge of my bed. Milo lifted his head from his dog-bed on the floor with one of his deep groans and a stretch, probably shocked that I was actually surfacing.

Him and me, both.

"But don't forget that I said this is a horrible, terrible idea and bad, bad, bad things are gonna come of it."

"Wah, wah, wah," she sang right back.

I punted her a glare. "You owe me, big time."

Carly rolled her eyes. "Believe me, it's me who's doin' you the favor."

Was pretty sure my eyebrows disappeared under my bangs. "A favor? The last thing I want to do today is go to the lake . . . with Jack . . . and everyone else." I pushed out the last through gritted teeth.

"It's got to happen sometime."

"Well, I'd prefer for it not to be today. Or ever. Sounds like a plan to me. I'll pencil it in on my calendar."

"You can't hide from him forever, Frankie Leigh. He's your family whether you're with him or not."

Oh, no, no, no. Family he was not.

Family didn't ditch you. Forget you.

They stuck firm.

No matter what.

Except . . . except that was a lie, wasn't it?

The boy forever etched so deep in me there would be no erasing the effects.

And now he was back and implying things that I couldn't afford for him to imply. His excuse one I sure didn't want to hear.

Then he'd gone and branded me with the mark of his touch. I could still feel it singed on my hip, the shape of his hand and the want in those eyes.

"Besides, you know he's gonna be out in the lake." She waggled her brows. I had half a mind to pluck all of them out. We'd see how she liked that.

"I hate you," I told her.

She pecked a kiss to my forehead. "You love me and you know it. Now get your ass in the shower and hurry up about it. I already have our things packed."

"This is a bad idea," I grumbled again as I stood, scratching at my lower back and giving into a big yawn as I shuffled on bare feet toward the bathroom.

Carly's expression shifted, a true frown marring her brow. "It's true, Frankie. You can't hide from this forever. You need to face it and embrace it, no matter which side you decide to land on."

Pained laughter rippled free. "There's no deciding."

Evan already decided that for me three years ago.

And that pain?

That was something I didn't ever want to experience again.

Twenty minutes later, we had most everything packed into the back of Josiah's old Tahoe. A cooler, bags of groceries, towels and blankets, and all our camping supplies.

I had to admit, I felt minimally better after a steaming hot shower. I'd pulled on some cutoff shorts and a tank over my favorite printed bikini and tied my hair up in a messy knot.

That was as good as it was goin' to get.

"Beer. Wine. Ice. Chips. Beer." Josiah ticked the all-important list off with his fingers.

"I think you're safe," I told him, totally droll.

He only had six 12-packs stacked in the back.

"You never know, Kit Kat."

So, the guy had a problem that he nicknamed everyone after his favorite candy bars. When I was thirteen, I'd wanted to reem him for it, but now I got it was nothin' but affection.

You knew you were in big, big trouble if he only deemed you worthy of calling you by your first name.

I leaned into the back of the SUV, trying to make room for a big umbrella.

A hand landed on one cheek of my butt and squeezed.

I jumped so high I nearly hit my head on the opened hatch, and I whirled around, doing my best to play it cool.

To pretend like my entire being hadn't just flinched with his touch.

To pretend like I wasn't carrying around this weight that was threatening to suffocate.

Jack shoved a small duffle bag into an open space, giving me a good side-eye.

I'd been avoiding him like he was the carrier of a brand-new plague. One that riddled you with guilt, and the shame you bore slowly killed you off.

But this was no love triangle.

Not when Evan and I were a constellation.

An intricate pattern that glimmered and twinkled in the deepest night. One that led you into the light like the sun breeching the horizon after you'd spent years wandering in the dark.

Old affection thrashed.

Tried to rise up and take hold.

How did I stop the flood? I couldn't entertain these thoughts. Couldn't.

Loving Evan Bryant had just hurt too bad.

I glanced at Jack. My chest squeezed tight. Even if I could never be with Evan, could never trust him that way again, I knew I had to end this. It wasn't fair to Jack. But how did you tell the guy who was supposed to be your boyfriend you were in love with someone else? That you'd always been and there was nothing in the world that was gonna change it?

That it would just be better that you weren't with either one of them?

Jack frowned through a smile. "What's goin' on with you, Frankie Leigh? You're acting weird."

I heaved out a strained breath, forced a smile of my own. "Nothin'. You startled me, that's all." Only it was *something* I was goin' to have to take care of and soon.

Carly shouldered around Jack, knocking him a couple feet back. She wedged a wicker tote on top of our pile of supplies. "I think that's it. We're ready to roll."

"Are you sure you brought enough shit?" Jack teased her, canting her one of his charming grins.

"No, actually, I'm not, but this was all that I could fit. Of course, you could hang back here, and I could fill your spot with some more of my things?"

If only I could get so lucky.

"Fine. Just don't ask me to drag all your crap to the camp spot," Jack returned, lifting his muscled, tattooed arms in surrender.

"Ha. You wish. That's the only reason we're letting you come." Carly gave him all her sass.

"You ready?" She turned her attention on me.

"It's gonna be a blast," I told her, nothing but sarcasm dripping from my tongue.

She reached up and slammed the hatch down. "Oh, it's gonna be a blast, all right."

Half an hour later, we were on the outskirts of Gingham Lakes where we hit the two-lane road that led out to the river and the lakes. Tall trees rose up at the sides of the road that curved and twisted through the lush, dense forest where it followed along the river.

We weren't even to the lakes yet, and I was already losing my breath.

That fluttery feeling of awe slipping into my bloodstream.

I'd been coming here for all my life, all the way back when it was just me and my daddy. We spent most every weekend out on the slippery rocks near the waterfalls that overlooked one of the lakes, Daddy grilling us hamburgers over a rock-rimmed fire while I'd danced and played and imagined I could be anything.

It was my favorite place in the world.

That world had expanded as our families had grown. As Rynna had become a sacred part of that vision. As Kale and Hope and Evan had become a part of it, as well as the rest of their tight-knit friends.

Children were born and our families multiplied and it became a haven all of us gravitated to. A place to get away and share in the most important things in life.

Time.

Experiences.

Laughter and support.

They would all be there, the second Saturday in September forever reserved for our campout.

Tradition.

No one dared miss it, and I was having the horrifying premonition that would again apply to Evan.

Evan who'd shared these days with me like we'd been born with the same DNA. Neither of us able to move one muscle without the other one moving one in return.

Magnets.

Beside me, Milo sat in the middle part of the backseat, his tongue hanging out as he panted and whined in his excitement, turning circles in the small spot. My fingers scratched through his fur in hopes to keep him from crawling all over the place.

My sweet old boy.

This was his favorite place, too.

Jack sat on the opposite side of me, Josiah was driving, and Carly rode in the front passenger seat.

Me? I was that girl in the right rear, getting eaten up by the disaster of emotions.

"So, you've been coming to this campout every year?" Jack asked Josiah, leaning forward to get his attention.

Josiah lifted his thumbs out from the steering wheel. "Nah, man . . . didn't start coming until high school. I guess Evan's parents figured I'd hung around enough through the years that I became some kind of honorable family member. Mars Bar begged 'em to let me come the summer before our freshman year. Have been coming ever since."

All it took was a single mention of his name for my heart to go skittering into overdrive.

"Mars Bar, huh?" Jack lifted a speculative brow.

Josiah chuckled. "Kid was fucking obsessed with the stars. It fit."

Could feel the weight of Jack's attention dragging over to me, heavier than it'd ever been.

Or maybe I was projecting.

"So this guy really got a heart transplant as a baby and is still breathing?"

Protectiveness welled. Sometimes Jack could be so callous and brash.

There was just something about Jack's tone that got under my skin.

Or maybe it was because that was where Evan really was.

Forever and ever under my skin.

Etched there.

Seared in the marrow and written in the bone.

"Can't fuckin' wait to see him," Josiah cut in, glancing at me in the rear-view mirror like he was wondering if I concurred. "He's cool as shit. You don't like Evan then you're basically a prick."

His gaze slid back to Jack.

Leave it to Josiah to make it sound like praise when he was delivering a warning.

"If I had to pick, I'd definitely trade both of these assholes for Evan," Carly said. "He's pretty much that awesome."

"Wow. Ruthless." Josiah chuckled under his breath.

"Huh," Jack mused, though it came out sounding more like an accusation, looking at me again. "You mean except for the fact he took off and left you all without a word, cool?"

Oh, this really was gonna be fun.

"Everyone deals with their shit in different ways," Josiah said like he'd already long since forgiven Evan for what he'd done. Understood it from the get-go.

My teeth were rubbing my bottom lip raw, hands going itchy at the way Josiah phrased it. And I couldn't help but remember the look on Evan's face that night. I should have known he'd gone to a dark, dark place.

Should have known he wasn't okay.

But the problem was, I hadn't been okay, either.

Josiah turned on his right blinker, slowing as we came to the turn off that veered north at an angle to round back up toward the cliff end of the lake. This road was rougher and narrower where it led to the secluded spot on the opposite end of the busy campgrounds.

The SUV jostled down the bumpy trail.

The trees were different here.

Spindly and thin with white, chalky bark. Packed so tight together it looked like they were in standing formation. An army that stretched so high the tops got lost in the bright rays of sunlight that burned from the endless sky.

Road climbing higher, we rounded a bend to a clearing where a ton of familiar vehicles were already parked.

My daddy's truck.

Ollie's teal historic one sat next to it. A secret grin pulled at one side of my mouth when I remembered how Evan had salivated over that truck, claiming one day he would own it.

Uncle Broderick and Aunt Lillith's Range Rover was parked at one side.

Next to it was Aunt Hope's Volvo.

And there went my breath again. Nerves scattering like the leaves tumbling along the rocky ground.

You can do this, Frankie Leigh. You can do this. You're a big girl. A brave girl.

But it was hard to convince myself of that when the wind kept gettin' knocked out of me.

Josiah pulled to a stop in an open spot and put it in park. "This is it. Let's get this party started, bitches."

I climbed out and gave in to the shiver of excitement that crawled under the surface of my skin.

I loved it here. God, I loved it so much. This place filled with so many amazing memories. Cherished moments that I never wanted to give up.

I went to the back, pulled out my bag, slung it over my shoulder, and grabbed as many of the food bags as I could manage.

"What can I get?" Jack offered.

"If you could get the umbrella and tent, that would be great."

"No problem. Just glad I'm here." His dark eyes roved over me, like he was looking for an affirmation.

Guilt twisted up my stomach in a thousand knots.

I hadn't even invited him. He'd just assumed, which I guessed I really couldn't fault him for.

It was long since passed time that I should have started including him in family events.

But the sad truth was that I hadn't. That I'd never felt ready and I was pretty sure that I never would be.

That should have been a warning right there.

But you know what they say . . .

Hindsight.

Even then, everything felt blurry. A daze of discomfort and these flickerings of joy that Evan had returned to where he belonged hazing up my sight and my mind.

Messing with my head.

Mixing up my heart.

I headed for the trail that twisted through the full bushes and the soaring trees. A breeze whistled through, dragging in the scent of the purple blazing star flowers that grew rampant in the fields.

I inhaled, breathing it in, my ear inclined to the sound of the rush of running water.

Struck with so many memories that a part of me wanted to weep.

For joy or sorrow, I wasn't quite sure.

All I knew was I felt this overwhelming sense of peace taking over.

The thicket of trees opened up at the end of the trail and revealed the expanse of the lake.

A calm, placid blue that stretched out to touch the base of the mountains in the distance.

I wound through the break in the rugged rocks that led down to the secluded cove and beach.

Massive rocks rose up on the right side. They went higher and higher until they became the cliffs on the north end of the lake.

At the highest point, the river took a tumble over the edge, and the roar of it filled my ears as it forever pounded into the waters.

Out on the beach, my family was setting up our camp. Voices shouting and laughing and a flurry of activity as tents were hoisted and umbrellas were erected.

Funny how my focus went to one place.

To the far-left side where Evan was working on putting up a tent.

Felt like he'd been there all along.

His red hair lighter, blonder than it'd been, the longer pieces whipping around the bold, striking angles of his face.

I knew he felt me.

Sensed my approach.

He recognized my presence the exact same way I recognized his.

Immediately, those eyes found mine from across the space.

Emerald fire.

He slowly straightened to his full height.

It probably wouldn't have mattered if he hadn't become the most beautiful man I'd ever seen.

My fingers still would have ached to caress his skin.

My body still would have begged to get lost in his touch.

And my heart . . . it would have always sung his name.

I could stare at his face all day except for the unfortunate fact that he wasn't wearing anything but swim trunks and there was no chance of resisting that.

My eyes dragged down.

Slowly.

Was pretty sure my jaw hit the floor as they traced over his shoulders that had widened, across his pecs that were now muscled and defined and sending another rumble through my shattered world.

Oh, but those masochistic tendencies didn't stop there, my

perusal raking down to his narrow waist, his abdomen chiseled and strong from the hours he clearly had been putting in at the gym.

Oh. My. God.

My belly throbbed and need pulsed between my thighs.

I begged it not to go there, but my selfish gaze shifted to the center of his chest, to the scar that ran all the way from the top of his sternum to the spot where his ribs ended. It had faded more and more as the years had passed, that little line that held him together.

What kept that beautiful heart in place.

I had the overwhelming urge to trace it with my fingertips.

"Uh, Frankie. You lost?"

Jack's voice jolted me out of the stupor. There was no missing the irritation in his expression when I jerked around to look at him.

Unease rumbled.

A premonition blew in with the breeze.

A feeling that I was right—this was a terrible, horrible, bad, bad idea.

"Frankie Leigh in the houuuuuuuuuuuuse!" my baby brother Preston hollered from where he was waist-deep in the lake, stealing the attention. "About time!"

And the only thing I could think was thank God for the distraction.

Family first.

You'd heard it said a million times. Tossed around like platitudes and the worst sort of cliché. Mostly because people rarely honored that philosophy. So busy and wrapped up in their worlds that they'd forgotten what it really meant.

Phones and errands and TV.

But that's what these weekends were about. Coming together. No other focus than cherishing the time. Wishing it would last.

So maybe I would have regretted it if I hadn't have come, but that didn't mean being here in the middle of it was easy, either.

All the guys were out in the lake, segmented into two teams, throwing the football, tackling each other before a swimmer could make it to the opposite side to their goal.

My daddy was the captain of one team.

My uncle, Ollie, the other.

They'd basically been trash-talking each other the entire day leading up to the big sporting event. Guessed that's what happened when you were lifelong friends.

Evan's little sister, Charlotte, and Uncle Ollie and Aunt Nikki's daughter, Becca, had both begged me to play.

Jack was on my daddy's team and Evan was on Uncle Ollie's.

You could safely say there was no chance in hell that I was gonna get in the middle of that.

All the tents were built on the perimeter of the camp. We'd made a gathering area in the middle and up a little closer to the beach, blankets and chairs set up together with big umbrellas overhead to offer shade.

Aunt Nikki, my mama, and Aunt Lillith were huddled around Aunt Hope where she sat on the edge of a blanket so she could watch Everett playing with some toys in the sand.

The little boy was wearing a beach hat and little sunglasses and probably an entire gallon of sun screen, his chubby belly hanging out all over the place in his adorable swim trunks.

I made sure to stay on the opposite end of where they were, where the summer sun beat down and I tried to pretend like I was napping while I suntanned, Milo curled up beside me. Pretended like I wasn't affected by all of this when every second made me feel like I was getting ripped to shreds.

I'd started to actually drift off. To relax.

But that was impossible when I heard the direction the conversation had shifted.

"How *are* you doing with all of this, Hope? I'm not the only one who thinks this is crazy, right? Is anyone else as shocked as me?" Aunt Nikki's voice was hushed and eager, tinged with a hue of worry.

Aunt Nikki never hesitated to say what was on her mind.

Maybe playing football would have been a safer bet.

Could feel Aunt Hope's hesitation, and I cracked open a single eye, unable to stop myself from eavesdropping. Her red hair glowed around her, and she was hugging her knees to her chest, glancing between Aunt Nikki and Everett who was babbling away and dumping shovelfuls of sand into a bucket.

"I don't even know how I'm doing with it. I think I'm still in shock, honestly. I mean, I have a *grandchild* that I didn't even know about."

"God, I can't even imagine. I mean, seriously, if Bo came home with a kid, I would absolutely lose my mind." Aunt Nikki sounded horrified by the thought. "I'd never let that boy leave his room again."

Her son, Bo, was barely fifteen. I sure hoped he didn't come dragging home a baby. And if he did? I'd ground him myself. Maybe even give him a good spankin' or two.

"Especially after Evan has been gone for all that time and then shows back up? I'm not sure if I'd be more pissed off or relieved that he'd returned."

Aunt Lillith smacked her in the shoulder. "Have you not learned when to keep your mouth shut yet? This is hard enough without you stirring up bad blood."

Aunt Nikki shook her head and lifted her brows. "Um . . . hello, Lily Pad. We are family. And families should be talking nothing but the truth. And I'm betting that Hope here probably needs to get a few things off her chest. It's not stirring up bad blood when I know Hope hasn't gotten this off her mind once in three years. I think it's about damn time we addressed it, don't you?"

Aunt Hope laughed a dubious sound. "Yeah, I think Nikki's right." She hummed for a second like she was trying to process her thoughts. "You know, it's crazy how we could be so upset with him and brought to our knees by relief at the same time."

Aunt Hope fidgeted, warring with the feelings that were clearly catching up to her.

I peeked a discrete eye her direction.

"We've been so worried about him all this time . . . so worried. It's the worst feeling in the world when your own child cuts you out of their life, but knowing for him to do it, he had to have been just as distraught? Hurtin' in a way there was no chance I really understood? That I missed it? I . . . I feel like I failed him somewhere along the way."

My heart clutched, and I realized I was starting to drift that way, getting called toward her devastation, knowing I'd been a partner to it, too.

That I understood it in every way.

Differently, but the same.

"There's no chance of that," I found myself whispering to her.

Her attention traveled to me. Sadness and love billowed out.

"You didn't fail him," I kept on. Like I could patch her up and take it away. "He just got lost somewhere along the way."

Lost to the fear.

I knew it.

I'd seen it so distinct in his eyes.

"I know . . . I just hate I wasn't there to help him find his way back."

My mama touched Aunt Hope's knee. "Of course, you were there, Hope. Why do you think he's here? Why do you think when he found himself in trouble, needing help, that he came right back here to you?"

A smile wobbled at the corner of Aunt Hope's mouth, and I was slowly sitting up, getting drawn into the conversation.

Obviously, they all knew a whole lot more about the situation than I did, considering I'd been hiding myself away for the last three days. Not wanting to know or face it.

My gaze dropped to the little boy.

Everett.

Like he felt me gazin' at him, he curled up his little nose, making these snorting noises as he grinned.

My spirit clutched. Nerves rattling.

The earth unsettled.

Somethin' like longing filling me full.

Shit.

But I couldn't turn away.

"He's adorable, Hope," Mama all but whispered, reaching out and fluttering her fingertips through Everett's hair. The little boy tilted his head back with the connection, like he was hungry for the attention.

For the love.

"Ehvie shovel." He held up the yellow plastic shovel with pride.

"I see it . . . you have a shovel, don't you," my mama was murmuring, still running her fingers through his hair.

Worry filled her expression, those eyes on Aunt Hope. "Is he . . ." I saw her war, hesitate, unsure if she should address the one thing I was sure that everyone was thinking. "Is his heart okay?"

The dread of that answer had been bumbling around somewhere in the back of my head where I hadn't let it take shape or form.

In that very second, it came into sharp, plain view.

My own seized for a beat.

Stalling out.

I all of a sudden felt like I was suffocating.

Worry shook Aunt Hope's head. "We don't know yet. Kale was able to get him into the clinic to do an examination. We got back the results of some preliminary tests, and so far, everything has been normal. He ordered a genetic workup and an appointment with the pediatric cardiologist. Even with Kale pulling some strings, it's going to be awhile before we know anything for certain."

My brow pulled together. "Wait. He hasn't been tested yet? I . . . don't . . . I don't understand."

I mean, wouldn't they have done that the second he was born? When his mother was pregnant?

Oh . . . that was such not a good vision . . . a young woman round with Evan's baby. Nausea curled and I was worried I was gonna lose it right there.

Aunt Hope frowned. "Evan just found out about Everett a week ago, Frankie."

She said it like she'd assumed I'd already been privy to that horrible information.

"What?"

My mind was wracked with so many thoughts all at once.

With worry and dread and a hurt for this man who'd already gone through so much. I was struck with the intense urge to jump to my feet, run right through the camp, and show all my stupid cards and hurl myself at Evan. Hold him and hug him and press my ear to his chest so I could hear the beat of his heart.

Or maybe that urge was to pick up the child.

To do the same.

Protect him when no one had been there to do it.

Silence fell over the group of them, everyone watching this kid coo and babble and drum and offer Aunt Hope a bucketful of sand like he was offering her his heart.

That lump was back. Blocking the flow of air. I turned my attention away, to the group out in the water, which was a terrible idea, too.

Evan was out there, the lake water lapping up by his belly button.

A vision where the water rippled out away from him.

The boy drenched. He lifted the football over his head to toss it to Ryland. Josiah was going in for the tackle, rushing him. Evan darted to one side to get the clear pass.

Body slick.

Sparkling under the shimmering light.

Every muscle highlighted.

Those eyes glinting beneath the glare. But he laughed.

Laughed like there was a way to find happiness again.

That maybe his depression hadn't fully stolen him away.

Burning up, I turned back to Aunt Hope, and I realized I was being blunt, but I was overcome by the crushing desperation to know. "What do you mean he didn't know about him until a week ago?"

Anger flashed through her expression. "Everett's mother never told Evan she was pregnant. He never knew until she showed up at his door and left him there with him."

A collective gasp went up. One of them was mine.

My eyes swung to Evan. Evan who was playing free. Like for a moment, a burden had been lifted from his shoulders. I wanted to hop up and rant and scream and track down whoever that bitch was that would up and leave her child.

Didn't she understand the gift she'd been given? Old feelings of abandonment crawled and shivered.

Had to tuck my hands under my thighs to keep myself from doing something stupid like making a move for the tiny boy.

Every cell in my body aching in the worst way.

To love and cherish.

Aunt Hope sighed a sound of confliction. "As angry as I am with her, I'm thankful she brought him to Evan. I guess she's in some kind of trouble, and I'm guessing that she didn't know Evan well enough to know about his genetic disorders to begin with. The whole thing is such a mess, and we're still trying to sift through the details of it. We have an attorney involved."

My mind spun.

This was all . . . too much. Too ugly and complicated and wrong.

It didn't matter if she was in trouble or not. If she understood Evan's history or not. It was no excuse for her not tellin' him.

"How could she do that? Who is she?"

Aunt Hope shook her head. "I think that's something you're going to have to talk with Evan about yourself, Frankie Leigh. It's not my right to be offering those details."

Right.

It was personal information.

Private.

Because that didn't include me anymore.

Distress wound and burned and stung, and I tried to gather myself up.

This seed of anger and possession I could feel gettin' ready to sprout.

That needed to be snuffed out really quick.

Sympathy filled Aunt Hope's expression, like she was offering me an apology. Her loyalty fierce to both of us. "Evan's gonna need support. Friends who love him most. Understand him most. I'm worried he can't handle all of this . . . he's been up all night, pacing like he thinks he needs to stand guard over his son. I think he's worried he's going to disappear as fast as he showed up. I guess now he knows exactly how it feels to fear for your child."

She said it like she was talking to everyone there, but she was looking directly at me, like she could see all the things rambling through my insides, the loss and the grief and that stupid love that I wanted to stamp out.

But that was the thing about truly loving someone.

It was unending.

My gaze drifted out to the man.

And I wondered if we could actually get back there.

My best friend. My best friend.

Maybe . . . maybe I could be there for him. For both of them.

I just was worried I wouldn't be able to handle it without my heart gettin' all mangled up again.

Oh, who was I kiddin'? It was already twisted and gnarled.

At least maybe I could get that one piece ironed out.

Set it to right.

"That's so, so good you gots a new a heart." Her voice came out a whisper. *"You want to be my best friend?"*

Because Frankie was sure Evan was her favorite, favorite.

The memory swam while I watched Mama reach out and touch Aunt Hope's knee again. "Blessings come in all forms of unexpected packages. And this little guy sure looks like a blessing to me. You know we'll be there for you all."

Aunt Hope squeezed her hand. "I know that. And I can't tell you how thankful we are to have you all. That we have a family that supports us like this. I'm not sure what we would have done through these years without you."

Love rolled.

That deep-seated loyalty.

I turned away, looked off into the distance toward the crash of the waterfalls, relishing in that peace while my aunts and my mama continued to talk and ask questions and offer solutions and promises of help. I got lost in it.

The warmth and the realness.

The goodness of it all.

The reminder that there was hope in the darkness.

Joy in the bleakness.

I nearly jumped straight out of my skin when a hand landed on my shoulder. Maybe it was because it sent a streak of warmth blazing down my arm.

Infiltrating.

That tiny hand eliciting too many feelings that I didn't know how to process yet somehow expected at the same time.

Everett held onto my shoulder, bouncing on his chubby legs, angling his head around to get into my line of sight.

"Hi!" he said with one of those grins and his tiny voice, patting at my shoulder and giving me a scrunched-up smile. And holy heck, I'd seen some adorable stuff in my life, but this little boy had gone and taken the cake.

Joy buzzed from his tiny body.

My chest squeezed.

"Hi, Everett," I murmured without any breath. I wondered if it made any sound.

"Puppy!" His index finger flexed and extended a hundred times.

"Yes, this is my sweet boy, Milo." I ran my hand over Milo's head. He dropped down onto his butt and crawled over and pressed his face into the fur of Milo's neck.

Milo's tail wagged like crazy, and when Everett pulled away, Milo licked him on the face.

Everett squealed and kicked.

Sound of it reverberating.

Sweet. Sweet. Sweet.

"Ball?" Everett asked, hopping from one topic to another.

A laugh ripped up my throat. "Oh, you remember that do you?"

Great. Now I was goin' to be the dessert lady. They always said you could win over any man with the promise of food. No wonder Aunt Hope had made a profession out of it.

"Bwue ball? Ehvie, please." He patted his chest and dipped his head down low in this adorable nod that was doing stupid things to me.

Aunt Hope's soft voice popped the bubble that I was gettin' ready to float away in. "Come here, Everett. Are you hungry?

Grammy will get you something to eat."

But he didn't respond to her. He just crawled right on top of my lap, still on his knees, facing me.

A direct line hooked into my spirit.

He patted my cheeks with both hands, jabbering a slur of words that I couldn't quite make out but completely understood. Something about a ball and his daddy and the puppy. Like a fool, I was brushing my fingers through his hair and inhaling deep and wishing everything didn't hurt so bad. Whole time praying all the prayers I could find that he was fine. Healthy. That this beautiful child wouldn't be stolen away.

I curled an arm around him like I could stop it from happening, and then my heart rammed against my ribs when I felt the presence approach.

Energy pulsing.

A shockwave through the heated air.

A shadow covered us whole.

Obliterating.

Penetrating.

A cyclone of that energy speeding across the ground.

Caught in a landslide of it, I peeked up.

Evan's jaw was clenched with restraint and his eyes were filled with need. Swore I could still feel the magnitude of his promise that had sent me into hiding for the last three days, unsure I could resist the pull of it.

You belong with me.

"Don't get too cozy with that baby, Frankie Leigh. Think we're not quite ready for that, yeah?" Jack's voice hit from the side. "Don't mind the practice, though."

I wanted to vomit.

Only saving grace was the fact that Evan had been staring at Everett and me the whole time and wouldn't have heard the profanity.

"Yo, Jack, catch." Josiah called him by his first name. He didn't give him time to prepare before the football was pelting the side of his head and ricocheting off to tumble onto the sand.

Jack's hand flew to the spot, anger spewing out. "What the

fuck, dude?"

"Ooops, my bad," Josiah said, lifting his hands like he hadn't done it on purpose.

Everett spun toward the action, pointed wildly, laughing and stamping his little feet that were chubbier than his hands. He turned to me, dramatically nodding his head and patting at his chest. "Ball! Ehvie, please, ball!"

Oh.

That ball.

I started to get up to go for it, when Evan took a step forward.

Then another.

I was glued to the spot.

Evan leaned down low, his chest and shoulders and those abs all up in my face.

Damn it all if I didn't want to paint every inch of his exposed flesh with my tongue.

Evan angled his head, his eyes narrowed like he was having a hard time being in my space too when he reached down and picked Everett up from under his arms.

"Come here, Chunky Monk. Daddy will play ball with you," he murmured in that raspy voice.

He kept me pinned with that unrelenting gaze as he slowly pushed back to standing, heated eyes sweeping me head to toe, lingering on my breasts that I didn't realize were spilling out.

Okay. So *spilling* was an exaggeration. There wasn't a lot there to brag about. But Evan was staring at them like they were an all-you-can-eat feast.

I readjusted my top that Everett had dislodged.

Swiveling away, Evan strode toward Jack who was still mumbling about getting sucker-punched by a ball, the ball Evan dipped down and snagged without saying a word, moving to where the sand was softer.

He set Everett on his feet. The little guy bounced at his knees and clapped his hands over his head, his tiny fingers wiggling like he was fully prepared to catch a pass.

Evan pretended like he tossed it, soaring it through the air before he carefully placed it in Everett's hands.

Everett's squeals filled the air with a ridiculous amount of delight. My head filled with worry for my well-being, my teeth back to chewing off my bottom lip.

Because I was pretty sure I heard my soul scream with delight, too.

ten

Evan

*W*as she for real?

I stole a peek back her direction where she'd pushed to standing and moved over by her and Carly's tent, two of them whispering their secrets where they were partially hidden by a tree.

Yep.

It was for real.

She was wearing a white bikini.

No big deal, right?

Except unicorns were printed all over it, like they were stamped on.

A statement.

Unicorn Girl.

Hadn't missed the fact that she was still wearing that necklace, too. Thought she might toss it in a bid to forget me, but nope, there it was, dangling between her tits that were making me insane.

Fuck. I was getting all messed up looking at her.

That body sleek yet toned.

Slim and muscled.

The subtlest curves that I was itching to remember if they were as soft as they looked.

Had to wonder if she was playing some sick game. Tormenting me. Showing up dressed like that, that douche in tow.

Dude was an asshole.

It was my fault. Wasn't trying to deny it or pretend like I hadn't caused all of this.

Didn't mean getting in the middle of it wasn't about to send me off the edge.

Out in the lake playing, prick had obviously been trying to make it clear that Frankie belonged to him.

Like he was pissing on his property.

Didn't think he had the first clue what belonging to Frankie meant. That give and take.

The uncontrollable connection.

I glanced back over to where she was in a heated conversation with Carly.

For a beat, those eyes dashed my way. A deeper-colored heat slashed through the hot summer air. My insides clenched in a tight fist.

Guts knotted.

Dick hard at the sight.

Basically, I had been dealing with that same unfortunate predicament since she'd come traipsing down the trail and hit the cove this morning.

All those wild brown curls blowing around her.

That look in her eyes.

Attraction bounding.

Thank fuck she was sharing a tent with Carly and Josiah was sharing one with Jack. Last thing I wanted was to have to commit murder tonight.

A little hand patted my knee.

My attention jerked that way, and a grin was taking to my face.

Affection bounding free. This feeling that I was willing to do absolutely anything to ensure his safety. His happiness.

Honestly, it felt good to get him away from my parents' house, this place a reprieve from the constant looking over my shoulder.

Every rumble and vibration and shift in the air putting me on edge.

Couldn't shake this nasty sensation that someone was watching.

Problem was, I didn't know who it was. If Ashley was some kind of threat or if she was the one being threatened.

If Everett could be in some kind of danger or if it was all just bullshit.

Dad had called his old friend, Seth, who was a cop. I told him everything I knew, and he said he would keep an eye out, told me to be vigilant, but he agreed with Dad. I needed my goddamn name on that birth certificate.

That had to come first.

Everett patted my knee again, and I looked down at my son. An outpouring of devotion flooded out.

Only thing that I made out from the babble was *Da*.

Was pretty sure it sounded better than a goddamn love song.

"Hey, little man." My mouth moved with the affection.

"Ehvie, up?" His little arms were over his head, his fingers moving like crazy, kid needing me.

I swung him into my arms and gave him a small toss into the air.

Carefully.

Protectively.

A riot of laughter tumbled from him, the crash of it a thunder I felt against my chest. His joy alive. I was going to be sure that I kept it that way. "Are you done playing ball?" I asked, tucking it between our chests after I shifted him over to my side.

"Milk." At least that's what I thought he said.

"Are you hungry?"

He gave me one of his ridiculously cute nods where his head dipped down so low his shoulders went to his ears.

"All right, let's feed you."

I headed up to camp where everyone had gathered after the football game.

We'd demolished Uncle Rex's team. Of course, they weren't so keen to agree.

"No way, Uncle Ollie. That call was bogus. I totally made it into the endzone." Preston was facing me, and even if I could have heard him, I thought the words would be slurred with the way he was shoving a hot dog into his mouth while he rambled.

I went to the cooler and grabbed the bag with the containers of food mom and I had prepared for Everett and carried it to the picnic table where the two teams had gathered, everyone hungry after playing in the water all morning.

I situated myself so that I could *hear*. My eyes flitting between the faces, finding moving mouths, *listening* to the conversations firing around me the best that I could.

I set the bag on the table, watching as I did.

"You wish, Preston. You were at least two feet away," Uncle Ollie told him before he tossed a potato chip into his mouth and chased it with a gulp of beer.

Ryland laughed and hooked a thumb in Preston's direction. "Dude right here is a sore loser. He wants to make varsity, he's going to have to give that shit up."

"Language," Uncle Rex scolded, and I chuckled considering I thought the only thing that had come out of Ryland's mouth the entire time we were playing were curses and jabs.

"Yeah, language," I said, covering Everett's exposed ear. Not that my poor little man wasn't constantly getting himself an earful. Guessed I was proof that it really didn't matter all that much if you could hear them or not.

I'd picked it up just the same.

Hell, all the kids in elementary school had begged me to teach them how to sign every bad word in the book.

You'd think I was a fucking comedian with the way they'd laughed like that shit was hysterical.

Ryland slapped a hand over his mouth and mumbled something behind it. Widening my eyes, I flipped a playful finger at my ear as I called him out for totally forgetting that I couldn't hear whatever nonsense he was mumbling behind his hand.

A thud of affection pulsed, seeing him changed so much.

Growing up so fast.

I'd missed Frankie's brothers like crazy. They'd been as close as brothers growing up. Of course, that'd had a ton to do with Frankie, the way we were tied at the hip. Was no surprise the two of them had always tried to follow us around.

Ryland was laughing hard when he pulled his hand away so I could see his mouth. "Sorry, man. Sometimes I forget."

"No worries, dude. Probably didn't want to hear what you had to say, anyway," I razzed.

"Asshole," he said through a grin.

Uncle Rex smacked him on the back of the head. Nothing more than a love tap.

I laughed.

Ryland rubbed at it and grumbled, "Dad, come on, man. Uncool. Uncool."

"Way more where that came from," Uncle Rex tossed out, though he was wearing all that care that shone in his eyes.

Could feel someone staring at me from the side, a piercing intrusion that hissed across my skin. I shifted my attention that way.

Jack took me in like he had assumptions to make. "Seems you hear a lot better than you're letting on."

Was he serious?

My brow rose in question.

Or maybe it was in challenge.

My blood ran hot.

Jealousy crawled down my spine.

Wasn't ashamed to admit it, either.

I was jealous. Fucking seeing green at the thought of this guy putting his hands on my girl.

My fault.

I knew it.

It didn't change how I felt.

Trying to hold the anger back, I sat Everett down on the edge of the table, wedging myself up close to him to keep him safe, and I dug into the bag and grabbed one of the small containers. I pulled off the lid so he could go to town on the diced-up pieces of grapes and honeydew while I tried to figure out how the hell I was supposed to deal with this bastard standing at my side without being a prick.

Josiah didn't seem so cautious, pushing out two hands from where he stood on the opposite side of the table. "Whoa, man, not cool. Probably should watch yourself with that kind of insinuation."

"Just sayin'." Jack shrugged.

What a dick. He wasn't *just sayin'.*

"That's fine, man," I said, canting a look at Jack before I turned my attention to Josiah and lifted my hands, signing quick. *GUESS MY PRESENCE SHOUTS A LITTLE TOO LOUD FOR HIM.*

Josiah laughed and tipped the neck of his beer in my direction. "Think you're right, Mars Bar."

Dad gave me a look that told me to cool it.

Sometimes I thought Dad could feel me the same way I felt everyone else. That he could sense the anger. Feel the rage.

I was feeling plenty of it right then.

For no other reason than the fact this sack-of-shit had my girl.

Thing was, I was pretty sure he was hating me even harder considering he knew I'd had her first. Because he'd already had the premonition that I was taking her back.

That the girl belonged to me the same way as I belonged to her.

Could feel the truth of it riding in with the wind.

All's fair in love and war and all that shit.

Jack lifted his chin with an amicable smile on his face, but it wasn't all that hard to read between the lines.

An invisible gauntlet had been thrown.

I didn't hesitate to pick it up.

eleven

Frankie Leigh

Sitting on a blanket on the ground, I hugged my knees to my chest.

Mesmerized by the fire. By the feel and the vibe and the peace I'd always found in this place.

Flames flickered and leapt toward the star-strewn sky. Small waves lapped at the lakeshore, and a speaker playing old indie songs my parents had listened to when I was growing up hummed with temptation, seducing the shadows to dance through the trees.

Uncle Ollie quietly strummed along, his guitar propped on his lap, his face tipped toward the heavens.

Most everyone had mellowed except for my brothers and Bo who were still out in the lake roughhousing, tossing each other around. Charlotte and Becca giggled from their tent, whispering teenaged scandal, while my mother and her friends shared a bottle of wine where we'd all gathered around the fire.

Carly was sitting on the ground to my left and Josiah was on the right in a chair where he was laughing at some tales my daddy and Uncle Kale were regaling him with.

Tales that seemed to get taller every time they were told.

Stories I'd heard so many times they'd become legend.

Behind me, Jack sat on a chair, tossing back beers. No question, he was feeling the tension that wound and whispered and thrashed.

It didn't help that Evan was sitting directly across the fire from me, holding that child who was fast asleep against his bare chest, his emerald eyes watching me.

Hotter than they'd ever been.

A shiver rolled the length of my spine, and I tried to rip my attention away. To stand against the lure and attraction that rose and lifted like it was fueled by the flames.

The problem was, it only seemed to dump gasoline on the inferno of mourning and need and love that toiled inside of me.

That power only increased with every erratic beat that thudded from my heart.

My best friend. My best friend.

My everything.

I wanted to reach through the distance to the way things used to be, but I was still having the hardest time trying to figure out my way back there after all the obstacles that had been dumped in our path.

The potholes and pitfalls.

The fathomless scars that grieved.

Maybe the hardest part of that was the way the wounds ached to be soothed, well aware that balm was sitting right there, five feet away.

"She was always gettin' into trouble, wasn't she?" My mother's soft voice touched my ears, and I barely turned that way to catch onto the conversation that was clearly going on about me, too much in a daze to notice until she'd mentioned the word *trouble*.

Daddy had once convinced me he'd actually changed my middle name to Trouble.

I'd cried for two days straight.

I guessed I had it coming considering I'd stuck a bobby pin in a socket to find out if it actually would shock me or not. Somehow, I'd rationalized that I really needed to know it for myself. Knocked

A.L. Jackson

the electricity out for an entire day and burned my hand really good.

Evan had freaked out, lecturing me about needing to be safe and to listen and to stop being so reckless for about fifteen hours, and Mama had cried for just as long.

Both terrified over what could have happened.

"Hey, are you all talkin' about me over there. That's hardly nice." My words were soft, filled with all the adoration I had for this woman.

God, coming here? I couldn't help but remember to be grateful for the way she'd come into my life. To never take for granted the sacrifices that had been made.

I'd experienced both sides of the token—sustained the most damaging sort of abandonment and witnessed the greatest forms of sacrifice and devotion.

I did my best to remember the sacrifices were the most important.

Mama giggled and pointed at me around the wine glass she clutched, the red sloshing close to the rim. "Well, all the worry you put us through was hardly nice, either. I don't remember a single time that we came out to the lake that you didn't get yourself into some mishap or another. I think Kale only came because he knew we were going to need a doctor on call."

"I was just exploring," I defended with a grin.

"More like you weren't listening." Daddy's gruff voice was suddenly in the conversation. My attention whipped over to where he sat. I was hit with a surge of the protective devotion he'd always watched me with. "You're lucky I'm still around with the way my heart damned near stopped every time you up and disappeared."

My heart did for the quickest flash.

Stopped beating.

People used that phrase so casually.

Flippantly.

Not that I could blame my daddy. It was an everyday expression.

Still, I hated it.

Hated it so much that it sent a crash of nausea spiraling

through my stomach.

I forced a smile.

"You told her one thing, she'd do the opposite," Uncle Kale added, watching me soft, the man my hero in so many ways.

He'd been there for me through the toughest time of my life.

Held my secrets in the palms of his hands.

Never looked at me any different when he did.

I couldn't love him more.

I hoped it wasn't stingy that some of it had to do with the fact he'd saved Evan.

Physically.

Emotionally.

He'd given him a family when he hadn't had a father to show him what a man should be like. Given him an example of what love should be. How to treat someone right. How could I not adore him for that?

"Hey, that's all y'alls fault." I pointed around at the faces who'd given me the best kind of childhood. "It wouldn't have been a problem if you wouldn't have forbidden me from doing all the fun things."

"Yeah because you ran right for danger," Daddy said. "Dove into it, half the time. Thinking you could fly when you didn't have wings."

"That's because you all kept trying to cut them off," I returned. "I even got in trouble for jumping off the cliffs, and if there's even an ounce of truth to the stories you've been tellin' my entire life, all of you were doin' way worse." I feigned my disappointment as I looked at Daddy, Uncle Kale, and Uncle Ollie.

Uncle Ollie chuckled a low rumble of guilt.

Evan shifted in his chair, something soft pulling at one side of his mouth.

And I knew he was thinking about all the times we'd been here.

Running.

Flying.

Soaring.

Our lives nothing but laughter and joy and hope.

Okay, and a whole lot of trouble, too. I think we'd found

ourselves in time out more than we'd had time to play. It was funny how those memories were just as wonderful.

Wistfulness pressed down on my chest.

Nostalgia.

A fierce kind of longing that pulsed and begged and whispered to be restored.

I'd do anything to reclaim it. To find that time again. When we'd truly believed that as long as we stuck together, we'd be okay.

Evan watched me like he was thinking the exact same thing.

The boy so gorgeous where he was lit up in the glimmer of the flames, the shadows tracing his and Everett's faces.

I wanted to reach out and touch the lines. To maybe claim the frame as my own.

I dropped my gaze when I realized I'd been staring too long, cleared my throat, and took a gulp of my wine.

"I had your back, Sweet Pea. I kept telling them to let you be. Girls need to figure out who they are, and it became clear really fast you were our wild child," Aunt Nikki told me with a wink. "And there's no use trying to take the wild out of a wild child."

"At least someone around here got me," I teased with a laugh.

Energy flashed. This enticing lure that wrapped me whole. Evan's attention trained, a promise that he had always gotten me.

Better than anyone else.

"Hey, don't forget about me. I had your back, too." Carly's voice was pure feigned affront. "I was always game for whatever escapade you conjured up. I mean, except for the one where you wanted to climb to the very top of that tree." Carly pointed at the massive Cyprus that grew off to the side of the lake.

"Hey, that was gonna make one heck of a tree house."

"And guess who volunteered to carry up the wood." Carly wasn't even asking, she was just staring across the fire at Evan.

My partner in crime.

My partner in everything.

"He had two big ol' planks strapped to his back, totally off balance, and he still thought he was going to scale that thing," Carly said.

"Frankie needs wood, she gets wood." That raw, raspy voice

hit the air, amusement fluttering all through Evan's expression.

Um, what?

My eyes bugged right out of my head, and I was trying to fight the urge to get up and run, or maybe laugh, or maybe just hug him because I thought it was the first joke I'd heard him make since he got back and it was so like something he would have said way back then.

Josiah spewed out the beer he had taken a gulp of, his hands fumbling like they were laughing as he signed. *OH, I BET MARS BAR WOULD BE HAPPY TO GIVE FRANKIE A LITTLE WOOD.*

The jerk actually waggled his brows.

Oh my God. It just got worse.

Evan chuckled a scraping laugh and shook his head like he was innocent of the whole thing.

I swear, Josiah should have been kicked out of ASL because he sure didn't need that as his secret language.

"I will cut off your hands," I whisper-shouted at Josiah. "You and Evan are not allowed to hang out. Put you two together, and you're worse than a pack of fourteen-year-old boys."

Josiah only hooted louder. Clearly the boy had put a dent in that stock of beer.

"Hardly," Mom cut in, "I have to live with Preston, remember? If I find one more penis drawn on something, I'm going to lose it."

Aunt Nikki giggled against the rim of her wine glass. "Well, maybe you shouldn't have left all those Lauren Rowe books lying around when he was learning to read."

"Bite your tongue, woman. Those are my most prized possessions."

From behind, I could feel Jack paying too close attention, trying to pick up on what was going on, the more than inappropriate innuendo being tossed around like it could possibly be funny.

Oh, my daddy sure didn't think it was.

He scowled like I was thirteen and he'd barged through my closed door thinking he was goin' to find Evan and me up to something salacious where we were lying in my bed, while Uncle Kale watched me with worry, waiting for the second that I fell apart.

Jack's fingers were suddenly playing in my ponytail.

Shit. Shit. Shit.

Could this get any worse?

Jack leaned over my shoulder. "How about you and I go for a walk?"

I didn't even have to be watching Evan to know that he flinched. There was nothing I could do but experience his turmoil.

To experience his pain.

A prisoner to the exact same thing.

Empathy shouted through our connection. This feeling that I understood it in every way and wanted to reject it just the same.

Didn't he know I'd never wanted it this way? That I would have given anything for him to stay? I wanted to hop up and scream and demand for him to tell me how he could have chosen to be so unfair and cruel when he'd always been the one I could count on most.

Suddenly feeling like it all weighed too much, I faked a yawn and an exaggerated stretch. "I'm actually gettin' a little tired. I'm going to call it a night. You ready, Carly?"

I gave her a look that she'd better be even if she wasn't. I needed back up. A voice of reason when I felt like I was losing my mind.

She drained her cocktail. "I am now."

"Uh, what? I don't think so," Josiah slurred. "This party is just getting started, my bitches. Get your asses off the lame train and sit down. It's shot time."

Carly pushed to standing. "Not happening. We are nothing like your gamer friends who will stay up all night listening to your nonsense."

He smacked his hand against his chest. "You wound me."

"Someone needs to wound you," she tossed back before she was stretching out a hand to help me up.

Awkwardly, I looked around, trying not to stare too long at Evan, failing at it miserably because my heart was getting all knotted up again when I looked at him.

My thoughts running rampant with what it might have been like. If we were still together and we were here as one. If we would have come clean to our families about who we really were to each other and who we wanted to be.

If Evan would have endured.

If he would have held on.

If he would have loved me enough.

"Night, everyone," I said over the scratchiness in my throat.

I started to take my first step toward the tent when Jack grabbed me by the wrist, whirling me around to look at him where he remained sitting. His face was twisted up in his own hurt.

A plea.

I never should have brought him here.

God. This was terrible.

So wrong.

Jack didn't deserve to get embroiled in our mess.

"Good night," I murmured to him, hoping he heard my apology.

Because I was no cheater, and I knew what Jack was thinking. Sorrow gripped me by the throat because that was the last thing I wanted to do—hurt someone I cared about.

Hell, I didn't want to hurt a soul.

But sometimes life was complicated and messy and there were casualties, no matter how hard we tried to keep it from happening.

Jack gave my hand a little tug.

An appeal.

I dipped down and kissed his temple.

It wasn't an affirmation of us.

It was an apology.

Then it was Carly who was tugging at my hand. "Come on, I need to pee. You need to hold the flashlight because there is no way I'm going out in those woods by myself. There might be bears or snakes or spiders out there. Or maybe there might be a Josiah. That would be a real horror story."

"Hey, I heard that," he cried, and everyone laughed, all except for me and Evan who I could still feel watching me.

The overpowering force of the boy hunting me down as I twisted out of Jack's hold. I didn't look back as I followed Carly over to our things set up by our tent. She grabbed a flashlight, and we waded out into the spindly forest that had become nothing but howling trees and the tranquil sounds of the night.

Once we got out of earshot, Carly spun around. Before she could say anything, the words tumbled out, "I told you I shouldn't come. I knew this was going to be a disaster."

Her face pinched in disbelief. "No, Frankie, this is exactly why you should have come. Because this is what you need to see. What's really important to you. Maybe then you'll stop faking it and go after what's real."

"I already know what's important . . . it was Evan who didn't grasp it."

She huffed, her voice held in a tight whisper. "You aren't really going to stand there and act like that's the truth, are you? Have you looked at him with that baby? Have you seen the way he looks at you? I promise you that man knows exactly what is important."

"He left me," I defended on a low hiss.

"And maybe he had to in order to become strong enough to find his way back to you." She hesitated, her eyes dropping in the glow of the flashlight as she sighed. It took her a few seconds to look back up at me. "I know you needed him, Frankie. I know what he did sucked balls and was all kinds of wrong and part of you wants to hate him for it, and that's okay. But I think you have to ask yourself how much time you two are gonna waste."

Grief constricted my heart, right along with the hope that wanted to burst up from the depths. I felt like I was suffocatin' on them both.

She stared me down for a second, waiting. I was completely incapable of answering her. She shook her head. "I really do have to pee."

Like the good friend that I was, I held the light while she squatted, and then we silently stumbled back through the rocks and dirt to our tent.

At the flap, I paused to peer out on the camp, the fire burning bright within the ring of rocks, all the faces of those who I loved lit up in the flames.

My chest clutched.

I gulped around the sorrow, crawled the rest of the way inside, and slipped into my sleeping bag. Carly climbed under hers and shut off the flashlight.

A few minutes later, her breathing evened out.

Voices carried, growing quieter and quieter the more time that past. I had no idea what time it was when the orange glow finally burned out the same as the conversation did.

Everyone calling it a night.

Footsteps crunched around the camp as everyone retreated to their designated tents.

It was almost silent when a cry jolted into the air.

Everett.

He was whimpering, crying these little bleats. "Ma-ma. Ma-ma."

Oh God. I could feel that little boy's pain. His own abandonment. The child so full of joy but also knowing he was missing something essential.

Evan's voice covered it.

Soothing.

Sweet.

Loving.

Everything ached.

So badly that I curled over onto my side in a ball.

And I let myself weep.

Quietly.

Trying to hold it in while I listened to the comfort bleeding through the thin tent walls.

Carly reached out and brushed the hair out of my face, her voice a desperate whisper. "I'm so sorry, Frankie. I know it hurts."

"It hurts so bad," I gasped, choking around the confession. "It hurts so bad."

"I know. I know."

twelve

Frankie Leigh
Five Years Old

Frankie Leigh inched down the hall, her back pressed to the wall, trying to make herself a secret.

She was supposed to be asleep, but she couldn't sleep when she could hear the voices coming into her room.

Quiet voices.

She didn't like the way they sounded, and her tummy felt funny as she moved closer and closer to the kitchen where the lights were shining bright.

She stopped right at the end of the hall, hidden in the shadows, her ear listening to her daddy who was talking to her new mama. Her good mama and not the bad one that was so, so mean and scary that Frankie's tummy got sick thinking about her, too.

Her daddy's voice was low, and she peeked out to see him sitting on a chair from the kitchen table that was turned around to face her mama. His elbows were on his knees and he was scrubbing both his hands over his face.

Her tummy twisted up.

"What do you mean?" her mama asked, sinking down onto her knees in front of him, touching him soft, trying to get his hands away so she could look at him.

"It's horrible, Rynna. That poor little boy. They don't think he's gonna make it through the night."

"Oh God." Her mama pressed her fingertips to her lips, and Frankie could see the tears making a stream down her face. "What happened?"

Her daddy shook his head. "There was some kind of altercation with his biological father. He had a cardiac arrest. They did emergency surgery, but things aren't looking good. Kale is a disaster."

What were they talkin' about?

Frankie tried to listen harder, to make sense of it when her mama started crying loud there on the floor. "Oh, poor Evan. Poor Hope. I just can't imagine."

Evan.

Evan.

Evan.

His name pounded on her ears.

Her favorite, favorite person in the whole world.

Her froggy boy.

Frankie all of a sudden felt freezing cold all over. Like she was in a pool of ice and all the big pieces were covering her and she couldn't get out and she was gonna drown.

Her lungs squeezed, funny sounds ripping from her throat that stung, everything feeling so ugly.

Her stomach got sicker and sicker she thought she was goin' to throw up.

She ran into the kitchen. "What do you mean, Daddy? Where is Evan? I want to go see my best friend right now."

Alarm filled up her daddy's face, and he was saying one of those bad words she wasn't allowed to say before he was standing. He reached out for her. She jumped back and stomped her feet. "Take me now, Daddy. I wants to go to Evan's house right now."

"I'm sorry, Sweet Pea. You can't." His voice cracked and

Frankie's eyes were all blurry and she couldn't see.

"Please, Daddy! Take me right now! I need to see him. I got to give him a toy."

And Frankie had never seen her daddy get tears before but he had them in his eyes, and she hurt all over like she fell down and her whole body got bloody. "Please, Daddy. Right now. We gots to go right now."

Her daddy dropped to his knees on the floor. "Sweet Pea." His voice was so sad when he said it, and she hated it so, so bad when it sounded like that. He brushed back her hair. "Evan's sick. Really sick. Remember how we told you he has a bad heart? It's really broken right now, and the doctors aren't sure they can fix it."

She clutched at hers, her shirt in her fists. "Then let me give him mines."

Her daddy's face crumpled up like a piece of paper, and he grabbed her, wrapped his arms that always made her feel so safe around her. But she didn't want him to hug her. They needed to hurry fast.

"Hurry, Daddy. You got to take me right now so I can give him my heart. He needs a good one."

"Sweet Pea . . . You can't give him your heart. People only have one."

"No. I want to give him mine. RIGHT. NOW!"

She was shouting and begging and her tears were big and hot, and her daddy was hugging her tight, and she thought that maybe she was gonna drown again. The way she'd felt when her mean mommy had left her alone and it was so scary and everything burned.

She didn't want Evan to be sick.

She had to make him better.

Her daddy stood up with her in his arms, and her face was in his neck, and his skin was getting all wet from her tears. "Daddy, please." Her voice sounded weaker.

He ran his hand over her back. "I'm sorry, Frankie Leigh. I'm sorry. I would change it if I could."

"We have to do something right now."

He hugged her tighter. "The only thing we can do is pray."

"Oh, Frankie, what are you doing?" her mama asked from Frankie's bedroom door.

But Frankie didn't have time to stop. She kept trying to cut open the stuffed froggy, her movements frantic and shaking and her finger stinging from where she cut it.

She wasn't allowed to have sharp scissors but she needed them really, really bad. So bad that she wouldn't even care if she got sent to her room for being in trouble for the whole day.

A fat droplet of blood dripped on the big green froggy, and she hoped that Evan wouldn't be mad that she got red on it.

"Frankie Leigh." A hand curled softly around her shoulder.

She shrugged it off. "I gots to do surgery like Uncle Kale, Mama. Shh. You gots to be so, so, so quiet. Did you knows Evan looks just like a froggy? I fink this is his favorite toy in the whole world."

Her mama climbed down beside her, touching the hearts Frankie had cut and colored and were spread out all over her bed.

Frankie's hearts.

At least a hundred of them.

Because Evan needed so many hearts.

Not just one like her daddy said.

When she got the froggy open wide, she started stuffing all of the hearts inside, saying all the prayers she could find.

Please, please, please make Evan okay. He's my bestest friend and I need him to stay here. It's too scary to be alone. Don't make Evan be alone. I'll be good. I promise.

Her mama softly brushed her fingers through Frankie's hair. "Do you want me to help you?"

Frankie frantically shook her head. "No. I gots to do it. They gots to be my hearts because he's my best friend and Grammy said best friends make all the problems gets all better."

"Okay," her mama agreed, but her face was still sad, and she stayed right there while Frankie got all the hearts where they belonged. Frankie took the big needle and the white thread and she sewed it up fast so they were all safe inside.

"There," she whispered. "All done."

Evan got all her hearts. Even when her daddy said she wasn't allowed to give it to him.

Thirteen

Frankie Leigh

I jolted upright with a gasp, drenched in sweat and clutching my sleeping bag.

My eyes darted around, everything dark save for the glow of the moon that seeped through the thin material of the tent.

The world was quiet.

Bugs trilled and an owl called from somewhere high in the copse of trees, the lake still doing its gentle patting at the shore, the waterfalls crashing in the distance. I felt drawn to the solitude. To the whisper of the world that promised it was all gonna be okay. That there was something bigger and better and more beautiful out there waiting for us.

I quietly crawled out of my sleeping bag and over to the tent flap. I cringed when I pulled down the zipper and it came off sounding about twenty times louder in the dead of night. I opened it only enough so I could squeeze through, and then I slipped on my flip-flops.

Quieting my footsteps, I started for the path at the back of the camp in the direction of a place that my heart would always know.

A place that was filled with memories of so much joy that it would always feel like stepping into a sanctuary.

The moon was high, close to full, the milky haze sweeping over the smooth gray rocks that had been my playground as a child.

I started to climb the path that felt so familiar.

Higher and higher to where the rocks became slick, smooth from the years of water flowing in different directions, small crevices carved out from ages ago.

Once I made it over the cusp of the ridge, the expanse of the lake came into quick view.

Glittering and dark.

Fascinating and foreboding.

I crossed the invisible barrier that I'd been forbidden to pass when I was little, and I climbed toward the summit.

With each step, the crash of the waterfalls grew louder, the vibration of them reverberating underfoot, my spirit feeling lighter as I made my way toward the place the felt like freedom.

It tasted of childhood dreams.

Murmured of teenaged hopes.

I kept going until I made it to the boulder that was almost shaped like a heart.

A big crack down the middle.

Evan and I had deemed it the Heart of Stone.

Fractured but unbreakable.

It had always been our favorite place.

Where we'd played and jumped and laughed before it'd become the place where we'd dreamed.

With a shaky hand, I dragged my fingertips through the narrow crater, as if maybe it was real and alive and would hold all the answers I was searching for.

We'd climbed this thing like we thought we had to conquer it, put a flag in it and call it our home, sneaking up here most every time we came to the lake.

Our sacred place.

A shiver rolled across my flesh when I felt the presence approaching from behind.

Like instinct.

Intuition.

The boy my sixth sense.

The same as I was his.

Both of us drawn here the same.

I slowly turned around.

Evan stood in the opalescent beams of the moon.

Wavering.

Hesitating.

Like he didn't know if he should trust to step into the thousand secrets and regrets that toiled in the distance between us.

His hair appeared almost white in the glow.

His face this mix of torment and desire.

Damn him.

He still wasn't wearing a shirt, and my gaze was gettin' unruly again, unable to stop myself from drooling over all that firm, packed muscle.

Never had I understood the phrase *a sight for sore eyes* better than in that very moment.

Finally, I managed to drag my attention back to his face. That wasn't any better because my pulse was racing through my veins like a freight train.

A collision right up ahead.

We stared, locked in that moment.

I didn't know for how long.

The only thing I did know was something fierce and unrelenting rose up in the middle of it.

Pushing and pulling and compelling.

WHERE IS EVERETT? I found myself asking. I thought it would be a safe topic, but there was no way to hide the way my hands moved like a plea.

A song.

Everett.

Evan gruffed an affectionate sigh. The sound of it wrapped me like a dream.

I wondered if that was what this was. If I was still back in my tent and the nightmare that had chosen to torture me tonight was this.

Loving him and never being able to touch him again.

My favorite froggy.

"My mom has him. He was fussing, and she claimed they have more space in their tent so he might be more comfortable, but I know she really just doesn't want to let him out of her sight."

"She's already madly in love with him," I murmured, knowing he would feel it, the emphasis of what I meant.

He gave a tight nod. "Yeah."

"They missed you."

"I missed them, too."

"God, Evan. I wish you wouldn't have gone away. I wish you wouldn't have done this to us."

It was out before I could stop it, and even if I could, I wouldn't have taken it back.

I needed him to know.

Pain radiated from Evan, his spirit echoing off the rocks, ricocheting back.

"Why did you?" I asked. Desperate.

He took a step forward.

The earth shook. A rumble of the caverns and a shiver of the cliffs.

I DIDN'T KNOW HOW TO STAY. His movements were fluid, mesmerizing as he signed.

"Why? Why would you ever think this wasn't where you belonged?"

His throat bobbed heavily as he swallowed, his own war raging inside of him. "My entire life, everyone always did everything for me. I figured it was my turn to return the favor." He edged closer, and my breaths were getting shallower, sorrow billowing and getting all mixed up with the insane attraction I felt for this boy.

This man who I was aching to touch. To caress and love and remind how important that he was.

"A favor?" I realized it was a cry. That I was pleading with him to help me understand. "How in the world could you possibly think leaving me was doing me a favor?"

He kept coming closer.

Energy sparked with each step.

A frisson in the air.

So vivid I could almost see the circuit glinting in the space.

Awareness churned, every hair on my body lifted and on edge.

I wondered what I was thinking, coming here.

To our secret place. I guessed it was the masochistic side of me knowing that he would follow. The part that needed to understand.

His head drifted to the side as he stopped two feet away. His overwhelming presence and the subtle scent he wore like cologne hit me in a crashing wave.

The lake and the masculine kiss of the sun.

"I was so tired of seeing the fear written in you and knowing I was the one who was responsible for it."

"And you think that fear was going to up and go away because you moved across the country? Because you ripped yourself away from me? You think it didn't grow a thousand times worse?"

Our conversation had become nothing but breaths and gasps. My pulse hammered so hard I could feel it pummeling against my skin, this thrum, thrum, thrum that climbed through the bare space that separated us.

"I wanted it to." The words quavered, and Evan was right there, his pants washing over my face, his presence making me weak.

"Did you really think I loved you so little? That my love was so superficial that you could leave and I'd forget you? Did you really think you could erase the spot where you are carved inside of me?"

He'd left a cavern so wide there was no chance of it filling. No way it could diminish or even cave in.

"That would be like believing we no longer needed the sun."

"Frankie," he rasped, erasing the last bit of space, and he leaned down to run his nose along the length of my jaw. Inhaling as he went.

I sucked in a sharp breath, shivers racing my flesh. I inched back, like I could possibly be strong enough to shun the pull this boy had on me.

Magnetic.

Hypnotic.

My back hit the cool, hard surface of the rock.

Pinned.

That's the way he'd always had me.

Completely trapped and never wishing to get away.

"Frankie . . . I missed you . . . so goddamn much," he murmured at my ear, and he pulled back a fraction to look down at me.

"You know that I missed you."

More than I wanted to admit.

Evan reached out and took a lock of my hair that was blowing around my face. He twisted it in his finger.

The air shivered and danced.

"It's killing me . . . killing me seeing you with him. Fucking torture, Frankie, having to watch my girl with someone else."

What the hell was I supposed to say to that? Tell him that I agreed?

Because it was.

It was torture.

Sheer, utter torture.

All of it.

Him leaving me and him coming back a daddy and the way that I still felt.

Those eyes watched me like they were looking for an answer, his chest heaving, and God, my stupid stomach was twisting in all these knots, butterflies scattering when they had no business taking flight.

"Only have one question for you, Frankie Leigh." That raspy voice was gruff. Hard and almost mad.

"What?"

"Do you love him?"

Flames lapped.

Singeing.

Searing.

We might as well have still been looking at each other through the fire.

Attraction and greed and everything we'd ever promised each

other roiled in that unending connection.

"I-I . . ." I turned away from him, unable to remain looking at him and not completely crumble.

Evan reached out and took me by the chin.

Softly.

I felt myself caving. Everything coming apart. I struggled to find defenses. "I don't owe you an explanation, Evan."

"You're right. You don't." He edged closer. The words a ragged growl. "But I need to know."

"Evan . . ."

TELL ME, he demanded, his movements harsh, his face in profile where the moon slanted down.

So gorgeous it was unfair.

"Why do you need to know?" It felt like a last-ditch effort that came bleeding out.

"So I can do this."

Evan's mouth crushed against mine.

Possessive and hard.

A desperate assault, though his hands took hold of my face like it might be a treasure.

"Tell me," he demanded at my mouth. "Do you love him?"

There was nothing else I could do. Nothing else to say. "No."

His lips closed over my bottom one, sucking slow, just the tip of his tongue running the flesh.

A stake of ecstasy plunged to the middle of me, way down deep in that cavern he'd left in the perfect shape of him.

I gasped in shock.

I knew he was swallowing the sound down, taking it in like a word, listening to what my heart would say.

Every inch of him tightened, his muscles flexing and bowing as he pressed me deeper against the boulder, his cock hard where it urged against my belly.

Oh God.

This was crazy.

Bad and wrong and I knew in an instant that I could never get enough.

Dizziness swept through my mind. My body drenched in need.

Desire and lust.

Something so much bigger than my consciousness swelled in the atmosphere.

Something profound and irresistible.

My fingertips raked against his bare skin, clinging to his shoulders.

"I missed you, I missed you, I missed you," I realized I was mumbling into his kiss. Like my soul was giving him my answer. The whole, bitter truth.

He groaned around it, the sound a tremor that tumbled down my spine and took a dive straight into that pool of need.

It sloshed in a slow-slide of chills that rippled beneath my flesh.

Evan coaxed me into submission with his maddening kisses.

Reservations dislodged.

Every molecule in my hypocrite body was screaming *hell yes*.

Wanting what it shouldn't have.

Demanding it.

Evan's lips were firm and tender and imploring as they moved and tugged and nipped, and he whispered my name over and over again.

"Frankie. God. Frankie. I missed you. Can't go on like this. Not anymore."

My hands moved in the space between us, right over his chest. *E-V-A-N*.

I knew he would feel it.

Hear it.

No one had ever listened to me the way that Evan Bryant did.

His name came like a promise.

A plea.

The second I said it, he took us deeper, into that blissful madness I had never been able to resist, his tongue sweeping into my mouth to tangle with mine.

At the contact, we were nothing but a chemical combustion.

Sparks and fire and greed.

All hands and panting moans, and Evan's eyes were wide open, tuned in to me as our worlds rocked and our bodies begged.

He spread a hand down my side and hooked it under one leg.

I opened up.

Muscle memory.

Knees going weak as he pressed me firmer to the boulder to keep me standing, so I wouldn't crumble at his feet, so he could fit his magnificent body between my thighs.

Pinning me.

Owning me.

Torturing me as his hand splayed across my neck and down over my breast.

He slid it under the fabric to tweak my nipple, and he exhaled a needy moan when he touched my flesh.

I whimpered. Arched for his touch.

"Unicorn girl," he mumbled against my lips, his fingers flitting across the necklace I still wore around my neck. "I'd never cut your wings."

Oh God.

I nearly lost it right there.

Nearly came apart in his arms and begged him to make it true.

Belief just teasing at the edges of my periphery.

Emotion pulsed and throbbed and wept, and his hand was moving lower, his erection still rubbing at my shorts.

Evan had always known how to work me, how my body would succumb to his magnificent hands.

He spread me wider, palm smoothing up the back of my thigh.

Chills raced, and he was slipping his hand through the leg of my short shorts to the soaked bottom of my bikini.

He pushed the fabric aside.

My heart stampeded.

My spirit sang.

Fingers dragged through my lips, plunging in once, before they were finding that sweet spot and sending me soaring before I could even process what the hell I thought it was that I was doing.

The recklessness that he evoked.

This boy who had always possessed me in every way.

The boy I wanted to hold.

An orgasm stormed through me like the bright, blinding flash of lightning followed by the low rolling rumble of thunder.

Shattering out to touch every one of those cells that had been so on board for this.

And I was whimpering, holding on tight before my mouth was moving across his jaw, his throat, before I was pressing a thousand kisses to the scar at the middle of his chest.

I didn't even realize I was sobbing until his hands were back on my face and prying me away, those eyes roving my face, reading me, pads of his thumbs working to gather up the moisture that was making it hard to see.

"Frankie." It was a command. Misery. A terrifying promise.

Panic surged in behind the aftershocks that left my legs trembling and weak, and I was choking, gasping, twisting out from where he had me pinned.

Stumbling, I got about ten feet away before I flipped around and looked at him in horror.

"Frankie."

"Why are you doing this, Evan?" I rushed through the vacant words, trying to wipe away the onslaught of moisture that rushed down my face. "Why?"

His jaw hardened. *BECAUSE I LOVE YOU.*

Oh God. How desperately I had wanted to hear those words.

To cling to their truth.

My hands were on my chest, trying to hold back my heart that was already crawling through the cracks, through my fingers, through my defenses. "You left me," I couldn't help but beg. *"You. Left. Me."* I could barely get it out I was crying so hard.

I wished he could take it back.

That he wouldn't have left all those scars written on me.

"I loved you, Evan. Needed you. If my love wasn't enough for you then, how would it be now?"

"I was wrong," he begged. "I never should have gone, Frankie. I know that now. But I wanted you to have the chance at a normal life. A family. Children. Everything I couldn't give you."

He took a step in my direction. "More than that? I never wanted to see you with that look on your face again, Frankie Leigh. I'll never forget it, you coming through that hospital door. Couldn't stand the thought of being the reason for that much fear."

Hot tears streamed out of my eyes. Soaking my face and trailing off my chin. All that pain was getting free. Everything I'd held inside threatening to climb right out to be set at his feet.

And I knew, standing there, that I had to tell him.

But how could I do it when I knew it would absolutely devastate him? What if it sent him running again?

"Evan." My throat tremored.

"I love you, Frankie. Tell me you still love me, too."

I blinked, wanting to just confess it all.

Memories rampaged through my mind. Us as children. The bond that should have been inseverable. Our love that had blossomed from the most beautiful place. The devotion I'd thought would come with that.

The pain. The betrayal.

The darkest night I'd ever spent.

I blinked through them all, and a sob caught in my throat.

Everything crushing down.

Unsure that I would survive that kind of pain again, I turned and I fled.

Problem was, the whole way back, I could hear him calling my heart back to his.

fourteen

Frankie Leigh

*T*ension curled through the cabin of Josiah's Tahoe as we headed back for our duplexes. Every mile it grew thicker. The silence denser. This dark echo that had followed us all morning like a heavy cloud.

We'd packed up and left early. I'd tiptoed over to my mama's tent and woke her, told her we had to take off because Carly wasn't feeling well.

Carly had told me I was welcome to throw her under the bus, but I owed her big time.

Thing was, I couldn't stand beneath the scrutiny and the questions.

Warily, I peeked over at Jack who was raging soundlessly in his seat. Knee going a hundred miles an hour. Even beneath his burly beard, I could see his jaw was hard as stone.

God, had everything gone downhill and fast last night. About as fast as I'd been scrambling back down the trail for my tent. The panic that had sent me spiraling. It'd only gotten ten times worse when I'd gotten to camp and I'd found Jack sitting outside his tent staring at the dead fire, tears staining my cheeks and my lips swollen from Evan's kisses.

Guilt written all over me like a brand.

I couldn't even face him. I'd fumbled back into my tent like I'd simply wandered out into the darkness to pee and had come right back, then lain swamped in shame until the sun had come up a couple hours later.

Thinking about it sent a tremble through my spirit. Never had I wanted it to go down like that. Never should I have let Evan touch me. Not when I hadn't ended things with Jack. Hell, I probably shouldn't have let it go down at all. Not when I couldn't get rid of the worry that I was setting myself up for a whole new brand of pain.

There was another part of me that knew it was worth it.

That every second I got to spend with Evan was one that was cherished.

Even if it was only one second of bliss.

The whole ride home, no one tried to make small talk considering there were no words that were going to make this okay.

No apology I could give.

It just was what it was.

Even though I hadn't wanted him to, Jack had become one of those casualties in the war Evan and I were fighting.

Josiah made the last turn into our neighborhood. The only sound in the SUV was the drone of the engine and Milo's whine, my boy sensing my distress. We made the left into the open lot in front of our duplex. Josiah pulled beside my car that was parked in front of our porch.

Somberly, we all piled out. Morning light spilled down, bright and hot and drenching my back in a slick of sweat.

Or maybe the dread was giving me a heatstroke.

Milo hobbled out, and I gave him a pet, angled my head at Carly in a plea. "Can you take him inside, please?"

She gave me a look of knowing sympathy before she whistled low and patted her thigh. "Come on, Milo Boy. Let's get you inside where it's cool."

No one even bothered to get anything out of the back. Josiah and Carly headed up the two short steps, and Josiah unlocked our door.

Milo was reluctant, looking back at me from the top of the steps. He finally gave in when Carly called him again.

The door slowly closed behind them, and I stood there facing away from the hostility that filled the air. I hugged my arms over my chest and fought the tears because this was not the time to be feeling sorry for myself.

This was my wrong.

Something I should have ended a long time ago.

Hell, I never should have let it get started in the first place.

But sometimes when you're just trying to survive, you'll do anything to make yourself feel normal. Do anything to fill up the vacant spaces. The best of intentions that time only proved faulty.

"Fuckin' knew it."

Anxiety flared, and I slowly turned around, knowing it was time to at least face one issue in my life.

Before I could get anything out, Jack cocked his head, rage seeping from his flesh as he fisted his hands. "Thought you said he was only your friend? Isn't that what you told me, Frankie? The boy you grew up with that you used to play fuckin' dolls and house and shit with?"

It was all a disgusted accusation.

I blinked. Those tears I'd been trying to hold back fell without permission. I sniffled and Jack laughed a disbelieving sound. "Knew that prick wanted you the second I saw him. Bastard thinking he could steal you away from me. Tell me he didn't touch you last night. I'll rip his goddamn hands off and then we'll see how much he likes making a fool out of me talking that bullshit language behind my back."

I winced. "Wow, Jack, that's awesome. Make light of his deafness. That's big of you."

I got it. He was pissed and I deserved it. That didn't mean I wasn't feeling defensive.

Protective over Evan. Over who we had been. Jack could never understand it, that kind of connection, especially when he and I hadn't come close to sharing it.

He'd asked me out to dinner one night, and I'd agreed. Lonely. Hoping to fill a little of the hollowness. We'd basically fallen into a routine, the emotion so thin that I doubted there was a day that we'd ever been real.

I should have stopped it before it started, but here we were.

Even if I never saw Evan again, I was ending this now like I should have done a long time ago.

Yeah, life was riddled with mistakes. Most of the ones I'd made I would take back if I could.

All except for the one I'd made by falling in love with Evan Bryant.

"I asked you a question, Frankie." Anger dripped from his words, a venom unlike anything I'd heard from Jack before.

Discomfort roiled.

That dread growing to something that almost resembled fear.

"It doesn't matter," I choked out.

His brow curled in disbelief. "It doesn't matter? It doesn't fucking matter? The way he was looking at you looked like it mattered a whole lot to me, Frankie. I'm not a fucking fool. I know you were out there with him last night."

I hugged myself tighter in an attempt to hold it together. "He's my best friend," I whispered, hoping he could feel the meaning of it without my having to say it aloud.

That just seemed unnecessarily cruel.

Jack nodded, voice close to taunting. "Best friend. So, nothing has ever happened between you two?"

My mouth grew dry, and I swallowed hard.

He laughed again.

Dark and disturbed.

Then he was in my face, making the demand. "Did you let that freak fuck you?"

Freak?

Revulsion flowed free. I couldn't believe he would say something like that. Be so callous. But I guessed that's what happened when I went and got myself into all sorts of trouble again.

Consequences unexpected and unfair.

I probably should accept it, but there was no chance I was going to stand there and let Jack spew that kind of hate.

I rasped out a sound of disbelief. "Did I let that *freak* fuck me?"

"Yeah." It was all a sneer.

I huffed out an incredulous sound, unwilling to give him the truth. That Evan was my life and my heart and my everything. My best friend. My first lover. The love that would burn inside of me until the day that I died.

That he was the kindest, most generous person I'd ever met.

If Jack wanted it that way, then fine.

"Yeah, I let that *freak* fuck me. And one time with him was better than a hundred times with you."

It was a low blow, but I'd never in my life stood aside and let someone call Evan names. It just wasn't in my makeup.

Maybe I should have thought better of it this one time because Jack was whirling away from me. A roar of rage ripped up his throat as he stooped down and grabbed something from the ground. Faster than I could make sense of it, he hurled it.

I screamed as glass shattered. Shock jerked my attention to my car that now was sporting a busted-out side window from the big rock he had thrown.

I reeled back, and Jack was gripping at his hair.

Enraged.

It was the most emotion that I'd ever seen from him. The ugliest kind.

That fear streaked. A flashfire. My heart raged in panic as he got back in my face. "Bullshit, Frankie. You and I belonged together. I fucking love you, and I'm not going to let some pretty boy asshole come in here and steal you away from me."

Dazed, I stumbled back, feet getting tripped up by disbelief and panic. "Are you crazy? You just threw a rock through my car window."

Maybe I was needing to repeat the obvious.

Unable to believe that Jack could be so volatile.

"I love you, Frankie Leigh." This time it was desperate.

He'd said it so many times. A casual *love you* or *love ya* or a heart at the end of a text.

I'd never said it back.

"Say it." His words were grit, hands in fists at his side. "Say it, Frankie Leigh."

Shaking my head, I stepped back. "I . . . I can't."

I could almost hear the shout coming up his throat before it was silenced by the door swinging open and the commotion on the porch.

"What the fuck?" Josiah's voice boomed through the air, busting through the vat of fury that held Jack hostage. Carly's shock spilled all over the place when she stumbled out behind him.

Milo started barking like crazy.

The three of them rallying at my side.

Jack stepped back, slanted a glare at the three of them standing guard before he glowered back at me. "This isn't over, Frankie. Not by a long shot."

Then he turned and stormed away, slamming into his house, leaving me staring there behind him.

fifteen

Frankie Leigh
Seven Years Old

"Come on, Evan, let's go!" Frankie scrambled up the rocks in front of her bestest friend in the whole wide world. She made sure to look back at him so he could read what she said since his ears didn't work.

She was learning her signs better and better, but sometimes she got them all wrong and Evan started cracking up laughing at her.

She liked it when he laughed.

Sometimes she messed up even worse so she could hear it.

He started up behind her.

"You comin', slow poke?" she asked, grinning over her shoulder.

"I'm comin'," he said in his rasping voice. "What, you think I can fly like you, you crazy unicorn girl? Just don't go jumping off a ledge. Last thing I need to do is have to come after you. Your daddy is right. You're nothin' but trouble."

She giggled when she looked back to watch him climb, his

reddish hair looking like flames of fire where it whipped all around his face, his green eyes so big behind his round glasses, his hands holding onto the slippery rocks as he climbed up behind her.

Her favorite, favorite froggy.

Frankie made it to the top, her chest feeling heavy with her breaths and her heart beating so fast from working so hard to get up there. She plopped down by their favorite rock, her back leaned against it, huffing up a storm.

Evan slumped down beside her.

"Whew," she exclaimed. "I didn't think I was gonna make it all the way up here. That was hard work. Did that feel like hard work? Does your heart feel funny?"

Evan giggled, his eyes watching her mouth. *YOU TALK TOO FAST,* he signed really slow so she could read it. *AND YOU WORRY TOO MUCH, TOO. MY HEART'S ALL FIXED!*

His eyes went wide like a bug's.

Frankie laughed. "I have to worry about you because you're my best friend and I have to take care of you."

He smiled that smile she loved, that one that made her chest feel tight and like she was the happiest person in the whole world. "No way, your dad said it's my job to take care of you. Said I have to make sure you don't go and hurt yourself again. You're the one who needs to be careful. You're gonna end up in the hospital if you don't and my daddy is gonna have to patch you and then your dad is gonna be mad at me."

He shoved his glasses up his nose.

Hospital.

She frowned at the mention of that gross, icky, creepy place.

Frankie's worst memory was when she had to go see him in the hospital. It was scary and there were so many wires and tubes and machines and everyone was cryin' all the time.

Frankie had been the one who was crying the most.

She thought it was even worse than when her old mean mommy had left her in the smoke.

But the good news was Evan got out of there really quick after she brought him the froggy with all her hearts, and he said it was his favorite thing in the world, and she made sure to remind him to bring it everywhere with him because she wanted to make sure he had it really fast if he needed it.

"We aren't even supposed to be up this high," he told her. "Your dad's gonna get mad all over again."

"Then how in the heck are we gonna get to our favorite rock? Maybe we can bring it down the hill so we can play on it all day."

Evan laughed like she was crazy. "Um . . . that thing weighs like a million pounds. No way are we getting it down there."

"We can roll it," she suggested.

He laughed. "You're crazy. No way."

She pouted. "Then I guess we better stay up here forever. Besides, this is where our weddin' was. It's our special place, remember? I think we should just live here."

Evan giggled a shy sound, and his cheeks were turning all pink. *THAT WAS FAKE.*

"Nu-uh, no way. My mama said it was real. Didn't you see my dress?"

"Yeah, I saw it, and you wore it yesterday, too." He was teasing her.

She huffed. "My mama said as long as I believe in something hard enough, I can make it mine or make it real or make it come to be. And I want the wedding to be real."

He laughed lighter. *OKAY. FINE. WE'LL CALL IT REAL. WE'LL JUST HAVE TO MAKE IT FOR REAL, REAL, LIKE MY MOM AND DAD, WHEN WE GET BIG.*

CAN WE HAVE FIFTEEN KIDS?

Evan curled his nose. *FIFTEEN? THAT SOUNDS LIKE TOO MANY. I DON'T THINK YOUR DAD WOULD WANT TO BUILD A HOUSE THAT BIG. HOW ABOUT SEVEN?*

She nodded. *PROMISE?*

PROMISE.

"Good. Because you aren't ever allowed to leave me."

Evan scrunched up his nose. "Where would I go without you, Frankie Leigh? If I go somewhere, then you have to come, too."

She looked over the blue lake that got mixed up with the blue sky, the mountains lookin' blue in the middle. This was her favorite place in the whole wide world as long as Evan was right there beside her.

She reached out and took his hand, loved the way it felt when he weaved their fingers together. "You're not ever allowed to die, okay?"

Evan laughed, sound raking on his throat. "I'm not gonna die. I've got all your hearts and the smartest, best doctor for a daddy. He said I'm good as new. I think I might be able to live forever."

She snuggled down against their rock. "You better. You got a heart of stone now. It can't get broken."

If it did, he still had all of her hearts.

And her mama told her love was always enough, and she prayed over those hearts every day that they were good enough to hold him together so he never had to get that line on his chest opened up again.

She squeezed his hand. "I love you the best, my froggy boy. You are my favorite."

Evan lifted his hands. *I LOVE YOU THE MOST, UNICORN GIRL. MY FAVORITE FOREVER.*

THEN WE STAY TOGETHER FOREVER. DEAL?

He reached out and shook her hand. "Deal."

sixteen

Evan

I glanced up at the jade-colored awning hanging over the storefront in front of us.

My mom's logo was printed on it like a beacon for the droves of people who flocked here each morning so they could make it through their days.

A Drop of Hope.

Had spent so much of my life within these walls that it felt like a second home.

A calling.

Or maybe it was the fact that Frankie had become such an intrinsic part of it.

My eyes darted around, making sure that prick from the other day was nowhere to be found.

Couldn't help it that I was constantly on edge.

Unease riding high.

I huffed out a sigh of relief when nothing seemed amiss.

Everett had plastered his face to the window of the cafe, kid going nuts with excitement, doing this little jig that looked like he was doing knee highs, flaunting that ridiculous grin with that scrunched up nose and eyebrows shooting toward the sky.

My chest tightened. Was starting to get worried that he affected me too much.

Protectiveness swelled. A silent promise that I would do absolutely anything to keep him safe.

"Oh, you want to go in there, do you?" I asked him.

Another adorable nod. "Ehvie, go?"

"Yeah, buddy, you can definitely go inside. We have some of our favorite people in there, don't we?" I murmured.

My mom and Carly and Aunt Jenna.

And Frankie.

Frankie. Frankie. Frankie.

Just her name twisted me in a thousand knots of anticipation.

Two days had passed since I'd seen her.

Two days since I'd had her pressed up against that rock.

Two days since I'd tasted her again. Felt her again.

Two days since I was reminded of exactly what I was supposed to be fighting for. Reminded of what I never should have given up.

I glanced down at Everett, heart getting all tangled up again.

It was getting harder and harder to hold onto the idea that I shouldn't have left. Kept getting the sense that maybe it'd been purposed. Required. Knowing this child wouldn't be here if I hadn't have gone off and given myself to the loneliness. Given myself to the recklessness.

I swung open the door.

Instantly, I was hit with the overpowering scent of sugar and cake and all things sweet.

It was mixed with the heavy aroma of fresh coffee brewing in the huge urns that were set up on the left side behind the counters. Rows of display cases ran to the right of that, filled with every delicious thing you could imagine.

Jenna was behind the counter. A huge smile split her face as she finished checking out the customer who was paying. As soon as the man stepped back and took a sip of his coffee, she was clapping. "Ah, you're here! I was wondering when you were going to come back and see me again. I had to work the whole weekend and miss out on all the fun out at the lake. Damn Susie for going and gettin' pregnant and being on maternity leave and making me have to step in to take her place. So uncool."

It was all a ramble of a tease.

"Seems everyone around here is up and having babies from out of nowhere." This time she was all raised brows and speculation.

I chuckled, roughing a hand through my hair, gazing over at Everett who'd made a beeline for the display cases and was currently slobbering all over the glass.

Remind me to take care of that.

"Life is full of surprises, isn't it?" I told her, totally droll.

She rounded the counter, came directly for me, and pulled me in for a tight hug. Stepping back, she set her hand on my cheek and met my eye. "It sure is. And I hope you're cherishing that surprise."

"I guess it's sometimes the least expected that come to mean the most to us."

Affection filled her expression, and she angled her head, brushing her thumb over the freckles under my eye the way she'd always done when I was a little boy. "That's the Evan I know. I sure missed him."

"I'm right here," I told her, knowing it was time I reclaimed what I'd thrown away. Praying it wasn't too late. That the bridges I'd burned could be rebuilt. The love I'd shunned could be rescued.

Movement in my periphery grabbed my attention, and I looked that way to see my mom come out the swinging door.

Mom's smile was so soft, so good, it flooded the entire room with warmth. "I was hoping you two would stop by to see me today. It's getting harder and harder to get up and leave each day and not get to see my rolly polly before he wakes up."

HE WAS ASKING FOR YOU, I signed.

WAS HE REALLY? Love gushed from her expression.

PRETTY SURE HE WAS ASKING FOR YOU BEFORE HE THOUGHT TO ASK FOR ME. WOKE UP TO HIM STANDING UP IN HIS CRIB, CLINGING TO THE SIDE

AND JUMPING AROUND AND SHOUTING 'GRAMMY'.

"Oh." Mom pressed a hand to her chest. Overcome by her love for this kid. This sweet child that had come from out of nowhere and now held all of our hearts in the palm of his tiny hand.

She headed around the counter, and Everett nearly lost his shit when he saw her.

"Gammy, Gammy, Gammy! Bwue ball?" He started nodding like crazy, dipping his head way down, looking like he was doing some kind of dance.

"How about some breakfast first, and then you can have a treat. Did he eat?" She turned her head to ask me.

"Had some Cheerios and milk a couple hours ago."

She tsked a little. "Cereal."

"Don't start judging my parenting skills." I cocked a teasing brow at her. Like I had the first clue what it took to be a good dad. But I was sure as hell going to figure it out. "Pretty sure I did just fine on a bowl or two of Cheerios growing up. They're good for the heart. I might live a year or two longer."

Mom scowled. "Evan."

"Bwue ball. Bwue ball," Everett chanted.

Was funny how I couldn't hear, and I still felt the chaotic nature of it. The way a child filled up a room, spirit so big and boisterous.

Filled with awe and untapped potential.

The reason we could recognize hope all over again after we'd thought we lost it.

And then Frankie went and appeared in the doorway, coming up short the second she saw us standing there.

A flashfire of energy dumped on the clutter.

This girl the cause of the pandemonium going down in my chest.

Clutching and pulsing and demanding.

Everything fucking ached for her.

Heart and body and mind.

This girl my picture of perfection.

Wild hair barely tamed in this messy twist on the top of her head, brown, frizzy curls getting loose, eyes wide and full of the same disarray of confusion and need and questions she'd watched me with Saturday night.

If I was being honest, she looked a little feral.

So what if I wanted to fucking pet her again.

Mom scooped Everett into her arms. Her attention darted between me and Frankie Leigh before she murmured to Everett something about eggs.

Figured she was talking food again but I was too wrapped in watching Frankie to get the full gist of it.

Mom rounded the counter and went for the heating station where there were a variety of breakfast sandwiches that were prepared each morning so people had a healthier option than a pound of sugar.

"Hi," Frankie mumbled, her teeth clamping down on her bottom lip, hesitating, like she didn't know whether to step out and act like nothing had gone down between us Saturday night or tuck tail and slip back through the door.

Pretend like this wasn't happening.

"Hey," I told her, letting the hint of a smirk ride up at one corner of my mouth.

She shook her head a little, half amused and half annoyed. "What are you doing here?"

"Just wanted to . . . check in," I settled on.

See you.

Talk to you.

Remind you again that we belong together.

So yeah. I'd been worried about her yesterday. Especially considering the last thing I'd told her was that I was in love with her and then she'd split. The four of them had packed up and left before anyone had even woken up Sunday morning. Apparently, Frankie had told her mom that Carly wasn't feeling well.

Except I'd had a pretty good idea where the illness was coming from. Frankie filled with the fear that I was going to hurt her again.

Wasn't going to stop until she understood that wasn't going to happen.

Part of me expected her to do it again—run, turn her back on me like I deserved for her to do. Instead, Frankie's expression turned soft, the girl glancing between me and Everett and back again.

"How is he today?"

God, didn't know if I could handle her extending her care to Everett. Had nearly come apart when I'd come up from the lake on Saturday to find her with my son in her arms.

That feeling that had taken hold.

I tried to clear the roughness from my throat. "He's great, Frankie. Wonderful."

So maybe I couldn't help but express to her a little the way he made me feel. The same way she did. Whole. Complete. Like there really was something worth living for. Fighting for.

I'd been a fool to let it go.

Wasn't going to repeat that same mistake again.

Her teeth were back to roughing up that bottom lip. "He is, isn't he?"

Emotion pressed between us. A circuit sparking. Awareness coming to life.

I peered over to where Mom was situating Everett at the tiny table that she'd set up for me and Frankie behind the far end of the counter all those years ago, where we'd share our after-school snacks and laugh and color and draw up our dreams.

Mom had broken up little bits of egg, sausage, and biscuit, and Everett was trying to pinch the pieces between his fingers and get them into his mouth.

All of it appeared so simple.

So right.

Still so fucking terrifying because I didn't know how long I was going to get to keep my son in my life this way. If things were going to shift and get shaken or if this fucking threat was real.

If I was going to lose all over again.

All I knew was I was going to fight, and I wanted to do it with Frankie at my side.

Friends or as a lover or whatever it had to be.

I just . . . needed her.

Needed her in my life.

Was tired of breathing without her.

Everything was better with a little Frankie Leigh.

"Mom?"

Mom looked back over her shoulder. "You mind keeping an eye on him for a second? Need to talk to Frankie."

Her eyes flitted between the two of us.

I wondered how much she knew. If it was plain as day to everyone else as it was to me. That this was just meant to be. "Sure. Of course."

Frankie frowned in worry, hesitating, then said, "I'll be right back. Let me know if you guys get busy."

I followed Frankie through the door and into the kitchen.

She stood facing away, the potent aura of this girl rippling into the space.

"Frankie." I touched her shoulder, let my hand glide down her arm, begging her to turn around. "Please. Look at me. I need to *hear* you."

Words were gravel. Hard and pained. The plea I'd made before she'd taken off Saturday night suddenly there, a barrier standing like a fortress between us.

"I love you, Frankie. Tell me you still love me, too."

Shivers raced her flesh, and Frankie slowly turned around. Cinnamon eyes flashed, affection and fear roiling all the way down deep in the depths.

I couldn't do anything but reach out and touch her face. Set my hand on her cheek. Run the pad of my thumb across her trembling lips.

She sighed with the action, her heat speeding up my arm and spreading across my skin.

"Hey, Unicorn Girl," I murmured.

The tears she'd been holding back suddenly fell. "Evan."

"Hey, please don't cry," I whispered. "I didn't come here to upset you."

"I know you didn't," she whispered back. She blinked a bunch of times. "But that doesn't just erase what you did. And you keep coming back here . . . pushing into my life . . . and I don't know how to handle it," she admitted.

I wanted to kiss away every tear. Promise her that I would make everything better. Hold all her fears and her pain the way she'd always held mine.

Be the man she deserved for me to be.

But I had to prove it.

"Frankie," I murmured. "Unicorn Girl. I never wanted to be the one to steal your sparkle."

I let a tiny bit of tease fill the last. This girl who'd basically bathed in glitter and color and capped it off with ridiculous outfits.

Affection and grief crested her features, and I kept brushing my thumbs over the soft skin of her cheeks. "I think that sparkle just shined brighter when you were in my life, Evan. That's the whole problem."

"I never should have gone."

"No."

I pulled my hands away so I could sign, so I could speak to her the way that I knew best. *I'M GOING TO PROVE TO YOU THAT I UNDERSTAND THAT, FRANKIE. THAT I KNOW THAT I DID IT ALL WRONG. I'M GOING TO PROVE TO YOU THAT YOU CAN TRUST ME TO STAY.*

I angled in closer, needing her to know. *MIGHT TAKE SOME TIME. A WEEK OR MONTH OR YEAR OR MY ENTIRE GODDAMN LIFE. BUT I'M WILLING TO PUT IN THAT TIME BECAUSE YOU ARE WORTH EVERY SINGLE DAY.*

Those eyes raced over my face, her fingertips fluttering up over the thunder at my chest. "And what if too much damage has been done, Evan? What if life has been so cruel and unfair to us that there are too many wounds for either of us to heal?"

I set my hand on her sweet face, splayed out wide like I could hold all those fears. "The cruelest thing that's ever happened to me was having to live without you."

Energy spun. Love spinning and spinning. Winding us tight.

I swallowed down the dread, just . . . needing to be up front because the truth of the matter was my life no longer looked the same. "And I don't know what's coming. I know you don't know all the details about what's happening with Everett. Hell, I don't, either. But the one thing I need you to know is I love him. He's my *son*. And I need him in my life, every bit as badly as I need you."

"Evan . . . I . . . I . . ." She fumbled for an answer.

"I get it, Frankie. I know you have a boyfriend—"

Her head shook, cutting off the direction I was going. "We broke up on Sunday after we got back home."

Didn't mean to exhale a gust of relief as intense as a desert windstorm. But it was there, filling the room.

She shook her head more. "It wasn't right . . . me being with him when I'm not over you."

I leaned in closer. "You make it sound like you're trying to get over me."

She huffed a self-deprecating laugh though everything about it was tender. "I'm been trying to get over you for years, Evan Bryant."

I edged forward, backing her to the counter, loving the way her breaths shallowed out and her heart beat faster. "Yeah? Well, I think you should give that up because there's no chance of me ever getting over you. Then we're even."

"Evan." My name was a whimper. "I just . . . need time. Need to find a way to forgiveness. You hurt me more than I think you know."

But that was the thing.

I did know.

Because even if she only hurt a fraction of the amount I'd felt without her? There was no questioning that shit was brutal.

Gaze searching her face, I let both hands weave into that wild mess of hair. "Frankie. I'm going to prove it to you. I promise."

Dipping down, I sealed it with the softest kiss to her lips.

She exhaled an even softer sigh.

I groaned when I inhaled the girl. "Cotton candy. You really are testing my will, aren't you, Unicorn Girl?"

She giggled a small sound. "Hey, don't go blamin' me. I do work in a bakery, after all. I was just whipping up something new and special. I might have felt inspired."

Another groan, my stomach twisting up with want. "You're

gonna have to stop with that."

She lifted her chin, the feisty girl I'd known emerging from that shell she never should have worn. "Oh yeah? What are you gonna do about it, Froggy Boy?"

I pressed myself a little closer, only an inch of fire separating us, our noses close to touching. "I think you really want to find out."

Her hand was about to fist in my shirt when I felt the movement at the door, and I whirled around to find my son pushing through, completely dazzled that the door swung.

My mom came in right behind him.

"Fi-Fi!" he said, pointing at Frankie Leigh, giggling as he went.

Something passed through her features. Something dark and overcast and still threatening to break with the day. He tottered over to her, and she only glanced at me for a second before she picked him up and pressed a kiss to his chubby cheek. "Hey there, little man."

"Puppy?"

"Oh, you remember my puppy, do you? I bet he remembers you, too."

She started bouncing him, walking him around the kitchen, showing off all the things.

Guessed I was getting way ahead of myself because I got the sudden, sharp sense that this was exactly the way it was supposed to be.

seventeen

Evan

*T*wo hours later, I pulled into the drive of my parents' house, soaring high. Feeling like I was finally making progress. Like everything was making sense. Everett was conked out in his car seat in the back, pooped from hanging out at the café for a while before the two of us had gone to the park to play.

Just . . . getting to know each other.

Truth was, it didn't matter that I'd known him for little more than a week. Felt like it'd been his whole life. Like there was no time missing and we'd been destined.

Like he was carved out of a piece of me that I recognized as myself.

I killed the engine and climbed out, going right for the back to unbuckle him. I hoisted him up high on my shoulder, cradling him as I made my way up the five porch steps.

Then I stopped in my tracks.

Breath leaving me on a punch.

Fear and dread and terror taking me hostage.

FREAK.

It was painted in big white letters across the entire expanse of the floorboards of the porch.

I whirled around. Ready for a fight.

I held Everett tight.

Protectively.

A feeling unlike anything I'd felt before came over me.

Could almost feel the adrenaline get dumped into my veins.

Rage and fury.

I tried to breathe, to focus.

Everett's tiny, chubby body was tucked close, the little pants coming from his nose hitting my cheek while the air stirred with an ominous silence that screamed through the late afternoon air.

A morbid kind of stillness echoed back.

A disordered calm.

I spun in a circle.

Looking for anything.

Anyone.

I stumbled a step when I noticed the note tacked to the front door.

Warily, I moved toward it and ripped it from where it was tapped to the wood.

Game's up, you're running out of time.
You and your perfect life.
I'm done standing aside and watching you win.
Fuck you, freak.
I'm taking back what is mine.

Ice slipped down my spine.

Frozen dread.

Spreading. Saturating. Seeping into every cell.

I slowly turned around and faced the echoing vacancy.

I clutched my child.

My son.

The cost and consequences didn't matter.

I would do anything, give up everything, to make sure he was safe.

Darkness filled my childhood room. The lamp on the nightstand shed a muted, dingy glow that barely illuminated the space. The glow-in-the dark constellations Dad had put up all over my ceiling when I was ten twinkled from above like we were actually out laying under the stars.

Should lull me to sleep.

But there was no chance I could close my eyes.

I'd texted the number I'd had of Ashley's from over two years ago at least a hundred times.

Dad had called it almost as many.

Nothing.

I needed to reach her.

Get an answer.

Find out what the fuck was happening.

How could she just . . . up and leave if she knew something was going down? If she knew Everett might be in danger?

Unease slithered across my flesh.

Worst part was this feeling that this was personal. That it didn't have a damn thing to do with Ashley.

I mean, what the fuck did that message mean? And who would give it if they didn't want something specific from me?

Apprehension blazing, I glanced down at where Everett was still lying at my side, sucking on the satin trim of the blankie, pointing at all those stars like he was as interested in them as the way I'd been.

I snuggled him closer. I should have put him down in his crib two hours ago, but I was having a hard time letting him get too far away.

He didn't seem to mind.

My own personal night owl.

Softly, I murmured the names of the constellations he was staring at, pointing at each one. Figured it was a good enough distraction.

Orion and Aquila and Ursa Major.

Pegasus.

"See that one," I murmured, pointing to the constellation that had always been *ours*. "I always liked to believe that one is about chasing your dreams. About allowing yourself to be free and believe. About being brave and tapping into the magical things you have inside of yourself. That one reminds me of Frankie Leigh."

His head popped up in acute interest. "Fi-Fi?"

A light chuckle rumbled out, and I smoothed my hand over the top of his head. "You like Fi-Fi?"

He got to his knees, nodding one of his nods and getting in my face. "Ehvie, Fi-Fi? Go?" He pointed at my door.

I laughed.

"Yeah, buddy, I want her, too. But we can't go right now. It's nigh-night time."

Everett leaned up higher on his knees, patting my chest, getting up close to my face with that grin that twisted me in two. His little lips moved erratically, his spirit speaking to me even though I wasn't sure exactly what he said.

Nothing except for, "Da."

Then he slobbered a kiss against my chin.

God.

I never thought I could feel like this.

So goddamn in love and terrified at the same time.

All of this bullshit dangling in the periphery.

Danger on the fringes.

If things around here weren't stressful enough, those fucking results still lingered out in no-man's land.

A threat of punishment and penalty.

A judgment coming.

Had I passed on this curse or not?

It was brutal.

Worry coming at us on all sides.

But somehow, this room? It felt safe. Right. Like nothing could tear me from this child.

I pressed my lips to his temple, breathing in all the sweet. "I love you, too, Chunky Monk."

Finally, he snuggled on the bed beside me with the old stuffed animal of mine I'd given him.

Crazy thing? I was already having a hard time remembering what my life had been like without him in it. But I had to remember that he'd been ripped from the normalcy of his.

Was still fucking worried that this poor kid didn't know what the hell was going on.

Knew at times he had to feel scared and abandoned and missing something important in his life.

A hole cut out of him in the shape of his mother.

Ashley.

He cried for her sometimes and that was about the roughest thing I'd experienced. Not being able to explain to my son why she wasn't here.

Couldn't come to terms with the way I felt about her. Pissed as all hell that she'd kept me in the dark, that she hadn't had the decency to tell me, and distraught for her at the same time.

No. We'd been no love match.

But she'd been cool.

A friend. If I really thought about it, she had probably been more into me than I was into her.

But the truth was, I really didn't know her all that well.

Didn't know her history or her hopes or spent enough time with her to even get the inclination that she could topple into depression.

Her brother's face streaked through my mind. That feeling I'd gotten.

Just . . . something about it didn't sit right.

And those two notes . . . the word left on my car and the porch.

My heart palpitated in fear. Knot filling up my throat.

I wrapped my arms around Everett and whispered at his head, "I'm going to take care of you. No matter what."

A flash of light in my periphery caught my attention, and I jerked to look at the window.

Ready to fucking go to war.

That was until I saw the throbbing rhythm. The same secret code Frankie and I had made when we were kids.

Our own private, flickering SOS.

I need you.

My pulse stuttered into a sprint.

Frankie and I had climbed up and down the trellis outside my window what had to have been a thousand times. Had no idea why she'd chosen to come this way rather than text and show at the front door. Wasn't like we were kids who needed to sneak around any longer. Guess what surprised me most was that she was actually there.

That she'd come at all.

"Dis?" Everett poked his head back up, his attention piqued. That little finger was pointing excitedly at the window.

I understood the reaction.

"Looks like our Frankie came to see us."

His green eyes went wide with approval. "Fi-Fi?"

He babbled something, still pointing away, while my chest grew tighter and tighter as she continued to flash the light at the window, the way she'd always gotten my attention as a child.

A signal.

A sign.

Her spirit calling out.

I slipped off the side of the bed, taking Everett with me. He dropped the stuffed animal, both hands fisted in my shirt.

Need clutched my stomach.

Apprehension.

Anticipation.

Everything rolled with thunder. My heart and my breaths and my mind.

I slowly crossed the room. Felt like I was stepping into unfound territory, unsure of where this was going to lead.

Every flash of her light slammed me with a fierce bolt of longing.

Energy shivering.

Rumbles of a storm underfoot.

Frankie Leigh was a silhouette in the window, but I'd recognize her anywhere. Wild curls flying around her, cinnamon eyes sparks of life in the darkest night.

She'd always been my sun. She'd called me out of the shadows that spun through the quiet in my mind. The girl finding me in the seclusion. Drawing me out of the isolation.

Lump in my throat, I fumbled around to push open the window with my free hand. Her aura flooded in, crashing against my chest and spilling onto the floor.

Could feel the weight of her gasp. The breath that she released. Like my presence struck her the exact same way.

I reached my hand out to help her through.

Energy crackled at the connection, this seething desperation, and I could tell she was trying to hold her breath while she climbed through the window.

Everett clung to my side, hiding his face, but peering out with one of his scrunched-up smiles. Frankie's gaze was on him, like she felt his pull. Like she couldn't resist him any more than I could.

"What are you still doing awake, little man?" Could tell she was whispering, and she reached out to touch his cheek before she grabbed his hand when he pointed at her again.

Wondered why the fuck if felt like she was reaching out to caress me at the same time.

"It's late," she said.

"Guess maybe he was staying awake, expecting you." My throat felt tight and heavy when I said it, tension bounding through the tense air.

Those eyes swung over to me, but she was still holding onto Everett's hand. I wondered if she even knew she was doing it. If she felt this affinity with him, too.

Didn't try to stop the smile from lighting on my mouth. "What are you doing here? Not that I'm complaining or anything."

She went to chewing on her lip again, action full of apology and worry and doubt. "I heard what happened this afternoon. That you had somethin' painted on the porch. Your mama left the store totally beside herself."

Frankie hesitated, those eyes dim. "It's my fault."

"What are you talking about? How is it your fault?"

She gave a regretful shake of her head. "I . . . I think it was Jack. The other mornin' . . . when we broke up?" She inhaled a heavy breath, and her shoulders hitched high. Clearly her worry extended to my son who she glanced at before she returned her gaze to me.

"When I told him about us, he threw a rock through my car window. Accused you of bein' a freak. I . . . I never in a million years thought he would pull somethin' like that. He was irate, Evan. Volatile. I mean, I knew he was gonna be upset, but I'd never expected him to come off like that. He told me he loved me and things weren't over between us."

"What?" I demanded, fully caught off guard.

Protectiveness struck like a match that burst into an inferno.

Consuming fury.

"Why didn't you tell me earlier? Fuck, Frankie . . . did that bastard hurt you?"

"No," she rushed. "I didn't want to upset you. Didn't want to get you tangled up in the mess that I'd already made. I figured he would cool off and see reason. I'm so sorry."

Guilt creased every line of that stunning face. I reached out and cupped it, that rage back in full force.

"This isn't your fault, Frankie. No matter what." My head shook as I tried to process through the information. "Honestly? I'm not sure that it was him. The note that was left? It felt . . . personal."

She huffed out a laugh that held zero amusement. "Oh, it's personal, Evan. He thinks you stole somethin' that is his. He's been weird about you from day one. The day you got here, he started wanting answers about who you are to me."

I moved into her space. Had to admit, I loved the sharp intake of air that she sucked in when I pressed up close to her. "Did I take something that was his? Seems to me like he had something that was mine."

Flustered, she stepped back, fidgeted with the hem of her shirt.

Damn, I wanted her.

Wanted to kiss her and love her and touch her. The way it was supposed to be.

She turned away and started roaming my room. Something wistful and soft filled the atmosphere. She reached out and traced the medals and trophies that still remained on my shelf, tenderly brushed her fingers over the framed pictures of us. I was holding Everett tight when she looked back. "It's been so long since I've been in here. How's it possible it feels so different and somehow exactly the same?"

I moved over for the bed and sat Everett down on it. On his hands and knees, he bounced around like a frog.

Frankie looked at him. There was so much affection coming from her it nearly dropped me to my knees.

"Our worlds might have spun off course, Frankie, but you and I are still here. You and I are still the same."

Shadows played across her face, across her body, and fuck, I knew she was asking for time, but I didn't know how to stand there and not claim this girl as mine.

Not when she'd always been.

Frankie sank down on the edge of the bed. She pulled one knee up so she could face me where I remained standing at the end of it.

I'M SCARED, EVAN.

Hatred pulsed. I was going to put an end to whoever this bastard was who was causing a threat. But if it was that prick, Jack? Thought of it made me see red.

I WON'T LET ANYTHING HAPPEN TO YOU. NOT TO YOU OR EVERETT.

She dropped her eyes, contemplating before she looked back up. "And what if what I'm really scared of is you leaving me again?"

I moved over to the opposite side of the bed and sat down, blocking Everett in between us. Like instinct, Frankie laid her head down on the pillow like she'd been doing it forever, the way we used to do when she'd sneak into my room and we'd stare at the constellations on the ceiling and dream and laugh and pretend.

Except this?

Nothing had ever felt so real.

"And even after everything? I don't think I know how to stay away from you." She said it like it was the confession of a sin. Like she was the one to blame.

Following her lead, I laid my head on the pillow and slipped my hand across the mattress. Grabbing onto a piece of her hair, I twirled it round and round my finger.

"I don't even know why you would try," I told her, our words vibrations that melded in the space between. "We get lost, and we'll always find our way back to each other."

"Evan." Sadness poured from her, all mixed up with the fierceness of the love that flooded the room.

A blanket wrapping us in security.

A shroud of sanctity.

The truth of who we were even if we weren't quite back there yet.

Everett sat up on his bottom, pointed toward the ceiling, his mouth making a little 'o', showing off what he had seen.

Frankie tipped her gaze up toward the stars. She shifted up onto her elbow so she could focus on him. "Do you like those, Everett? Aren't they amazing? Your daddy loves the stars. I think it only makes sense that you do, too."

"I showed him yours," I told her.

Wistfulness washed through her expression, and she turned to look at Pegasus.

Shit. Had the unbearable need to hear her voice in that moment. Wanted to experience it all. The sound and the taste and the brush of it across my skin.

"I always thought I could soar so high I could touch the stars."

"You did . . . and I was always right there, trying to keep up with you."

"I think I was always beggin' for your attention so you'd follow."

A somber smile played around that sexy mouth.

I was having a hard time keeping myself in check.

Could see Everett was finally fading, so I grabbed the stuffed animal he'd dropped on the floor.

The green frog I'd carried around my whole life like it was a lifeline. Guess I wanted to offer that to him, the same comfort it'd always given me, this girl always within reach. "You want this, Chunky Monk?"

His eyes lit up. "Ehvie, dis?"

Adoration and disbelief sparked in Frankie's expression. She looked over at me as Everett threw his arms around it. Hugging it to his chest, he buried his face in the dingy, worn fabric.

"You still have it?" she whispered in surprise.

"Of course, I still have it. You gave it to me. Day you told me you were giving me your heart, remember? You think I ever would have thrown that away?" Tried to tease, but the words reverberated with old misery.

Three years lost.

Three years wandering.

Three years of wishing I could be someone different.

Someone better. Someone right. Someone healthy who could offer this woman a good life.

She stretched her hand out across the bed, her fingertips fluttering over the thunder of my heart. "It's always been yours."

"Frankie." It was a plea.

Everett suddenly toppled himself forward like he was as desperate as me to get into her hold, kid spreading out on his stomach while pressing his face into the crook of her elbow. Wasn't sure if he was mumbling a bunch of words against her skin or giving her kisses, but I could see his mouth moving.

He was so tired that I was thinking he was probably getting delusional.

Frankie began to rub his back. Softly. Tenderly.

"Shh," she whispered.

Like it was intuition.

Second nature.

"Are you tired, sweet boy? Shh . . . just relax. We're right here."

Love squeezed my chest. So damn tight I could hardly breathe. Could hardly see anything but the beauty of this.

His little thumb snaked its way into his mouth.

Fuck.

How many times had I dreamed of a picture like this? Frankie with my kid? Only in that fantasy, the child would be ours. We'd be married and have a family and this fucked-up plague wouldn't stand the chance of following us. In that dream, those kids would never be put at risk and I'd live to an old age out on some porch in a rocking chair with Frankie at my side, watching our children grow.

A gush of sorrow swamped me.

Overwhelming.

Fact I'd probably never have a chance to watch this little boy become a man. That I might not get the chance to witness the amazing things he would become.

More terrifying was that I'd been so careless that he might be put in the same position, too. That I'd already cast his lot.

Condemned him to a life that I would never want him to have to live.

They were almost the exact same thoughts I'd had that night three years ago, when leaving had felt like the only option, the only thing I could do to make a fucked-up situation right.

I struggled around it, those thoughts that wanted to creep in and take me hostage.

A soft hand grazed my jaw, drawing me out of the spiral. My gaze drifted up to find Frankie watching me, like she'd witnessed every single thought that had run through my mind.

"Evan," she murmured.

"Are you scared?" she asked.

TERRIFIED.

Terrified of the love that felt like too much.

"He's so beautiful. He looks so healthy. So much like you."

My head shook in disbelief. "Never thought I'd get to be a dad."

A flash of longing swept through Frankie Leigh's being at my admission. I hoped she would get it. Understand me on the level that she always had. "I shouldn't be."

"Evan—"

My head shook a little harder, cutting her off. "And I sure didn't expect to be a single dad. Going this alone. Especially when I didn't even know he existed."

Tenderly, she ran her hand down his back. "You're not alone, Evan. Look at everyone around you. Everyone who loves you. I . . . I can't believe she didn't tell you. That you found out this way."

She kept rubbing his back.

A sweet, sweet consolation.

Like she wanted to wipe away Ashley's stain. Make up for her deficit.

Emotion trembled through my body. "I love him so much, Frankie. I hardly know this child, and I'd give up everything for him."

"Love for a child is instant." I barely caught the words on her lips, felt them more than anything.

"Tell me about her," she finally asked. The torment on her face was nothing but a flash.

Still, there was no missing it.

"Her name's Ashley. She was just this girl at my apartment complex. She seemed cool. We started hanging out. She didn't seem to care that I was different . . . liked it even."

Frankie flinched at that.

TMI, apparently.

Exhaling, I roughed an agitated hand through my hair and forced myself to continue. "I was lonely . . . drinking a bunch at that time. Think she liked that, too. Kind of became a thing. We'd get trashed and hook up."

Hurt slashed through the air.

The bitter stab of a dull, rusted blade.

Didn't want to wound her. But I wasn't about to lie to her, either. "It wasn't like we were a couple or anything, so I didn't really make a whole lot of it when she didn't come around for a while. Finally stopped by her place and knocked at the door. Apartment was empty. All of her things gone."

My eyes held Frankie's, that space separating us charged, our voices held in whispers and secrets. "Didn't hear from her again until she was banging on my door in the middle of the night last week."

Frankie's hands flowed with emphasis. *I AM SO SORRY, EVAN. SO SORRY THAT SHE WOULD BE SO COLD TO LEAVE YOU OUT OF HIS LIFE. SO SORRY THAT SHE TOOK THAT TIME AWAY FROM YOU. BUT I AM SO GRATEFUL THAT SHE BROUGHT THIS BABY TO YOU.*

Cinnamon eyes deepened. Love spilling free.

HE NEEDS YOU.

I sat up farther, angling her way when I signed. *I'M TERRIFIED THAT SHE'S GOING TO GET IT TOGETHER AND COME BACK FOR HIM. TAKE HIM AWAY FROM ME.*

Intensity flared, this fierce, unrelenting force that radiated from Frankie. Her hand was on Everett's back where he slept, her fingers splayed wide, a hedge of protection.

"She can't do that."

"She might try, but I will fight for him, Frankie. Whatever the hell is going down, I'll fight for him."

"I wouldn't expect anything less." She switched to signing. *HE'S YOUR SON.*

Realized I had nothing to lose. The only thing I could do was cut myself wide open. "I'm scared I won't be enough. That the courts will take one look at me and see the risk. A fucking deaf dude with a broken heart who's already surpassed his life expectancy."

Fully sitting up, she reached over my son to hold my face in her hands. "I think what they'll see is an amazing man with an amazing heart. They'll see a man who will live every single day for the ones that he loves. They'll see a man who's still livin' because this is where he needs to be. Because he belongs with us."

I grasped one of her hands and pressed it tighter to my face. "That's who I want to be, Frankie. That's the man I want to show up. The one who is here loving you. The one who is loving him."

"And that is who is sittin' here, right now. This is the boy who grew into a man—one who was taught to never give up on hope. We hold it. Fight for it until it's ours."

"You were always my hope, Frankie Leigh."

My faith.

My dream.

The end game.

Her lips trembled. I traced my fingertips across the lush curves.

Flashes of energy. Rising and thrashing.

Swore I could feel the room begin to spin.

The two of us caught up in a second flat.

I pinned Frankie with my eyes as I edged back and picked up my son. He stretched and his mouth moved, but his eyes never opened as I carried him to his crib and settled him onto the mattress. He heaved a sigh and his little body settled down into the comfort of his bed, his thumb back in his mouth and the frog tucked under one arm.

Everything fisted.

Love and adoration.

Felt the shift of the potency behind me. Greed and desire. A river rushing with need.

I slowly turned around.

Frankie had stood from the bed. She was back to wringing her fingers, those eyes wild and unsure, the girl wearing this tank and shorts that made my mouth water, all that skin aglow in the murky light that hovered around her.

My hands twitched and everything hardened.

She gestured toward the window. "I really should go."

I took a step her direction. "Yeah? Why's that?" I took another step forward.

Energy streaked.

A thunderbolt.

She chuckled a little, the girl antsy and needy as she shifted on her feet. "I think you know the answer to that, Evan."

DO YOU NEED TO GO OR DO YOU WANT TO GO? My head angled to the side as I asked it, edging forward, drawn to this girl.

She lifted her chin. Surrender and defiance. "I don't know how to be in your space and not want you, Evan. I don't remember how not to be yours."

That was all it took for every reservation holding us back to topple. For every wall to crumble to the ground. Nothing but rubble and debris strewn in the middle of us.

I scaled right over it.

I had Frankie in my arms in a second flat, one hand twisted up in her mess of hair and the other bound tight around her waist.

Her face was a couple inches higher than mine, and I gazed up at her in the same second I was pulling her down to my mouth.

Devouring her in a mind-altering kiss.

Greedy as I stroked my tongue between her lips, groaning deep as hers twisted with mine in a reckless rhythm that I wanted to dance to forever.

Fuck. This girl always tasted the same.

So goddamn sweet.

"That's because you're mine, Frankie," I rumbled at her mouth. "You've always been. Nothing is gonna change that."

"I missed you. So much. Oh God, Evan, I missed you. You are makin' me crazy."

I drank down every word, read them against my lips, savored each one like it had been carved into the pages of our story.

"Just let me touch you, Frankie. Let me make you remember what we were like. The way we were supposed to be."

Her mouth was on mine, the whisper of her words hitting me like a storm as I deciphered her meaning. "Please, Evan. I don't want to hurt anymore. I don't want to hurt anymore. Make it stop."

Fuck.

I hated that I was the one who was responsible for it. That I'd been the one to divvy out this pain. Knew I had to be careful with her. That I had to prove it.

"Shh . . ." I murmured. "I've got you. I've got you."

Her fingers were in my hair, yanking and tugging in her play to get closer.

Our spirits surged into the air.

"Please . . . touch me . . . just let me feel."

Frankie suddenly jerked free of the kiss, and her attention darted to the crib. I followed her line of sight to find Everett stirring a bit. I didn't hesitate, I just carried her across the room and through the door of the attached bathroom.

I glanced back to make sure that he had settled. "Can you hear him if he needs us?" I asked as I snapped the door closed.

Frankie nodded frantically before she dove for me.

Fingers frenzied. Lips frantic. This girl a live wire I held in the palms of my hands.

A bomb. Mortar.

Exploding into my world and changing its makeup. I spun and pressed her to the wall, taking some weight off so I could run my hands down her sides.

Clutching. Searching. I wanted to rediscover every inch.

Felt her moan in my mouth, her back arch, hungry for my touch. She clawed at my shirt, tugging it free, and I slipped my hands under her tank, sliding it up and doing the same.

It only mussed up her hair more, that frizz flying free.

Those cinnamon eyes sparked with desire.

Frankie wore this pink frilly bra, all lace and ribbons and temptation, the cups pushing up her small tits, the charm of that necklace dangling in the middle of it.

I brushed my fingertips over it. "I can't believe you still have this."

"I've never taken it off."

I ran my hands over her breasts before I tugged down the fabric of her bra. It exposed her even pinker nipples that were so pebbled and pretty that I couldn't do anything but lean down and take one hard tip into my mouth.

Swirled it like a sucker.

Sweeter than candy.

Fuck. She was gonna undo me. Almost forgot what it was like when she was mine.

How she'd always been a little wicked.

Incautious in her need.

Not afraid to demand exactly what she wanted.

She gave a good yank at my hair, my head pricking in a delicious-sort of pain as she begged for more. For me to push her harder and deeper and farther.

Spinning her around, I pushed her belly up against the bathroom counter. Her hands flew out to steady herself.

Our eyes met in the mirror where I towered over her from behind.

Her expression turbulent.

Untamed and ferocious.

She'd always left me feeling a bit savage.

Like I was two seconds from coming unhinged.

Usually did.

Getting lost in Frankie Leigh was the best feeling in the world.

Her chest heaved, and I slipped my arms around her so I could cup her tits. I plastered myself to her back. Heart hammering out of control and my dick begging at the curve of her ass.

I rubbed against her there, searching for any kind of friction. Relief.

This girl an oasis when I'd been dying of thirst in a parched, rainless desert.

Knew she was making all these needy sounds, felt the breaths panting from her lungs.

She rested her head on my shoulder.

Succumbing to my hold.

I watched her through the mirror, the flat planes of her stomach quivering, her deep belly button so sexy it made my head spin with greed.

"Please, Evan. I need you. I need you so bad I can't see straight. Can't think straight. I haven't slept in two days, remembering the feel of you." Only picked up on every word or two. But I knew what she was saying.

Frankie was a love song I'd memorized a long time ago.

I splayed my hands over her trembling belly, kissed along the soft curve of her neck and shoulder, breathed her in as I went.

Cotton candy and sugarplum drizzle.

My stomach clenched, cock desperate to get free, lust a shockwave that boomed through the dense air.

Reverberating in the tight, cramped space.

"You want me, Frankie Leigh?" I flicked the button of her jean shorts, and I slowly eased them down over her slight hips.

They slipped down her legs, leaving her there in nothing but a matching pair of underwear that I was pretty sure had been designed with the single task of driving me out of my mind.

Sending me over the edge.

Straight into a freefall of ecstasy.

"God . . . yes." Could feel her plea. Tasted her confession.

I kissed down her spine. A streak of chills lifted everywhere my mouth explored. Kept traveling lower and lower, hands on her hips as I kissed into the dip at the small of her back and down the lace of her underwear, my nose running her cleft.

It brought me to my knees.

And I was kneeling behind her on the floor and trying to see through the insanity that was threatening to take me over.

Inhaling this girl like I was issuing up a prayer.

A promise.

Frankie pushed back, begging for more.

Delirium.

I reached up, hooked my fingers in her panties, and dragged them all the way down.

Want fisted my guts.

I wound the fabric free of her ankles, and I urged her slim legs apart.

Felt her exhale in anticipation.

Whimper in excitement.

I kissed up the back of her thigh, hands following suit until I had her bottom in my hands, kneading the flesh, spreading her apart.

Knew words were tumbling from her mouth.

Deep urges.

Desperate pleas.

Felt them crash against my body.

Flames and fire.

I dragged my tongue through her slit, all the way to her ass.

Frankie trembled.

And I thought maybe I was going to die, my dick so damned hard and needy that I was going to explode.

Pushing to standing, I shoved down the elastic band of my shorts, needing the contact of our skin, even if it were only for a second. They slipped all the way down my legs, and I kicked them away.

Heat blistered through my body, and I stood up and rocked my dick through the crease of her ass, gripping her cheeks while I did.

"Frankie."

A groan was tumbling out, and Frankie was falling forward,

those eyes meeting mine in a fury of heedlessness through the mirror.

"Evan."

Our connection screamed to be unchained.

Unbound and set free.

I spun her around.

Frankie lunged at me, pressing reckless kisses at my jaw. At my throat. At my chest.

I NEED YOU. I NEED YOU. She signed the erratic revelation at my chest. *YOU ARE MY FAVORITE.*

Hot hands landed on my sides. Exploring. Seeking. Remembering.

Then she hoisted herself up onto the counter.

She met my gaze, unwavering.

Got the sense this girl was ripping out her heart and offering it to me anew.

She brought up her legs, hooking her feet on the edge of the counter, spreading her knees in invitation.

"Be careful with me, Evan." Felt the words punch the air. "I know you've always thought I was the strong one, but it's always been you who has had the power to destroy me."

Regret struck me like a blow to the head.

Reared me back.

This girl so gorgeous she was making it hard to see.

She had always been so fun and free, but I'd always seen her vulnerability.

I'd loved that about her, too. That she was brave and loved with everything and still was scared over losing herself.

I was committed to holding all those pieces together.

I threaded my fingers through her hair. "No, Frankie, it's you who owns me. Did me in the first time I saw you. I never looked back. It's you who did all the wrecking."

Still, just because I was a glutton for punishment, desperate for the pain, I nudged only the aching head of my cock into the slick clutch of her body before I was pulling out and rubbing it on her clit.

Sweet fucking torture.

Could feel her rasp of pleasure, her breath on my bare skin.

Before I could give myself over to another mistake, I grabbed her by the outside of the thighs and dove down to lick deep into her pussy.

When Kale had given me *the talk*, he'd told me girls were like a flower. Treat them right, and they'd flourish and blossom.

Frankie was like a whole fucking garden.

A thousand acres blooming in my hands.

Her body a rainbow.

Her soul the sun.

She writhed, and she sank her fingernails into my shoulders, dragging and raking them across my skin before they were twisting back in my hair.

I didn't hesitate, just went to work on her clit, stroking her with my tongue, slipping two fingers into that tight, wet heat.

She bucked, and fuck, it was another of those moments that I'd give anything to hear, to relish her sighs and her pants and the tumble of praises that I could feel rolling off her tongue.

I edged back, watching as my fingers sank deep into her cunt, letting the tips of my free hand slip through her crease, just teasing her ass.

I met her eye, needing to know. "Good?"

Knew her response was a wisp, thin and barely there, the girl struggling to open herself more, like she couldn't get close enough. "Nothing has ever felt as good as you touching me."

"Tell me, Frankie."

"I need you. I need you so bad. In every way. In any way."

I angled down, lapping at that sweet, swollen spot, fingers thrusting harder and deeper, winding this girl so tight I could feel her getting ready to burst.

Tension rising.

Everything dense and tight and rippling.

Energy creaked under the fissures.

Two seconds later, Frankie shattered under the pressure.

Pinpoint pleasure that I could see streaking through her entire body.

I held her there, driving her higher, feeling her quiver and shake as she came undone.

Heaven.

I stayed with her in that place while she soared, while she squirmed and panted and thrashed.

Something toppled from the counter as she fumbled to get hold of me. Like if she let go, she might float out in the blackened night for all of eternity.

Our spirits shouted.

Uncontained.

Felt her ragged gasps slip across the skin of my back while every cell in my body screamed for release.

To just give in.

To let go.

But I knew I needed to give her time. Tonight wasn't about me.

I pried myself away.

Motherfucking torture.

The girl panted, her chest jutting where she remained spread out on the counter.

I struggled to get a breath into my lungs.

To steel myself.

To gather it up and force it down and pretend like I wasn't absolutely dying to get inside this girl.

To touch her and love her.

Take it all because I wouldn't settle for anything less.

Managing a grin, I gestured to my raging hard on. "Think I'm going to need a cold shower."

I helped her down onto unsteady feet, the girl's eyes still unfocused while I reached over and turned on the showerhead.

She blinked incoherently, her head slowly shaking like she was trying to find a new foundation after the one we'd been standing on had been demolished. I leaned down and let my mouth brush across the shell of her ear. "Getting to touch you again, Frankie Leigh? It's the best feeling in the world. But I want you to know . . . no matter what happens, you will always be my best friend."

Turning, I stepped into the spray of the shower, letting the frosted door swing shut behind me.

I struggled to kick the lust that was still raging through my body.

Mind told me to wait, but the rest of me was figuring we'd wasted enough time.

A rush of that energy slammed me from behind, the girl a windstorm, a tornado and the softest, coolest breeze. She slipped into the shower, and I slowly turned around to face her, and Frankie was climbing down to her knees.

The spray pounded into my back. Only a slight drizzle made it onto her body.

She stroked me once, looked up at me with those cinnamon eyes, the lapping darkness filled with emotion. Drawing me into their depths. Right where I wanted to drown.

"You will always be my best friend, Evan. My first love and my last. You will always be my everything."

And then Frankie took me into her mouth, silencing everything but the bliss of her touch.

Frankie Leigh
Eight Years Old

*J*eers echoed through the air, rolling over the field at the back of the school.

"Haha . . . that's right, run away, you freak."

"Run off and cry, you pussy!"

"He's such a pussy, he's probably really a girl."

Frankie stood at the edge of the sidewalk that led to the trail where they normally met to walk home. Evan wasn't in their meeting spot. He was in middle school now, sixth grade, and he always waited for her right there.

Not today.

Her stomach twisted with that nasty sickness that made her feel like she was going to throw up, a pool of black dread, and her eyes immediately searched, terrified these boys were talking about Evan.

That dread nearly spilled all the way out when she saw he was already all the way down by the fence, walking faster than normal, like he wanted to run but wanted to pretend like he didn't care about anything at the same time.

His backpack bounced fitfully with each of his hard steps while the ugly words were spewed at his back.

She was happy Evan couldn't hear what they were saying, but she was bettin' that he'd heard plenty enough when he'd been looking at their gross faces. She bet all these stupid jerks had said all kinds of things that made her want to rip them to shreds.

This feeling crawled over her body. Like she couldn't breathe and couldn't see and the only thing she wanted was to make them cry when they kept shouting horrible things at her best friend.

They were huddled in a circle over by the swings. She was already moving that way. "Shut up, you stupid buttholes!" she yelled.

Brent swiveled around to face her. He was the meanest of the mean. Her daddy told her to stay far, far away from him, but she didn't care. She was going to teach him a lesson once and for all.

"Awww . . . look . . . the poor freak needs a little girl to stick up for him. Talk about pathetic," he taunted, cracking up with laughter when he did.

Without giving it a thought, she shrugged out of her backpack, letting it thud to the ground behind her as she started to race their direction. A roar came up her throat like thunder rolling through the air. "You stupid bullies."

"Ha . . . look at her . . . freaks actually do stick together. Check this weirdo out. Thinks she's tough." He gestured at her like he thought it was funny.

Frankie wasn't laughing.

She didn't slow. She attacked. Jumped on him, scratching and clawing and kicking as best as she could.

In less than a second, he'd shoved her off, and she stumbled back, landing on her butt on the hard winter ground.

"What the hell?" he spat. "Are you crazy?"

Jumping up before he expected her to, she grabbed his arm and bit down hard. Until she could tell she was breaking the flesh of his wrist and making him bleed, the taste of a penny filling her mouth.

He'd see who to make fun of now.

He jerked back, swearing like a sailor. "Motherfucker. You bitch. I'm bleeding. You are fucking crazy. You're lucky my dad would kick my ass if I hit a girl."

Frankie wanted to swear at him, too.

Tell him he was a mother-trucking blowhole and she wanted to kick his skinny butt from here to New Amsterdam. Maybe she would.

But instead she grinned, hoped that blood was coloring her teeth. "Hit me," she taunted. See what happened then. Her daddy would lose his ever-lovin' mind and then this stupid jerkface would get a taste of his own medicine.

"Frankie!" Evan's voice was suddenly filling her ears, scratching and raspy the way it always was, but this time it was covered in something mad and angry.

"You better watch out," she told the pack of boys, ignoring Evan who she could feel racing back her direction. She wanted to jump in front of him. Protect him. Scream for him to run and hide.

But Evan was dipping down and picking up a big rock and shouting instead. "You touch her and you are not gonna like what happens."

"Whatever, you freaks aren't worth it. Let's go." Brent lifted a hand and twirled it in the air.

All the stupid boys followed his lead, grumbling and throwing more mean things over their shoulders. Frankie was half inclined to chase them the rest of the way down the street.

But she was too wrapped up in the weird feeling that was coming from Evan, all hard and annoyed.

When he saw the boys were going away, he threw the rock down, and he turned to take back off for the trail.

Frankie darted over to where she'd dropped her backpack and scooped it up by a strap, running after him and trying to sling it back onto her shoulder. "Evan, hey, wait up."

He couldn't hear her words, but she knew that he felt them. Knew he knew she was calling out for him.

Her heart started beating funny when he wouldn't turn around to look at her. He just walked faster and faster, angling through the break in the fence and rushing out into the woods that separated the school from their neighborhood. He hit the trail that led toward their houses before he veered off in the direction of their second secret meeting spot.

They had to have a bunch of them so they'd always know where to find each other.

Only this time, it didn't seem like Evan wanted her to follow.

She rushed to keep up, out of breath and a step behind him when they finally made it out into the clearing. Big trees touched the blue sky on all sides of the circle. There was only one in the middle where they'd made their fort with Carly and Josiah this last summer.

The grasses that covered the ground had turned brown, crunchy leaves scattered in piles, the kind they used to make leaf angels with.

Evan tossed down his backpack in frustration and threw himself to sitting on a fallen log.

Frankie chewed at her bottom lip and slowly approached.

WHAT'S WRONG? she signed, having to dip down to get in his line of sight when he was trying to ignore her which was just rude after she'd gone sticking up for him, trying not to let her heart quiver and shake.

She hated it when he was mad. Got worried that he might get too upset and make his heart quit.

Fear beaded up in a slick of sweat at her neck, and she suddenly wanted to cry. She rubbed at her eyes really quick to erase the feeling.

He huffed a sigh. "Nothin'."

"It's not nothin'." YOU'RE MAD. "I know you're mad. You've got that look on your face, and you're all red." She mixed the two languages together, moving in and out of one, not sure the best way to reach him when he looked so far away.

Distant.

She wanted to reach out and make him come back to her.

Why did people have to be so mean? Hurt bottled up on her insides, this wish that she could take away all the words and the looks and the pity. Everyone thought he was different and she didn't like it at all. The mean words and the weird looks and the way some adults talked to him like he was stupid.

Even some of the teachers did.

He was the smartest, smartest person that she knew.

She plopped down at his side, planting her elbow on a knee so she could rest her chin in her hand.

He kicked at a rock under his foot, staring at it, finally huffing out a breath and turning to look at her. "You don't need to stick up for me, Frankie. I'm not a baby. And you're a girl and younger than me."

"You're my best friend. That's what best friend's do. Doesn't matter how old you are. Duh." She lifted her eyebrows so high they touched her bangs.

He fought a smile, shaking his head more before he let the sad come back in. "I don't want people to think I'm weak. That I can't take care of myself. That I can't take care of you."

Frankie edged forward, getting on her knees in front of him. *YOU'RE NOT WEAK. YOU'RE THE STRONGEST PERSON I KNOW.*

"That's just dumb. You know I'm not."

YOU'RE THE BRAVEST.

I'M SUPPOSED TO TAKE CARE OF YOU. NOT THE OTHER WAY AROUND. She watched his movements, enthralled by the motion of his hands, enthralled by the flash of his green eyes that made her feel like she was the most important thing in the world. She wanted him to feel that way, too.

She touched his arm. *WE'RE SUPPOSED TO TAKE CARE OF EACH OTHER.*

Evan huffed.

"We're married, remember?" She figured the reminder would make him laugh.

So what if she spent too much time looking at the pictures her mama had taken of them out at the lake at their special rock. So what if she'd made a special book out of them and kept it under her bed.

Evan laughed that scraping sound. "That was fake. We were just little kids."

"It's not fake. We just have to do it again when we get big. You promised. Remember?"

He huffed like he thought she was ridiculous.

Her stomach hurt.

She didn't like it when he was like this.

They were supposed to be happy together forever.

"What were those stupid boys bein' mean to you about this time? They're so dumb I don't even know how they can say any words."

He heaved a breath, all kinds of reluctance seeping from him before he finally reached over and quickly unzipped his backpack to reveal the stuffed froggy tucked inside.

Frankie knew it was stupid, that her daddy told her to be careful not to fill her head too full of fairytales, but she was sure this froggy kept Evan safe.

She peeked over at him, and it was hard to say it, but she made herself, anyway. "You don't have to carry it everywhere. I won't be mad."

Evan looked angry again before he breathed a bunch of hard breaths and shook his head. *NO, I WANT TO. I LIKE KNOWING IT'S THERE. I LIKE HAVING YOU WITH ME ALWAYS.*

"That's because I'm the best, best, best friend in the world, right?"

And she wanted to beg him to never, ever leave her, either. She wanted to press her hands to his chest and feel the drum of his heart that she'd promised she would hold together forever.

No matter what it took.

"I guess . . . even though you are a girl."

Emerald eyes twinkled with the tease.

"Hey!" Frankie shouted, "that's just rude," and then she was hopping up, reaching out to flick him on the back of the head.

Snap attack.

"You're it!" she hollered.

Then Frankie ran, and she knew the only thing in the world she wanted was for him to chase her.

nineteen

Frankie Leigh

The front door creaked as I slipped inside. The sun was just rising over the horizon and steadily climbing to the sky, everything stilled and hushed except for the birds that were twittering through the trees.

I kept my footsteps light as I stepped into the house, carefully clicking the door shut behind me and twisting the lock. I tiptoed the rest of the way in, head down as I headed for my room.

"Where have you been all night, young lady?"

I nearly jumped out of my skin, hand smacking across my chest, a shocked shriek echoing through the living room. Trying to quiet my raging pulse and slow my breaths, I glared at Carly where she was sitting on the couch, legs curled under her and an arm leaned on the armrest.

"What the hell is wrong with you? You scared the shit out of me," I whisper shouted, looking around to make sure we hadn't disturbed Josiah.

"What the hell is wrong with me? What the hell is wrong with you? Sneaking out in the middle of the night? I've been beside myself worried about you."

My eyes narrowed at her. "You mean you noticed I was gone and you're nosy AF and were dying to know where I went."

She shrugged. "Same diff. Now sit your butt down and spill."

"Nothing to spill. I woke up early and went for a walk."

This time it was her eyes narrowing, calling my lie. "You should probs take a look at yourself in the mirror before you start making claims like that. You look like a scarecrow. Have you seen your hair? And I know exactly what that hair means." She spun her finger around me in a circle like she was offering up the evidence.

Unease spiraled, and I shifted on my feet, trying not to sneak a peek at myself in the mirror hanging in the hall.

Too late.

Good lord.

I ruffled my fingers through the rat's nest, all frizzy, matted curls sticking out two feet from my head, smashed down on one side from where I'd fallen asleep with it wet.

Rivers of mascara ran beneath my eyes.

Lips red and swollen.

Cherry on top?

My shirt was on backward.

I was giving the walk of shame a whole new name.

"So, I took a shower last night before I went to sleep." I hiked my shoulder in what I hoped looked like indifference.

Totally casual.

Zero guilt.

While this smidgen of worry and a whole ton of bliss were vying for dominance.

Both roared through my veins. Inciting a feeling I knew there would be no escaping.

Hell, there'd never be any escaping that boy. I'd been his since the moment I'd met him. I'd been a fool trying to pretend like it wasn't the truth.

"Uh, yeah. Question is, just where did you take this shower? Now haul your skinny ass over here and dish the dirty deets." She pointed at the spot beside her.

My lips pursed.

She reached out and grabbed a wine glass from the table, pointing at me around it. "Don't even try it to deny it."

Blowing out a sigh, I shuffled over and flopped onto the couch with a big groan. "What have I done?"

"Evan, I'm thinkin'."

I smacked her thigh. "Not funny."

She giggled into the rim of her glass. "It's hysterical, actually."

I glared up at her. "Don't make fun of the craziness that is my life. Maybe pay a little attention to yours. You are the one who is drinking at six in the mornin'."

"Well, when my ass has been up since one when you went sneaking out the door, I'm not sure what else you expected me to do."

"Sleep?"

She released a giddy laugh. "Sleep when I'm this excited? I do not think so, my friend. Might as well be a kid getting ready to go on a trip to Disneyland in the morning. I bet Josiah my next month's rent that you and Evan would hook up by the end of the week. This girl here is going on a shopping spree. Score!"

She lifted her glass like she was offering herself a congratulatory cheer.

"You are sick, you know that? And I hate to break it to you, but we did not hook up. I just went over there to talk to him."

My mind flashed through a sequence of images.

Jarring and whipping and stirring.

The desperate kisses. The gripping and clutching. His mouth and his hands and the boy who blurred all the lines.

Heat rushed over my body.

Whatever had gone down last night? When it came to Evan, I refused to recognize it as that term because there was nothing that we ever shared that could be considered *hooking up.*

That was sheer and utter defamation.

"You didn't hook up?" She gestured to my knees that I didn't even realize were rubbed raw and bright red. "Let me guess, you just tripped and fell and ended up with his dick in your mouth?"

My mouth flapped open.

"Just like that." She grinned.

"It wasn't anything like that," I defended.

It was beautiful and wonderful and completely terrifying.

Because I was pretty sure if this boy left me again, I wouldn't survive it this time.

In too deep.

That baby's face flashed through my mind, pulsed through my spirit, and seated itself firmly in my heart.

I groaned with the impact of it, burying my face in my hands. "God . . . I really did go over there just to talk to him. Warn him about Jack goin' off the rails. Hash out a little bit about what had happened Saturday night. Set some boundaries."

I'd come to the resolution that I had to tell him we needed to wait.

That he had to give me time like I'd asked for.

Become friends again and see if we could mend the wounds enough so we could start thinkin' about maybe going back the direction we'd been heading three years ago.

Before destruction had swooped in and annihilated the joy.

That maybe, just maybe we could lean on each other enough, trust in each other enough, that I could tell him what had happened.

Confide the truth.

Pray it wouldn't rip him apart the way it'd done me.

"Then he went to looking at me the way he does and those boundaries went poof." I lifted my hand in the air in a little exploding plume. "I truly have no control when it comes to him."

Carly fanned herself. "I understand why you lose your mind when you're around him. Seriously, I don't know what happened, but that man became downright lickable. Like, ridiculous. He was always cute and all . . . but holy hot damn. And when he's wearing those glasses? He's like the male version of a hot librarian."

I sat forward and leaned my arms on my knees, talking to the floor. "He was always beautiful to me."

Even when he was my nerdy little froggy boy with his big glasses and wide eyes.

Shifting around to face me, Carly crisscrossed her legs. Could feel the mood grow serious. She touched my shoulder. "Hey . . .

I'm teasing you. I stayed up waiting for you to get home because I was actually worried about you. I know this can't be easy."

Sadness crawled through my spirit, and I chewed at the inside of my cheek as I tried to figure out what it was that I was feeling. To process through the panic that had overtaken me when I'd awaken, curled up in Evan's arms just as dawn was cracking the sky.

This feeling that no matter what direction I went, I was going to lose.

There were so many complications. So many unknowns. More tragedy than he knew. Part of me wanted to protect him from it, sure he would be destroyed when he found out the truth, the other was still angry that he hadn't been there to share in that pain with me.

I glanced at her, words close to a plea. "I'm worried I'm already in too deep, Carly. That little boy . . ." I trailed off, not even able to complete the thought.

That I was terrified I was going to lose them both. Terrified of the way I'd been drawn to that crib when I'd awoken. The way I couldn't help but reach down and rub Everett's little back, pray that he was whole and well, that he would have the chance to soar and fly.

Pray that his mother wouldn't harm him in some way. That she wouldn't harm Evan by trying to steal him away.

Scariest was the realization that I was praying that it wouldn't harm me.

Attached.

Connected.

In love.

Overcome with it, I'd crawled out Evan's window without making a sound, knowing I needed some time to process it all. To figure out where we were headed and if I was ready to go there because I sure as hell couldn't seem to put on the brakes when Evan was in my space.

From zero to a hundred in a second flat.

No looking back.

"What do you feel when you look at Everett?" Her question

was careful.

I swiped at the single tear that streaked down my cheek, huffing out a sound of disbelief. "Too much. Everything. Fear and jealousy and this bright, blinding love that I can't stop."

"You have to tell him," she quietly urged, a supportive hand on my knee.

Sorrow gathered in my throat, thick and wobbly, and I struggled to swallow it down. "I know. I'm just . . . not sure I'm ready. Not sure that he is."

Carly frowned. "You can't keep it from him, Frankie. It's not right. And with Everett . . ." she trailed off.

Guilt teetered around on unsteady feet.

"I'll tell him. I will. I just . . . have to find the right time."

The right way. The right words.

And pray they didn't send him crumbling once and for all.

"You think there's ever going to be the perfect time? That it will change how it will affect him? You've carried that around for years, Frankie, and it's nearly destroyed you. You can't keep shouldering all of that yourself. He needs to know."

A tremble rolled through. "I know."

"After that?" she pressed.

"We hope it doesn't send him running across the country again."

Milo came trotting out of my room, his nails clicking on the tile. He came right for me and burrowed his face in my lap. I petted him, fingers in his fur, a kiss to his head. "Hi, boy. You need to go outside? I'm sorry I was gone all night."

He hopped around, all too excited for a pee.

Dog life.

If only ours could be that simple.

Carly waved me off. "Pssh . . . he didn't even notice. I went in there to check on him a couple of times, and he was snoring away like an old man."

"That's because you are an old man, aren't you?" I cooed as I rubbed both sides of his snout and kissed his wet nose.

I pushed to standing. "Come on, let's go," I called to him, heading toward the door where I kept his leash on a hook.

I hooked it to his collar and opened the door to the blazing morning light, the sun shining through the branches of the trees to warm the coming day. I led Milo across the porch and down the steps. He lifted his leg before my old boy went to sniffing away.

Movement startled me from behind, and I whipped around, a shriek getting free when I found Jack lurking ten feet away.

I scowled his direction, trying to look mad and irritated, praying it would cover up the creeping fear that slithered beneath my skin when I saw him leaned on the post of his porch.

"Mornin'," he said, his hands stuffed in his pockets.

"I don't want to talk to you," I told him, turning my back.

"I'm sorry," he said anyway.

I tossed a glare his way. "You threw a rock through my car window. I'm not sure apologies are accepted at this point."

He heaved out a heavy sigh. "That was unacceptable. I know it. Surprised you didn't have me hauled off to jail, honestly, or your dad over here to kick my ass."

Gathering myself, I turned and stared at him.

Sure, he was a little burly and rough, but I'd never expected him to do something so explosive.

Did I not know him at all?

I wavered, taking him in like I might be able to see the guilt written on him. "Did you do it?"

He frowned. "You saw me do it, Frankie. Lost my temper. Know it was wrong. Like I said, I'm sorry."

I didn't see any flicker of recognition. No flash of guilt before it was tucked away.

I lifted my chin. "I'm not talkin' about my window. I'm asking if you went over to Evan's parents' house yesterday."

Genuine confusion filled his expression. "Don't know what you're talking about. If I go over there? You'll know it because that punk will be getting his ass handed to him."

Worry and disappointment shook my head.

Defiance lifted my chin, and I stared him down, showing no fear or submission. "Stay the hell away from him, Jack. I'm warning you."

He laughed.

He took a step forward.

I took one back.

"You're the one who always said never stop fighting for what's most important to you. Never stop believing in what you want. Didn't you, Frankie Leigh?" Thing was, when he said it, it was bitter.

Acid burning from his tongue. Apparently, he'd missed the memo on the meanin'.

Agitation flinted in the rays of the rising sun.

Palpable.

Visible.

"Just . . . stay away. From both of us," I warned him again.

He chuckled low. "You act like I'm the intruder here, Frankie. Think it's that prick who needs to watch his back. Maybe go back where he came from."

Milo gave this weird, uneasy growl, like he felt the animosity clogging the air. I stood my ground, petting his head while I tried to wrap mine around the idea that Jack could have been responsible for this.

Act like I was his possession.

Like I'd made him promises when I hadn't.

Without saying anything else, he strode over to his car and hopped inside, peeling out without looking back.

twenty

Frankie Leigh
Thirteen Years Old

*Y*OU *AREN'T SUPPOSED TO GO THIS FAR.*

Frankie grinned as she looked at Evan from over her shoulder, the way his hands bled with worry and protection, that look in his eye as he watched her, following her close up the slippery rocks toward the cliffs.

"Oh, come on, Evan. I want to jump!"

YOUR DAD IS GOING TO KICK MY ASS.

ARE YOU SCARED? she taunted.

He rolled his eyes. "Hardly. Only thing I'm scared of is you getting hurt." His rough, scraping voice touched her ears, and her stomach did another flip.

She turned and started to climb, trying to ignore the feeling.

"Every time we come out here, I end up having to carry you back to camp to get patched up," he complained.

"That's because I want you to carry me." She said it aloud, but straight ahead so he couldn't hear.

Needing to say it but not wanting him to know.

The roar of the waterfalls thundered through the air, the spray from the gushing waters hitting the lake below rising up to cover their heated skin as they played beneath the sun.

Evan couldn't hear it.

But she knew he could feel it.

The vibration and the hum.

She wondered if he felt her heart doing the same. Going thrum, thrum, thrum as she looked back at him in his bathing suit as he climbed up behind her.

He was still skinny, but somehow, this summer he looked different. The red of his hair had lightened in the sun. His lips fuller. His shoulders wider.

Her eyes traced his scar, the whitened line that seemed to get smaller and less noticeable with every year that passed. She watched it like maybe she could keep it together, love him hard enough that it would never split open or fail, her eyes a glue that kept guard.

They made it to the top, where the cliffs opened up to the lake.

Breathtaking.

She looked back, and her lungs squeezed tighter.

Their family was below, swimming in the lake, splashing and roughhousing in the blue, tranquil waters.

Frankie ran across the streams, water splashing beneath her feet, and she raced over to her and Evan's rock.

The one that looked like a cracked open heart. She climbed to the top of it and threw up her hands. "If we jumped from here, how high do you think we could fly?"

She almost sang it, a huge smile splitting her face.

He laughed a little, but he didn't play along the way he used to when they were young. When he'd said he wished he could fly so incredibly high that they would soar to the stars.

"More like you're going to fall and crack your head," he grumbled.

She jumped anyway. But she lost her balance the second she hit the smooth, slick rock below.

Before she could tumble and fall, Evan rushed forward and

grabbed her.

His hands on her skin.

He whirled her around, worry carved in his expression. "Damn it, Frankie. Would you be careful?" Emerald eyes traced her face, his mouth twisted in concern. "Don't you know I can't stand it when you get hurt? I swear, you ask for it."

She touched his chest. Lightly. Just her fingertips. But she swore she saw the burst of light that came with it. This feeling that only existed with Evan Bryant. Something that kept growing and growing and was getting more confusing with each day that passed. "I can't stand for you to hurt, either."

For a moment, he stared, his chest rising fuller. Then he cracked a smile. "Only pain I've got is you . . . you know, the pain in my ass."

She frowned. "Stop being a jerk, Evan. I'm bein' serious. You're my best friend."

His brow drew together, somberly, and he pressed her hand tight over the spot on his chest that drummed. She wanted to press her ear to it so she could listen. "You're my best friend, too. Always."

Frankie suddenly felt all nervous and sweaty.

"What if I want you to be more than that?"

Her voice felt rough and scraggly, her stomach twisting with nerves. She was never shy, but she felt shy right then.

His eyes moved over her, dipping to her mouth. All of a sudden, he stepped back. "Don't be stupid, Frankie."

"I'm not. I mean it."

He shook his head like he was mad. "You're too young to even get it."

Anger flashed through her like a fire. "I'm thirteen . . . you're fifteen. Big whoop."

They were in that one month when he was only two years older than her, and it'd become her favorite month of the year. She couldn't stand the thought of him growing up without her. With him looking at her like she was stupid and small. She really, really hated it when he pointed it out.

He laughed a frustrated sound, and his hands were flying.

FRANKIE, WE AREN'T GETTING MARRIED OR HAVING BABIES OR LIVING HAPPILY EVER AFTER. WE WERE JUST LITTLE KIDS. YOU NEED TO GET OVER THAT.

I DON'T WANT TO GET OVER IT. She signed the words between them, mad and hard and trying to ignore the urge to shove him against the chest.

"Well, we don't always get what we want, do we?" His weird voice that she loved gushed across her face.

"If we fight hard enough for it, we do."

He turned his face away, like now he really was in pain, then he looked back at her and took her by the hand. "Let's just jump, Frankie. Jump. Maybe if we jump high enough, we can soar to another place where I could be different. Normal."

He used to say stuff like that when they were little and it felt fun and hopeful and the only thing they needed in the world was to believe.

Today the only thing those words did was make her sad.

"I don't want you normal. I want you just like this."

His head shook. "You don't even know what you're asking for."

Evan – Fifteen Years Old

Do you know that moment in life when you realize you're a complete idiot? When you slam face-first into reality after you've been living in some kind of fantasy?

A world where everything is glitter and gold and words are magic.

Hope.

Belief.

Faith.

Evan guessed he'd lost every single one of them that day. Earlier that morning when he was sitting in the doctor's office for his regular check-up and the doctor had told him that he wanted to talk, man-to-man.

Evan was fifteen. He figured it was about fucking time since most people treated him like he was a little kid.

Dumb and stupid and ignorant.

Turned out, he was ignorant after all.

Sure, he'd always known he would die young.

Was he okay with it?

No.

But somewhere along the way, he'd accepted it would be his fate even though that meant living with the normalcy of fear, a huge burden he'd carried around day to day, like his backpack always weighed just a little bit heavier.

Only thing that made it okay was he'd never stopped believing that there was a place after death, that this world was too full of miracles and wonders and beauty to believe there wasn't something waiting out there that might even be better.

Still, there were so many nights he'd lain awake as a little boy with his broken heart pounding out of control, hammering at his chest with a suffocating kind of anxiety.

Wondering which day would be the end. But he thought he'd always been more scared of leaving behind the ones that he loved most than anything. The one's that worried for him.

Mostly his mother.

Kale, of course.

His baby sister once she was born.

Hardest part was Frankie Leigh, this girl who had always been by his side.

His best friend, even though he'd always known they were more than that.

Intertwined in an extraordinary way.

Like they were part of the same person, and it'd seemed impossible to separate the two.

She'd always been this light . . . this feeling that would come over him when she came into the room . . . shining this bright ray of hope that whispered that maybe he could be normal after all.

That maybe their connection and bond was so great she could keep him bound here in this world for longer. That all those silly games they'd played as kids, ones where they got married and played house and had ten kids might actually be in their future.

Something meant for him.

Evan realized he'd never really even contemplated it before

then.

It'd just felt natural.

Like it was the most logical progression they would take as they grew up and got older and just kept living for each other because he couldn't imagine being with anyone else.

Maybe that'd started to dwindle a bit when he'd hit about twelve or thirteen.

When the illusion had begun to fade and reality had started to infiltrate his consciousness.

It'd finally hit him like a sledgehammer this morning when the doctor had cracked some joke about him betting that Evan was a ladies' man before his expression had gone grim, like he'd been trying to lighten the mood before he'd dragged Evan into a darkness he hadn't been prepared to walk.

His doctor had carefully explained what his genetic defects actually meant.

Of course, Evan had known he'd inherited his bad heart and deafness from his biological father's side of the family. Knew fragments of the messed-up story about how his aunt had died from cardiac failure when she was in her twenties without anyone knowing she was even sick.

How Kale had said thank God Evan's had been discovered early.

That he was lucky.

For years, Evan had heard the murmurs and the rumors and secrets his mom and dad had whispered to each other when they'd been protecting him so fiercely and trying to offer him the most normal life that they could.

He'd just never fully put two and two together.

Not until the doctor was telling him he had to take every precaution, especially now that he was older. How the man had told him it didn't matter if he had a girlfriend yet or not, he wanted him to start carrying condoms around wherever he went. He'd gone as far to suggest that if Evan could handle it, it would be best for him to just abstain like some kind of fucking monk without a voice.

How he was a carrier.

A disease.

A fucking threat to family and society.

Evan finally realized in that moment that his life was never fucking going to be *normal* because he wasn't *normal*. Didn't matter how badly everyone around him wanted to pretend that he was.

Case in point: Frankie Leigh.

Fucking Frankie Leigh who was dancing around the campfire like the wild child that she was, her brown hair nothing but gold streaks and flames, wearing one of her ridiculous pink tutu skirts and these godawful socks and her pink Chucks that were getting covered in soot and ash.

She didn't care.

All she cared about was soaring.

Flying.

His unicorn girl.

Their families were laughing as they told stories by the fire where they camped out in their favorite spot by the lake. Same place they'd been coming for years.

Same place they would probably still be coming long after he was gone.

The moon was high, and he was still itching from what Frankie had said up at the falls earlier this afternoon, still itching from his checkup with his doctor.

Unable to handle it for a second longer, he stood and slipped away into the darkness. His mom cast him one worried glance as he headed for the woods.

He smiled a big smile for her, wishing it felt as real as it used to. Last thing he wanted was to hurt her. To cause her more worry than she'd already had.

Evan started to climb the narrow trail, the one that weaved up the back way to the cliffs, though it sat farther back where the smoothed rocks met the trees in a tapestry of landscapes.

Nothing but peace and serenity.

Where he could sense the sounds and the rustles and the vibrations rushing over his skin. He sank down on a patch of leaves and turned his face to the night.

Stared up at the stars written in the sky.

A history that went on for eternity.

He felt the shiver of energy break through the perimeter of the trees.

He didn't even have to look that way to know it was her.

She was always like a burst of light.

He released a heavy sigh. Wasn't sure if he could handle her right then.

Evan glanced her way, signed with his elbows still rested on his knees. *YOU NEED TO GO BACK TO CAMP.*

She rolled her eyes like his request was ridiculous and kept coming closer. He tried to hold his breath when he felt her aura swirl around him like a cotton candy breeze.

DON'T WANT TO. She plopped down at his side. *WHY ARE YOU BEIN' SUCH A BUTTHOLE TODAY, ANYWAY? DID YOU EAT A WHOLE BAG OF SOUR CANDY? YOU'RE MAKING THAT FACE.*

She puckered up her entire face like she was sucking on something bitter.

Almost laughing, Evan hugged his knees closer to his chest.

"You shouldn't do that. Not a great look for you, Frankie Leigh. Your face might get stuck like that."

She smiled wide then looked at him in worry, like she could read his mood the same way as he could read hers.

"Sorry." He knew it had to be a mumble. He wasn't even sure she could understand it.

"You don't have anything to be sorry for." She grinned at him. *I JUST LIKE YOUR FROGGY FACE BETTER.*

His head shook in playful disbelief and a little bit of truth. "So I'm nothin' but a toad, huh?"

"I'll have to kiss you to find out."

"Frankie," he warned, sighing again, roughing his hands through his hair before he forced himself to look back at her, letting himself get washed in the heaviness that had been following him all day.

He decided just to lay it out.

No more tiptoeing.

No more pretending.

WHAT ARE YOU GOING TO DO WHEN I DIE, FRANKIE LEIGH?

He saw it.

Felt it. Grief pierced through her being.

Arrows of sorrow that impaled her spirit.

Gutting.

Crushing.

No thirteen-year-old should ever have to look like that.

But Evan wondered if either of them had ever truly gotten to be kids with the things they'd gone through.

"Don't say that, Evan. Don't ever say that."

Evan's brow pinched as he looked at her. *YOU NEED TO FACE IT, FRANKIE. ACCEPT IT. IT'S TIME YOU STOPPED FOLLOWING ME AROUND LIKE I'M THE ONLY PERSON IN THE WORLD AND LIVE YOUR OWN LIFE.*

He knew her well enough to know it was anger that blazed through her tiny body, and she was scrambling around to get on her knees in front of him, the movements of her hands chaotic. *JUST SHUT UP, EVAN. SHUT UP! YOU CAN'T SAY THINGS LIKE THAT. YOU HAVE TO KEEP BELIEVING THAT YOU'LL BE OKAY AND YOU WILL.*

"Life and death don't work that way."

She pressed her lips together like she was trying to keep them from trembling. "Fine. Maybe you won't be here forever. Maybe I won't, either. Maybe I'll trip right off this cliff and hit my head and die right now. Or maybe I'll get run over tomorrow. Or maybe when I'm thirty. None of us know. The only thing I know is while we're here, you're supposed to be with me. Together."

She gestured wildly between them, her fingers reaching out to trace over his heart.

Heat streaked across his skin.

Their connection fierce.

He had the flash of the thought that maybe she was right because something that powerful shouldn't be possible.

"You're my best friend. My everything. Remember what we promised?" she begged. "That when we're grown, we're gonna get married for real? We belong together."

Her lips moved and Evan watched and his heart hurt more than it ever had. He knew her words shook with a sob, that they were all messed up with her worry and her hope that she continually tried to get him to hold on to.

Emotion crashed, and his stomach fisted, and crap . . . he needed to get her out of there because she made him feel too many things all at once.

That belief that was threatening to go missing tried to climb back to the surface. The girl shining all her light on his dark.

"I can't ever have kids, you know that right? Even if I live until I'm a hundred, I can't have kids or have a normal life and that is not something you want. If I do, they're going to end up like me, and I can't do that. And believe me, you're going to want the things I can't give you."

I'M BROKEN, FRANKIE.

He knew it was all kinds of wrong that he was having this discussion with a thirteen-year-old. That he was even giving a thought to these things.

Like they were adults and having to make important decisions about their lives.

But Evan didn't have the luxury of waiting.

Not when he didn't know if he'd even have tomorrow.

"I don't care, Evan. I don't care about any of that. The only thing I'll ever want is you." Frankie promised it like she actually knew it as the truth, and he knew in that moment, she meant it, but she didn't have the first clue what that meant she would be giving up.

NO, FRANKIE.

She completely ignored him and crawled forward and signed against his chest, the energy flashing with each stroke of her hand. *YOU ARE MY FAVORITE.*

Evan wanted to weep.

He wanted to hold her.

Keep her.

Fuck, he'd do anything to be different. To be normal and right. To be free of the affliction.

She leaned forward, her dark eyes watching him, flecks of

cinnamon that danced in the night.

Her sweet intensity crashed over him, filling him up and draining him dry.

She leaned in and kissed him on the lips.

Pressing firm and lingering.

They'd kissed before. Little pecks. But never had it been like this.

The two of them breathed each other's breaths, their eyes locked and staring the whole time. And Evan knew he knew her better than anyone else, but that was the moment he thought he saw into her soul.

The true kindness that was there.

Belief without barriers.

Faith without doubt.

This girl the brightest gift.

Wiser than a woman and more innocent than a child.

He wanted to cling to it.

Believe in it.

Be thankful for it because he doubted there were many people who got to experience a connection like this even if they were given old age.

Still, he pushed her away by the shoulders. "Frankie," he rasped, fighting to gather his feelings. To get himself back in check. "You can't go kissing me."

"Why not?" She was back to pouting.

"Because you're thirteen."

"Doesn't change the way I feel."

"Yeah, well, I'm almost sixteen, and if your dad found out I was even thinking about it, he'd chop off my dick."

Okay.

So maybe that might be a solid plan.

Just get rid of the problem.

Frankie giggled, her face half embarrassed and half interested, a reminder that she was way too young to be having this conversation, anyway.

But then she was getting serious again.

Perceptive and discerning.

"Do you remember what your mama always told us, Evan? When we were little? All those suckers we made to try to help out other kids? That all you needed was a lick of hope. Do you remember what that felt like? When we knew we could do anything? Have anything we wanted in this life?"

She touched his cheek.

"Do you know what I want?"

"What's that?" he asked.

"Someday, I want you to kiss me again. Without this fear I see in your eyes right now. That's what I want."

There was no chance he could let that happen. She deserved so much more than his wounds that would only in the end make her bleed.

Still, he was following her line of sight toward the skies. In sync, the two of them laid back on the ground to stare upon the stars.

WHICH ONE IS ME? she signed, though he'd shown her a thousand times.

He didn't mind.

He'd sit there forever and whisper their mysteries.

He threaded his fingers through hers, their arms not quite touching, the way they'd always done.

And for the first time that day, he didn't feel like he was going to drown.

twenty-one

Frankie Leigh

Evan: You left.

So probably grinnin' like a loon at the text message that came in was the exact opposite of what my response should be, but the fact that Evan was back and communicating and that my body was still hummin' from last night was making me feel like I was flyin'.

Teetering right on the edge of something magnificent.

I just couldn't help it.

Couldn't help the butterflies that went scattering and lifting and fluttering wild, wings tickling my belly and fluttering higher to quiver my heart.

From where I stood at the counter at A Drop of Hope, I peeked around, making sure the coast was clear.

Jenna was helping a customer, Aunt Hope was wiping down the tables in the dining area, and Carly was in the back putting the finishing touches on something delicious.

No one was paying any mind to me or my scandalous activities.

There we were—sneaking around again. Thing was, I was more

unclear now about who and what we were than I'd ever been.

I was scared to trust him, and I wasn't scared to admit it. It was just a bitter, ugly consequence of what he had done.

Still, my fingers were flying across the screen.

Me: I did. I'm sorry. I guess I just needed to clear my head.

I stood there staring at the phone, anxious as I waited for a response. Seemed to take forever before one buzzed through.

Evan: Are you already regretting me?

Got the feeling it was somewhere between a tease and a serious question. That was the problem when things went amiss. When connections got broken. You were suddenly walking on thin, cracked ice, tryin' to be careful not to make a wrong move that would send you tumbling through.

I worried at my bottom lip. I almost laughed, thinking about my gramma on my daddy's side who'd passed a couple years back. She was the one who'd taught me that phrase, said it was my tell when I was upset, the worrying that I did.

God, I missed her.

She would have had a whole ton to say about this.

Probably like jump in and get wet and see how good it felt to get drenched.

I just wished I could grab back on to that philosophy.

Me: I don't think I could ever regret you, Evan Bryant.

Evan: That's good because I have to admit I kinda enjoyed last night. Best night's sleep I've had in a long time. Only thing that could have made it better would have been waking up with you by my side.

Redness streaked. Heat rising fast. Wondering what that might be like. To wake up in this boy's arms each day. God, how badly had I wanted that? Dreamed of it for all my life?

I needed to tamp that down before I got ahead of myself.

Me: Kinda?

All right, so I couldn't help the tease.

Took all of two seconds for him to respond.

Evan: Getting to touch you is the best feeling in the world, Frankie Leigh. You touching me? That's a fucking miracle.

My grin was getting ridiculous as I peeked around, being sly as I tapped out a response.

Me: I am pretty amazing, aren't I?

A string of texts started bleeping through.

Evan: Spectacular. Breathtaking. Sexy as fuck.

Evan: Glittery.

Evan: So damn sweet.

Oh God.

My belly was flip-flopping with those feelings I hadn't come close to forgettin', but had come to the acceptance that they were just something that were going to be missing from my life.

Another message came through.

Evan: You need more?

I could feel his amusement from across the space. I loved it more than I wanted to admit.

Me: Well, it doesn't hurt.

Evan: Don't ever want it to hurt.

I sighed a little. Could it really be that easy? Could he just come back here and we could pick up right where we left off? Could I forget three years of hurt and worry and torment? Most of all, could I be certain that he wouldn't regress into that boy who I'd hardly recognized?

Although, if I were being honest, if I looked hard enough, the warnings were there. The way he'd go far away.

Distressed and disturbed.

The overwhelming weight of the burden he'd carried.

I just wished he would have understood that I wanted to carry some of it, too. Hold it for him. Hold his hope and his faith and his fear.

That way, both of us would know we were never alone.

I guessed that was what made me the most hesitant.

I glanced over at Aunt Hope who I could feel peeking at me.

I wondered how badly she was experiencing the same fears, too.

Though now, it was multiplied, that little boy suddenly filling up the space and the air and their lives.

I turned away and tapped out a message.

Me: I just don't know where to go from here, Evan. Only thing I know for certain is I am so thankful that you're home. So thankful that you have found a reason. You think I'm amazing? That little boy is the miracle.

I did my best to dodge the stake of pain. An arrow impaled at my back. Whispered a thousand prayers for an actual miracle.

That this child would be spared.

Before I completely got lost, I tucked my phone in my back pocket, deciding I'd better get my tail back to work. I was definitely slacking.

Call me distracted.

I checked the displays for what needed to be restocked and

pushed back into the kitchen to grab a few things while my phone continued to go off.

Carly pointed at the back of my jeans. "Your butt's having its own personal dance party. Why do I get the feelin' only you're invited? What's he saying?"

I rolled my eyes. "We were only saying hi. You are so damned nosy."

"That seems like a whole lot more than just hi. And hello . . ." She gestured at herself. "Being nosy is my job."

"He was just wondering why I took off this mornin' without saying goodbye," I grumbled a little.

"And did you figure that out yet?" she asked as she rinsed a big silver mixing bowl and put it into the dishwasher.

A self-deprecating huff filtered between my lips. "Uh . . . let's see. I think it goes something like I'm scarred and a little broken and a whole lot chicken."

Carly scowled. "Chicken? Hardly. I mean, maybe one with its head chopped off half the time," she razzed, "but you, girl, are no coward. If you're guilty of anything, it's self-preservation, and you know full well that's not even close to being the same thing."

I started arranging an assortment of cupcakes onto a tray. "Yeah, and what's it called when you know you want something so bad—when you know it's right for you—and you're still afraid to reach out and take it?"

"When it's already bitten you on the hand? That's called protectin' yourself."

I sent her a scowl. "I thought you were the one who was all about us hookin' up and putting down money on the fact it was gonna happen? Hell, I'm pretty sure you were pushing me at him the first time he walked through that door."

"Oh, I'm all for you two. There is no other duo like the duo of Evan and Frankie Leigh. All's I'm saying is you don't have to feel bad that you're having these reservations. That it's okay to be cautious."

She eyed me from across the large prep island. "What I want most is for you to demand that the two of you are up front and honest about everything. Things went south real fast when you both started making decisions about what was best for the other without asking the other for their opinion."

"I didn't—"

Her barking laugh cut me off. "You did. You thought you needed to carry more of his burden, protect him, and he did the same for you by removing himself from the picture. Look where that got both of you."

My pants pocket continued to go off like the Fourth of July. A new message came in every few seconds.

She angled her head. "So, talk to him. Let him know where you stand. And I'm asking you as a friend and someone who cares about you both . . . no more secrets, Frankie Leigh."

She grabbed a big jug of creamer, not looking back when she left me alone in the kitchen.

Wow.

Okay then.

Sighing, I pulled out my phone to read the string of waiting messages.

Evan: I can think of all kinds of places for us to go, Frankie.

Evan: My bed.

Evan: The kitchen.

Evan: The shower.

Oh, it was a fine time for desire to spark right in the middle of the morning rush. Memories of his mouth and those hands and that body.

Evan: The park with my son.

Evan: Dinner.

Evan: Go to dinner with me, Frankie. A date. You and me.

Let's start again. Figure this out together.

Evan: I'm finished living my life without you in it.

Another had come in behind it. It was a selfie. Evan and Everett with their faces smooshed together, the cutest thing I'd ever seen. Green eyes matching, sweetness gushing out from the lens.

Evan: Someone has been asking for his Fi-Fi.

Evan: And you're right. He is a miracle. Just like you.

My chest squeezed so damned tight I was wondering if I'd up and developed myself a severe case of asthma.

Because feeling like this shouldn't be right, and I was a little worried that it wasn't healthy.

Falling so hard and so fast.

One thing for certain, Evan Bryant was not fighting fair.

I hesitated, searching for the right thing to say. I let my fingers tap out the message.

Me: Dinner would be nice. I think it's a great idea to get to know each other again. Talk. Take some time to reconnect.

He'd know it was code for I thought we should maybe put on the brakes. He'd know he'd completely knocked me for a loop. That I was terrified I was going to get sucked right back into his vortex. Problem was, the whole other side of me was thinking I wouldn't mind that one bit considering all that talk about his bed and the shower and the kitchen sounded really damn nice.

Me: And if you're having fantasies about a kitchen counter, I think you're gonna need to figure out some other living arrangements because I'm pretty sure your mama and daddy wouldn't be all that keen to finding us

buck naked on the island in the middle of the night, and I'm afraid Carly might like it too much.

Maybe I was askin' for it, but I couldn't help myself. Bantering with Evan had always been about as easy as it'd come. Teasing each other. Laughing constantly. Making each other blush. It was pretty much our favorite game until those blushes had grown into flames.

Evan: I think that can be arranged.

I bit at my lip like it was goin' to stop my grin while I typed away.

Me: Getting your own place or dinner?

His response was instant.

Evan: Carly watching.

I busted out laughing.

Me: Um . . . not in your dreams, big boy.

Evan: You're my only dream, Frankie Leigh.

Damn him.

I was giggling like I used to, having the urge to do a couple twirls and a skip and a jump or two.

The door swung open, and I shrieked in surprise, so wrapped up in the two of us. Which basically was the way it'd always been. Evan and I living out those fantasies.

Innocently.

Maybe even naively.

But that was okay.

We'd deserved those years.

"Aunt Hope." I fumbled to get my phone back into my pocket.

I pinned on a bright smile, rocking back on my heels and huffing a piece of hair out of my face.

She waved a flippant hand in the air. "Oh, don't even try to play coy, Frankie Leigh. You think I don't know who you're talking to? You should see your face. And believe me, it looks way happier right now than it did when you were sneaking out Evan's window at the crack of dawn this morning."

She cocked a brow.

A gasp of guilt and shock and oh shit blundered out of my mouth.

"Wha . . . I . . . I just . . ."

Well, that wasn't helpin' things.

She rolled her eyes. "Oh come on, Sweet Pea. You think I don't know you've been in love with my son for his whole life? Same as he has been with you? You think it was some kind of secret? Because I promise you, it was not."

Unease shivered.

"You knew?"

I guessed the question was, how much? What did Uncle Kale tell her? Because I'd wanted to spare her that grief, too.

"I'm his mama. Of course, I knew. Not sure why you two thought you needed to keep it a secret."

"We were gonna tell y'all."

I mean, I'd just turned eighteen. My daddy wasn't gonna be all that thrilled about it, but he would have gotten over it.

She seemed to war with what to say, hesitating before she seemed to decide differently and headed for the door, only to pause to look back at me from over her shoulder. "Just . . . be careful, Frankie Leigh. For both of you. There are a whole lot of hearts at stake right now."

Without giving me time to respond, like I even would have been able to with the instant pressure crushing my ribs, she disappeared back through the door.

I fought my own war, pulling out my phone and looking at it again before I typed out another message.

Me: Dinner. Friday. Let's talk.

I went to chewing at my lip again, added a couple more words.

Me: And just . . . watch out for Jack. Let me know if you see him. I don't trust him.

I was the last to leave that evening, closing up the café, making sure the front doors were secured and double-checking that the ovens were off and the refrigerators were running.

When I verified everything was set, I flipped off the lights and stepped out the back door, locking it up tight.

Gravel crunched under my shoes as I made my way to my car, clicked the lock, and got inside. I pushed the button to turn the ignition, the headlights instantly coming to life, and I put it in reverse and started to pull out.

It was just a flash of something that I caught out of the corner of my eye.

A shadow.

A vapor.

A horrible, terrible premonition.

The hairs lifted at the back of my neck, and I struggled to see into the darkness, the shape gone as fast as I'd noticed it.

Shaking it off, I hit the road and headed for home.

But that sensation wouldn't leave me. The phantom feeling that I was being watched.

Tailed.

Tracked.

I slowed my car, searching through the rear-view mirror. The car right behind me slowed, and when I made a sudden left, it did the same.

My heart rate spiked and dread slicked my flesh in a sticky sweat.

I made a quick right.

The car did the same.

I made another, then rasped out in relief when it went left.

With the headlights shining bright, I could barely make it out, the black car that could be anybody's. But something about it felt familiar. Like I'd seen it before.

I gave a harsh shake of my head. I was being paranoid.

Winding back to my normal route, I drove the rest of the way toward home and took the last right into our neighborhood.

Everything was quiet, the sun giving up its hold on the day, twilight sinking into the atmosphere.

Strewing the sky with blues and purples and one twinkling star that made itself known just above the horizon.

I made the left into our duplex. The front porch light was on, but the lights were out. Carly and Josiah would be off doing their thing for their bowling league which basically was slamming more drinks than pins that they would topple.

My gaze moved to the duplex to the left that was just as vacant. Jack's car was nowhere to be found.

Blowing out a strained breath, I came to a stop, killed the engine, and cranked open the door.

Shivers rolled across my flesh the second I stepped out.

That creeping dread chasing me home.

I slung my bag up high on my shoulder. Well, that was right after I'd fumbled around to find the mace that Dad had insisted on when I started driving and had been sittin' in the bottomless pit of my bag for the last five years.

My footsteps were slowed, and my breaths were heavy and hard, punting into the air.

I was being ridiculous.

Completely ridiculous.

That was until I took the two steps onto the porch and my eyes hit the disgusting words that had been painted in huge letters across the wood.

FREAK FUCKER.

My hand flew to my mouth to try to stop the sob from ripping out. It got loose anyway, my vision blurry from the instant tears as I stumbled around and searched the dusky vacancy.

Only the howl of the trees murmured back.

I fumbled for my phone and typed out the text.

Me: I need you.

Evan

I flew the streets of Gingham Lakes in the direction of Frankie

Leigh's house.

Pulse pounding so fiercely it was making it difficult to see. Difficult to think.

Rage flooded my bloodstream as streetlamps flickered to life above. Day fading to darkness and night settling in a dreary cloud over the city.

Every second that ticked by made me feel like I was going insane.

Felt hostage to this mess I wasn't sure how to get out of.

How could I ensure that the ones I loved weren't getting put in the path of a firing squad when I had no fucking clue what the sin had been?

Mind going crazy trying to figure out why the fuck someone would do this.

Unless it was Jack.

Violence skated the surface of my skin at the thought.

Still, my mind rejected it. I knew Frankie thought he was

responsible, but hadn't this been going on before I'd met him? That note in the diaper bag? The word on my car? Or were they separate? A coincidence?

Either way, knew the Jack was pissed.

I didn't trust him for a second.

Second the text had come in, I'd rushed downstairs and asked my parents to watch Everett, told them something was going down at Frankie's place, my fingers tapping out a quick message to Seth to let him know there had been another message.

He'd texted back that he would head over to check it out.

Didn't matter that I knew he was going to be there. Couldn't stop myself from speeding down the streets to get to her.

Needing to know she was okay.

That she was fine.

Squeezing the steering wheel, I took a right a little sharper than prudent, tires skidding through the curve, the vibration of the pull at the rear of my car filling my nerves with another shock of aggression.

The silence in my head screamed.

I had to get to her.

Had to.

I slowed only a fraction when I hit the neighborhood street, eyes scanning the house numbers that whizzed by.

Guessed I already knew which address was going to be hers, the way I was jerking the car to the left in a sharp turn, jamming on my brakes in the gravel lot in the front.

I hauled out of my car the second I put it in park, jumping out, noticing the black muscle car that was sitting at an angle in front of the duplex attached to Frankie's.

Shit.

Frankie had said that bastard wasn't there. That his car was gone. Told me she was fine, she just needed me there.

Fury lit. Hands in fists as I started up the two steps onto Frankie's porch, vision going red when I saw the entirety of it covered in the two words. She was jerking the door open like she'd been standing on the other side waiting for me to get there, my heart nearly cracking in relief at the sight of her before I sensed the movement coming at me from behind.

I glanced over my shoulder to find that piece of shit charging for me.

Rage pumped out of control.

A shock of adrenaline to my system.

Before I could get turned around, asshole grabbed me by the shoulder and yanked me back down the steps.

Jack was this beefy motherfucker.

Twice as wide as me.

I was too goddamn pissed to even consider that he might be twice as strong.

He dragged me backward down the steps, but somehow, I managed to keep my balance enough to whirl around and throw a punch that landed in his gut.

Hard enough that I could feel the air gush from his lungs, asshole bending at the waist.

Of course, he was throwing a fist at the same fucking time, clocking me on the jaw.

Pain splintered across my face. A ringing sort of pain. Like I could actually hear the crack of agony as it fractured through my brain.

Frantically, I blinked, fought to remain upright. To remain coherent.

I swayed to the left, staggered forward.

Was pretty sure it was only the surging anger I felt that kept me standing. The disgust that cleared my mind enough so I could focus on what I was fighting for.

What had me throwing a sidekick, sole of my shoe hitting him square in the chest. It sent him stumbling back, and I was moving his way, throwing another hit to the side of his head, trying to get a hold of him so I could take him to the ground.

He lurched forward. Rammed me in the chest with his shoulder.

Air bashed from my lungs.

Could feel the crazed energy rushing all over me, the dread and the fear and the horror. Frankie Leigh was suddenly a blur at the edge of my sight.

Could tell she was screaming, losing her damn mind as she clawed and kicked and tried to get in the middle of us.

"Frankie!" I yelled. "Get back, Frankie."

That was right when Jack flung an arm out and tossed her out of the way. He sent her a scathing glare as she toppled to the ground.

He shouted something I couldn't read.

Hatred howled, beat through my mind and thundered in my chest.

I flew for him, unprepared for the fist that struck me at the corner of my mouth. I barely even felt it. Barely felt the blinding pain or the blood that was gushing free. The only thing I felt was the fury. The desperation to end this.

My arms wrapped around his waist in an attempt to tackle him to the ground. Frankie was there again, trying to get on his back, screaming, "No, no, no, you're going to hurt him. His heart. His heart."

Didn't she fucking get that it beat for her?

Rage pummeled through my senses, a frenzy of fear spinning through the air, Frankie so terrified I wanted to weep. To tell her it was my job to protect her.

Not the other way around.

I came at him. One fist then the other. One clipping his jaw the other striking his nose as his head jolted one direction.

"Get out of the way, Frankie," I shouted as I started to go in for another hit as headlights burst across the yard. Red and blue lights suddenly whirled into action as the car slid to a stop behind my car.

Seth jumped out with his gun drawn. I reared back, and Frankie dropped to the ground in relief. Could tell she was rasping around her shock. Completely freaked. The feel of her shaking rushed across the ground. Her fear slamming me, crash after crash.

I wanted to go for her, but Seth was yelling, "Sit the fuck down, both of you."

I dropped to my ass, chest heaving from the exertion.

The agony from the blows I'd sustained rushed me in one acute wave.

I squinted at the lights, trying not to topple over on my side from the adrenaline bleeding out.

From the relief that Seth was there.

"Evan didn't do anything, Seth. It was Jack. He came after him on my porch."

"Stay right there," he told Jack. Jack who didn't move. Jack who stood there glowering at me like he was getting ready to come in for another attack.

I'd be happy to go another round.

"Told you to get down," Seth repeated.

"Fuck this," Jack spat as he charged for me again.

Gun trained, Seth rushed him. "Get down. Face down. On the ground. Not joking around, Jack. Do not make me do something I don't want to do."

Seth had to grab him by the shoulder to force him down before he finally conceded, fighting the cuffs Seth snapped around his wrists. He hauled him onto his feet, saying something to him that I couldn't see.

Could only feel the hostility blistering from the prick who'd come undone.

Blood dripping from a nostril and bitterness in his eyes when he glared at me.

Guy could hate me all he fuckin' wanted. But if he turned that aggression on Frankie Leigh? That story wasn't going to end in his favor.

Seth shoved Jack into the backseat of his cruiser while I sat there trying not to pass the fuck out.

Getting in a fist fight with that asshole was like getting in a wrestling match with a grizzly bear.

Groaning, I slumped back onto the ground, just trying to breathe.

Unease sloshed around in the deepest part of me. Where awareness and trepidation met.

Wanting it to be over, but none of it adding up.

Ashley and that note and the one that was tacked to my door.

Could feel the shockwaves of worry blast through the atmosphere, the spiral of energy and the rustle of movement vibrating the ground floor.

I forced myself to peel open an eye, finding Frankie leaning over me, all frantic and tremoring, her fingers fluttering over my face.

Wanted to welcome her touch, but I flinched.

"Are you okay? God, what were you thinkin'? What were you thinkin'?" Frankie was pleading, those eyes searching my face, girl trying to hold back tears. "You're a mess, Evan. Oh my gosh, I'm so sorry."

"What are you apologizing for?"

"For dragging you into my mess."

A frown deepened my brow, and I started to answer her until a shadow fell over us. I forced myself to sit up, fighting the rush of dizziness that spun my head.

"You good?" Seth asked.

I swiped at the blood I could feel dripping down my chin. "Yup. Good as fucking new."

"You're not fine. Look at you. You are a mess. I can't believe this. I can't believe this. We need to get you to a hospital."

I DON'T NEED A HOSPITAL, FRANKIE. I let a bit of frustration weave into the response.

She shook her head. *YES, YOU DO.*

NO, I DON'T.

Seth bent his knees to sink down in front of me. "You sure you're good?"

"Yeah," I told him.

He gave a tight nod. "Okay then. I'm going to take him down and process him. See if I can get him to confess about what's been going on around here. You two try not to touch anything on the porch. I'll have someone come tomorrow to dust for prints. Problem is, Jack lives next door. A print of his on Frankie's porch isn't going to be all that condemning."

Seth looked skeptical.

About everything.

I was, too.

"Okay."

Seth straightened to standing, hesitated. "You're sure you're good? Face is busted up pretty bad, man."

"I'm good."

Frankie and I watched Seth head back to his cruiser.

Tension bound the air, something unsettled and wrong.

When he pulled back out onto the street, Frankie moved to get onto her feet, still bent over and extending a hand. "Come on, let's get you inside and cleaned up."

I took it, groaning a bit as I forced myself to standing.

Warily, I followed behind her, our fingers loosely threaded as she slowly made her way up to the house. Neither of us touched the railing, and we were careful to sidestep the letters the best that we could. She opened the door to Milo who looked like he'd been scratching at the window the entire time, frantic and worried himself, trying to get out to do a little protecting of his own.

I scratched his head when he did a circle around my legs. "Good boy."

I followed Frankie through the great room of her house to a small hallway that opened up to two bedrooms on each side. She led me into the one on the right, not slowing as she started toward the bathroom attached at the back.

My gaze jumped around to take it all in.

It was so completely Frankie Leigh it was ridiculous.

A pink comforter and purple sheets and a ton of mismatched pillows piled on her unmade bed. Bright pictures covered every inch of the walls. Covering the floor was about everything she owned, the room a disaster, clothes strewn everywhere, clearly the girl trying things on and tossing them to the floor before she went to digging through her closet again.

A whirlwind.

A tornado.

My unicorn girl.

I followed her the rest of the way into the bathroom. She flipped on the light and I finally got a good look at myself in the mirror. I cringed.

"Do you get it now?" she demanded. No question, the words had come out mad.

"Get what, Frankie? That I would do anything for you? Protect you? Fight for you? Love you? Whatever the hell it takes?"

She went to gnawing at her bottom lip, and I was having to fight the urge to do it for her. She reached into the cabinet under the sink, grabbed a hand towel, and ran it under water. She didn't look at me for the longest time, the energy thick in the small space, banging against the walls.

Finally, she turned and peeked up at me, dabbing the towel on the corner of my mouth where I had a cut.

I winced as she cleaned it.

"I can't stand to see you hurt," she murmured.

My head shook, and I grabbed her by the waist so I could set her on the counter. I planted my hands on either side of her, dipping down so we were close enough that our noses brushed and our breaths mingled and I was inhaling all the sweetness that was this girl.

She tried to look down, and I reached out and tipped up her chin, forcing her to look at me. Roughness scraped my throat, fragments of aggression still twitching through my muscles. I brushed back the hair that was matted to her face. "You always thought you were supposed to take care of me, Frankie Leigh, when it's always been my job to take care of you."

She shook her head. "No. It's . . . it's not safe for you to get yourself in the middle of what just went down. God, Evan, what would have happened if—" She stopped mid-sentence like she couldn't bring herself to say it.

Figured I would finish for her. "If my heart stopped?" I swallowed down the bitterness. The feelings of inadequacy. "Don't you get it, Frankie? Don't you get that was part of the reason I had to go? I couldn't stand to live my life with you thinking you had to take care of me. Thinking I was weak. Like I was some sort of pathetic kid."

I spread my hand across her cheek, holding her, praying she could feel the truth of what I was trying to say. "All I ever wanted was to love you right. Be enough of a man to do it. To stand for you. To protect you. To take care of you. I never wanted you to see me as a burden. As a weight."

Her fingertips fluttered over my jaw, barely touching my lips.

Thing was, I didn't give a fuck about a few scrapes or bruises. Only thing I cared about was making this right.

Protecting my family.

Loving her the way she needed.

Those fingers kept tracing my face. "I never thought that, Evan. Not even once. You were my hero. The one I looked up to. You were the one I needed most."

I dipped down lower, inhaling the girl, nose running the length of her jaw.

Cotton candy and sugarplum drizzle.

"Then let me take care of you, Frankie. Let me stand in the fire. Let me be the one who fights for you. For Everett. For *us*."

I spread my hands around her waist, stretching out my fingers so I could hold her tight. I pressed my lips against hers and whispered the words. "Let me love you."

Cinnamon eyes flared, fingers digging into my shoulders. "As long as you promise you'll never stop."

"Never." My mouth crashed against hers, and she was in my arms.

I was kissing her like my life depended on it, and I was pretty damned sure that was the case. This gorgeous girl who had been purposed for my life.

Written in my stars.

I thought maybe every single one of us had our own constellation.

A map drawn out in the heavens.

An intricate design that had been created just for us.

If that were the case?

Then Frankie Leigh was my North Star.

twenty-three

Frankie Leigh

*E*van carried me into my bedroom.

Like that was exactly what he had been made to do. His arms made in the perfect shape to hold me. To cherish and adore me.

The same as I had been made for him.

A flawless give and take.

He wrapped a hand in my hair, the man controlling the desperate, urgent kiss as he moved for my bed.

With each step he took, he stirred the energy that flash-fired through the space.

Lapping up and rising higher.

Flames licking my flesh. A need unlike anything I'd ever experienced pouring into my body.

"Frankie," he rumbled at my mouth. So seductive. So right. "Never. I'll never stop loving you. I never did. How could I? Not when it's always supposed to have been me and Frankie Leigh."

Oh God.

His words hit me like a straight shot to the heart, everything a thunder as it raced through my veins, my spirit desperate to reclaim what I'd thought would be lost forever.

My hands made a desperate play to touch him everywhere. Rushing over the rugged sides of his face and smoothing at his neck, fingertips digging into his shoulders.

His lips pushed and pulled and danced over mine.

Tongues tangling as we fought to get as close to the other as we possibly could.

Distance was no longer an option.

"Evan," I whimpered at his mouth, knowing he could feel me. That he would drink down my words through the fierce connection that only he and I could share. "I love you. I never stopped for a day. Not for a second."

It was a murmur of need.

A flood of desire.

A declaration of devotion.

Our connection spun through my room.

Fierce.

Stronger than it had ever been.

He grunted a rugged sound. Every touch of his hands read every innuendo and intimation, his breaths jutting out to brush my heated skin.

I shook in anticipation. In this want that had simmered for years that now had reached an all-out boil.

It felt like all the molecules that had been scattered in our separation, lost in our dissolution, had gathered to a pinpoint.

A ferocious, unrelenting force that wrapped and knitted and interlaced.

Threading us together in the most intricate way.

In a way that could never be undone.

Every stitch dependent on the other.

Carefully, he laid me out on the mattress before he straightened.

I pushed up on my hands, soul arching for him. "Promise you'll never leave me."

He stood at the side of my bed and looked down at me like I was the rising sun when for so long his world had gone dim. Tenderly, he cupped my cheek. "I will stay with you for as long as my heart will allow. It's always belonged to you, anyway."

He was cast in lapping shadows, a silhouette of everything I'd ever dreamed could be mine.

His wide chest was still heavin' from the exertion, his face battered and bruised and the most beautiful thing that I'd ever seen.

I WAS MADE FOR YOU, FRANKIE LEIGH. JUST LIKE YOU WERE MADE FOR ME.

The stroke of his hands was powerful.

A current raced with each movement, a promise reaching out to rush over me as he signed his forever in the dense, dense air.

Something flashed across that beautiful face.

Hesitancy and resolution.

"Just have to make sure this is the life you want, Frankie Leigh." His rough voice scraped the air, words like blades that cut through every question and worry and hurt.

He fisted his hands at his sides. "Because I think we both know there is no coming back from this. I touch you tonight? It's done. I've gone without you for too long, and I promise you, I'm not about to let go of you again. But you need to know . . . Everett is now a part of me. You want me? He's going to be a part of that package. And I don't know if he's inherited this affliction. If this life is going to be spent fighting for his health the way my life was."

He fisted a hand at his chest, torment bleeding out of him at the idea.

"This life might not be easy, and you need to know what you're signing up for."

Emotion gripped every cell, that atmosphere charged.

A crack that shifted everything.

Our worlds and our minds.

I sat up so I could sign, a torrent of passion in my hands.

AM I SURE I WANT THIS LIFE?

My head angled in emphasis.

ARE YOU ASKING ME IF I BELIEVE IN WHO WE WERE MEANT TO BE? IF I CAN LOVE YOUR SON? BECAUSE I THINK A PART OF ME FELL IN LOVE WITH EVERETT THE MOMENT I SAW HIM. I COULD FEEL

HIM, EVAN, THE SAME WAY AS I ALWAYS FELT YOU. AND HE IS WORTH EVERY SECOND OF WORRY.

My motions tightened, a confession that cut through the tension.

SO YOU WANT TO KNOW IF THIS IS THE LIFE I WANT TO LIVE?

Could feel my brow knitting with the severity.

A LIFE WITHOUT YOU WOULD BE LIVING WITH A HOLE CARVED INSIDE OF ME IN THE SHAPE OF YOU. AND I'M SITTING HERE, RIGHT NOW, ASKING YOU TO FILL IT.

I leaned back on my elbows, begging him to meet me there.

Evan exhaled a harsh breath, the man never taking his eyes off me as he slowly peeled his shirt over his head. The ridges of his defined abs came into view, his chest, his shoulders, that face.

The scar.

Love blistered, a searing heatwave that blasted through my room.

He tossed the soiled fabric to the floor before he kicked off his shoes. He flicked through the buttons on his jeans at the same time.

Energy crashed.

Need rising so fast that I was immediately drenched.

I pressed my knees together like that might be able to staunch the desire that begged and throbbed as I watched him undress. His jeans getting shoved down off his hips and free of his ankles, muscle packed and sinewy, his strength that others had refused to recognize so distinct.

My fighter.

My survivor.

The man the utter breath of existence.

The sight of him standing there in my room stole a gasp from my lungs and twisted my belly into a thousand needy knots.

"How's it possible you are so beautiful, Evan? How's it possible that you make me feel this way?"

Planting a knee on the bed, he began to climb over me, coming closer and closer until he was the only thing I could breathe. Those eyes drank me in as he gathered my shirt at the hem. "You are the definition of beauty, Frankie Leigh."

He slowly dragged it off, the long curls of my hair falling down to tickle my bare shoulders and back.

I was overcome with the weight of Evan's attention as he gazed down at me as he tossed the fabric aside.

The raw hunger.

The infinite love.

He angled in to brush his lips against the corner of my mouth. "So stunning you make me shake."

Then he moved to whisper against the shell of my ear. "So sexy and free and stunning my guts get twisted up every time I look at you."

Edging back a fraction, he let his fingers drift down my neck so he could splay his hand out on the center of my chest. "This heart that radiates goodness."

He gently urged me down to lie against the bed. Fingertips fluttered over the lids of my eyes. "These eyes that see the world in a way that shouldn't be possible."

He moved to trace my lips. "This mouth that speaks beauty."

I writhed.

He ran his palm over my breast.

My nipples pebbled into hard, needy peaks.

Evan released a groan that sent a rush of goosebumps racing as he ran his hand down to the waist of my jeans. "All wrapped up in the most gorgeous package. This body, Frankie—you made me understand what it means for a woman to bring a man to his knees."

He flicked the button. "You are the beauty of my life."

The man leaned back on his knees, every masculine line of his body demonstrating how desperate he was for me.

He edged my jeans down, taking my underwear with them, the slow slide of the rough fabric dragging down my legs nearly driving me insane.

"You are the definition of my joy," he continued, talking with those grating words that had always been my favorite song.

He tugged the clothing free of my ankles, and I was lying there a quivering, shaking mess.

"How did we get to here?" I rasped, my heart going boom, boom, boom as that boy stared down at me with those eyes that took me in like I was a dream.

"Because this is where we belong."

Heat streaked over my flesh as he crawled over me, planting both hands on the mattress on either side of my head.

Hovering.

Anticipating.

And I could feel that hole carved out inside of me in the shape of him shiver with need. To be filled and restored and healed.

That energy went wild. Jerking at the chains that had kept us restrained.

Everything getting ready to rupture.

To burst.

To come together.

"I need you, Evan. I need you so bad I can't breathe," I whimpered.

It was true. Felt like my chest was gonna cave by the weight of wanting this man.

A smirk ticked up at the corner of his mouth as he wound his hand behind my back so he could flick the hook of my bra. He slowly peeled the lace down my arms.

"You need me, huh?"

Tease.

God.

I forgot that he could be such a tease.

And I loved it and I wanted to play but the other part of me was just needing to feel all of this man.

It'd been too long.

Too long.

Still, I couldn't stop the smile. "It was always me chasin' you, Evan Bryant. It was kinda embarrassing. Don't make me keep doing it."

A slight chuckle tumbled from his throat before emotion twisted his brow, and he started fiddling with a strand of my hair. "I think I was running from what I thought I'd never deserve.

Because believe me, Frankie, the only thing I ever wanted was you."

I reached out to trace his strong jaw, this boy so much more than he'd ever believed. "You deserve everything in this world, Evan. Maybe it was me who was praying she could be enough to be what you needed. To hold you and love you."

"Frankie." My name tumbled from his tongue like a promise.

"Maybe what we should accept is that neither of us should be ashamed of the love we have for each other. Maybe together, we are more than enough for each other."

Emotion pressed, and that energy sizzled. The hum that vibrated in the air almost glowing with the intensity of it.

Reaching out, I signed against the scar on his chest where his beautiful heart hammered at his ribs. *YOU ARE MY FAVORITE.*

Evan dropped his forehead to mine. "You are my everything."

I could almost see the walls that had separated us crumble at our feet.

Come crashing down in a blinding storm that ended with us.

Evan took my mouth in a possessive kiss, hands close to frantic as they began to explore.

Running over my breasts and my sides and gripping at my hips.

A groan of objection was starting to form when he took his mouth from mine, but then he was making a path down the sensitive skin of my throat and that groan was turning into one of need.

Tiny spikes of pleasure lighting up everywhere his lips traveled.

Down, down, down, the boy licked a path over the raging thunder of my heart, over the swell of my breast, and I was crying out when he took the tight bud into the well of his mouth.

He sucked hard, teeth scraping the flesh, tongue swirling, and all those sensations were hitting me all at once, and my fingers were digging into his shoulders, raking in their plea.

"Evan. Evan. Oh God. I missed this. I missed you."

And I knew he couldn't hear what I was saying, but that he could feel the brush of the words on his skin. I knew it in the way he exhaled in his own surrender.

"Yes," he murmured at my breast, his tongue coming out to flick one last time before he pushed up onto his hands to stare down at me. "I missed you. I missed this. Touching you. Loving you. Now I'm not ever going to stop."

"You better not." There would have been the threat of a tease in the words except for the fact I was physically shaking like a windstorm was coming through, my heart palpitating and sending all that anticipation pounding through my bloodstream.

Every nerve alive.

Every cell on high alert.

Tuned into this man.

The hint of a smirk lifted at the corner of his mouth. "That's a warning I plan to make good on."

Then there was no more laughing because Evan was winding out of his underwear, the last barrier keeping us apart. His abdomen jerked and flexed and ticked in these pulses of need as he slowly twisted out of his briefs.

His cock got free.

Hard and bulging at the tip.

My insides clutched. The man so damn beautiful it just wasn't fair to my sanity.

Because I could feel myself slipping away.

I gripped him and ran my thumb over his engorged crown, then fisted my hand over all that hard, velvet flesh.

Stroking once.

Then twice.

Evan's mouth dropped open in a straight-shot of pleasure, a low rumble echoing from his throat and covering me in his need.

"Frankie. Shit. Don't stop. Don't ever stop."

Loved being in control of it.

Loved knowing that I could cause this reaction in him.

I rushed to dig around in my nightstand for a condom, ripping into it and slipping it over his cock that was twitching in my hand.

He wound a spot for himself between my thighs, and he was staring down at me in awe as I continued to pump my hand along his length while guiding him to me.

"Fuck, Frankie . . . you are killing me, sweet girl. You just touching me and I'm already dying. Dying to be inside of you."

"Please."

I wasn't too proud to beg.

He shifted, took himself in his hand, the man watching me something fierce as he barely pressed himself at my center.

Anticipation so thick neither of us could breathe.

Everything dense and tight and completely hinged on this moment.

Evan nudged himself deeper, slowly spreadin' me, and my nails were scratching into his back and his forehead was dropping to mine and he was filling me so full that the only thing I could feel was his body consuming me.

Heart and body and soul and spirit.

His eyes were open, and I knew he was experiencing me the same way as I was experiencing him.

Wholly.

Utterly profound.

The feel of him as he began to rock, the drive of his hips deep and slow and measured. Like he wanted to savor every second of the bliss that surged into my body.

He gathered me up, bringing us chest to chest, our hearts beating a reckless rhythm. "Unicorn Girl," he murmured, those eyes striking in the shadows as he watched down on me.

As he loved me and I loved him and our bodies moved in time.

In slow desperation.

In a perfect union that started to take me to the highest places.

To the stars where he'd always said we'd been written.

Little sparks of pleasure lit our flesh, and Evan quickened his pace, every muscle in his body taught with glorious strain.

Evan grunted, panting as he drove and loved and kissed me mad.

And we were suddenly a mess of hands and pleading words and desperate mouths.

"Please."

"I need you."

"Never stop."

Vibrant colors flashed at the corners of my eyes.

Ecstasy gathering fast.

Pleasure spiked in the middle of us, the ties that bound ablaze, our skin slick with sweat as we moved in the most decadent dance.

It only grew with each thrust of his body. An explosion of desperation as we climbed toward the peak.

Evan gripped me by the back of one leg, spreading me wider, driving hard and fast, completely letting go.

And that pleasure surged.

The feeling gathering to a pinpoint.

Our gasps ragged and hard and both of us begging for mercy.

"Evan . . . I love you. I love you."

Our bodies slapped and clutched.

The hurricane coming at us was one I didn't think either of us were prepared to experience.

Because the second it hit, I was done for.

Annihilated.

Decimated.

A crack of thunder that rang of paradise.

Otherworldly.

Our connection unlike anything possible.

This boy the other half of my soul.

And we were there together, shooting toward the stars where we soared.

I clung to him tighter as he jerked and drove, his mouth open at my neck as he pounded me into oblivion.

Higher and higher.

And I thought I couldn't take it, that I was going to die, my entire body clinging to his as everything rushed to come together in the eye of the most breathtaking storm.

It fractured through the middle of me.

Blinding pleasure.

Euphoria.

Rapture.

Bliss. Bliss. Bliss.

His orgasm chased him down at the heels of mine.

Evan roared this massive sound that banged against my walls, body jerking as he came, hands everywhere, sinking into my flesh like he refused to ever let me go.

Savage satisfaction.

And he was panting and I was still lingering out there with him, where it was the two of us and nothing could ever come between.

Where we'd always stand for the other.

Where our dreams were bigger than our obstacles.

Where our fears were destroyed by our belief.

Darkness swam through my room, peace a covering that kept us shrouded.

Held and protected.

Our hearts beat in time.

Contented and fulfilled.

We were under the covers, on our sides and just staring at each other.

Relishing in the restoration.

Reveling in the revival.

Evan had the fingers of our hands threaded, and he lifted them through the rays of moonlight, studying the connection.

There was no resisting the force of the giddy smile that was working to break loose.

No shame in this surrender.

He shifted his head on the pillow to fully look at me. With our fingers still twined, he reached up and dragged his knuckles down my cheek. "I love it when you look like this."

Heat flooded my face, warmth gushing through my body. I bit down on my bottom lip. "And what do I look like?"

"Like you've been fucked and thoroughly satisfied."

A smirk took to the corner of his mouth, his tease so easy.

"Oh, you're pretty satisfied with yourself, are you?"

"Oh yeah," he said with that gruff, rasping voice.

God, I couldn't believe how much I'd missed it. How much I needed it.

He pulled my hand to his mouth and pressed a kiss to the back of it, inhaling deep. "Being with you feels like the greatest gift I've been given, Frankie. You and Everett. Both of you are something I didn't think I would have."

Emotion crested his brow, those eyes darkening in the shifting shadows of my room. "A family."

My heart clutched, nearly gave, and I was tracing the line on his chest, peeking up at him. "Is that what we are? A family?"

His throat bobbed as he swallowed. "That's what I want, Frankie. A family. That's what I've always wanted us to be."

Love blistered across the surface of my skin. Etching and searing. Branding me with forever. "I want that more than I could ever tell you."

My chest squeezed, and I had to turn my gaze from the penetrating ferocity of his.

I turned to lie on my back, staring at the ceiling, at the dance of shadows that cast their comfort on my room.

I lifted my hands. *DO YOU REMEMBER EVERYTHING WE'D DREAMED OF? ALL OF OUR CHILDHOOD FANTASIES?*

Three years ago, I'd accepted them as nothin' but fairytales and fiction.

I shifted back to meet his eyes. "I never stopped wanting that," I confessed.

I hesitated, searched through all the notions and wishes that had gotten banged up by our separation.

I took his hand, needing something to do with my trembling fingers. "I always imagined that we'd have a big family."

Regret rippled through Evan's features. "You know that's not possible."

My head shook. "No, Evan, it is. I'd always imagined our family would be made of patches and pieces. Children who needed to be loved because they'd been cast out by this world. Because the world looked at them like they were broken and deemed unworthy. Because they needed to be loved in a way that only we could love them."

"Frankie." His eyes squeezed closed for a beat, and then he was back to looking at me like I was his treasure.

I couldn't stop the tear that seeped out of the corner of my eye and dripped into my pillow. "I'd always imagined that we'd take over your mama's café, that in some way you would be involved in A Lick of Hope . . . that it would remain a part of who you are. That you'd run the charity and I be the one standing beside you to watch it flourish and grow."

Wistfulness throbbed in the space between us.

Drawing us together.

Back to those days.

His voice was gruff and scratching, the words barely there. "Yeah. I remember dreaming those dreams with you."

"What made you give them up?"

Lightly, he brushed his fingers across the trail of moisture on my cheek. "I didn't want you to have to wait around for the pain to come."

My head shook. "No, Evan. A single day spent with you is worth a thousand years of pain. I love you. And it's not a small love. It's not a love dependent on you bein' healthy. It's not a love contingent on life being easy. Because the only thing I want to do is do life with you. Whatever that looks like."

He reached over and took my face in both of his hands. He squeezed tight. "How did I get so lucky that I found you?"

"I was meant for you, remember?" The words raked the air.

Dense and mesmerizing.

This man my surrender.

My love.

My light.

My everything.

"I remember . . . and I promise I won't ever forget. I will fight for you . . . love you and protect you with everything I have. And I promise I will never make the decision for you again. You choose to love me? I will choose to love you back."

Grief and affection and every emotion that I'd ever felt bottled in my chest. I needed to tell him. God, I needed to tell him. I tried to force it from my tongue, to give him this burden that I knew was going to destroy a piece of him.

But the front door was banging open and Milo was going crazy, his nails echoing over the wood floors from the other side of the door.

"Milo, sweet boy!" I could hear Carly coo way too loud for midnight. "You are the sweetest, sweetest boy in the whole wide world, aren't you? Come and give Auntie Carly some love. Apparently doggie kisses are the only kind that I can get."

Josiah's voice boomed right behind hers. "Oh, come on, Carly, you want some kisses, I'd be glad to do you the favor. Have you looked at me? There is some major hotness you are missin' out on."

"Ew, gross, kissin' you would be like kissin' my brother."

Josiah cracked up. "You're right. On second thought, keep kissing that dog. Way better than your last boyfriend."

"I will stab you."

More laughter echoed through the house.

Apparently, Carly and Josiah had done it up right, their voices ringing through the house, slurred and ridiculous.

A giggle slipped free of my mouth, affection so fierce that there was no way I could stop it, and Evan quirked a questioning brow.

Sometimes it made me sad that he was missing out on something that so many took for granted. But I also knew he made up for it in so many extraordinary ways. It was everyone else who was truly missing out.

Being observed by Evan Bryant suddenly made you feel as if you had fifteen thousand senses. All of them firing at the exact same time, touching you everywhere, making you feel like you were the most important thing in the world.

That's what I wanted Everett and me to be.

His world.

And I was gonna make both of them mine.

"Carly and Josiah just got here," I explained, sitting up and taking the sheet with me.

He sat up, too, roughed a hand through his hair, something cocky riding through his demeanor. "Should we be concerned?" He said with no concern at all.

Hell, I was pretty sure those words were packed with nothin' but pride.

"Oh, we should definitely be concerned. Carly is gonna want

to throw a party."

Evan touched my chin with his knuckle. "Sounds like a good plan. I think we have plenty of reason to celebrate."

twenty-four

Evan

Frankie: Here.

Couldn't stop the big-assed grin that pulled to my mouth when my phone buzzed in my hand.

I headed for the door.

So yeah, I wanted to throw a goddamn party.

The biggest one ever.

I'd gotten word yesterday that my paternity test had confirmed me Everett's father. Not that I'd ever questioned it. But the fact my attorney was currently getting my name on the birth certificate so we could have his previous medical records ordered was a huge fucking relief.

Well, that and the fact that I'd spent the last three nights wrapped up in Frankie Leigh.

Two of us rediscovering.

Sometimes slow and soft and sweet.

Other times wild and reckless and hard.

Everything in between.

Neither of us could get enough.

I opened the front door of my parents' house to find her standing on the porch.

All those curls chaotic around her face. Girl was wearing a T-shirt with a frog printed on it and this frilly black skirt.

A smirk threatened, and I leaned up against the doorframe, hands lifted so I could sign. *SOMEONE LOOKS AWFUL CUTE TODAY.*

She did a little curtsey, grabbing her skirt at the sides and flailing it around a bit.

Yeah, fucking cute.

"Well, I might have been dressing up for someone real special."

My grin widened. "Oh, and who might that be?"

She stepped up to me, her hand on my chest and sliding up to my face. "My favorite froggy, of course."

I drifted forward, wrapping an arm around her waist and tugging her close. Just loving the heat of her body against mine. "And tell me . . . once you kissed this frog, did he turn into your prince?"

She giggled. I could feel the sensation of it running up my throat, this girl instantly making me ache to reach out and take a little more.

She peeked up at me, her fingers playing with a button of my collared shirt. "Better than a prince."

My brow lifted in a tease. "Better?"

She gave an overexaggerated nod. "Oh, yeah. Turns out he's kinda a god."

"God, huh? Wow, that's pretty impressive."

She raked her teeth over that lip. "Mmhmm . . . and he's been reignin' from my bed."

A groan rumbled in my chest. Half laughter. Half need. I gathered her closer, feeling the press of her joy. "You are ridiculous and perfect, Frankie Leigh," I told her where I was pressing my lips to her forehead.

"I'm kinda great, right?" she teased as she looked at me so I could see what she was saying.

"Don't get too carried away."

Easiness bled between us.

A quieted, sated gratefulness. Still couldn't believe we'd gotten to this place. Wasn't ever going to leave it.

Her eyes went soft. "Where is Everett?"

"He's in the backyard with everyone. Pretty sure he's getting smothered with kisses this afternoon."

"I think I need some of those kisses." She lifted her hands. *COME ON, WE'D BETTER GET BACK THERE BEFORE SOMEONE SENDS OUT A SEARCH PARTY.*

I roughed a hand through my hair. "You're probably right. You ready for this?"

"I think it's something we should have done a long time ago, Evan. When we first started. There was no reason to hide what we are."

WELL, EXCEPT FOR YOUR DAD.

I smirked down at her.

Another giggle. "He's not so bad."

"Uh, have you seen him?"

She took my hand, resting her head on my arm as we started through the house toward the back porch where everyone had already gathered.

Frankie'd had to work, so she was later than most. Basically, I'd been standing around like some kind of antsy asshole for the last hour and a half waiting for her to get here.

Knowing we were finally going to make a statement.

Claim us.

Frankie grinned up at me. "You took on Jack. I'm pretty sure you'll do just fine."

"Think that was pure adrenaline."

"I think you're way stronger than you give yourself credit for."

I pressed a kiss to the top of her head as we took the left down the short hall toward the kitchen. Could feel the energy in the air, the clatter of voices and activity that I couldn't hear but could sense as we made our way to the backyard.

On top of that?

I could feel the way Frankie was suddenly a little wary as she held onto my hand tighter as we headed for the french doors at the back.

"You okay?" I asked, glancing down at her, watching for her response.

"More than okay. I just can't believe we finally *are*."

I shifted so I could take her by both sides of the face. "We've always been. Now it's time for the world to know it."

Her smile was tender, this girl touching me deep, and God, I was having a hard time believing that this had become our reality, too. "Come on, let's go show them exactly what that is."

Taking her hand, I pushed open the door and led Frankie out behind me.

Was funny how you could tell when every single pair of eyes landed on you. Like it was catching. A domino effect.

Every single one of them felt the shift in the air.

A statement being written in the sky.

Everyone was there. Frankie's family. All of mine. Aunt Nikki and Uncle Ollie. Their kids, too.

Not like we hadn't been seen holding hands before. But I think they all knew this was different.

Think they heard the proclamation.

The declaration.

Could feel the force of my parents' gazes, Frankie's parents coming to stark attention.

I squeezed her hand a little tighter, and Frankie waved her free hand. "Hey, guys."

Mom popped up, holding Everett, and she came our way. "Oh good, Frankie is here."

She gave us a soft smile as she approached, and Everett was going crazy, babbling away as he reached his arms for Frankie.

Frankie immediately took him, held him to her chest, kissed his cheek as she started whispering words that I knew were nothing but adoration. Pure devotion.

Mom gave me a look that promised she'd known it all along.

That she was happy for us.

Frankie glanced back at me as she headed for her parents and Aunt Nikki and Uncle Ollie where they sat at a table under an umbrella, this look on her face that blew me away.

You wouldn't think one look could say it all.

Love. Love. Love.

Infinite. Definite.

My broken heart expanded, making space that I didn't think was possible.

And I knew . . . I knew.

I'd finally found what I'd been meant for all along.

"Your dad hates me." I licked the vanilla cone as I smiled at Frankie where she sat across from me at the ice cream parlor. We'd left the barbecue forty minutes before, wanting a little time to ourselves.

She held out her cone for Everett, kid's face completely smeared with the pink concoction, adorable as all hell.

Frankie giggled a little as he tried to bury his entire face in it and she tried to keep the situation under control.

Thought if Everett was given the chance, he would swallow it whole.

"My daddy does not hate you," she said.

"Uh, I beg to differ. He shot daggers at me the entire afternoon. Was waiting around for him to push me up against a wall and tell me to stay away from his baby girl."

Truth? He'd done it when I was seventeen.

Couldn't say I blamed him.

Of course, when he'd done it then, he'd patted me on the cheek and told me I was a good kid and to watch myself because he wouldn't want to have to hurt me.

Frankie tsked. "I've long since stopped being his baby girl. He was just . . . speculatin'." With a shrug, she took a lick of the same cone she was sharing with Everett. That was cute, too.

"Speculating?" I asked, amusement filling the question.

"You know, to engage in a course of reason based on inconclusive evidence. To conjecture or theorize. Speculatin'."

It was all a casual ramble.

So, it was hell having to watch her lips so closely when we were in a public place. I had this crazy urge to lean over the table and just kiss her.

Or maybe it was that we had Everett right there in a high chair.

No doubt, the poor kid was going to grow up subjected to constant PDA because I couldn't help myself. Leaning up and over the entire table, I kissed her soft and slow, just little plucks of her lips, the tiniest fleck of my tongue. "Mmmm . . . cotton candy."

She giggled against my mouth. "You like?"

Felt the words vibrating my skin.

"Very much. And did you just quote the definition of speculating to me?"

She giggled some more, this sexy tremor that rolled down my throat. I angled back so I could take in her eyes and her face and that mouth. "I might have. Seemed you were having trouble figuring out its meanin'."

"No trouble. I was just disagreeing."

"Okay, so my daddy used to be a tad bit overprotective. He's over that now."

"He glared at me over his beer the entire barbecue and didn't say one word to me."

Frankie turned serious, her hand brushing through Everett's hair, her gaze on him so soft before she was turning it on me. "Honestly? He is protective, Evan. And you know what, that's a good thing. I'd much rather have parents who care than ones who don't give it a second thought. And after Jack . . ."

Anger flared at his name.

"I think he's worried about what I'm getting myself in the middle of," she admitted. I could tell her voice dropped with the admission.

I got that. Respected it. Hell, I was still worried that I was getting her in the middle of something that she shouldn't be in myself. But like I'd promised her—I was over making that decision for her.

AND EVERETT? I asked, feeling my teeth clench at the thought of someone rejecting him.

Confusion knitted her brow. "How could anyone not love him, Evan? Stop worrying."

I blew out a reluctant sigh and then I let a grin tug at one corner of my mouth. "Maybe I could buy your dad off?"

She rolled her eyes. "If you really want him to hate you, then go for it. Believe me, he cares about your money about as much as I do."

I laughed. *SO MONEY WON'T WIN ME ANY POINTS. WHAT WILL?*

Everett had his hand wrapped around her finger, and she was swinging it around, making him laugh.

But she was looking at me. "I think the only thing you have to do is love me. The rest is goin' to fall in line."

Ten minutes later, we'd cleaned our table and gathered our things. Everett was getting sleepy, the evening coming on fast, and he pretty much slumped down on my shoulder when I pulled him out of his high chair.

My phone vibrated in my pocket. Frankie must have heard it because she reached for Everett. "Here, let me take him."

He cuddled onto her shoulder, taking a big handful of her hair and rubbing it on his face. Apparently, he liked Frankie about as much as I did.

I touched his cheek, sent her a smile as I pulled my phone out of my pocket and thumbed into it so I could check the text.

Seth: Hey, man, wanted to touch base about the situation. I'm 99.9% sure Jack is not the one responsible for the letters or any of the paintings.

Dread curled in the pit of my stomach.

I think I'd been just as sure. This sense that something was off. Still, I'd been hoping.

Praying it was something as simple as that.

Jealousy.

A man scorned.

That I could handle.

Could feel Frankie's unease from the side, the way she was trying to make sense of what was going on.

Another text buzzed through.

Seth: I've dealt with bad guys my whole life, and I'd bet the deed on my house that he didn't do it. He seemed completely oblivious to any messages being left, and he was all too keen to admit to being responsible for the fight. Said he was pissed and lost his temper.

Seth: There's no evidence to think otherwise and my gut says he's telling the truth.

My nod was slow, like he could see my response.

Seth: Sorry I don't have better news. I'm changing the focus of the investigation to his mother. Now that you have proven paternity, I can get in front of a judge and get an order to dig into her records. Hang tight, man. Let me know if you see ANYTHING that doesn't sit right.

I looked up at Frankie who was watching me close. "What is it?"

"It wasn't Jack."

Fear streaked through her features. "Are you . . . sure? I . . . I mean, I knew he was released the next mornin' and all, but I heard he's been staying with his brother, hidin' out. If that isn't an admission of guilt then I don't know what is."

She hugged Everett tighter, like she recognized it, too. We'd both wanted it to be. An easy answer. A quick fix.

But pinning this on Jack didn't fit.

"I think he didn't want to be around you, Frankie."

Wise choice.

A shiver of that fury slid beneath the surface of my skin.

I sucked it down.

We had bigger problems than that.

Apprehension moved through her body, her eyes narrowing as she attempted to process. "I'm scared, Evan." Could tell she was whispering the words. Offering them to me with the trust she'd given me. "Scared for him."

She nuzzled the side of Everett's face, breathed him in, loved him in a way that I knew only an amazing girl like Frankie Leigh could.

I reached out and cupped her face. "We're going to figure this out, Frankie. I promise. I won't let anything happen to him."

Her throat wobbled as she swallowed, but she was nodding her head against my hand. "Okay."

"Okay."

I led them out of the parlor, eyes darting everywhere like I actually thought I was going to see something. Like the truth was all of a sudden going to jump out at me.

Nothing but a fool's game.

Except I did.

In my periphery.

At the very fringes of consciousness where the deepest sort of recognition lived. Where the base instinct to protect the ones I loved was bred.

That was the thing about being me.

The heightened senses were sometimes a blessing. Sometimes a curse.

Vibes that tingled and itched and pricked at my skin.

Barbs and hooks and knifes.

Because I felt her staring from where she was hiding in a doorway that was tucked back in a cove up the sidewalk in the distance. Head barely peeking out.

Like she'd been tailing us. Following us.

Watching us.

My heart skidded then jumped into a sprint, a thunder of desperation and anger filling me to the brim.

Her eyes went wide the second she saw that I'd noticed her. Fear taking her hostage.

Wasn't even close to being as severe as mine.

Could feel Frankie getting confused from my side, protectiveness instantly lining her bones as she hugged Everett to her so fiercely while I started in the direction of Ashley.

Ashley whose head was shaking like she was begging me not

to approach her.

Ashley who I could tell was starting to panic as I slowly started to weave through the people on the sidewalk like I was approaching a wild animal.

I was getting frantic myself when I saw that she was preparing to bolt.

She wavered, attention darting around, like she was searching for the best escape route.

Twilight had settled, blues and silvers strewn across the road as lamps blinked to life, a dusky haze pushing down from the heavens and gathering on the street.

She started to duck into it.

To get lost.

To disappear.

Vapor and mist.

"Ashley!" I shouted, shoving out from around a man who was taking a picture with his girl. I didn't even take the time to give an apology.

She looked back at me.

Terror froze her expression.

My spirit clutched.

My senses coiled.

This awareness that everything was bad.

So goddamn bad, and if I was going to fix it, I had to get to her. She was the only one who held the answer.

The fate of my son.

"Ashley," I yelled again as I got closer.

She started to push through the crowd.

Distraught.

Frenzied.

Deranged.

Panic gripped me, and I started to run, started to plea. "Ashely, stop! Wait!"

People were looking at me like I was the deranged one as I pushed through them. I shouted her name over and over.

While I felt like I was a second from everything coming apart.

Everything dependent on this moment.

On me getting through to her.

Ashley's straight-brown ponytail bobbed furiously as she fled. I followed it like it was a flare streaking into the sky.

A shout for help.

Because my chest was tight. This feeling that she was not alright sliding into my bloodstream, knowledge pounding and beating and screaming.

"Ashley!"

She suddenly ducked across the street. A car skidded and swerved to miss her. She stumbled a bit, shocked, so terrified that she kept running to the other side.

I chased her down, dodging one car, then another, sure they were probably blaring their horns at me but not giving a shit about anything but getting to her.

I hit the sidewalk, finally catching up. The sheer fear radiating from her slipped across my sweaty flesh like a bad omen.

I grabbed her by the arm, and she whipped around, her eyes so big I was wondering if her brother was right.

If this girl was manic.

Maybe even crazy.

"Ashley," I pled, knowing it was probably too loud and hard, but not knowing how to stop the outright desperation from flooding out. I gripped her by the outside of both shoulders to keep her from running. "Stop. Need to talk to you."

Frantically, her head shook. "Let me go."

"No . . . not until you tell me what the hell is going on."

Knots of dread curled her brow, and I could feel the agony radiating from her pores. "I . . . I just wanted to check on him. To make sure he is fine. That's all."

"Bullshit," I gritted, probably holding her too tight. I had to beat down the urge to shake the truth out of her. I dragged her over to the building, into another doorway that was tucked back from the wall, the shop closed up for the night. "Tell me what's happening."

"I just need to be sure that you'll take care of him. Protect him, no matter what."

"Of course, I will, but you've got to tell me what the hell is going on here. I don't know how to help him if I don't know anything about his past."

Harshly, she shook her head. "I'm sorry. I'm so sorry. I-I-I didn't mean for this to happen. I love him, Evan. I do. I'm sorry."

I blinked, trying to make sense of the ramble of words she was releasing, faster than I could process them all. "If you're sick, you need to tell me. So I can help take care of him. So I can help take care of you."

Her brow pinched, dread and confusion. "Sick? I'm not sick, Evan. You just . . . you need to protect him."

She kept looking over her shoulder. Terror ridging her spine. Making her tremble and quake.

"But your brother—"

She yelped when I said that, and she jerked back, holding her arms over her chest as she backed away. "I'm sorry . . . I didn't mean for this to happen. I'll try to stop it. I will. I promise. Just . . . take care of him. Please."

"Ashley." I started for her, and I saw her mouth form a screech when I grabbed her again, like she was getting burned from my touch.

Misery.

She yanked her arm to try to break from my hold. "You have to let me go."

A man who was walking the street shouldered between us.

"Hey, asshole. You bothering her? She said to let her go."

My surprise at him cutting between us gave her enough time to dart across the street, the guy blocking my way as she jumped into a car waiting at the curb. Then she was gone.

Dread curled and shivered and rushed.

Fear a whirlwind that gusted and blew.

I looked back up at the street where Frankie was holding Everett, bouncing him, a protective hand on the back of his head.

There was a moment in my life when I'd thought I had no purpose.

When I'd believed I was more of a hindrance than a remedy.

No more.

Because standing there, I saw my life staring back at me.

And I was going to do whatever it took to protect it.

twenty-five

Evan

I followed Frankie up the steps to my parents' porch. She still

was refusing to let Everett go, cradling him as he slept against her chest, his thumb in his mouth.

We'd been down at the station telling Seth everything we knew, which was a whole lot of nothing except for the fact that I believed Ashley was in some kind of danger.

And she was here.

In Gingham Lakes.

Fact she would follow us here was pretty huge.

Seth had taken a description of both her and her brother. They were searching for them both.

While I watched.

Vigilant.

Distrustful.

Unable to shake this feeling that things were way worse than I'd wanted to admit.

I moved around them and opened the door to the lapping darkness that flooded out.

Silence palpable in the oppressive air.

We stepped through the door, and my attention moved to the end of the stairs where my dad was waiting.

WHAT HAPPENED?

Could feel his anxiety.

The angst riding through the atmosphere.

My head shook. *WE DON'T KNOW MUCH ELSE EXCEPT HIS MOTHER IS HERE.*

He nodded. He'd already known that *minor* detail since I'd filled him in as best as I could via text. His attention slanted to Frankie who cuddled my son, slowly swaying him in the comfort of her arms.

Something passed through Dad's eyes, something that looked too close to grief, and I was wondering if he was more terrified over the idea that Ashley might take Everett away from us or if he might be a carrier of this sickness.

He turned back to me. *AND WHAT DID SETH SAY?*

THEY'RE LOOKING FOR ASHLEY AND HER BROTHER. GOAL IS TO BRING THEM IN FOR QUESTIONING. NEITHER ARE WANTED FOR ANYTHING, BUT HE SAID HE'LL DO HIS BEST TO FIND OUT IF EITHER OF THEM ARE INVOLVED IN THE MESSAGES. FIGURE OUT IF SHE NEEDS HELP AND WHAT WE CAN DO. TRY TO FIND OUT WHAT HER INTENTIONS ARE.

If this was a severe depressive episode or something entirely different.

And fuck, I wanted to help her, but not at the cost of my son.

Not at the cost of losing him to her.

My stomach turned with the possibilities, with the unknowns, and my thoughts drifted back to that guy on the sidewalk in front of A Drop of Hope who'd called me a freak for no reason at all. The letter on my car when I'd come back out.

I tried to focus. To dig through my mind to find if he was familiar in any way. To pinpoint if he might have a reason for this insanity.

Problem was, I was coming up dry.

Unable to sort through the mess.

Unable to make the frayed ends fit.

Dad nodded. *OKAY. IF THERE'S ANYTHING WE CAN DO, LET US KNOW.*

THANK YOU, I told him, so honestly, so sincerely. Wishing there was a way I could express to him how much I appreciated all he'd done. All the way back to when I was a child to the present. To make amends for letting him down.

But I realized the only thing I could do was never repeat it.

Prove to him what it meant rather than trying to find the words to make it true.

FRANKIE IS STAYING, I added.

I was pretty sure the sound he made was an affectionate scoff, and he gave a slight shake of his head. *FIGURED THAT. GUESS IT'S BETTER THAN HER SNEAKING IN THE WINDOW THE WAY SHE USED TO DO.*

Affection filled his expression when he looked at her, and Frankie was trying to subdue a guilty laugh, the tiniest bit of lightness breaking into the heaviness. "We were just friends."

"Liars. Both of you." Dad pointed between us, grinning soft.

Busted.

Like they didn't always know.

Felt the movement from above, and I glanced up to find Mom coming down the darkened staircase, wearing a nightgown and her hair twisted up on her head. "Oh, you are here. I thought I heard something." Worry crested her features. "Are you all okay? I hate that this is happening. I just . . . want some peace for y'all. For this baby."

She hit the landing and moved directly for Frankie, her arms outstretched. "May I?"

"Of course." Frankie handed him off to her, though she clearly didn't want to let him go.

Thought maybe she would stand right in that spot and hold him forever.

Mom pressed a bunch of kisses to Everett's temple, bouncing him a little when he stirred from sleep. "Did you get anything to eat?" she asked us.

"No, not yet," I told her.

"There are some leftovers in the fridge. Why don't you two go heat yourself up a plate, and I'll take this little guy upstairs. He can hang out with me for a while . . . or spend the night in Grammy's room, if that works best."

She angled her head between Frankie and me like she was offering us some privacy. A reprieve.

I couldn't be more grateful, and still, there was a huge part of me that didn't want to let him out of my sight.

"That'd be nice, thank you. I'll probably pop in and get him before we go to sleep."

"Well, leave him as long as you like. Believe me . . . getting Grammy time is no problem at all."

I sent her a soft smile, and Dad wrapped his arm around her waist.

Two of them were the picture of devotion.

Dad started to lead them up the staircase, but he hesitated. "I'm glad you two are finally figuring this out. Last few years have been rough on all of us . . . think the thing we need to remember is to be honest with each other. Open. Talk about our pasts and our futures."

I nodded, and he did, too, before they turned to climb the stairs.

I moved for Frankie. "Are you hungry?"

She ran her hands up her arms. "I should probably eat."

I set my hand on the small of her back. Figured we both needed the connection. Never close enough.

We headed in the direction of the kitchen, but Frankie surprised me by taking my hand and ducking us into the den off to the left.

Pulling me into the darkened room, she clicked the door shut behind us.

WHAT ARE YOU DOING? I asked, hands getting slowed in the tension as Frankie rounded around me.

Shadows danced and played and leapt through the oversized room. The drapes that hung over the massive windows that overlooked the backyard were parted a foot, the sheer fabric exposed letting the moon flood the room in a milky glow.

A huge bookcase took up one large wall, floor to ceiling, and two big sofas faced each other in the middle, a pool table toward the back.

That energy banged against the walls.

Two of us bottled in the force of it.

Our connection bounding and shivering.

I JUST NEEDED TO BE ALONE WITH YOU.

Could see the bob of her throat as she swallowed, the moisture clouding her eyes. "Your dad is right—we need to be honest—and I have to be honest right now and tell you how scared I am of losing him. When I saw you runnin' after her? I knew it. I knew it was her and I was already feeling a crater getting carved out of the middle of me at the thought of having to let him go. I still can't understand how she could possibly leave him in the first place."

She'd turned her head a bit in profile, so I had to decipher part of what she was saying, but I got it. Understood it on a level that terrified me, too.

When she turned back to me, helplessness had taken hold of her features.

I started to edge her way. Slowly. The energy shifted as I moved for her. "Unicorn girl." My fingers reached out to trace the angle of her face. "What did you tell me? One day together is worth a thousand years of pain?"

Her eyes dropped closed. Lingered there. Her mouth forming a quiet, "Yes."

"Then we fight for every day that we can. We fight for Everett. We fight for us."

E-V-A-N.

She signed it up close to my body, her fingers flitting out to touch my chest. I grabbed her by them, dragging her arm up and curling it around my neck. I started to edge her deeper into the room.

"Evan," she said this time, her breath caressing my face.

"We do this together, Frankie. No more walls. No more barriers," I murmured down at her.

Remorse twisted through her face, and I shook my head to

stunt it.

Last thing I wanted was her focusing on the time we'd lost.

We didn't have time to regret the past when the only thing we had was our future.

"It's you and me, Frankie Leigh."

She released a gush of air, and I swallowed it down, took her in a kiss that I poured into her with everything that I had.

I hoisted her up on the edge of the pool table.

Could feel her needy gasp.

Desire a lightning burst that flashed through her body.

I stepped back so I could stare at her sitting there in that skirt and that shirt.

Her brown hair was as wild as it came, mussed and frizzy, kinked up curls that I reached out and grabbed a fistful of. I spread my opposite hand out on her hip and dragged her back to me.

Dick already hard. Lust speeding out of control, the need to get lost in this girl overwhelming.

To forget. To remember.

To touch and take and tease.

I was kissing her again.

Deep and hard and demanding.

Unchecked.

Could taste her moan, and I swallowed it down, taking our kiss deeper. Tongues flicking and our hands losing the little control that we'd had.

She slipped hers under my shirt, palms rushing up my abdomen as she drew it over my head. Need thundered, and I did the same, ripping the fabric from her body so I could get to what was underneath.

Chills lifted in a flash across her skin, gooseflesh racing.

I dipped down to chase it with my tongue, kissing along the delicate curve of her neck and across her collarbone, dragging all the way down to pull her nipple into my mouth through the lace of her bra.

Nails dug into my shoulders. Sharp pricks of perfect pain as I sucked at the hard as stone peak. "Evan." Could feel the breath of my name skate across my back.

A.L. Jackson

A shiver of a pledge.

I pushed up the fabric so I could get a better taste, sucking her tight bud into my mouth, swirling with my tongue, loving it when she was fisting my hair in her hands.

I flicked my tongue out to the opposite side while I reached out to unclasp the hook of her bra.

Frankie Leigh arched as I peeled the black lace from her arms.

Begging for more.

"Fucking gorgeous, Frankie Leigh. You have any idea what you look like right now? How sexy you are? Most beautiful thing I've ever seen."

I edged back, dragging my fingertip from her lips, running it down the length of her trembling throat to her quivering belly. "What do you need, Frankie Leigh?"

Her hands flew in a rash plea. *YOU, EVAN. YOU HAVE ALWAYS BEEN THE ONE THING I'VE NEEDED.*

My palms slipped up the tops of her thighs, chasing the goosebumps that lifted on her flesh, riding all the way under the fabric of her skirt.

It bunched up around her waist.

I took her by the knees, spreading her, a matching scrap of black lace covering her drenched pussy.

I dragged it down her legs, watching her, the way her entire being convulsed with anticipation.

Second I dropped her panties to the floor, I pushed two fingers inside her heat, her walls clutching in a needy throb.

"Evan. Please. Don't tease me. I don't think I can handle it tonight."

A smirk pulled to my mouth as I pumped my fingers slowly. "You teased me my whole damn life, Frankie Leigh. Think you deserve a little of it, don't you?"

Knew the words had to be coming off as gruff. Scraping with a demand. Because the truth was, I was just teasing myself.

Cock so damned hard it was painful.

Mind getting swept up in a rush of dizziness.

This lingering disbelief that I was worthy to touch her this way.

"You're a liar," she rasped. "I was always the one who was

beggin' you. Chasin' you. You were the one who kept me waitin'."

She angled back, planting her hands on the table behind her, spreading herself wider.

An offering.

A gift.

Everything.

"And I don't want to wait anymore."

I didn't hesitate, I nuzzled my head between her thighs, going right for her swollen clit, fingers fucking her hard and fast, driving her straight into oblivion.

Frankie writhed, pressed herself closer, wanting everything I could give.

Thirty seconds later, she busted apart. A shockwave of bliss detonated.

Fracturing.

Splintering.

I led her through her orgasm, kept suckling at that sweet spot, girl panting for air as she tried to come back down.

I kept thrusting my fingers when I edged back. "Don't get too relaxed, Unicorn Girl. I'm not done with you yet."

Greed jutted her chest at that, and I pulled her off the pool table and spun her around.

Her hands flew out to steady herself, the girl arching back as I pushed that frilly skirt up over her waist.

Girl bare.

Her slit was perfect. Pink and wet. Her puckered asshole just as sweet.

My cocked twitched, desperate to let go.

Wanted it all. Every inch. Every cell. Every moment. All her heartache and all her joy.

I found her reflection in the huge ornate mirror that sat on the ground with the top rested up high on the wall to our right.

Taking in the whole scene.

The pool table.

Frankie Leigh.

Me.

Us.

Those eyes flashed need.

Surrender.

I smoothed a hand over her bottom. "You wore this just to drive me insane, didn't you? You knew exactly what it'd do to me, didn't you?"

She pushed back, begging for my touch, our eyes locked in the reflection. "I told you I was dressin' for someone special."

I let my knuckle run the course of her slit.

She was shaking, holding on, her ass in the air as I wound her back up again.

I stepped back so I could flick through the buttons on my jeans, shoved them and my underwear free while I relished in the sight of her shivering with anticipation.

Still was having a hell of a time realizing that this was us. That she was mine. That she was always going to be.

"You are every fantasy I've ever had, Unicorn Girl." I twisted her hair up again, tugging her back an inch, meeting her eye in the mirror. "Did you know that? Look at you."

I leaned over so I could kiss along the curve of her shoulder, tongue licking out, eyes watching her in the mirror through the shadows.

That energy rushed. Boomed and simmered. Coming to a head.

Like it was getting ready to turn into something brand new.

Her head shook, wild mane flying all over. "I can't believe it's even half as good as looking at you. You keep stealin' my breath, Evan. Same way as you stole my heart the first day I saw you."

F-R-A-N-K-I-E.

I signed it out against her back.

A brand.

A tattoo.

I LOVE YOU. LOVE YOU SO FUCKING MUCH. NEVER GOING TO LET YOU GO. NOT EVER AGAIN.

I gripped her by the waist, shifting languages, loving that Frankie could hear me in every way.

Our senses tied.

Our spirits bound.

"Tell me you want me as badly as I want you."

She strained back, pressing her ass against my dick. "Yes. Please. Always. Forever. Any way you want me, I'm yours."

I slipped a single finger through the cleft of her ass, dipped it into her needy pussy.

Frankie Leigh squirmed, desperate for more.

Body nothing but a plea.

This time, it was me who was groaning when I grabbed myself, pressed the head of my cock to her lips.

I slowly spread her. Nudged in an inch.

Lust clutched my guts, and I took her in one solid thrust.

Frankie jolted forward, nails scraping at the green felt of the pool table, girl bent over this way the most seductive thing I'd ever seen.

Paradise.

This girl was paradise. The feel of her clutching my dick, the constant throb of our bodies as we begged for the other.

Bare.

Frankie was on the pill, and I was clean, and there was no better feeling than zero space between us.

"You are perfect," I raked out, splaying my hand out to run up the small of her back, riding up her spine as I pressed her chest against the table.

I wound my other hand around to find her clit.

Rubbing her fast.

Fucking her hard.

My attention turned to the mirror.

To the silhouette of us as I rocked my hips, as she fought to meet me thrust for thrust.

The intensity swelled and the energy flashed.

Strikes of lightning.

Thunderbolts of greed.

Devotion tightened my chest and the impending pleasure knotted my guts.

I drove faster and faster, words tumbling from my tongue, "You are my life, Frankie Leigh. I'm going to give you everything."

"Everything," she confessed, giving me the same.

Her pants rose into the air. Meshed with mine.

Our hearts racing to meet.

Boom. Boom. Boom.

Bodies smacking. Her sweet body getting ready to blow.

Could feel her clamping down on my cock. The friction and the slide.

Took her as deep as I could, until her mouth was dropped open, riding a fine line of pain and pleasure.

Felt it the second she shattered.

Splintering into a million pieces.

Her body an earthquake.

She throbbed and pulsed and it set me off.

That ball of greed fracturing out.

Broken.

Coming together.

Two of us one.

And it shouldn't be possible, but after today? After the highs and the lows? I didn't think we had ever been so close.

I stayed there bent over her, holding her in my arms as our chests heaved and our pulses thundered.

As our spirits swam.

I inhaled a tight, ragged breath, pushed back the mess of her hair with my nose so I could nuzzle against her cheek, both my hands winding around to hold her by the chest. My mouth moved to her ear. "Want to marry you, Frankie Leigh. Want to build a home. Want to be with you like this every day."

She twisted her face around so she could look at me, hooked her arm back to wrap around my neck. "I am yours."

I knocked lightly on my parents' bedroom door. Sure my hair was a disaster and I smelled like sex, but I didn't care. Couldn't wait for their call, so I carefully cracked open the door and peeked inside.

Mom was sitting up against the headboard, her readers perched on her nose, reading a book. Dad was passed out with a sleeping Everett draped across his chest, his hand protectively set on his back.

Emotion surged.

Thick and overwhelming.

Mom took off her glasses and smiled, gesturing for me to enter. "Hey." Could tell she was whispering.

"Hi." I kept mine the same as I crept inside. "He's out, huh?"

"He never even stirred." She turned her gaze on Dad and Everett before she turned the weight of it on me. "That's one beautiful sight, isn't it?"

My smile was almost wistful. "Yeah. Never thought I'd get to witness a sight like that. Never thought I'd get to have it." I eased down to sit on the edge of her bed.

Mom reached out and touched my cheek. "I'm so glad you have this chance."

I cut my gaze over to Everett before I returned it to her. "I get it now, Mom, how you always told me I was perfect to you, no matter my disabilities. Don't think I ever really believed it before. Thought it was something you and Dad told me to make me feel better. But I get it. It doesn't matter how this turns out, I will love him the same."

Her nod was slow. "I don't think a child can ever understand the extent of a parent's love until they get to experience that for themselves."

Sitting there, memories assailed me, the fear I'd felt when my mother had been trying to protect me against the wrath of my biological father.

God, even at eight, I'd fucking hated him.

Wanted to protect her no matter what.

But it had been Mom who'd done the protecting.

She and Kale.

They were the ones who'd stood for what was right.

I swallowed hard. "Do you remember what you used to say . . . what you used to tell me when I was a little boy?"

She angled her head, brow pinched, unsure.

I lifted my hands.

THIS HOUSE IS LOVE.

It was an assertion we'd made.

A command.

A rule.

Tenderness filled her expression. "Of course, I remember."

"That's what I want, Mom. I want a house, and I want to fill it with love."

"That's always been my hope for you, Evan. I've always hoped you'd find love and you'd hold onto it . . . because there is nothing more wonderful than that." Her eyes darted to the door. "Love her." That gaze slipped to Everett and back to me. "Love him."

She squeezed my hand.

"If there's one thing I've learned in my life and one thing I hope you hold onto for all of yours—never let go of what you love most."

twenty-six

Frankie Leigh

$\mathcal{E}$van was sprawled out, face down, his naked back exposed where he slept.

My tummy turned and a blister of the need that showed no hope of dying out seared through my body.

Not that I was complainin'.

But I was supposed to be to work in twenty minutes, and if I wanted to get there on time, I was going to have to tear myself from the warmth of his glorious body. I mean, I could just stay there all day, right?

I pouted a little.

Nope.

That was just not gonna happen.

I couldn't go letting Aunt Hope down that way. Gettin' flaky just because her son was back in town. But with everything, I wondered if she would blame me.

I crawled over him, running my nose from the sexy dimples just above his butt up the length of his spine, all the way into his hair. Breathing this boy in. There went my tummy again.

Yum.

He stirred, and I could feel the force of his smile where half of his face was pressed to the pillow. He flipped over and pulled me across his hard, chiseled body.

Flaking was sounding like a mighty good plan right about then.

"Mornin'," he rumbled in his sleepy voice, that scraping sound wrapping me whole.

My favorite song.

One I wanted to listen to every single morning.

"Hey," I whispered. "I've got to go."

He tightened his hold. "No. Stay in this bed with me all day."

A giggle slipped free. "Don't tempt me. The last thing I need is my boss to come barging through the door later to find me here after Jenna said I called in sick."

And I was pretty sure *lovesick* didn't count.

A smirk tugged at his sexy mouth. "She won't mind."

I fiddled with a lock of his bedhead hair, voice going serious. "No, she probably wouldn't, but I never want to let her down."

Evan reached up and brushed the hair out of my face, cupping my cheek, staring up at me like I was his treasure.

My heart banged against my ribs.

Beatin' for him.

"You are so good, Frankie Leigh. Have me in awe. Every second. Every day."

My head shook. "The only thing we can do in this life is try to be the best person we can be. From lovin' to workin' to helpin'."

"And that is what makes you so good. That you recognize it. I hope one day I can stand beside you and you see the same thing in me."

I trembled my fingertips across his full lips. "I already do."

Could feel that Evan was hard. From the twitch of the packed muscle on his abdomen to his erection that was straining through the sheets.

I groaned. "I've got to go or I'm really going to be here all day. I've got to run home to change really quick."

"Grab a few changes . . . need you here with me. And honestly, I really don't want you out there by yourself."

Was I blushin'? It didn't have a thing to do with being shy, it was pure giddiness. Pure gratefulness. "You really want that? Me to be here with you?"

"You think I was lying last night?"

My eyes searched the depths of his. The sincerity and devotion. Could stay there forever.

He gripped my bottom, making me squeak. I tried to subdue it, tried to silence the giggle that was breaking free so I didn't disturb Everett who was fast asleep in his crib.

"We're goin' to have to figure out something with Milo. I can't be leaving him with Carly and Josiah all the time."

He nodded, something passing through his expression. "We'll figure it out." He lifted his chin with a grin. "Go on. Hurry up and go to work so you can come back to me."

"Bossy pants," I told him, slipping out from his bed and pulling on my skirt. Was just going to wear the T-shirt I'd borrowed from him back to my place.

He quirked a brow, watching me dress with a hungry gaze. "You want me to show you bossy? Don't tempt me, woman."

I edged back over for him, brushed a kiss to his lips, inched back so he could read me. "I'll tempt you all I want. You better get used to it, Froggy Boy."

He clutched me by the inside of the thigh. "Get the hell out of here before I have you tied to my bed."

I laughed.

He shook his head.

And it didn't matter how much was going on in our worlds. How scary things could be. I didn't think I'd ever been as happy as right then.

Both of my boys lying in their beds waitin' on me to come back to them.

I crept out the door and downstairs as quietly as I could, figuring everyone would be trying to sleep in on Sunday morning.

I hit the bottom landing, making a beeline for the door only to freeze when I heard the words hit me from behind. "You going to tell him, Frankie Leigh?"

I flinched.

Body and soul.

Warily, I turned around to face Uncle Kale who was leaning against the back of the couch.

There was no judgment on his face.

Just the expectation that I would do what was right.

I gulped for clarity.

For my own resolution.

I stared at my uncle who'd always stood by my side, even before Evan had come into our lives. Emotion fisted. "I will . . . I just . . . I'm not sure it's the right time with everything happening with Everett."

Sadly, he shook his head. "It's never going to be the right time, Sweet Pea. You know that. And it's only going to get harder to find the words the longer you keep them hidden. He has a right to know. *Especially* with what is happening with Everett."

Grief fired from that place where I'd tried to keep it locked down. Where I'd lived the best way that I could with it until Evan had come back into my life. "I know that. It's so hard, Uncle. I don't want to hurt him."

"You can't protect him from that, Frankie Leigh. Just like he couldn't protect you from his disability."

Uncle Kale was right, but that sure didn't make it any easier.

"I will do it soon. I promise."

His nod was full of understanding, and he straightened to standing. "It wasn't your fault, just like it wasn't his."

I swallowed down the old wounds, forced a smile that was as brittle as the thought of telling Evan made me feel, and I slipped out the door without saying anything else.

Thankfully my car was still sitting out front from when I'd gotten there yesterday afternoon, and I got in and made the quick drive to my duplex.

Unease coiled my stomach when I saw that Jack had returned, his car parked the way that it always was. But I wasn't goin' to live my life in fear, and if Seth believed that he was innocent of the letters, then I had to believe it, too.

I thought I probably had always believed it way down deep, anyway. Doin' something like that just didn't seem Jack's style.

It was too petty.

Too cowardly.

He came out fists blazin'.

Obviously.

Which I wasn't so keen about, either, but at least there was some honesty to it, and I got the feeling he wouldn't be bugging me anymore. Still, I was quivering a bit when I stepped out into the cool dawn air, and I rushed for the porch, my key already in hand.

Carly and Josiah would be here, so I knew I really didn't have anything to worry about.

But I was on edge. Fighting the creeps chasing me down. Hair lifting at the nape of my neck.

A slick of awareness sent my pulse into overdrive.

I whirled around, Jack's name on the tip of my tongue, ready for a fight or to scream or to just plain run, only for it to die right there when I saw the stranger slink out from the trees.

A misty etching in the morning.

My eyes narrowed while my heart drum, drum, drummed, taking the guy in. Shaggy dark brown hair, medium height, thin build.

Completely ambiguous.

I realized he fit the description that Evan had given Seth of Ashley's brother.

Chris.

Chris was his name.

And my hand started shaking, fumbling around to get to my phone, when he started to speak.

"Are you Frankie Leigh?" he called, shoving his hands in his pockets and rocking back on his heels.

I relaxed a fraction when I realized he bore no threat. That he was remaining way out behind my car.

"Yeah," I told him, keeping myself planted in the spot, ready to bolt inside if I needed to. "Are you Chris?"

He nodded. "I am. Ashley's brother. Have you seen her?"

I didn't answer him, instead I was blinking, trying to sort through the disaster of questions that tumbled through my mind.

"How do you know who I am? How do you know where I live?"

How do you even know about me?

That one I didn't ask aloud, too scared to voice it.

He gave a harsh shake of his head, looking away in frustration before he turned back to me. "Sorry. I apologize for showing up here out of the blue, but I thought I finally caught up with her yesterday. She told me what hotel she was staying at and left me a key at the front desk, but when I went inside her room, she was gone. Took most of her things except for a few scraps of paper . . . one that had your name and address written on it. Thought you might know where she was. Guessing you know Evan? The guy she dumped her kid on?"

Wasn't sure why that phrase dug at me, but it did.

"I wouldn't call it dumpin'. He's Everett's father."

Chris raked a hand through his hair. "Listen, I'm just trying to track down my sister. I'm not here to cause any trouble. She needs her medication, and she hasn't been on it for over a month. I'm worried about her. She calls me, tells me she is ready to go home, and then when I get there, she's vanished again. Was hoping there was a chance she'd been here since she had your address."

He appeared a little helpless, and damn it, I felt bad for jumping to conclusions. I shook my head. "She hasn't been here that I know of, but we did see her yesterday downtown."

He heaved out a sigh of relief. "Where?"

"Down by Patty's Ice Cream Parlor on Macaber."

He nodded, attention drifting for a beat, like he was calculating where she might have gone after that.

If only we knew.

"She was super freaked out," I added. "She took off running when we saw her."

I edged up closer to the railing. "Would she . . . would she be the type to vandalize? Paint on someone's property?"

Sadness had him pursing his lips. "Not normally. But about a year ago, she . . . she left a really hateful message for our mom written on her windshield in lipstick. Our mom hasn't talked to her since . . . it was that bad."

God, I hated to think that Everett's mother could be this

disturbed. Hated the idea that he had the possibility of ever being in her care again.

Protectiveness swelled.

So fast I could feel my spirit squeeze.

"I'm sorry to hear that."

"I am, too. I really need to find her so we can get her stabilized."

I nodded slow. "I understand. I wish I could help you more, but I can't. But one of the officers here in town is looking for her and would like to have a word with you. He wants to help her as well."

More relief. "Yeah, that would be awesome to have someone on my side."

"Let me call him really quick, I'm sure he can come right over."

"Actually, could you give him my number? I really want to get back out on the streets and see if I can find her this morning."

I flipped into my phone. "Sure . . . what is it?"

I inputted the number as he rattled it off.

"All right, I'll give it to him."

"Thanks, Frankie Leigh. I appreciate your help. And if you see anything, please let me know."

"Absolutely."

He started to walk back down the drive, then he hesitated, slowly turned back around. "Is . . . Everett okay?"

Affection burned so bright inside me that I thought I might physically glow. "He's wonderful."

Softness filled his expression. "You and Evan are close."

He didn't phrase it like a question. It was just a quiet satisfaction. "He's the love of my life," I said simply. "And I promise you, we'll take care of Everett. Provide everything that he needs."

He gave a gentle smile. "That's great, Frankie Leigh. That's great."

Then he turned and disappeared from where he'd come.

Quickly, I dialed Seth so I could give him the number. It was early so I wasn't all that surprised that it went straight to voicemail. Rather than leaving one, I tapped out a message as I rushed inside, hoping that we were getting closer to being able to put this behind us.

twenty-seven

Evan

"You have money for this?"

Uncle Rex was in the middle of the kitchen spinning a circle in his work boots.

He was wearing his typical. Tattered jeans and an old flannel, the guy printed in grit and tenacity.

"Yeah."

He eyed me with more of the *speculation* Frankie had been talking about.

Thing was, he knew me as well as everyone else, and I was nervous as fuck.

"Going to pay cash for it, actually," I amended, making it clear.

He nodded slow, calculating, eyes making another circuit around the brand-new custom kitchen, the brand-new floors, the brand-new windows—the brand-new everything.

Yeah, house was brand new.

Had never been lived in.

No expense had been spared. Place gorgeous.

Best thing about it?

It was a street away from mine and Frankie Leigh's parents.

Skeptical, he turned his attention back to me. "Why do I get the feeling you don't have me here to get a remodeling quote?"

So maybe I'd lured him here under false pretenses.

Sue me.

I needed to see him. Face-to-face. Without anyone else around.

Felt like the right thing to do. Because I was finished being a pussy. Finished being a coward. Finished not standing up and fighting for what was most important in my life.

Still, I exhaled a strained breath, nervously rubbed my palms together. "Might need an awesome playground out back."

He huffed out what I was pretty sure was a disbelieving laugh. "Little below my pay grade, don't you think?"

Okay, so Rex's company, RG Construction, was the largest, most successful builder in the area. He'd grown it from the ground up, a few remodels here and there, to building the high-rise apartments that had gone in downtown, not to mention the entire community he and Uncle Broderick had collaborated on down by the river that now was one of the most popular resort destinations in Alabama.

He wasn't exactly begging for work.

I'd texted him and told him I was calling in that favor that he really didn't owe me.

I was only half shocked that he'd shown.

I wrapped my hands around the counter to keep myself from twitching, nerves a riot as I hedged the real reason I had him there. "Seems to me it's something you'd do for family."

He ran his hand over the scruff on his jaw, eyes closing for a second before he leaned back against the opposite counter. "Cut to it, Evan. This about Frankie Leigh?"

My chest squeezed at the thought, and I looked around the house before I let my gaze slide back to him. Straight truth bleeding free. "Know I don't deserve it, after what I did, but I hope I get lucky enough that she will want to live here with me."

His nod was slight, though I could read that his words were a challenge. "And what does this have to do with me?"

I chuckled what I knew was a rough sound, and I scratched

uncomfortably behind my ear, head dropping for a beat before I forced myself to look at him. "Come on, Uncle Rex. I know you have something to say about this. Know you're pissed. Thing is, I'm not sure if it's because I left or came back or have a kid or if it was because I was with Frankie in the first place."

He wanted me to cut to it, then so be it.

He blew a sigh into his palms and rubbed his face before he dropped his hands. "A little bit of all of them, Evan."

Acceptance had me nodding, but it wasn't close to being in surrender. "I get that."

He chewed at the edge of his lip. "Thing is, when you have a daughter you were solely responsible for until she was five-years-old? When you love her so damn much you can't see straight? When she is your entire world and the only thing you want is for her to have the very best? I think it's not hard to imagine that I would have a problem accepting there was someone that could ever be good enough to fit the bill."

Wasn't sure if it was an objection or agreement that was getting ready to come off my tongue, but he held up his hand to stop me from saying anything. "And it's even harder when you realize she found that person at such a young age. Hard to watch a little girl love with everything she has. It's terrifying being afraid she might be crushed if she lost it."

Guessed Frankie and I hadn't even come close to managing to hide it.

His mouth pinched when he shook his head. "And when you took yourself from her? Made the choice to leave her? That was the hardest thing I've ever had to witness. Watching my child crumble, fall apart, and be helpless to do anything about it."

Emotion clotted the airflow at the base of my throat, knives of regret impaling my skin. "I never wanted to hurt her."

"Don't imagine much that you did, but the fact of the matter is you left her, Evan. You up and left her without a word and then came riding back with a kid three years later. After she's finally, finally moved on."

Knew his voice was strained with emphasis.

My brow twisted, half apology, half aggression. "Jack's an

asshole. She doesn't belong with him. She belongs with me."

His nod was slow. "You're right. She belongs with you." He pushed off the counter, cocked his head to the side as he took one step my direction. "So don't you dare stand behind your disability and say you are protecting her when who you are protecting is yourself. When it's you who is scared of losing her. You love her? Fucking prove it."

Lifting my jaw, I gave him all the honesty I had. "That's why I wanted you to come, Uncle Rex. To tell you that is exactly what I intend to do. To tell you it was wrong that we kept it from you, and I was a fool to leave. It is the biggest regret of my life. But I'm here, and I'm not going anywhere."

He huffed a breath through his nose, and he moved toward me, shocking the hell out of me when he pulled me in for an overbearing hug. Arms tight for a full two seconds. He clapped me on the shoulder and then squeezed it when he pulled away. "It's good to have you home, Evan. We missed you."

Frankie Leigh fumbled along the sidewalk as I led her toward the single step, the blindfold hiding the thrill I knew would be waiting behind those gorgeous eyes.

"What are we doing, Evan?"

"I told you, I have a surprise for you."

"I know you did, but I've been wearing this thing since you showed up at the café and kidnapped me."

"Believe me, it will be worth it."

Unable to see, she focused all of her excitement on that bottom lip she was chewing to shreds.

Fucking loved it.

Loved her.

Loved it all.

It bottled in my chest.

Pushing and expanding.

Getting ready to blow.

I'd never been so happy in my entire life.

"Easy, there's a step," I warned her as I helped her up it. The white wooden planks thudded under our feet.

Could see the questioning grin quirk at the corner of her mouth. "Where are we?" she asked, already in awe before she even knew what to be in awe about.

"Where I want you to be," I told her. Wondering if she could feel the disturbance.

The restless harmony.

The peaceful anxiety.

Yeah, I was excited.

So goddamn excited I was sweating.

I led her to a stop right in front of the door, then I inhaled the deepest breath as I swung it open. I let my fingertips flutter across her mouth, her nose, her cheek before I finally removed the blindfold from her eyes and urged her across the threshold.

Confusion contorted every line on her stunning face, her eyes rushing to take in the massive room we stepped into.

Hope and a future echoing back.

So it turned out if you had enough money you could make things happen quick.

I'd sped through the process of buying and had the house furnished in a handful of days.

I stood back and watched her as she took the whole place in. Bewilderment that slowly turned into a soft wonder. She finally turned back to me. *EVAN, WHAT IS THIS?*

I slowly edged her way. *IT'S LOVE, FRANKIE. THIS HOUSE IS LOVE.*

Knew she was trying to stop them, but tears streamed from her eyes. *FOR US?*

IF YOU WANT IT.

There was a question there.

A petition.

A call.

I dropped to a knee and pulled out the ring I had in my pocket.

Frankie's hands went to her mouth.

No, I couldn't see what she was saying.

But I felt it.

I knew it.

"When I was eight, I promised you I'd marry you for real, Frankie Leigh. I told you again when you were eighteen. I think it's time I kept that promise."

twenty-eight

Frankie Leigh
Eighteen Years Old

Frankie Leigh blew out the candles on her birthday cake. She was pretty danged proud of herself when she snuffed out all eighteen in one fell swoop. Oh, but she was determined to get that one wish.

It cast the entire kitchen into darkness as a roar of cheers and hollers echoed through her parents' house.

The lights flicked back on. She blinked against the brightness, and she grinned when she saw all her family and friends staring back. Still shouting and clapping where they were gathered around the table.

"Happy birthday, Frankie Leigh!"

"Whoop, whoop, Frankie's an adult!"

"Watch out, Sweet Pea is getting ready to take on the world."

Love overflowed. Frankie Leigh was so grateful to everyone who had gathered to celebrate her. She thought literally every person in her family had to be there, plus a mess of friends from high school and a few other people she'd met along the way.

All of them were stuffed into the kitchen and overflowing into the living room.

Maybe it was wrong, but her heart sought out only one person. Evan.

Her eyes immediately raced to where she knew that he would be. That gorgeous boy was up against the wall just outside of the commotion, like he wasn't sure that he wanted to slip into the fray.

On the outskirts when the only thing she wanted was him by her side.

Sipping at a beer, he watched her in a way that made her tummy shiver.

Twisted inside out.

God, she'd been lovin' that boy her whole life, and she was praying it was time that he would finally love her back. The way she'd been dying for him to. In the way that she'd lie awake at night with her heart pounding and this vacant place inside of her throbbing, aching for him to fill it.

Her mama and her aunt Hope wedged their way through the chaos. "I hope you're ready to taste this, Frankie Leigh. I know what a sweet tooth you have," her aunt Hope teased as she gestured to the cake she'd made.

"Um, yes, please. That looks delicious."

"Well, you know I made it special just for you. A brand-new recipe."

"I think it's a perfect match," her mama said with a laugh.

Frankie Leigh gestured to herself. "I guess you two know me well, don't you?"

Her mama and her aunt Hope started cutting it into pieces and placing the small squares of cake on party plates.

It was this huge sheet-cake that was about as big as the table. In cursive letters, it read, "Even unicorns become adults one day," and it had a soaring unicorn flying for the moon.

It was frosted in a rainbow of colors and sprinkled with edible glitter.

Yeah, it was pretty much perfect, and Frankie's heart swelled again, loving that they knew her so well.

"Here you go, Sweet Pea Frankie Leigh. This one's for you." Her aunt Hope handed her the piece that had the unicorn horn that was made out of a waffle cone cookie and white chocolate. "I think this is worth a second wish."

But the thing was, Frankie would wish for the same wish all over again.

She only wanted one thing and it didn't cost a cent.

Frankie gave her the biggest hug. "Thank you, Aunt Hope. Thank you so much for being such an important part of my life for all these years. I hope you know how much I love you."

Pulling back, her aunt set her hand on Frankie's cheek. "It's me who's thankful for you, Frankie Leigh. My son would never have had the childhood that he did without you. I love you like you're one of my own, and I'm praying that you find all the joy in this world that you deserve."

Emotion welled up so fast that there was the threat of tears. The last thing Frankie wanted to be doing was crying on her birthday.

That would just suck.

This was a night to celebrate.

So she did.

She celebrated with her family and friends while she and Evan seemed to orbit around the other.

He remained distant, like he couldn't bear the thought of gettin' too close, all the while remaining the closest person to her there.

And she wanted to call to him. Gesture with her hands in the language they knew best.

To tell him to come stand by her side because that was where he belonged. But there was something about him tonight that knotted a ball of apprehension in her belly. Something that was sad and distant.

Like that boy felt he didn't fit in.

Everyone at the party ate and talked and danced.

Frankie Leigh opened presents. Clothes and money and gag gifts.

Frankie received a sweet ring from her parents, her uncle Ollie and aunt Nikki gave her her own camping gear, and then she opened a ridiculous check from her uncle Broderick and aunt Lillith that they said was to help with her college education.

Next, Frankie was handed a tiny box that was wrapped so pretty. The paper a shimmering pink, the ribbon streaks of silver.

Her hands started shaking when she saw it was from Evan. He was still standing way back in the back, but she knew he could feel the tremors of her anticipation. Knew he could feel her love that was already pouring out when she slipped off the ribbon, tore off the paper, and lifted the lid.

A shocked gasp raked her throat.

Pure affection.

Unending thankfulness.

Ceaseless love.

Trembling out of control, she reached and pulled the necklace from where it was nestled on a satin bed.

Never Cut Your Wings was written in a dainty white gold, and a unicorn hung from the 's', a diamond on its horn.

Heart beating so hard it almost hurt, Frankie stood. She met his eye. Energy flashed. Their connection that they'd always shared so intense, making it difficult to walk, but she did it anyway.

Weaving through the crowd toward the one who invaded her thoughts and her mind.

Her best friend.

Her best friend who she wanted to be more.

Her best friend who she wanted to be her everything.

The only thing she wanted was for him to finally really see her the way she saw him.

All those wishes she'd cast praying for that very thing.

Would he see her now?

Could he feel the depth of her love?

He almost looked sad when she made it to him, something so tender and full of wistful devotion awash in those green eyes.

"Evan," she whispered before she threw herself at him, hugging him so fiercely that she thought she could sink in and disappear in him forever. She kinda wanted to cry when he did the same, his arms firm and strong, so right when they were wrapped around her body. He murmured in her ear, "I want the world for you, Unicorn Girl. Go out and own it. It's waiting on you."

Pulling away, she brushed away her tears, hands on his shoulders as she offered him a smile that she hoped he could read.

One that promised him that he was her favorite person in the world.

That he had always been and that was never going to change.

That she was the one who was *waiting* on him.

"Happy birthday," he gruffed aloud in that raw, sexy voice, and she was so desperate for him to kiss her right there.

Right out in the open.

He'd kissed her twice before.

Once when she was thirteen. One other time last year.

Both times it'd been her begging for it. Pushing through the attraction until he'd caved, groaning when his body reacted.

Both times Evan had torn himself away like he was committing some kind of mortal sin.

She wanted to wipe that from his consciousness. Show him there was no shame in the way that they felt.

Before she could throw herself at him, her friend Nina, cut in. "Hey, I have to leave in a few minutes. I wanted to give this to you before I go."

"Oh, of course."

Reluctantly, Frankie Leigh stepped away from Evan, hating that she was so rude that she was wishing that it was just the two of them right then.

Alone.

She gave him a soft look that promised *later*, and she turned away and dug into the gift.

Guests surrounded her as the celebration continued.

Rowdy and lively and fun.

But still, she couldn't stop the anxious feeling that slithered into her spirit.

Unsettled and vacant.

Restless, she let her gaze hunt through the crowd.

Searching for him.

Already knowing he was gone before her eyes could confirm

it.

She did her best to just wait. To enjoy her party.

She waited until the last person left, and she hugged each guest tight, telling them how grateful she was that they came.

She stayed and helped clean up the mess. Her daddy and her brothers took all the folding chairs and tables out to the shed, and she and her mama swept up the floors and loaded the dishwasher.

When they finished, her daddy looked at her from across the kitchen, his smile soft. "I can't believe my baby girl is eighteen. Blows my mind . . . seein' you all grown up. Wild Child."

Tenderness filled his words.

Wistfulness overflowed, and Frankie wondered how much more affection she could take before she completely burst with it. Her voice quivered with sincerity, "I am so thankful that I got to have my childhood with you as my daddy. You were the best one I ever could have asked for."

Emotion crested in his eyes. "You will always be my little girl."

Crossing the room, Frankie hugged him tight. "And you will always be my daddy. Age doesn't change that. Things just look a little different now."

"That's what I'm afraid of," he said with a rough chuckle. Nostalgia rimming his features, he touched her chin. "Good night, Sweet Pea."

Frankie Leigh turned to her mama and hugged her just as tight. "Thank you, Mama, for being the woman I needed. The woman my daddy needed. Our lives were made complete in you."

Only Frankie knew she was still missing one person.

Her mama touched her face, her smile full of wonder. "It has been my absolute honor to get to be your mama, Frankie Leigh, and I am so excited to see what you do with this new stage of your life."

"I love you."

"I love you more than you'll ever know," her mama said before she released her and retreated upstairs as well.

Frankie climbed the stairs behind her, only she had no intention of turning in.

She rushed into her room and changed her clothes and slipped right back out the door. She hopped in her car and drove to the small apartment complex by the college where he now lived.

She parked and got out, nerves coiling her stomach in a gazillion intricate knots. Excitement declaring anarchy on any bit of self-control that she had.

Above, the heavens were strewn with a cascade of stars, the air crisp and cool and brushing her overheated skin.

Frankie moved for his door, and she rang the doorbell that she knew would trigger the light inside.

It felt so much like she was flashing her SOS at Evan's window, the way she'd done all their years growing up.

I need you.

I need you.

I need you.

Only tonight, it was meant in an entirely different way.

A second later, the door cracked open and he peered out.

"Frankie Leigh." He mumbled it like he hadn't expected her to come which was ridiculous in itself.

"Hi."

"Hey."

Wary, he widened the door and stepped back, and she slipped all the way into his tiny apartment. Standing just inside, she gazed at the boy who had somehow become a man.

So beautiful in every way.

His hair mussed like he'd been tugging his fingers through it.

He was wearing no shirt, only a pair of dark jeans.

His feet bare.

God. Why did she think that was sexy, too?

FRANKIE LEIGH, WHAT ARE YOU DOING HERE?

She took a single step his direction. He took one back. *YOU ACT LIKE YOU DIDN'T KNOW I WOULD COME.*

He sighed, and moved over to the chair he'd been sitting on, took a sip of his beer before he set it aside. He seemed to hesitate before he lifted his hands to speak. *YOU SHOULD BE OUT WITH YOUR FRIENDS.*

She was certain he didn't believe that statement any more than she did. Her head slowly shook, that energy gaining momentum, her heart going thug, thug, thug as she confessed her truth.

YOU ARE THE ONLY PERSON I WANT TO BE WITH.

He leaned over, and he roughed a hand over the top of his head.

Sadness gushed out.

She edged forward, wearing the outfit she knew he would like, wanting to catch his attention. But more than that she wanted him to know how special that he was. What he meant to her. The way he made her feel.

She inched all the way forward until her fingers were taking the place of his, and she urged him to look up at her in the shadows of his living room.

"What's wrong?" she asked, a shiver taking her whole at the way his eyes watched her mouth. She bet this boy could read her like a book.

The way she was shaking.

The way she was trembling all over.

Her nerves running wild.

His attention flitted to the neckless she already wore around her neck.

One she was never goin' to take off.

His throat bobbed when he swallowed. "Wanted to give you something special for your birthday."

She fiddled with the white gold. "You did. I love it. I'll cherish it forever."

Sorrow left him on a breath, so heavy, and he hung his head again. She brushed her fingers down his jaw, and he finally returned his gaze to her, his eyes pinching at the sides. "I . . . I wanted to try to be better, Frankie. I thought maybe . . . maybe I could be good enough for you."

Confusion twisted through her spirit, worry catching hold, and she wriggled herself closer until the outside of her legs were wedged between his knees. "What are you talking about, Evan?" she asked quietly, loving that he could hear her that way even when he couldn't really hear her at all.

He blinked a bunch of times. Like he wanted to reject what he needed to say.

I'M NOT A CANDIDATE.

There was so much pain, so much surrender in his movements, that Frankie's lungs squeezed tight.

So hard that she was hit with a swell of dizziness.

So tight that she suddenly couldn't breathe.

Was . . . was he talking about his heart?

Was he sick again?

Frankie tried with all her might not to drop to her knees in dread, but she did anyway when he hung his head.

Climbing to the floor so she could reach him.

Trembling like mad, she grasped both sides of his face. "Not a candidate for what?"

In frustration, he gestured at his ear. "For cochlear implants. I . . ." *I JUST WANTED TO BE HALFWAY NORMAL FOR YOU, FRANKIE LEIGH. FIX ONE GODDAMN THING. BE THE KIND OF MAN YOU NEED. I'M SORRY, FRANKIE. I'M SORRY.*

He slipped so quickly into his first language.

The movements of his hands beautiful.

Sensuous.

But Frankie was horrified by what he said.

She grabbed him by the wrists to stop him. "Why in the world would you say that? Why would you ever think I want you any different than you are? I love you, Evan."

His eyes pinched closed for a flash, and she reached out to sign against the scar that ran down his chest. *YOU ARE MY FAVORITE.*

His eyes weren't even open, but she knew he could feel it anyway.

He finally opened his lids and the confession was tumbling the second their gazes met. "I'm in love with you, Evan."

"Frankie." He said it like a warning. Like it was absurd.

She didn't care. Shying away wasn't exactly her style. She held him tighter, her frantic stare locked on him.

"Tell me you don't love me back, and we can curl up on your couch and watch a movie the way we always do, but don't you dare lie to me."

Frankie was shocked by how quickly he gripped her by the side of the neck.

Her pulse stampeded out of control as the man gazed up at her.

Intensity bloomed in the space.

A flashfire that shocked straight to her soul.

"I have always loved you, Frankie Leigh. Always. I love you so fucking much it hurts."

Frankie's heart slammed against her ribs. A frantic bam, bam, bam. Her pulse a thunder in her ears as she listened to the words that were the most perfect harmony.

He loved her.

He loved her.

She wasn't going to waste any time.

She slowly stood.

Everything grew dense.

The air and their breaths and the weight of their stare.

I LOVE MY NECKLACE, BUT THE ONLY THING I EVER WANTED IS YOU. I WISHED FOR THIS, EVAN. I WISHED FOR YOU.

Evan groaned, and his palm was running up the side of her bare leg. Chills scattered in its wake.

"I shouldn't do this, Frankie," he muttered in that scraping way. "It's not right. I meant what I said tonight. I want the best things in this life for you, and I can't give that to you."

She set her hand on the side of his head, and the man leaned into it, desperate for her touch. "You're wrong. You are the best thing. Don't take that away from me."

"You don't want this life. Believe me."

"I do. I do. I do."

Could he hear her chanting it?

Could he hear her soul singing it?

His hand tremored at her flesh.

Nerves and hesitation.

"Please," she whimpered. Begging him to just give himself to her.

Once and for all.

Throat quivering, he slid his palm higher up her leg.

That connection raced.

Spun and sped.

He slipped his hand all the way up under her skirt.

That was right when his restraint turned into a long moan. "Shit . . . Frankie. Why aren't you wearing underwear?"

"I figured you'd want me only in this skirt. It is your favorite, isn't it?" she mouthed right up close to his lips.

She put on the short pink tutu that she normally wore with leggings underneath.

Not tonight.

"Yes." The word was a breath, and he was reaching around to grip her by the bare bottom.

Tingles flashed.

That severity flared.

And Frankie was shaking like crazy when she reached up and pulled off her shirt.

She wasn't wearing a bra underneath.

"Shit," Evan hissed, and he was gripping her ass tighter.

She slowly climbed onto his lap.

Evan watched her like he was the one receiving the gift.

But this was what they both deserved.

To be each other's treasure.

Their breaths mingled and their hearts hammered and Frankie was so nervous she thought she was gonna pass out.

Getting brave, she let her fingertips trace down his abdomen. God, she loved the way he reacted, the way his muscles ticked at her touch and the way he inhaled a jagged breath when she flicked the button of his jeans.

She thought he might protest, but she saw all the reservations drain out of his eyes and hunger fill them instead.

He lifted a fraction to help her nudge his jeans and underwear down his thighs, the pants jutting from his mouth hard and shallow.

He gripped her by both sides of the waist.

Fingers burrowing into her flesh.

"Frankie . . . what are you doing to me?"

"What you did to me a long time ago."

Tension bound between them.

Pressing and pulsing and suffocating.

Turbulence a shock that quivered through every cell in her body.

Because Evan was bare below her, and he was fumbling around in the drawer of the end table beside him and producing a condom. She knew he'd have them. He always did. Something his doctor had impressed upon him. That he was always prepared.

He ripped into it and, a second later, he was rolling it down his hard length that was so much bigger than she'd anticipated.

Her daddy had always told her she needed a good dose of fear, but she didn't want to feel a lick of it right then, and she was leaning up so she could mouth the words down at Evan.

Asking him to hold them.

To hold her.

To take care of her.

"You are my favorite, Evan."

"You know that you're mine."

"I saved myself for you," she barely forced out.

He threaded his fingers through her hair, those eyes so sincere. So real and open. Exposing everything she'd wanted to see. "I know, Unicorn Girl. I know. I wouldn't even have known how to be with someone else than you."

E-V-A-N.

"I love you, Frankie."

Nodding frantically, she wrapped her arms around his neck and held on with all her might as he positioned himself between her trembling thighs.

His hands were back on her hips, and he was slowly guiding her to sink down on top of him. Heat seared her to the core, too hot and too full and all wrong and just right, and oh God, she really was gonna cry. She pressed her face into his neck as he seated himself way down deep inside of her.

His hands were in her hair, tugging her back, forcing her to look at him.

And he didn't say he was sorry because she knew neither of

them were. She knew he just needed to see her face, to *hear* her as he guided her to move.

It was choppy at first. She thought maybe both of them were shocked. Overcome. Just . . . feeling the other.

Evan seemed to catch on really quick. "Frankie, oh fuck . . . shit. You feel so good. So good." He mumbled it as he started to move in these erratic juts.

Quick, desperate urges of his body.

They were gasping and gripping and clutching the other.

Their mouths open. Lips barely touching as they watched each other.

And it was short and fast and the most intense thing she'd ever experienced.

She didn't come, and that was so perfectly fine with her because Carly had already warned her it wasn't going to be great the first time, and she still thought it was the most wonderful thing she'd ever done.

Then she was learning a whole new level of wonderful when Evan kissed her tenderly, his arm around her waist as he pulled her off of him and laid her out on his rug on the middle of his living room floor.

He buried his head between her thighs and softly, slowly sent her to oblivion.

And she experienced that ecstasy all over again after she'd been fast asleep curled up in his arms and he rolled her onto her back. As he crawled back over her, watched down on her like they were both lost to a dream as he took her gently.

Tenderly.

One of her knees tucked up under his chest and his hands running her entire body.

Bliss coming on like the slow fall of snow on a Christmas mornin'.

And oh God, did she ever feel it the next morning when he perched her on the edge of the island in his kitchen, when he loved her a little harder.

And she and Evan were suddenly having each other everywhere.

Sneaking away every chance that they could get.

Laughing and loving and kissing and touching.

Dreaming and hoping and making all the promises that they could give.

She already loved him with all her heart, but she loved him even more loving him in this brand-new way.

The two of them learned the other. Experienced all they had to give and all they had to take.

Shared their fantasies and found no shame in it.

He fucked her in the shower and she sucked him off in the front seat of his car and he pinned her to the wall in the storage pantry of the café where she was pretty sure they were committing every health code violation in existence.

And he made love to her out on the soft grasses where their old treehouse was falling apart and he bent her over the back of his parents' couch with the sunlight shining through the window while everyone else was out back.

Frankie was quick to discover that she liked it a little rough. Hard and raw and full of demands, and she didn't mind at all when he wanted to try dirty, decadent things.

The boy took her in every way. Body and soul and heart and mind.

And they got so recklessly in love. So in love that nothing else mattered. Evan made promises that Frankie had wanted to hear for her whole life, and he was finally believing all the things she'd always wanted him to believe.

"I love you."
"You're mine."
"I'm going to marry you."
"Nothing can ever come between us."
And they forgot about everything except for them.
And he loved her on the Heart of Stone that could never be broken.
With the stars shining so bright above them.
Their bodies joined together.
No barrier between.
No separation.
ONE.

And everything was so perfectly right until that unbreakable rock split right down the middle.

Until the foundation they'd built crumbled beneath their feet.

twenty-nine

Frankie Leigh

*S*unlight poured in through the window, nudging me from sleep. The arms that were wrapped around me from behind curled tighter.

Their hold fierce and secure.

It seemed almost unreal. Hard to believe.

This man my haven.

A sanctuary.

Evan peppered a line of kisses along the length of my shoulder. Chills spreading across my flesh while he was makin' all these grumbly, sexy, sleepy sounds that I felt way down deep into my soul. He slipped his palm all the way down my arm until he was threading his fingers through mine where they rested on the bed.

The ring he'd put on my finger yesterday glinted in the morning light.

Surreal.

I guessed that's what this felt. A dream that I'd had for all my life that was finally coming true.

"Mornin'," he rumbled up toward my ear. He gave the lobe a

gentle nip.

Tingles spread in a slow slide of warmth.

I rolled over so I could see him, talk to him, struck again by his face and that mouth and those eyes.

I couldn't do anything but reach out to trace across every line. Mesmerized.

Belly shaking with the need that he instantly stirred up in me.

"I don't think there's anything better than wakin' up next to you," I murmured, teeth raking my bottom lip as my fingertips danced across the plush line of his, his mouth so perfect and pretty and hitting my head with a wave of dizziness.

He snuggled me closer until I was flush with every line of his naked body. "I was just getting ready to say the exact same thing."

"Then I guess we really better do this together forever." Softness came out with my words.

Amazement that we had made it to this place. Racing for the finish line. My spirit shivered, wishin' we could just dodge the obstacles that still remained in our course.

Evan kissed across my fingertips that were busy running the edges of his lips. "Why do you think I put that ring on your finger? That way I get to get lost in this sweet body every single night."

A giggle rippled free.

"Oh, you think that's the way it's gonna work, do you?"

He gave a little rock against me. "I didn't hear you complaining last night."

He gave me this wicked grin. My insides twisted up in glee. Heat skating my flesh as my mind went back to last night.

You could say we'd done a bang-up job of christening this room.

I burrowed my face in his throat to hide my smile.

Evan rolled me onto my back. Gathering me up in those strong arms, he stared down at me like I was the falling star he had wished upon. "You are so beautiful, Frankie Leigh. Do you know what you mean to me? Fact you let me put that ring on your finger? After everything? For your forgiveness? For your belief?"

Apprehension pooled in my stomach. Guilt for the unspoken words I'd yet to confess.

Uncle Kale was right. The longer I'd held onto them, the harder it was to find the right time to release them. The more it felt as if I'd been keeping a secret. The more my silence had begun to feel like I was doing nothin' but telling a lie.

I wasn't to blame. Of course, I knew that. But that didn't mean I didn't owe him the truth.

I reached up and played with the flop of hair that had fallen over his eye. "I think I'm gettin' the idea," I whispered, searching for the right way to open up. My chest tightened. I didn't know how to steal this joy from him when we finally were feeling it. When we finally had it.

I didn't want to let it go.

He brushed his fingers through my hair, his smile turning into something wistful and sweet. "I can't wait to spend my life with you."

"We're already doing it," I told him because we didn't need a wedding day to tell us we were forever.

His eyes dropped closed for a beat, and he leaned down and pressed the softest kiss to my lips. "Every day."

"Every day," I whispered back.

His phone buzzed from the nightstand. I didn't think he noticed, so I nudged him a little. "Your phone is going off."

He dipped down and pecked me on the lips before he sat up on the edge of the bed and put on his glasses.

He looked so damn good in them they should be illegal in all fifty states. A crime for him to wear them any time he wasn't looking at me.

He swiped into his phone. Could feel the mood shift. Tension ridged his back.

Worry slammed me. I couldn't help it. Couldn't help that I was immediately on edge.

Everett's mother was still out there, at large. No word in days. Seth hadn't been able to get in touch with her brother, either.

All of it sat so wrong that it left a bubble of dread sitting permanently right at the center of me.

I climbed onto my knees so I could move over and wrap myself around Evan's back. I angled around enough so that he could see me. "What is it?"

He looked up, and where I was expecting to see him upset, he was bleeding relief, his eyes flooded with hope. "It's my attorney. He got the approval from the judge to get my name on the birth certificate. He needs me to come down to his office this morning and sign some papers so he can request Everett's medical records."

I swore I could feel it—deliverance rumbling through the air. Blistering and streaking. Wrapping us in it.

Joy split my face, and I eased around farther. "I'm so happy. This is such good news."

He set one of those big palms on my face. "It's all coming together, Frankie. Our home. Our family. *Us.*"

Emotion pulsed.

I swallowed around the severity of it. "Us," I repeated.

He gave a tight nod and then pressed a kiss to my forehead. "I need to get over there. Are you okay with Everett for a couple hours so he doesn't have to sit in an office for so long?"

Awe tugged at my mouth. The fact that this was goin' to be my life. "It's my honor to care for him, Evan. Always. Every day. Without question."

Understanding moved through his features, and he dropped his forehead to mine. "Thank you, Frankie. Thank you for being you." He inhaled deep before he brushed his lips to mine.

It didn't matter how many times he kissed me—every time, the boy managed to hitch my breath. He pried himself away, the softest smirk hooking at the corner of his delicious mouth as he stood and headed for the en suite bathroom.

His glorious ass bare and on display.

God, the man was gorgeous.

I nibbled at my thumbnail, watching him go, wonderin' again if I was dreaming, but knowing if something felt this good, it had to be real.

I heard the showerhead turn on, and I laid there just listening to the sounds of life happening around me. The stark, sudden change in my path that I'd been destined for all along.

Evan was quick, in and out of the shower and dressed in ten

minutes flat.

Excited.

Anxious.

I walked him to the front door and he dipped down, kissed my mouth, smiled so sweet. "I love you, Frankie Leigh."

I clung to his shirt for the beat of a second, couldn't do anything but sign against his chest, *YOU ARE MY FAVORITE.*

I knew when he got back, today had to be the day. I couldn't keep this in any longer. It wasn't fair or right or good.

The last wedge between us.

One he didn't even know existed.

It was going to hurt.

Slash and cut and flay.

But we were strong enough to make it through it.

We had to be.

Milo did circles at my ankles, as happy as could be as I locked the door behind Evan.

I petted him behind the ears. "Hey, Milo Boy. What do you think about all of this? Completely crazy, right?"

He whimpered approval, and I dipped down to kiss him on his snout before I straightened, struck again by this house that Evan had asked me to help him make a home.

Evan had been nervous that he was bein' bold, making another decision for the two of us without my input. But he'd wanted to surprise me. To give me a gift when he'd said he'd missed so many. He'd been adamant that if I didn't love it, we could pick a different place. He'd wanted to snag it quickly since it was so close to our parents' neighborhood, and he knew he wanted to raise Everett with his grandparents nearby.

I couldn't have agreed more.

Bonus points?

The man had really good taste.

The house?

It was magic.

Gorgeous and warm and more than I ever could have imagined.

Bigger than any fairytale I could have conjured.

I knew Evan had inherited a ton of money from his grandfather, money he'd never wanted, blood relatives that he would have just as soon have forgotten.

But sometimes life brought you a buoy that you didn't anticipate.

There for you when you needed it most.

I went into the kitchen that I was sure would even make Aunt Hope jealous, and believe me, she had a kitchen to envy. I dug into the fridge that had already been stocked to find something to make for breakfast.

I chopped and hummed and swayed, my heart lighting up when the baby monitor I had sitting on the counter next to me crackled. Immediately, I glanced at the image of Everett climbing to his feet, taking hold of the railing, and jumpin' up and down.

"Da? Fi-fi? Da?"

There was no staunching the rush of affection that flooded me. Head to toe.

It wasn't like I wanted to stop it, anyway.

It was a welcomed invasion.

Setting aside the knife, I walked down the hall to his room and opened the door. The second I did, Everett started clapping his welcome. "Fi-Fi! Fi-Fi! Puppy!"

He pointed at Milo who was hot on my heels, Everett's smile so wide and open and full of joy.

"Good mornin', sweet boy. Did you have a good sleep?"

"Ehvie up." He did that adorable nod where his head bobbed all the way to his scrunched shoulders, and I got that melty feeling I felt every time I looked at this child.

I didn't hesitate, I picked him up from under the arms and swung him into mine. I cuddled him close, kissed his temple, inhaled his sweet baby scent. "Hey there, my little man."

He rubbed his entire face on my chest, and I hugged him tight as I carried him over to his changing table. I laid him down, staring down at this boy who looked so much like his daddy, all emerald trusting eyes and wide sloppy grins as he bounced his fist in the air and blabbered me a story that I cooed right back.

And I felt it.

The connection.

Our spirits twined.

I changed him out of his diaper and into fresh clothes. "There we go, my sweet Ehvie."

So, it was catchin'.

His little voice embedded in my mind and written on my soul.

I picked him back up. "Are you hungry?"

"Eat. Ehvie eat." Another nod.

We went into the kitchen, Milo trailing us, wagging his tail, Everett babbling and pointing to him as we went.

Joy pressed down on my chest. The tightness no longer a feeling of wrong or something missing, but rather that I was getting too full with all that was right.

Setting him onto his feet on the floor, I filled a plastic sectioned plate with the eggs I'd already scrambled and a few pieces of fruit I'd chopped.

"Side?" he asked, tottering over for the door to the backyard.

"Do you want to eat outside?"

He smacked his hands on the glass.

I guessed that was a yes.

Laughing under my breath, I grabbed his plate and his sippy cup.

With my elbow, I edged open the massive sliding door that basically was a wall.

Did I mention this house was magic?

I was still in awe.

Couldn't believe this was our home.

Couldn't believe this was our life.

That Evan now was legally Everett's father.

That we were so close to getting all of this figured out.

I wasn't such a fool to think that Ashley wouldn't come knocking one day. I just hoped Evan would have taken enough steps that Everett's home would be established.

That there was no chance that she could ever fully take him away.

We stepped out onto the patio that was ground-height, something that would make it easy for Everett to run out and play in the fenced backyard.

My mama and daddy had brought by the cutest toddler patio table set as a house warming gift last night, but I think it was a whole lot more of a statement than anything else.

That they were accepting him, too.

That he was goin' to be their grandchild every bit as much as he was going to be my son.

I knew Evan had spoken with them.

That he'd gone old-fashioned and pretty much asked my daddy for my hand.

I had to admit, I appreciated it, that he'd come right out and had been straightforward and admitted the things we should have confessed in the past. That this time we were doing it right.

Now I just had to take that one last step.

Fear threatened to take hold, but I stamped it down.

It no longer had any place.

I settled Everett down on one chair and placed his food in front of him.

"There you go, my sweet boy."

Tenderly, I ran my hand over the top of his head. He tipped it up when I did, rubbing his head around like he loved the connection, and he scrunched up his adorable nose, making a snorting noise.

I was a puddle of heart-warmed bliss.

Giggles flooded into the warm morning air, everything his joy, and he pinched some eggs between his chubby fingers and offered them to me. "Fi-Fi, eat."

I pretended to gobble it all up, and he laughed his belly laugh, and I didn't think I'd ever felt so happy in my entire life.

"Okay, Everett's turn. He has to eat all the rest so he can grow so, so, so big."

He started shoveling the eggs and the diced pieces of fruit into his mouth, babbling at Milo who was sitting at the ready to get whatever scraps fell to the ground.

The bounty promised to be plenty.

"*Awwa* gone," he proclaimed, his plate only left with a few bits of egg that he couldn't get, and he guzzled down a drink of his milk before he was climbing up and toddling across the lawn to the sandbox that was set up under the shade of a tree.

I watched.

Affection overflowing.

My cell rang and I glanced at it where I'd left it on the patio table.

Carly.

I grinned as I answered it. "Hey."

"Oh my God. You are in so much trouble. Tell me you did not get engaged and then didn't call and tell me."

Oh crap.

Light laughter slipped free, and I was biting at my bottom lip, trying to stop the rush of joy as I looked back at Everett.

"I was kinda busy last night," I told her.

"Um. Hello. Rude. You are never supposed to be too busy for me."

I giggled. "I'm sorry."

"I'll forgive you just as long as I get to pick your dress."

"Ha. Not gonna happen. You'll have me wearin' some boring old thing."

"Yeah, and I'll be savin' you from picking some tulled-out disaster. If you aren't careful, you're going to look like a bad rendition of Madonna from the 80s."

I chuckled a little. "Bite your tongue. I will be rockin' that vibe. You know that's exactly what I'll be going after—except in pink."

"Oh lord help us . . . I can only imagine what atrocity the bridesmaid's dresses are gonna be."

On a smile, I gazed out at Everett who was inside the sandbox. Standing there facing away. Holding a yellow shovel. Milo whined, doing a circle around him.

There was just . . . something off.

He stood there.

Unmoving.

Like he was in a daze.

Confused, maybe?

A feeling that hit the air.

That ugly, horrible spot inside of me flared.

"I've got to go," I told Carly, not even giving her a chance to say goodbye before I was sprinting across the yard.

Milo started yipping, making these whining, howling noises.

That was right when Everett toppled forward.

Face-first into the sand.

Oh my god.

Images flashed.

Evan only a little boy. Hooked up to all those machines. Her favorite, favorite froggy.

"Hurry, Daddy. You got to take me right now so I can give him my heart. He needs a good one."

I raced across the lawn. Refusing it. This couldn't be happening. "No. No, no, no, Everett, no."

Pain lanced.

Cutting me open wide.

Grief cutting me in two.

The loss. The loss.

She's gone. She's gone.

Dizziness swept in, and my mind spun, and my world tipped out onto the ground.

And I wanted to give them all my hearts. Patch them up and make them better and love them hard enough that they could never be stolen away.

So that they could breathe and live and smile.

I dropped to my knees at his side, trying not to shout out in grief when I rolled him over.

When I saw his face was purpled and swollen, his lips turning blue.

A scream bubbled up from my soul.

Agony. Agony.

I struggled to remain upright.

Not to pass out.

I was shaking. Shaking and shaking. Sickness curled my stomach. Bile crawled up my throat.

"Everett . . . sweet boy, no," I pled, blackness sweeping in to blind me at the edges of my sight. "Please, Ehvie, no."

Fingers trembling, I touched his neck, searching for a pulse.

Thready and dulled.

Not him. Please, God, not him, too.

I begged it a thousand times as I dialed 9-1-1, begged it harder when the operator came on the line when I shouted, "Please, someone help."

thirty

Evan

"This should be the last one." My attorney slid another document across the desk for me to sign.

I scanned over the words, anxiousness riding through my being.

Couldn't wait to get this done. Needed it finished. Needed to know my son would have the best care possible.

My phone buzzed where I had it rested on my thigh.

Again.

For about the fifth time.

Anxiety flared.

I tried to ignore it, to give this my entire focus.

When it buzzed with an actual call which was something my parents had done when they needed to get my attention, a sort of SOS, I quickly signed the few lines on the page and lifted my finger. "Excuse me for a second, but I need to check this."

"Not a problem," he said, thumbing through the last documents that were sitting in front of him.

I flipped into my phone, trying to shake the uneasy feeling, trying to convince myself that it was only Frankie texting to ask something about the house or Everett or an inconsequential thing, but hating that I knew she wouldn't interrupt a meeting that was so important if what she needed to say wasn't more so.

My eyes flew over the words.

Frankie Leigh: Come to GL General. Hurry.

My sight blurred, and I was pretty sure I swayed to the side as I staggered to my feet.

Everett. Everett. Everett.

My soul chanted his name.

This little boy who had swept into my life like a windstorm to rearrange everything.

To set it back to right.

No.

This couldn't be happening.

It couldn't.

He was going to be spared. I'd felt it. Prayed so damn hard for it.

"Mr. Bryant?" At least that was what I thought the attorney said, but I wasn't sure I was seeing straight when his mouth moved.

No capacity to read the words or feel their meaning.

Because the only thing I felt was *this*.

This consuming, gutting pain.

I blinked a thousand times, trying to get my bearings. "I have to go," I told him, not waiting for a response before I bolted out the door and down the long corridor to the lobby. The whole way, I tried to process through the rest of the texts that were waiting for me as I fumbled to get to my car.

Dad: Evan, you need to get down to GL General.

Dad: I can come pick you up.

Dad: Are you there?

Dad: Goddamn it, Evan, answer your phone.

Jumping into my car, I turned over the ignition and gunned it, car skidding around the corner.

Sweat slicking my skin in dread.

My heart twisted up tight in the horror.

I made the six-minute drive in three.

I blinked frantically, trying to remain coherent.

Rejecting this idea.

The curse. He couldn't have inherited it.

Grief grabbed me by the throat. Squeezed so tight I was pretty sure I was going to pass out by the time I flew into the hospital parking lot. I came to a jolting stop in the wrap-around drive. Didn't even bother to turn off the engine. I jumped out and raced for the double doors. They skated open, the cold air inside blasting me in the face.

Chills spread.

Ice cold.

I started for the emergency room desk, only to come to a dead stop when I saw Dad coming through the double doors.

Torment on this face.

Agony clawing my insides.

I shifted directions, hands moving as I raced for him.

OH GOD. WHERE'S EVERETT? IS HE OKAY? WHAT HAPPENED?

Dad quickly signed, *HE'S OKAY. HE'S OKAY.*

I nearly crumbled to the ground right there.

Relief.

I slammed into a wall of it.

Stumbling forward.

Walls spinning, disoriented by the magnitude of it.

Dad grabbed me by the outside of the shoulders to steady me. "He's okay," he reiterated.

"Oh God." It raked up my throat, and I was blinking, trying to rearrange the picture of what I'd thought I was going to be walking in on. Chest heaving, I stared at my dad. "What happened?"

Dad put up a hand like it was a sign of caution. Like he needed me to slow down so he could talk to me through the storm clouding my mind. "They are running more tests to make sure he is clear, but it looks like he had a severe allergic reaction with anaphylaxis. The pediatric cardiologist came in to see him. They aren't going to release him until they are completely certain, but right now, it doesn't appear to have anything to do with his heart."

That might not have been good news to some parents.

A severe allergy.

But for me? It was like telling me my kid had won the lottery.

I swallowed around the rocks in my throat. "Thank God," I breathed out, still blinking, trying to slow the racing of my pulse. "I thought . . . I thought . . ."

Fuck. I couldn't even say it.

He tightened his hold on the outside of my arms. "I know what you thought, Evan. All of us did. It was Frankie who was there with him, and she . . ."

His expression went dim.

I roughed a hand through my hair.

I knew exactly where her mind had gone. The terror she had to have felt. My poor, sweet girl. It was something I'd wanted to protect her from. The constant fear that you were riding the edge of losing something you loved most.

One slip, one second, and it was gone.

I NEED TO GET BACK THERE. I NEED TO GET TO THEM.

I started to round him, but Dad stopped me, and he angled his head down to make sure I was seeing him.

"Before you go in there, I need to warn you, Frankie is not okay."

My brow pinched. "Everett is okay. That's all that matters. We'll be okay." I was rambling it, my head nodding, all the adrenaline and fear I'd felt on the trip over draining out of my system.

I just wanted to get to my family.

Dad squeezed my shoulders harder. "Evan. Listen to me. The doctor needs to talk with you, and I know this is about Everett, but listen to me hard . . . talk to her. Today. It is the only way you two are going to make it in the future."

Dread clamped down on my ribs. A frown pulled across my brow, misunderstanding seeping through. "What are you saying?"

Sorrow filled his expression. "Just talk to her, Evan."

Then he turned his back and motioned for the door to the emergency room to be opened, expecting me to follow.

Legs still shaking, I did, not sure how the hell to handle the overwhelming relief that was dampened by the urgency of what Dad had said.

By what he'd implied.

I walked deeper into the depths of the emergency department.

Nurses were quick as they came and went in the small private rooms, most with the blinds drawn, and there was a large work station in the middle.

Dad led me through, and I caught the vibe of the stares. No doubt, most everyone knew him there, his reputation as one of the best physicians in Gingham Lakes preceding him.

He slowed in front of a closed door, glancing back at me once in some kind of warning before he opened it.

My heart bottomed out again when I walked through and Everett was in this odd crib. Super high railings on all sides, the front of it dropped open while a physician was checking one of the monitors he was attached to.

It didn't matter that she was there. Didn't matter that he was hooked up to a ton of wires and monitors, an oxygen tube in his nose and taped on his face to keep it in place.

I rushed for him.

Didn't say a word to the doctor when I picked him up and held him. Needing to feel him chest to chest. Heart to heart.

Overwrought with the need to feel the life running through his veins.

His little fingers dug into my shirt and I thought maybe he was relieved, too.

I breathed out, hugging him closer before I finally felt confident enough to turn my attention to the physician.

She sent me a careful smile. "You must be Evan Bryant."

"I am." I shook her hand when she extended hers.

"It's nice to meet you. I'm Dr. Lucero. I'm the pediatric cardiologist who was supposed to see Everett in my office next week, but it looks like he was impatient to see me."

She attempted to inject some humor into the mood.

I wasn't exactly feeling it.

Hugging Everett tight, I glanced around. Mom was there, anxious, tears staining her face, pacing in her worry.

But it was Frankie who was huddled in the very back corner that sent a riot of worry stampeding through me, the girl appearing so small. Like she'd been cracked wide open and she no longer knew how to hold herself together.

She refused to look at me.

But I felt her.

God. I felt her.

Hugging herself as tight as I was hugging Everett.

I wanted to go to her. Call to her. Promise her it was okay. Tell her how thankful I was that she was with him when this happened. Or maybe just bury my face in her hair and sob my guts out, so goddamn thankful that Everett was okay when I'd been certain that a day that had started out pure and perfect was going to end in tragedy.

Instead, I focused on the physician, trying to keep the trembling out of my hand when I shook hers. "It's nice to meet you."

Encouragement filled her smile. "I spoke with your father at length about your disabilities as well as the concern for Everett. I took him for an emergency echocardiogram, and I see no abnormalities. I want to order an MRI in order to be certain, but I'm confident this test will be negative as well."

I wanted to drop to my knees with the sheer magnitude of the relief.

My nose went to Everett's cheek, inhaling his sweet scent.

The innocence and vulnerability.

Overwhelmed by the miracle.

Overcome by the grace.

It was all mixed up with the flickers of grief and shame and guilt that had crowded in, crawling out from where I'd had them chained, threatening to take me over.

Thinking I'd condemned my son.

After everything, I didn't think there was a chance I would have been able to stand under the misery of that.

"God." My eyes pressed closed, relishing in the deliverance. I blew out a heavy breath.

Dr. Lucero continued to explain, "The emergency room physician will be in to speak with you. He is the one who treated the allergic reaction with anaphylactic shock. There will need to be further testing with that, but all symptoms point to a severe food allergy. He responded quickly to the epinephrine dosage. But in light of his emergency room visit, I've made a call to expedite the rest of his genetic testing so we can clear him before he is discharged. I hope to have a definitive answer for you this evening, even though I would still like him to keep his appointment with me next Wednesday so we can go over the results in detail."

I nodded understanding. "Okay. Yes. Good."

So maybe I wanted to shout.

To sing.

To chant with this joy.

She turned her gaze to Everett with a sympathetic smile. "It's a huge relief, I know. He is such a sweet boy."

She cast a slight nod to everyone in the room. "Someone will be in momentarily to take him for the MRI. I'll be back in to speak with you as soon as I have the outcome of that test."

My dad spoke at my side, "Thank you, Dr. Lucero."

"It's my pleasure. I'll talk with you soon."

She glanced around at everyone in the room, offering a soft, reassuring smile as she exited.

The door shut behind her.

The aura in the room shivered.

Rays of relief and streaks of sorrow.

Mom sniffled, swiped at her tears. "Evan. Thank God."

She threw herself at me. Hugged us hard. Letting go of the fear she'd been holding.

Maybe it was the first time I got a real glimpse into what she must have felt when I was a child.

When I'd been clinging to life.

Skating the edge of death.

I was certain it was only her faith that had kept me here.

She leaned back, her cheeks wet, her gaze soft. She set her hand on my cheek. "Thank God."

I nodded at her, though it felt difficult to move beneath the torment that still flooded the room.

Thick and dense and unrelenting.

"Can you take him?" I asked, knowing I needed to get to Frankie Leigh.

"Absolutely."

Mom took him, and I planted a kiss to his temple before I warily turned around to where she was tucked back in the farthest corner, still hugging herself with her head dropped, like she could disappear into the wall.

Could see she was trying to restrain the sobs that wracked her body.

Had only seen her like this once before—the last time we'd been together in this hospital.

Regret gusted and blew.

And I wondered what she'd thought. What she'd had to go through this morning.

I inched her way. "Frankie."

Could feel her name slice through the dense air.

Could feel her flinch.

I kept moving that way, and with each cautious step I took, she slowly lifted her head.

"Frankie," I murmured.

She turned to look up at me.

My chest squeezed.

The girl demolished.

Crushed.

Eyes red-rimmed and swollen.

Her spirit tortured.

Thrashing and flailing as it seeped into the atmosphere.

"Frankie, sweet girl." The words barely made it over the gravel lining my throat. "It's not your fault."

Her mouth twisted, the girl choking out a sound that I knew shouted with misery. She pressed her face into both her hands, and I tried to pry them away.

"Frankie. Please, Frankie. Stop crying, sweetheart. It's good news. It's such good news."

We needed to be celebrating.

Loving and laughing and hugging.

But her head shook in rejection.

Trembles tumbling down her spine and wracking through her body.

I could feel the piercing gaze of my dad, and I glanced that way, remembering the dire warning he'd given. He angled his head for us to follow him.

"Hey, sweet girl. Please . . . come with me. We need to talk."

She clutched her chest at that, but she was nodding through the tears that kept pouring out, her head tipped down, refusing to fully face me.

Gulping around the distress, this alarm that screamed and pounded and roared in my chest, I took her by the elbow to guide her out.

Dad led us to a private waiting room, didn't say anything as we stepped inside, let the door swing shut behind him.

As soon as he did, I turned and took her by the face.

Forced her to look at me.

"Frankie . . . what is it?"

Tears raced into my hands.

"Evan, I'm so sorry. I'm so, so sorry."

thirty-one

Frankie Leigh
Eighteen Years Old

*F*rankie Leigh knocked quietly at the office door. She was so
nervous she thought she was going to throw up.

Nausea coiled in her stomach.

Nerves frayed and sparking and making her twitch.

From the other side of the door, she heard her uncle Kale call,
"It's open."

Visibly shaking, she turned the knob.

This was the only place she could go.

Surprise curled her uncle Kale's face into a questioning smile.
"Frankie Leigh. What are you doing here? Come in and have a
seat."

He gestured to the two chairs that sat opposite his desk.
Probably thousands of his patients had sat right there in front of
him through the years, and she knew he would have given gentle
diagnoses and plans and words of hope.

Frankie was almost afraid to feel any of it.

Terrified. Scared. Overjoyed.

Hope.

But it was there, and she prayed he would be able to help her. That he would know what to do.

She shuffled into his office and uneasily took a seat. Nervously, she twined her fingers over and over, trying not to rock to soothe herself, but doing it anyway.

Her uncle immediately caught on to her distress, and he stood from the desk. Rounding it, he came to kneel in front of her. He touched her knee. "Sweet Pea. What is going on?"

"I need your help, Uncle."

He searched her face. "Of course. I've always told you that you could come to me for anything."

She sniffled. "I know. That's why I'm here. Because you're the only person I can trust, and the only person who will really understand."

Worry passed through his features, but he just knelt there, waiting.

The supporter he'd always been.

How many times had she sat in front of him as his patient? As a tiny girl, her daddy used to constantly rush her to the ER for any little scrape or bruise. Her daddy always so terrified to lose her. That this cruel world might steal her away from him.

Right then, Frankie Leigh fully understood.

"What's going on, Frankie. You can tell me, trust me, with anything."

A tear slipped free, and she frantically brushed at her cheek, that worry bottling in her chest and spinning her head and making her sick all over again. "I'm pregnant."

She guessed that maybe he didn't look all that shocked. She was eighteen and known to be wild and reckless and the first to experience every single thing in life.

What else would she be coming to him this way for? A freaking cough?

She knew he knew better than that.

But the thing was, he was also Evan's father.

Even though she knew he was trying to hide it, she saw the

distress that blazed through his expression.

She twisted her fingers so tight they were blanching white, cutting off circulation.

He exhaled a heavy sigh, contemplated, glancing to the wall before he looked back at her. His voice cracked. "Is it Evan's?"

Her nod was jerky, and the tears started coming faster. She sniffed, reached up to try to wipe the moisture away. "Yes."

She and Evan hadn't told anyone about their relationship.

Maybe they'd been having too much fun sneaking around.

Loving the feel of something scandalous and secret and special even when them being together made perfect sense.

She wondered just how obvious they were.

If she was obvious then.

If anyone else would know.

"Oh, God, Frankie." His brow pinched. "Are you okay?"

She choked out a disbelieving sound. Of course, he would think to ask her how she felt. Exude all his care. She gave a harsh shake of her head. "No, Uncle Kale, I don't think that I am. I'm . . . I'm scared. I'm so scared and I don't know how to keep this inside any longer."

Evan had crammed it into her head thousands of times that he could never give her a family. That he could never take that chance. Told her to chase after something better. Told her to go after what he believed was a better life because there was a part of him that believed he was nothing but a sickness and disease.

But the thought of this child as something different than extraordinary broke her heart right in half.

"We were careful, Uncle."

Except for the couple times that they weren't.

When they'd been so caught up in the other that they didn't have time to think about anything else.

Consequences or gifts.

Guilt seared through her flesh, cutting her open wide.

God, what had she done?

"I . . . I don't know what to do," she admitted, feeling her mouth tremble all over the place.

Her uncle's brow pinched. "He doesn't know?"

Her throat bobbed, and she tried to swallow around the mountain of jagged rocks that were gathered there, boulders pressing down on her chest.

The weight too much.

"No. Oh God, Uncle. He's . . . he's going to be so upset. He's told me so many times that this can *never* happen."

But it was already happening.

"He has a right to know, Frankie."

"I know. I'm going to tell him. I will. I just . . . have to make a plan. Figure out what we're going to do."

His nod was one of reluctance. "Do you know when your last period was?"

She dropped her head, more of that shame streaking free, whispered toward her lap, "Almost four months ago."

"God, Frankie." That was the first amount of disappointment he'd shown.

But she'd ignored it for too long. Tried to will it away before she'd started to beg for it to stay.

He shook his head like he was trying to shake off any judgment. His voice softened. "What do you want to do, Frankie Leigh? Do you know?"

It was the one thing she did know in all this mess.

She ran her hand tenderly over her belly, a wistful smile breaking through the tears that kept streaming down her face. "I love her, Uncle. I love her so much."

Her uncle seemed to struggle, both trying to be the man he'd always promised her he would be. Supportive. But it was up against the outright worry that instantly sagged his shoulders. Dimmed his eyes. "Okay. We need to start with some testing."

"No, Uncle. Please. Don't say that." It was a whimper.

Sorrow rushed and spilled and spun the walls. She couldn't see. Refused to hear.

"I'm sorry, Frankie Leigh, but her heart abnormalities are incredibly severe. There is little chance of her making it to term, let alone through delivery."

She tried to hold it back, but the sob broke free. She pressed her hand to her mouth.

Trying to keep in the hope. Not to let it go. If she believed hard enough, it would be.

She rocked in the same chair she'd been sitting in for the last five hours. She'd been there waiting and waiting and waiting in a private office after she'd been sent for a special echocardiography in Birmingham.

Her uncle Kale had driven her there after he'd arranged for her to meet with a fetal cardiologist.

Her entire world had dropped out from under her when it had only been him coming through the door to give her the results.

She'd known it the second she'd seem him.

Mourning already engraved on his face.

She pressed her hands to her chest, angling forward. "There has to be something that can be done. There has to be. She . . . she can get a transplant like Evan did. Evan is perfect. She'll be perfect, too." The words tumbled free. A prayer. A plea.

Sadness shook his head. "Frankie."

"No, Uncle, no."

It wasn't fair. Wasn't fair that this curse could steal the life right out of her hands.

Evan.

Oh God, Evan was going to be destroyed.

Blame himself forever.

She gasped for a breath.

It felt like her lungs were collapsing.

Closing in.

Shutting down.

"Please," she begged, pain sheering through her insides. Twisting her in half. Cutting her in two.

He climbed down to his knees in front of her. "I am sorry, Frankie. I . . . I am devastated over this, and I know it doesn't come close to what you are feeling right now." He took her by the hand. "If there was anything . . . anything in this world that I could do, you know that I would. I have to recommend you terminate this pregnancy, Frankie Leigh."

She clutched at her chest, feeling like her heart was getting ripped right out. "No. No. I can't do that."

"Frankie."

"I can't." She clawed away from him, flying from the chair, shaking her hands out in front of her like it could possibly wake her up from this nightmare. She paced, stumbled, tried not to fall to her knees.

But she was breaking.

Breaking, breaking, breaking.

And she had no idea how she was going to come back from this.

How would she ever tell Evan?

The movement of his hands flew behind her eyes. Memories ingrained.

The statements that he'd made.

FRANKIE, WE AREN'T GETTING MARRIED OR HAVING BABIES OR LIVING HAPPILY EVER AFTER. WE WERE JUST LITTLE KIDS. YOU NEED TO GET OVER THAT.

Oh God. Oh God.

Tears raced and her pulse shuddered and her mind whirred with the thoughts.

Flashes of hopes and dreams and dread and fear.

She remembered her childhood belief. All the hearts she'd sewn into that froggy for Evan. Believing there would always be one there for him if he needed it.

If only she could do that for this child. Believe hard enough, and it would be.

She clutched at the bump that was just beginning to show.

Agony clawed as a rush of love flooded into her system.

She looked back at her uncle Kale. "I can't."

They drove in silence back to Gingham Lakes. Music quietly playing. A melody that was meant to soothe, but there was no comfort that Frankie Leigh could find.

She rubbed mindlessly at the bump.

Baby girl. Baby girl.

And she prayed with all she had that she could feel her. That she would know, even if she never got to hold her, that she would be forever loved. That Evan wouldn't take it on as a burden.

As a sin.

The phone ringing through the speakers nearly made her jump out of her skin. Everything too sensitive. Too sharp. Too shrill.

Hope's name came up on the dash screen. "Hey, baby," Uncle Kale answered, though his voice was subdued. Different than his normal casual easiness.

But Aunt Hope. Aunt Hope was screaming on the other end of the line. "It's Evan. He collapsed in class. They brought him by ambulance . . . he wasn't breathing. Oh, God. Kale."

A guttural sob tore from Frankie's throat.

Instant.

Like it'd been waiting right there to explode.

Climbing out from where it had rotted and decayed. From the deepest, most sinister place. From that place that would whisper its menace in her ear, tell her she was going to lose everything that meant the most to her.

It was the first time she believed it might speak the truth.

E-V-A-N.

She rushed into the hospital room.

He was breathing.

Alive.

Whole.

She dropped to her knees at his bedside.

Sobbing and sobbing and sobbing.

Because she couldn't control it anymore.

She was weak.

Losing the battle.

"Oh God," she whimpered, pressing her face into his arm, fingers digging into his skin, inhaling him, wanting to crawl on top of him and hug him tight and beg him to never leave her alone.

She wanted to attach herself to him in some fundamental way. Seep into his bloodstream and heal all that was wrong. Do it for their child who would never know what it was like to run and play.

"I can't, Evan, oh God, I can't."

A swell of sickness slammed her, and fumbled for the trash bin next to his bed, and she puked up the little that was in her stomach.

No longer able to keep it together.

No longer able to keep herself from fallin' apart.

He reached for her.

Squeezed her hand.

So much sorrow in his expression. Green eyes overflowing with an apology.

"I'm sorry," he said, brushing his thumb across the tears soaking her cheek. "I am sorry, Frankie."

She kept weeping, unable to stop.

"I can't, Evan. I can't," she was rumbling, tears a blanket down her face, wanting to tell him about the baby but unable to force the words from her tongue. "I can't."

Evan pulled her close, ran his fingers through her hair, pressed a kiss to the top of her head. "It's okay."

But it was so, so not okay.

Frankie Leigh.

My Sunshine.

My Unicorn Girl.

I am the most selfish man. I've been taking what I never should have. Stealing more time than I should have been given.

But I saw it today.

I saw that look on your beautiful face.

I saw more pain than any person should have to suffer.

I saw the childless.

I saw a widow.

I saw a life of unreasonable sorrow.

I can't be responsible for that. I can't hold you back. I can't stand in your way.

Loving you will always be my greatest treasure.

Letting you go my greatest pain.

Soar to the stars, Unicorn Girl. And don't ever, ever let anyone clip your wings. I won't let that be me, anymore.

Evan

Clutching the letter to her chest, Frankie Leigh dropped to her knees.

Finally conquered by the pain.

Nothing left to give.

No hope left.

"Evan. Evan. Evan. I need you. Oh God, I need you."

She whimpered his name again and again. Praying for him to come back to her. To wrap her up and tell her it would be all right. To remind her where they had been written in the stars. Her constellation.

Emptiness howled.

Vacancy echoed back.

Frankie Leigh alone. Abandoned. The way Evan had warned.

Only he was the one who chose it.

When she awoke in the middle of the night, she knew. It was the quietest kind of heartache. The kind she waded through slowly. The kind that hitched her soul up in a surrendered sort of agony.

The stillness that echoed inside of her.

The little soul she could no longer feel.

Tears streamed silently down her face, everything numb except for her heart.

Her mind and her spirit and her body that felt like they had floated out into the universe, chasing after what was lost.

She didn't change out of her pajamas. She just slipped into her flipflops, took her purse, and eased out the door.

She moved right toward Evan's parents' house.

She'd crossed that road a million times.

But tonight—tonight the sky was starless.

As if all the constellations had fallen.

Pure darkness taking its place.

She rapt at the door, listened to the creak of the stairs and squinted when the porch light flickered on overhead. Her uncle Kale slowly opened the door.

He looked like he'd aged fifteen years in the six weeks since Evan had left.

Depression taking hold.

Frankie couldn't even bring herself to look in the mirror.

Couldn't bring herself to see the hollowness staring back.

"Frankie," he murmured urgently.

She set her hand on her belly, and she whispered, "She's gone."

She'd thought that maybe she could handle it all.

Had thought maybe she was strong enough.

But that splintered Heart of Stone that couldn't be broken?

It finally completely split in two.

Evan

I dropped to my knees.

Reduced to a puddle of tears and heartbreak and apology.

I buried my face in her stomach, held her by the hips like I could breathe healing into her body, into her soul, while Frankie Leigh just kept weeping.

Though I could feel it.

She was detached.

Hovering somewhere in the periphery.

Gone to the story she had just told.

Swept away in the grief.

"Oh, God. Frankie. I'm so sorry. I'm so sorry."

I tried to gather her closer, but her head shook, her knees week. Girl so distraught I could feel the pulses of misery shuddering through her shaking body. Or maybe it was only mine ricocheting back.

Pain searing through the atmosphere.

More than either of us could bear.

I'd been responsible for the one thing I'd sworn I would never be.

Reckless with Frankie.

Reckless with life.

It was an affliction that was supposed to have ended with me.

I never should have let it happen.

A child. Our child. Our little girl.

"Frankie," I begged again, trying to get her to focus on my face. To look at me. To see me.

But she'd retreated.

Withdrawn into herself.

Everything going dim and dark.

"Frankie, please, look at me."

Her head shook, her eyes distant as she tried to back away.

"I'm so sorry, Frankie. Fuck. I never meant to hurt you this way."

I watched her mouth, her lips moving slow, like she was speaking from someplace faraway.

From three years ago when I'd betrayed her.

Left her when she needed me most.

"I was so mad at you for leavin' me, Evan. So angry, and still, I totally understood why you did it. Accepted it. Forgave you a long time ago."

Sorrow trembled on the edges of her gorgeous mouth that was soaked with her tears.

An apology written in this smile that ripped me in two. "But this mornin'? I think . . . I think I'd buried it, never really dealt with the grief of it. I just stuffed it down and let it fester and thought it would get better. And today it got loose. And right now, I don't know how to handle it."

Shame eclipsed her light, and she fumbled to step back.

Agony filled her movements, the closest she'd let her spirit come to me since she'd started confiding the truth I should have been man enough to hold then.

WHAT IF I'M TOO AFRAID TO LOVE HIM RIGHT? WHAT IF I'M NOT ENOUGH? I . . . I CAN'T BREATHE, EVAN . . . CAN'T BREATHE AT THE THOUGHT OF LOSING A CHILD ALL OVER AGAIN.

Pushing to standing, I tried to wrap my hands around hers. To stop this madness. To stop this girl from shouldering any more blame. "No, Frankie. You saved him. He needed you, and you did exactly what he needed you to do. That's what parents do. They do the best that they can. This is *my* fault. The sorrow you've harbored. The child. The fact you were alone. My. Fault."

Knew my voice was cracking. Begging this girl to see. To once and for all be the man she needed me to be.

"Please, let me hold the sorrow. It hurts so goddamn bad, Frankie, knowing what we created. That we lost it. That I wasn't there to hold you through it. But I need you to know how badly we need you. Everett and I. Right now. Today. Forever. And I know you need us, too."

Squeezing her eyes closed, she stepped back, rejecting what I said. "I . . . I think I need to go, Evan. I need . . ."

She blinked like she didn't know what that was.

Lost in the wreckage of what I'd done.

"Frankie."

She put up a hand. "Please, Evan . . . I just . . . please."

She started for the door.

"Frankie." My voice stopped her when she was halfway out, her broken gaze meeting mine from over her shoulder. "I ran, Frankie, because I was scared. Because my life and who I was and the hardship of it felt like it was too much. I was wrong. I belong here. Just like you belong with us."

Tears kept falling down her face, and her teeth clamped down on her bottom lip. "It hurts, Evan, and I'm scared I might love him too much."

Then she slipped out. Taking the storm of energy with her.

Staring at the closed door, I realized it only took one mistake to change the trajectory of our lives.

One mistake to cause a fallout that would rain forever.

One mistake and the consequences were more than we could afford.

But sometimes . . . sometimes we received mercy for our sins.

Grace in our errors.

A blessing given in the middle of the curse.

She might be scared, but Frankie needed to see that Everett was ours.

He was our second chance.

Our vindication.

And the three of us, we belonged together.

thirty-three

Frankie Leigh

*N*ight crawled along the ceiling where I lie sleepless in my old bed at Carly and Josiah's. Swimming in a sea of anxiety. A vat of misery. Lying in a pool of sweaty, sticky suffering that made me feel like I was gonna drown.

I kicked my legs free of the covers, feeling like I was being incinerated.

Burned at the stake.

I tossed, and I tossed again, unable to get comfortable because I knew all the way deep down that this wasn't where I belonged.

My sweet boy Milo wasn't here.

Everett wasn't here.

Evan wasn't here.

This wasn't my home, but I didn't know how to return to it.

Didn't know how to stand up. How to wade through the shame.

And I realized that was what it was.

Maybe I'd never gotten to the point where I'd fully allowed myself to feel it before. I'd been too worried about what the truth would do to Evan. Terrified that he would slip into a deep depression and blame himself.

Thing was, that meant I'd never allowed myself to process.

To accept.

To heal what was inside.

It wasn't anyone's fault.

Logically, I knew that. Of course, I did. But once the scabs had been ripped from the old wounds, I'd felt it in a sudden rush.

Realized what I'd been harboring.

Shame.

There was a huge part of me that felt as if I'd failed as a mother. Failed that innocent girl who I was supposed to protect and give life.

If only I would have slept more or eaten differently or did something better, she might have had a chance.

If only I would have gone in earlier.

Sought help rather than hidden it away.

I'd felt it all over again this morning.

The feeling that I had failed so miserably that I really didn't deserve the chance.

With it, came the stunning fear that had come in for a rebound.

The terror of losing it all over again.

What ifs slamming me as I'd replayed it over and over.

Me in that kitchen dicing up those strawberries without a care in the world because I'd felt so utterly blissed out this morning.

No thought given that I might be harmin' him. That beautiful, sweet boy who had been given into my care who I'd come to love with all my soul.

Like his little life had found a way to beat inside of me.

God.

Losing him?

Shivers rolled across my flesh.

Sickness roiling. I couldn't. I just . . . couldn't. But on the same token, I didn't think there was a chance I could stay away.

Grief curled and twisted and sucked me a little deeper into the dark, lapping waters I couldn't get free of.

Loneliness consuming.

It was all mixed up with the regret of taking off the way I did. Guilt of not staying and being there for Evan after he'd found out this way.

Knowing he had to be home by now. Destroyed the way that I'd known he would be. Left alone to deal with it, and I knew firsthand that was not a good place to be.

Knowing he would be harboring all that guilt too when really it was neither of our faults.

Lots cast long before either of us had been born.

And then that cycle would just repeat, and I'd get sucked a little deeper into the vortex of what if and guilt and the need to get up and fight for what was right.

I ached.

I ached to hold him.

For him to hold me.

For him to come to me and tell me I was forgiven, tell me he didn't blame me, so I could tell him that I had forgiven him and didn't blame him either.

So we could cry together and finally begin to heal.

My mouth opened on that disorder of thoughts, a silent cry cast to the heavens. For the clarity for us to finally figure out how to make this right.

I nearly hit the ceiling I jumped out of bed so quickly when I heard the doorbell ring.

He was here.

Maybe his presence slammed me face-first into the realization.

The realization that it didn't matter how terrified I was to be put in the same position—to love someone so hard that it felt impossible.

Maybe that was when I realized that was just what loving a child was.

Maybe that was when I realized the full magnitude of it.

It didn't matter if they were healthy or sick or young or old.

That love remained the same.

I raced for the door, my bare feet echoing on the hardwood planks, the errant sensation that it was so wrong that Milo wasn't there right beside me.

This place that I'd considered a home for two years suddenly feeling vacant.

And I was ready. I was ready to go home.

To confess and forgive and love.

I jerked the door open only to stumble back a step when I saw who was standing on the other side.

Not Evan.

My thundering heart stuttered a beat before it jumped into a jagged sprint. I stared dumbfounded at Chris who was standing on the porch, his dark hair hanging over his forehead and his hands stuffed in the pockets of his jeans.

He blew out of a sigh of relief when he saw me.

"Frankie Leigh, thank God. I went to Evan's parents' house and no one answered. Do you know where he is? I found my sister . . . she's in bad shape. Really bad shape."

Dread curled. "What? What happened?" I demanded, pissed that he'd disappeared for all these days when he'd been the one asking for help.

"Think she tried to overdose. I found her in her motel room passed out with a bunch of empty bottles scattered around her." His voice quavered. "She is okay, but she needs serious help. But she's worried about that kid. She's going to try to take him back and that is the last thing she needs right now. We need to talk some sense into her. Convince her he is better off with you and Evan."

Agony tightened my chest, the thought of that little boy being snatched away.

But this woman obviously needed help, and I wasn't going to stand in the way of that.

"Where is she? We have been trying to get in touch with you for several days."

I rubbed my hands up my arms, trying to quell the chills that lifted.

A frown crawled to his brow. "What do you mean? I haven't heard from anyone. Figured your cop friend didn't give a crap about another basket case roaming the streets." Bitterness filled his short laugh, and he shook his head. "I gave up and headed back for California then turned back around when I got another call from her yesterday."

The constricting lump that had been in my throat was back, although this time it was all different. The need to protect this little boy greater than anything I'd ever felt.

Bigger than my fears.

Bigger than the wounds.

He started to back away, his demeanor urgent. "Listen . . . do you know where Evan is? I need to talk to him . . . see if I can get him to come down and talk some sense into her."

My nod was frantic. "Yes. We . . . he moved just a short while ago. Let me grab my keys and my phone and you can follow me over there."

"You sure? It's late."

My tongue swept across my dried lips, the words rushed and haggard. "Yes."

Absolutely.

Yes.

I needed to do this. Be there for Evan. Fight for what was right for that little boy.

My spirit shivered in awareness. In fullness. I'd already felt it—experienced it—the depth of the love I had for him. Maybe right then was the first time I really felt like I had the right to feel it.

"I'll be right back, let me grab a couple things," I told him, and I rushed back through the quiet house and into my old room, trying to keep my footsteps from banging through the house and waking Josiah and Carly. I grabbed my keys, phone, and wallet from the nightstand and slipped my feet into some sandals, didn't take the time to change out of my sleep shorts and tee.

I was back at the door in less than two minutes.

Chris gave me a grateful smile. "Thank you for doing this, Frankie Leigh."

I returned a wary one because I really didn't think he should be thankin' me.

Yes, I hoped his sister could find a way to heal.

To be well.

But I was no liar, and the truth was, I was doing this for Everett and Evan. "You can follow me over there."

I hurried down the two steps to my car, and I backed out onto the street. Headlights lit behind me from where his car was parked, and I started toward home.

Home.

Knot in my throat, I told my phone to dial Seth. It was past midnight, and I cringed thinking about waking him, but he told us to call immediately if we had information.

It went to voicemail, so I left a message. "Hey, Seth. It's Frankie Leigh. Could you give me a call as soon as you get a chance? Chris showed back up. Said he found his sister yesterday. He wants Evan to go and talk with her. He said he hadn't heard from you, and well, I just . . . I wanted to let you know what was happening. We're heading over to the new house right now. I'll talk to you later."

By the time I ended the call, I was already to the new neighborhood. I made the right and then the left, easing into the short driveway of the slumbering house.

All the lights dimmed.

Everything quiet and still.

Though that energy echoed back.

Alive and warm and inviting.

And I knew . . . I knew that this was where I belonged.

Cracking the door open to get out and getting ready to shut off the engine, I jumped when my phone started ringing through the speakers. Seth's name lit on the dash. I quickly answered it. "Seth, hey."

"Frankie," he said, sounding out of breath. "Where are you?"

"We just got to the new house. I'm sitting out front in my car."

"Do not get out," he shouted.

"What?"

"Do not get out, Frankie. He is not who he said he is. I've been following a lead and I just got confirmation. Get as far away from him as you can."

"Oh God, what?"

Panic kicked in, pulse pounding out of control, and I fumbled to get the door shut so I could lock it, so I could hang up and text Evan and pray he saw his phone light up so I could tell him not to open the door. To wait for Seth. That I didn't know what was happening, but I knew help would be on its way.

But a hand was in the way of the door, forcing it open. Gasping, I fought to shut it, but he was too strong, and he was right there standing in it.

Chris grinning down.

But it wasn't close to being that innocent smile he always wore.

It was . . . deranged.

Eyes wired.

He reached over and pushed the button to kill the engine and ripped my phone from my hand. He tossed it to the ground on the driveway. "You won't be needing that."

"Wh-wh-what are you doing? Who are you?"

"Get out, bitch."

I felt the prick at my ribs.

The tip of a knife.

My hands started shaking uncontrollably. As uncontrollably as the words that were spilling from my mouth. "Please . . . don't do this . . . I'll give you anything."

He laughed a menacing sound, and he forced me out of the car. He pulled my back against his chest, an arm locked around the front of me, his mouth at the back of my ear. "Sorry, gorgeous, but you don't have a thing that I want. All except for your pathetic fiancé's heart on a silver platter."

Fear spiraled.

Sweat slicking my flesh.

Pulse thundering out of control.

"Please, I don't know what you want, but I know you don't want to do this." The words tumbled out in a panicked plea, and I was dragging my feet, trying to slow him down. To distract him. To do anything to keep him from getting to that house.

Out of the corner of my eye, I noticed the car he'd pulled in beside mine. Realized it was the same car I'd thought had been following me last week.

Panic pulsed, heart racing mad.

"Why are you doing this? Those messages . . . they were from you?" I guessed it was a tumble of confusion that came bleeding out.

Maybe it took that long for awareness to take hold. For it to sink in that he was the reason that Ashley had been terrified that day on the street. I gulped around the realization. The unwanted thought that he was probably the reason she had abandoned Everett in the first place.

The terror Evan had explained she'd possessed that night.

It wasn't Ashley who was crazy.

Wasn't Ashley who was unhinged.

He dug the knife in a little deeper. Pain pricked, and I bit back the cry. Last thing I wanted to do was give this asshole ammunition. From the look in those eyes, he would be feedin' off the fear.

Loving it.

He shoved me up the single step, making me stumble for the door, jerking me back right before I hit it. Fingers digging into my arm to keep me in place, he reached out with his other hand and pressed the bell that would trigger the lights inside about fifteen times in a row.

A couple seconds later, a light flicked on inside.

Horror raced.

No, Evan, no. Do not open that door, I silently prayed. Prayed that he would somehow hear me.

But I thought the energy was all mixed.

Chaos.

The turmoil from earlier in the day too much for either of us to process. Because Evan was seeing me through the window and his face was bleeding relief while I was sure I was going to crumble to my knees.

He unlocked the door while I screamed, "No! Evan, No!"

But he couldn't hear me.

Couldn't hear me.

Oh god.

Please.

He jerked open the door like he was going to welcome me home with open arms and I was getting shoved again. Flying forward, I slammed into Evan's chest. Those arms were already there to steady me, and we floundered back two steps.

Disoriented and confused.

Chris entered behind me and before I could even turn around, he slammed the door shut and turned the deadbolt.

It rang through the air like a death sentence.

I struggled to hold onto Evan, to get him to look at me, for him to *hear* what I needed to say.

Run.

Save Everett.

I'm sorry.

I love you.

But all his attention was trained on the malice infiltrating the house. The sickness that encroached.

I yelped when Chris grabbed a fistful of my hair and yanked me back.

Evan fought to keep hold of me, but he let go when the blade was placed at my throat. "Move, motherfucker, and she dies."

Evan froze in horror.

My head snapped back in a sharp bite of pain, and I let go, gave as the monster jerked my back to his chest.

The tip of that knife danced at my pulse point.

A thready drum raced through my brain and pounded through my body.

Evan was slowly moving, his arms out like he was placating the devil.

But I saw it.

His eyes narrowed.

Clearly calculating a retaliation.

Violence covered him like a new layer of skin.

Muscles shivering with it.

Fury.

"I don't know what is going on, but let her go," Evan demanded, his voice cracking and raw. "Clearly, this is about you and me."

Chris laughed this crazed sound. The sound of it banged off the walls and vibrated the windows with nothing but cruelty.

"Fucking freak. Listen to you. Can't even fucking talk like a real man, can you?"

Fucking freak.

Fucking freak.

The taunt ricocheted through the room.

Why? Why was he so angry?

Besides, he was the one with a knife to my throat. Definitely not my definition of a man. But I knew better than to say a word.

My lips moved silently, begging Evan to see, *"You save Everett first."*

Evan's throat bobbed as he swallowed, and that aggression only increased. Evan took a step forward. Chris forced us back one. "Put the knife down, Chris. Let's talk. Tell me what you want? Where is Ashley?"

"Ashley?" Chris choked a delirious sound. "You worried about that freak fucker, too?"

Uncertainty and confusion and anger puffed out of Evan's chest. An explosion of a plea.

"She's your sister. My son's mother. Of course, I'm concerned about her. Just . . . put down the knife and we'll talk about it. You can hate me for having a kid with her, but listen to me, man, I didn't know she was pregnant. I didn't desert her or leave her alone or any of that bullshit. She packed up and left. I didn't know a thing."

Knew Evan was trying to assuage him. Talk him down from the ledge.

Chris laughed a scraping, mocking sound. "You always had to take everything that was mine, didn't you?"

Confusion deepened the lines on Evan's face, frustration oozing out, his brows twisting in a tight knot. "What are you talking about? I don't even know you."

More laughter, this time bitter. "Come on, Evan, tell me you don't even recognize your own brother? Now that is pretty sad, don't you think? And here I thought maybe you and I could become best friends." Could feel the crack of his vicious smile at the side of my head. "Probably not, though, right?"

His brother?

I watched the commotion go down in Evan's mind.

Disoriented.

Flustered.

Agitated.

The three of them got whipped up in a pit of fear.

So intense Evan paled and his body shook.

Saw the way his knees went weak. But he fought it. Remained upright. "I have no idea what you are talking about, Chris. But this madness needs to stop before someone gets hurt. Please. I'm begging you to put down that knife."

Chris shook his head, carried on like Evan hadn't said anything at all. "You have any idea what it's like to live in the shadow of you? This fucking freak who can't even fucking hear with his fake fucking heart?"

The arm locked around me tightened in a frisson of rage.

Irrational hostility.

I could see the stark fear streak through Evan's expression, but he was trying to keep calm, trying not to set Chris off. "I don't know what you're talking about, I promise, but whatever you're upset about, we can figure out. You can let her go."

Chris chuckled a dark sound. "No can do, Big Brother. You took everything from me. You have any idea what it was like to grow up as me? *Daddy* fucking hated my mom because she wasn't your bitch of a mother. Treated her like shit. Nothing but a punching bag for the rich prick to take his anger out on. A whore he came to in the middle of the night."

Hate blistered through Evan's features.

Our worlds spinning.

The frayed threads we hadn't been able to put together knitting into a blanket of horrified realization.

Chris's face pinched with disdain where he had his jaw pressed tight against mine, the sensation of it scraping my skin. "Then that piece of shit who was supposed to be my grandfather? He owed me *one* thing. One fucking thing. And guess who got that five-million dollars our daddy promised me to keep me from squealing to the counselors at school?" He whittled the knife a little deeper into my throat. "Ding, ding, ding. Not. Me."

Hatred seeped into the room.

Venom.

Pure wickedness.

I gasped out in relief when he jerked the knife away from my throat and waved it around in the air. "Nice place you have here, by the way. What do you say we paint it red?"

Evan lunged forward.

Chris jerked me back, waving the knife again. "Wouldn't do that."

"I'll give anything . . . all the fucking money. I don't care. Just let her go. I didn't know about you. I promise. You're right. Our father is a prick. This is all on him. Let's figure this out together."

Could feel the air puff from Chris's mouth, a sticky hot disease that blew through my hair, his unhinged mind spinning away.

And I knew . . . I knew in that moment there was going to be no talking him down from this.

Felt him crack a perverse smirk. "You know, I really thought it would be the kid that did you in. Ashley and I figured we'd get what was owed to us. Loved her, you know. Fucking loved that bitch. Turns out, she was a whore, just like my mother. She was only supposed to seduce you once. Tease you with the idea of a kid since I knew there was no chance you were going to have one. Bitch actually got herself knocked up. And then what did she do? Ran off the second she found out she was pregnant."

My heart fell to the floor.

Ashley had been in on this?

Some sort of twisted, messed up plan to steal from Evan?

How could people be so terrible and cruel?

We'd started circling, and I knew Evan couldn't hear the sirens that were approaching in the distance.

Oh, but Chris surely could. Knew he'd be gettin' desperate. "Took me close to two years to find her . . . should have known she'd try to run again. I finally caught up to her, though, made her pay for what she did."

A tiny yelp of agony jutted from my spirit.

Oh God.

Oh God.

"You took my childhood. My mother. The money. My girl.

Time to pay up, asshole."

"This is crazy, Chris. Just think about what you're doing. I'll give you all the money. All of it. Just let her go."

Evan's eyes kept darting to me. Telling me to hold on. That he was going to protect me. Not to be afraid when I knew neither of us had ever been so afraid in all our lives.

Chris carried on so casually. "I'm thinking there might be something in this world that is more important to you than the kid, though," he mused.

He wielded the knife, dragging the blade close enough that it nicked my jaw in a slow, searing sting. I tried not to whimper. Tried not to cry. "She is pretty, isn't she?"

Milo was in the hall, whimpering and whining, turning in circles.

Feeling the distress.

Chris pulled the knife away and waved it back and forth in front of my face. "The baby or the girl? The baby or the girl?" He singsonged the threat. "What's it gonna be? Which one will make us even for what you have taken from me?"

There are moments in your life when everything comes into sharp, clear view.

When it crystallizes.

When you realize all the hope and love and belief you had was meant to be directed at one thing.

I think Evan and I had lost so much time thinking we were sacrificing for the other. Him protecting me from the life he thought would burden me, and me protectin' him from the burden I didn't think he could bear.

I guessed it was right that second we both accepted that was the meaning of love. We would sacrifice it all, give it up for the other.

But more importantly, we both gladly give that sacrifice for Everett.

Pay any cost.

Lay down our lives.

Those emerald eyes were on me.

Conveying the same message I was giving.

Our connection shivered and shook and trembled. So different. So different than it'd ever been before. Fierce and unrelenting and all-knowing.

We were in this together.

To the end.

Everett. Everett. Everett.

Evan jumped into action before Chris could process the shift in the atmosphere. Evan spun, bolted down the hall in the direction of Everett's room.

Chris tossed me aside, seeing the choice was made, running after his revenge.

Sirens whirred and the severity flashed and our worlds gathered to a pinpoint.

The second strung out like it would go on for eternity.

Chris darted down the hall.

The door banged to Everett's room, and Evan was rounding around, a punch thrown that caught Chris off guard, fist ramming into his face.

He staggered back, not anticipating that Evan was gonna fight with everything he had.

It left him disoriented for the one second needed to isolate him.

Make him vulnerable.

I shouted, "Attack."

And Milo—my sweet old boy—he did.

He protected the way he'd been trained to do.

Milo went for his arm, mauling at the flesh, teeth tearing and ripping.

Chris dropped to his knees.

Howling in pain.

When Chris scrambled back for the knife that had dropped to the floor, Milo went for his neck.

Lights spun through the windows, flash after flash, and I raced for the door and flicked the lock just in time to allow a herd of officers to come stampeding through. Seth was at the helm with his gun drawn, eyes on me before they were dragging to where Milo tore into Chris's neck, going for the throat, because my boy knew this was a fight to the death.

Evan stood right outside Everett's door.

His breaths heaving.

His eyes meeting mine as the officers swarmed the house.

And we might have had hurts stretched out between us.

Wounds that had been inflicted.

Traumas we didn't know how to navigate.

But we knew—we knew what we were fighting for.

He was fighting for me.

For Everett.

For us.

Exactly the same as I would forever fight for them.

Evan

*L*ying in our bed, I gazed at her through the early morning light that trickled in through the drapes of our bedroom window. The girl stared back at me. No chance we could tear ourselves away.

It was what we'd done the entire night, neither of us able to sleep after what had happened.

No words really said.

Just silent, unspoken resolution.

Everett was fast asleep in the middle of us because we couldn't bear for him to be out of our sights, and Milo was in the mix of it, curled up at the bottom of the bed at our feet.

Our family.

She slid her hand across the mattress over Everett's head, reaching out to trace the lines of my face. "I am so thankful you came back to me."

I knew she was whispering it so quietly, words little more than a breath that caressed my face.

"And I'm so thankful you came back to me."

Her head shook slightly. "I guess I really didn't leave you,

Evan. I just got lost in the fear for a while. The same way as you did. You were just gone a little longer." A wistful smile tugged at one side of her mouth.

Emotion clogged my throat. Trying to process through all the information and facts and raveled ends. How was it possible to be so repentant, to want to beg for forgiveness for your greatest transgression, and know you would never take it back, would never change it, if given the chance?

Everett was the gift that had been given.

I brought her hand to my mouth. "You're right, Frankie. That is exactly what I was. Lost. Lost without you." I reached out, toying with one of those untamed curls, tucking it back behind her ear as I stared at my best friend.

My partner.

The girl who had always been meant for me.

Maybe it'd taken a little while to finally get to where we both fully knew it. Where there was no going back. No questions or barriers left between us.

"Could ask you for forgiveness again." No doubt, the words were nothing but shards of broken sounds coming up my throat. My gaze dipped to Everett before it returned to her. "But I won't. I won't because I already know that you know how much I regret hurting you. You already know how much it kills me that you went through that alone. But I also know it would only hurt you and Everett more if I lived in that regret."

I swallowed hard, chest stretched tight, my love and devotion so thick I was sure it had manifested in the room.

Become a living, thriving entity.

I laid my hand on her cheek, brushed my thumb over her trembling bottom lip. "You have taught me the most important lesson in life, Unicorn Girl. Every day that you ran free and loved without question and pushed me to love you back? You were teaching me that every single day counts. None of us know how many we're going to be given, but what we do know is each one we take for granted is one that has been lost. And I don't want to waste any more. Not a single one."

I tightened my hold on her face. "And I am ready to chase after every single one of those dreams."

Her teeth clamped down on her bottom lip, those brown eyes soft and warm and drinking me down. "I don't think I ever really let go of them, never stopped believing in them, and they were granted when I least expected them."

Her attention had drifted to Everett, her hand slowly rubbing his back the way that she did. She looked up at me. "I will love him for all the days I have, Evan. I will choose to protect him. I will choose to stand for him. The same as I choose to stand for you."

"Frankie," I murmured, brushing her cheek, her nose, her chin. My insides twisted in affection.

I loved her.

Loved her so badly it hurt.

Her brow pinched, and her tongue darted out to wet her lips. "I'm sorry for what happened to her. He's going to need us to love him even harder because of it."

Disbelief pulled through my senses. A wash of quiet sadness.

Ashley was gone.

Found strangled in a hotel room in the next town over. *Freak Fucker* carved in her forearm with what was thought to be the same knife he'd brought here.

Did I hate her for doing it? For trying to set me up? Manipulate me out of money? Did I hate her for putting Everett in the danger that she had?

Yeah.

But I also respected the fact she'd run when she'd found out she was pregnant. That she'd done what she had to protect him, as stupid and greedy as she'd been. But I had to believe that maybe she'd simply gotten mixed up with the wrong person. Was being manipulated herself before she'd realized what she was doing and changed course.

Kristoff Manning, aka Chris, the piece-of-shit half-brother I'd had no clue existed, would survive.

They'd finally linked the description I'd given with a fingerprint that had been lifted from Frankie Leigh's house. It'd hit, but rather than coming back with information about Ashley's brother, that fingerprint had belonged to a twenty-two-year old from Birmingham, Alabama who'd grown up with a single-mom and had a history of mental illness and a string of arrests for petty crimes.

Fathered by Dane Gentry. Same as me.

Maybe he'd been manipulated, too. Brought up in a chaos and fear and hatred so extreme it had shaped him into a vile, sadistic bastard.

But that didn't change what he'd done.

The horrible crimes he'd committed and the ones he'd intended to carry out.

Hating me because he felt like I'd had some kind of relevance in the fucked-up family tree that needed to be ripped up from the roots.

"I hate that Everett will forever have that part of him missing, but you and I both know what it's like for a parent not to want us. To abandon us. We both know what it feels like. And the only thing we can do is fill him with all the love we can give him and support him in the times when he's feeling the loss. That's what Rynna did for you and what Kale did for me."

She chewed at her lip. "But our parents didn't love us or want us, Evan. My heart tells me that his did. That she loved him so much she was willing to sacrifice everything for him."

I nodded, hating to agree but knowing it was true.

Frankie Leigh slowly sat up, crisscrossing her long legs and facing me, hair falling around her, shirt falling off one shoulder.

So damn pretty in the rising morning light.

She lifted her hands, earnestness bleeding out.

YESTERDAY I WAS TERRIFIED I WASN'T ENOUGH FOR HIM, EVAN. TERRIFIED THAT I MIGHT FAIL HIM. THAT I WOULDN'T BE GOOD ENOUGH. BUT I HAVE NO QUESTION THAT HE NEEDS ME, EVERY BIT AS MUCH AS I NEED HIM. EVERY BIT AS MUCH AS I NEED YOU.

I eased up, getting onto my knees, leaning over the girl and taking her by the face. "I saw what you were willing to do last night. I saw it, and I know you meant it. You are more than enough. You are everything."

I leaned in.

Kissed her slow.

Loved her soft.

Silently promised her that was what they were going to be.

My everything.

I grinned at her lips when I felt the movement on the mattress, my forehead dropping to hers as I looked to the side to find Everett on his knees. Giving us one of his scrunched up, adorable grins.

Pointing at us with that little finger. "Da, Fi-Fi, Ehvie!"

He laughed like it was the funniest thing, and I was laughing, too. I swiped him into my arms.

Felt his giggles float into the air.

Ricochet from the walls and echo in our hearts.

Milo perked up, ears twitching, old guy crawling slowly up to get snuggled in with us.

Our real hero from last night.

Holding Everett in one arm, I reached out and cupped Frankie's cheek. "Unicorn Girl . . . let's soar for the stars."

Emotion crested her face, and she brushed her fingers through Everett's hair, kid bobbing an arm at her to get her to take him into hers. "Just as long as you two are flying by my side."

Frankie Leigh
Two Years Later

*S*unshine poured into the backyard. The Alabama sky as blue as
could be. The trees surrounding our home were full and lush.
Surrounding the yard in a hedge of protection.

My pulse thudded when I glanced at the clock.

Almost noon.

I stepped the rest of the way out onto the patio.

Everett noticed me the second that I did, and he hopped up
from where he was playing in the yard and raced my direction.
"Mommy! Is it time? Is it time? Daddy said he was going to be
here when the sun got way, way, way up high in the sky, and look
it. It's so high."

Kai did circles around Everett's ankles, yipping and barking
and wagging her tiny tail in excitement.

I wondered if the sweet girl could feel it. The anticipation in
the air. The feeling that everything was getting ready to change.

"It is way up high, isn't it? It's almost time. You should come inside."

Everett stopped where the lawn met the wood and hopped onto the patio with two feet. "Dids you see that? I jumped so high. Almost as high as the sky."

Love overflowing, I ran my fingers through his soft hair. He grinned up at me, sending me one of those smiles that shattered me. Tied him to me.

Sometimes it was hard to fathom the love that I had for this child.

I knelt down a little so I could kiss him on the forehead. "You are such a big boy. I'm so proud of you."

I searched his emerald eyes. "Are you ready for this?"

"Yes! It's my favorite day!"

I heard the car pulling into the front yard. Everett's eyes bugged out in excitement.

God, he looked so much like his daddy in that second that I couldn't stand it.

"He's here, he's here, he's here!" He clapped and did some kind of dancing jig that pulled a giggle right out of me. "*Wet's* go. Come on, Kai. We gotta go fast."

Everett bolted through the house, his footsteps banging on the wood floors, Kai's nails clicking as she raced alongside him. The girl basically refused to leave his side.

Chest tight, I followed them to the door where Everett stood antsy, waiting on me to unlock it. The car came to a stop, and we stepped out.

I met Evan's gaze through the windshield of his car.

That energy surged.

I'd always thought it impossible. The connection that I shared with this man. But it'd only grown.

Amplified.

Deepened with the commitment we shared.

This life.

This home.

This family.

Those emerald eyes flashed devotion.

Admiration.

But it was me who was so incredibly proud of him.

Evan had stepped up to take a chair on the board of A Lick of Hope. He'd committed his life that he'd once feared inconsequential campaigning for awareness for genetic heart disorders.

I'd taken over the marketing of the actual lollipops. Getting them into stores across the country to help spread the word.

Together, as a team, we were making a difference.

Evan cracked open the door while Everett was jumping all around at my side, clapping his hands over his head and shouting, "You see my puppy."

Affection pulled at the corner of my mouth, and Evan stood from the car.

Emotion crashed.

Tugged and strobed and pulsed.

My smile trembled.

Evan sent me that look that promised he understood me in every way. That he would never cut my wings. That he would be there with me every step of the way.

That we were doing this together.

That it was right.

Finally, I moved, knees weak, heart in my throat.

Every sensation heightened.

I reached my hand out for Everett. "Come on, little man."

"Okays!" He hopped down the step at my side, and we followed the walkway to where Evan had moved to the backdoor of the car.

He opened it, dipping down for a minute before it shut.

The little boy stood there with his hand wrapped up in Evan's.

Scared and unsure and nervous.

Evan heard about this little boy who'd been in the system for the last two years.

Abandoned.

Forgotten as if he couldn't be heard.

His dark eyes met mine. My spirit shivered. And I realized my breaths had gone short and my heart was racing and the world was spinning a little faster than it had been before.

I got down onto my knees in front of him.

Gravity.

He tightened his hold on Evan. Evan watched down on me with a tender smile.

I lifted my hands. *HI, DOMINIC.*

His eyes lit. Shyly, he signed, *HI,* before he buried his face in Evan's leg. Warily, he peeked out.

Nerves and hope.

And that was the only thing we wanted to give him.

Everett chattered at my side, going on about all his toys and asking Dominic if he wanted to play.

My smile was soft, and I edged forward a fraction. *WE ARE SO HAPPY YOU ARE HERE.*

I gestured behind me before I turned back to him and lifted my hands with the promise.

THIS HOUSE IS LOVE.

It was, and the only thing Evan and I wanted to do was fill it with more.

Let it overflow.

I took Dominic's hand.

Energy flashed up my arm.

I felt staggered.

Unprepared for what I would feel.

I glanced back at Evan. My heart clutched in my chest.

The man so beautiful and strong and right.

I was floored by the love.

By the joy.

By the belief that this was where we were supposed to be.

No. None of us knew the number of our days. None of us knew what each of those days would bring.

But Evan and I?

We chose to live for every single one.

We chose to live life loving with everything that we had. Chose to never let go of the ones that we loved most.

And no matter what life brought our way, we would forever hold on to hope . . .

the end

Thank you for reading *Hold* ON TO *Hope*!

I hope you loved Evan, Frankie Leigh, and Everett as much I loved writing them! They are forever going to be in my heart.

Can't get enough of this family? Start where it all began with Rex and Rynna in *Show Me the Way*

http://smarturl.it/SMTHAmzn2

New to me and want more? I recommend starting with my super-hot, raw rockstar series, Bleeding Stars!

Start with *A Stone in the Sea*

http://smarturl.it/ASITSamzn2

Text "aljackson" to 33222 to get your LIVE release mobile alert
(US Only)
or
Sign up for my newsletter
http://smarturl.it./NewsFromALJackson

More from A.L. Jackson

ABOUT THE AUTHOR

A.L. Jackson is the New York Times & USA Today Bestselling author of contemporary romance. She writes emotional, sexy, heart-filled stories about boys who usually like to be a little bit bad.

Her bestselling series include THE REGRET SERIES, CLOSER TO YOU, BLEEDING STARS, FIGHT FOR ME, and CONFESSIONS OF THE HEART.

If she's not writing, you can find her hanging out by the pool with her family, sipping cocktails with her friends, or of course with her nose buried in a book.

Be sure not to miss new releases and sales from A.L. Jackson - Sign up to receive her newsletter http://smarturl.it/NewsFromALJackson or text "aljackson" to 33222 to receive short but sweet updates on all the important news.

Connect with A.L. Jackson online:

Page **http://smarturl.it/ALJacksonPage**
Newsletter **http://smarturl.it/NewsFromALJackson**
Angels **http://smarturl.it/AmysAngelsRock**
Amazon **http://smarturl.it/ALJacksonAmzn**
Book Bub **http://smarturl.it/ALJacksonBookbub**
Text "aljackson" to 33222 to receive short but sweet updates on all the important news.

Made in the USA
Monee, IL
19 April 2024

57185066R00225